THE BALL BOUNCED BACKWARD

A Novel

Cav A. Badger

THE BALL BOUNCED BACKWARD

1405 SW 6th Avenue • Ocala, Florida 34471 • Phone 352-622-1825 • Fax 352-622-1875
Website: www.atlantic-pub.com • Email: sales@atlantic-pub.com
SAN Number: 268-1250

Library of Congress Control Number: 2020914895

Printed in the United States

PROJECT MANAGER: Crystal Edwards

ACKNOWLEDGMENTS

I'd wanted to tell the story you are about read for a long time. But when I was prepared to start writing, something else always seemed to have priority. A little more than two years ago, my across-the-street neighbor, John Wasowicz, told me he had recently published a novel, his first, a murder mystery, *Daingerfield Island.* I bought a copy. John's book gave me more than a fun read, however; it gave me a good kick in the pants. His example pushed me to stop cogitating and start working. I would never have written *The Ball Bounced Backward* without it. Thank you, John.

Jackson Lassiter and I were colleagues in the business school at The George Washington University where I learned he had an avocation as a creative writer and writing coach. I was just starting this novel and asked his help. Jackson agreed and taught me more about writing in his commentaries on an early draft than I've learned before or since. He was pointed while encouraging, a marvelous teaching blend, particularly for me as a beginner. I know he'll be displeased that the final text contains far, far, far more adverbs than he would prefer, and that I often substitute jarring verbs for 'said' and 'replied'. But without Jackson's thoughtful advice, this work would be much inferior.

Two close friends and avid readers, Judy Stone Weaver and Kevin Wilkinson, volunteered to review a mid-course draft. They independently reached similar conclusions about the work, the most important that initial portions of the novel didn't hang together and needed a major rewrite. They were correct. I took my friends' advice and rewrote relevant portions as well as incorporated many suggestions of lesser consequence. The story is much improved because of their help. For their efforts, I would offer both a share of the profits from this venture, but I suspect my lasting gratitude and friendship, which I sincerely offer in lieu thereof, will have substantially greater value.

My wife, Kathy, plowed through the initial draft. She gave me a thumbs up and told me to complete the novel. While she surreptitiously may now recant that judgment given the many months spent editing the work contrasted to the few months writing it, I always know that she'll be my greatest advocate. Finished, I promise to now spend more time with her.

I would also like to thank Andrew Peacock, an editor at Atlantic Publishing, for his helpful comments and Cathy Cline and Crystal Edwards, also at Atlantic, for their production assistance.

Lastly, but most importantly, I would like to thank the kids who played on the teams I coached. With them, even a bad day was a good one.

Cav A. Badger

June, 2021

TABLE OF CONTENTS

NAMED CHARACTERS

The Elliot Family

Doug Elliot
Maddie Elliot
Travis Elliot

Players

Casey Costello }
Rickie Hansen } *The Troika*
Travis Elliot }
Zack (no last name)
George Kovac
Andy Novak
Wilfredo (Willie) Hernandez
Randal Wise
Carleton Whitely - son of Jordan Whitley
Freddie Marnoca - friend of Carleton Whitley
Tommy Ferguson - St. Joseph's player and son of Toby Ferguson

Coaches and League Officials

Jordan Whitley - St. Jerome's coach and friend of Doug Elliot
Bob Kartz - St. Jerome's fifth-grade coach
Bart Anderson - director of the basketball program at St. Jerome's Elementary School
Paul Spenser - league commissioner
Fred Bauer - St. Leo's coach and acquaintance of Doug Elliot
Toby Ferguson - St. Joseph's fourth-grade coach
Adrian Atkinson - St. Joseph's fifth-grade coach
Major William Taylor - Little League coach

Employees of Steiger Bros.

Ty Finchly - manager of local Steiger Bros. office and Doug Elliot's boss

Mae (no last name) - senior employee of Steiger Bros. in the local office

Barney Ambrose - director of public relations for the local office of Steiger Bros.

Robert Bonson - director of Steiger Bros. public relations

Peter Robichaeux - public relations staffer at Steiger Bros. headquarters

Clergy

Monsignor Schreiber - pastor at St. Joseph's

Sister Cecelia - principal at St. Jerome's Elementary School

Father John Doering - pastor at St. Jerome's

Others

John and Celeste Hansen - parents of Rickie Hansen

Jill Whitley - Jordan Whitley's wife

Montgomery Wise - father of Randal Wise

Rita Horvath - friend of Maddie's, volunteer at St. Jerome's Elementary School and a source of intelligence about school activities and people

Mr. and Mrs. Hernandez - Willie's parents

Bert Pratt - professional sports photographer

Mr. Louganis - janitor at St. Jerome's elementary school

Detective Ludlum - local police detective

Frankie Marnoca - Freddie Marnoca's brother

PART I
THE FIRST HALF

PROLOGUE

The Troika

"Hi, Dad."

"Travis."

"How are you this morning?"

"A little stiff. My concession to age."

"If you did the stretching exercises I showed you, you wouldn't have that problem."

"Ugh." I could hear my son snicker on the other end of the line. He knew I hated to exercise.

"Okay. I get it," Travis said, dropping the exercise dig. "How's Mom?"

"Not much different than when you saw her last month. She has good days and bad. Her memory frustrates her, particularly when we're cleaning out the house. We go back and forth. Today she wants to pack something that yesterday she wanted to toss. Then she gets annoyed because she can't remember why she put whatever it was on the toss pile in the first place. Unfortunately, her contradictory choices slow the culling process, and after forty years in the same house we've got a lot of culling yet to do."

"Any change in the prognosis?"

"Nah. We're dealing with gradual, at least for now. Day-to-day changes are imperceptible. Even week-to-week. The worst is your mother's exasperation with her memory lapses."

"When are you putting the house on the market?"

"This spring."

"After all those years in northern Indiana, Arizona'll be a big change."

"Remember, we've spent the last few winters there. Made some friends. Your mom's found a handful of card-playing buddies, so that'll help her stay mentally active. We'll be out of the cold and come visit you when it gets too hot. So, yeah, it'll be a change, but a welcome one for both of us."

My wife, Maddie, and I met at Eastern Illinois University. EIU's home, Charleston, Illinois, was a modest place by any standard, even when it included Mattoon, the neighboring town to the west 12 miles or so down IL-16. But the university was huge, at least to Maddie and me, and we were immediately swallowed by it. We both walked on campus neither knowing anyone nor understanding how to make friends in the university metropolis. The dorms became our social and psychological savior, and when the first fliers appeared announcing a freshmen mixer for our adjacent housing, we eagerly, if apprehensively, joined the event.

I can't remember the circumstances, but Maddie and I ended that evening in a small group with maybe six or seven other freshmen chatting about how we decided to attend EIU rather than someplace else. It was only a short step from there to cross-referencing our rural roots and first in the family to attend college status. I can't say it was love at first sight, but it was comfort at first conversation. By our junior year we were engaged. We married three days after graduation.

The newly formed Elliot family settled in northern Indiana. Travis was born a few years later. We wanted more children, but they never came. Aside from that disappointment, life was good. We lived comfortably and uneventfully, enjoyed several close friends, and watched our son, and then our three grandchildren, grow. Maddie was over 60 when we first noticed that she struggled with lapses in memory. We thought little of them given our preoccupation with consequential decisions surrounding my retirement. But they eventually became too frequent to ignore.

"Did I catch you in the middle of anything?" Travis asked.

"I'm in the garage, rummaging through some old boxes I haven't looked at in ages. Part of the culling process." I shifted the phone to the other ear so I could free my right hand to open a dust-covered plastic bin. "You'll never guess what I unearthed this morning. Action photos of your fourth-grade basketball team playing St. Katherine's. Remember them? I found a manila envelope full of pictures tucked into a copy of my old employer's annual report, the one with that cheesy feature on the team."

"My God. How many years ago was that? Twenty-five?"

"About." I pulled the envelope from the bin with my free hand and clumsily started perusing the photos. "There're some great shots here of everybody on the team, including you."

The old photos pictured Travis as larger than the average fourth grader, both in height and bulk. He was pudgy though not fat, with dishwater-blonde hair topping a creamy-complexioned, round face. What the photos couldn't show was that the round face smiled often, underscoring an easy-going disposition that felt comfortable around people and served as a wellspring of conversation.

"I'll hold them if you want. You can pick up everything when you come over next weekend. If you don't, they're going into the toss pile. Your mother and I have no use for extra memorabilia these days."

"Take photos of everything, including the cheesy feature, and shoot them to me," Travis said. "Rickie, Casey and I are getting together Wednesday night. They'll get a big kick out of seeing them."

"*The Troika*'s alive and well? I haven't thought of those two guys in ages."

"Not like fourth-grade, is it? We've gone our separate ways, but we stay in touch. Facebook. Linked-In with Casey. An occasional call. Some get togethers, like this Wednesday, though I can't tell you when the last one was. A year or two ago maybe."

Rickie Hansen, Casey Costello, and Travis Elliot flew to one another like a pile of metal filings to a magnet their first day at St. Jerome's Elementary School and quickly became inseparable, like brothers without the fighting. The boys were so close Casey's mother dubbed them *The Troika* after reading a cold war spy novel, and the nickname stuck. Even when summer vacation distanced them, they finagled two weeks together at Camp Sunk Boat and often assembled on one another's turf to do what boys do after parents chauffeur them 25 minutes across town. Driver's licenses in high school eventually eliminated the parents' chauffeur roles, but only enhanced the boys' relationships.

"What's Casey doing these days? I always liked him. Last time I heard he was in law school. Has to be a success."

"That he is, Dad. That he is. Casey's already a partner at a big-time law firm in downtown Chicago. I can't remember the name of the place. All law firms sound alike, an endless list of dead lawyers' last names. He's a litigator there."

"A litigator? I'd never have guessed that." Casey was a smart kid and well-spoken as a youngster, but he was also laid-back, collegial, and polite. Exceedingly polite. I could see him schmoozing a client or figuring out a legal subtlety. But a litigator? Mixing it up in a courtroom?"

"That's what he says," Travis assured.

"Has he changed? Personality-wise, I mean."

"Casey? Nah. Same guy. Has a couple of kids, both in school, and at a parochial school, I might add. His wife's a teacher. We kid him about getting old. He's graying around the temples."

"Gray temples against that coal black hair. Distinguished. Good for a lawyer, though I hope he has a better haircut than that flopover job he had as a kid. Just don't tell me he's balding. It'd ruin the image."

I remember Casey Costello as the most complex member of *The Troika*. The piercing dark eyes, his most distinctive and attractive feature, appeared as deep crevasses, cloaking extraordinary intelligence and maturity. A long and somewhat extended nose interrupted an otherwise handsome face and the small clef in his chin aged him beyond his years. He exhibited youthful traces of awkward and gangly movement, but he was a boy with seemingly unlimited potential.

"Casey? No way. Full head of hair," Travis said. "Rickie's a different story though, pronounced thinning."

"You're kidding. I recall Rickie's hair was fine, and almost blanched. Like his skin. White-blonde threads flying in every direction." Rickie was shorter than both Casey and Travis. He moved quickly and abruptly with a personality to match. The kid was restless, even hyper, and mouthy with his peers but spooky-silent around adults. He was never a favorite of mine and grew less so the longer I knew him.

"What's Rickie doing now?"

"He's a long-haul truck driver, working out of the Indianapolis area."

"What?" He was willow thin as I recalled. An air-conditioning unit set to 'High' would have toppled him. "You're telling me he's driving a big rig? The hydraulics in his truck must be amazing. Is that his career now?"

"I don't know if the trucking job's permanent. Rickie's had a few careers before. This one seems to suit him now. He just went through another divorce. Divorce and long-haul are probably connected."

"Second divorce? Mid-thirties? Wow."

"He doesn't have any kids. I suppose that's good. His folks still live in northern Indiana, but other than that he seems rootless. I feel sorry for the guy."

"Where's *The Troika* meeting Wednesday?"

"Some place outside Dayton. Rickie recommended it. I've got a name and address, but that's all I know. Probably a dive that'll make Casey do a double take. But so long as we have a place to talk and a bartender who'll keep our glasses full, who cares?"

"Dayton? The garden spot of Ohio."

"Only luxury for *The Troika*," Travis chuckled. "We all had business there the same day. Some coincidence, huh."

"Tell you what, Son. Let me overnight these pictures and the annual report. Glossy photos don't always come out over the phone. Too many reflections. Plus,

I've got several. You can pass them around instead of just flipping through them on your phone. If anybody wants one, or two, or the even whole bunch … give it to them."

"Thanks, Dad. The guys'll love seeing those shots."

"Are you in contact with any other members of that fourth-grade team?"

"A couple."

"Send them any pictures they're in. The more, the better. Get rid of everything."

"*The Troika* and fourth-grade basketball, relived. Man, does that bring back memories," Travis said.

"Good, I hope."

"Oh, yeah."

Twenty-five years ago. So many years; so little time, I thought. "What's your team going to be like this fall, Travis? Any feel for it yet?"

"Since I'm the new guy in the league, I'm sure the rest of the coaches are licking their chops waiting to play us. We'll surprise a few folks, though. I saw the team play last season from the opposite sideline and watched a lot of film of the returning players before I even interviewed for the job. I told the school administration, 'don't expect miracles, but your football team's better than your record was last year'. They seemed to agree."

"Will you teach junior year American history, too?"

"My purgatory."

"Arizona's a little far to travel to watch your Friday night games, but we'll be rooting for you. We'll keep up. The local paper's Web site will carry a story if nothing else. Want to talk to your mom?"

"Sure."

I walked out of the garage into the kitchen where my wife sat drinking a cup of coffee and reading the morning paper.

"Maddie. Travis is on the phone."

RECRUITED

"Dad. You've got to be our coach." Travis hopped into the car and turned off the radio. On the off chance I hadn't heard, he repeated his plea. Only louder. "Dad! You've got to be our coach!"

Travis's mind was three steps ahead of his tongue. He abbreviated ideas, often making him difficult to follow. Even more so when he was excited, which he frequently was. Maddie and I learned that rapid patter from Travis usually meant something was up and he wanted affirmation, not questions.

"What's this all about?" I asked.

"We've a basketball team and no coach. I talked to Casey and Rickie. They agreed. They thought you'd be a good coach, too."

I exited St. Jerome's Elementary School parking lot, taking pains to follow the flailing arms of the school's safety officer.

"Slow down. Start at the beginning." I couldn't help but smile at Travis's enthusiasm.

"Mr. Anderson came to school today and …"

"Who's Mr. Anderson?"

"I don't know. He's not one of our teachers. I guess he runs basketball for the school or something. Anyway, Mr. Anderson went to all the classes and told everybody all about it. Well, just the upper classes. He didn't talk to the little kids. The fourth-grade's going to have a basketball team and play fourth-grade teams from other schools in the diocese. We need a coach. Casey's dad is out of town all the time, so he can't do it. Rickie's dad doesn't know anything about basketball. We all agreed you'd be the best coach."

"Thank you and thank the other members of *The Troika.* Now, calm down and let's think about this for a minute." Travis wanted immediate acquiescence; I wanted to slow him down. "More than the three of you'll be on the team. Right? Maybe there're other dads who want to coach. One of them might be a great coach. Have you checked that out?" I gave Travis time to consider the possibility. The three, as a group, were so assertive they often took over before anyone else could say or do a thing.

"No," he said and grew quiet. Repressed silence didn't fit Travis. His normal behavior resembled a dog off his leash in the middle of a park. Now he appeared tethered and kenneled besides.

"There're other things to think about. I have a job. Remember? It pays the bills, including your tuition to St Jerome's. I can't walk out of work in the middle of the afternoon to go to a fourth-grade basketball game."

I suspected coaching Travis and his friends would be fun, but a lot of things would be fun, and I couldn't do them, either. The world has a nasty way of intruding, and if I forgot my responsibilities to it, Maddie would remind me.

"When do you practice? It takes a good 45 minutes to an hour for me to drive from work to school. The only reason I'm picking you up today is because the office is closed."

"You'd be a good coach, Dad."

My concern was logistics, not my ability to coach a grade school basketball team. I'd led a sixth-grade team for two seasons at a local parochial school when I was in college. With considerable success. The kids seemed to like me, though it may have been because we won. Over the two seasons we came out on top in 39 of 43 games.

"I can't believe Mr. Anderson just came in and said that there'll be a fourth-grade basketball team and that it needs a coach. Didn't he say anything more?"

"That's about it. He said we have to keep our grades up and stuff. We already knew that. Our games are on Sundays. And, um … we have uniforms. Rickie said they're nice ones, too." Travis's fingers swept across his forehead as if he were trying to think of anything else.

"I'm interested in what Mr. Anderson said about needing a coach. He must have said something more."

"Oh, yeah. I almost forgot." Travis twisted and fished a tightly folded paper from his back pocket. "Mr. Anderson gave us this to take home."

Travis unfolded the paper and tried to hand it to me. I waved him off. "I'm driving, Son."

"Yup. It's all here," he said, scanning both sides of the single page. "Mr. Anderson even put his telephone number on the paper, so you can call and tell him you'll be our coach."

"That makes more sense. I'll read the handout when we get home. Then, we'll talk about it. Fair enough?"

"Okay. But you'd make a good coach, Dad."

The short drive from school ended as the car rolled up the driveway and into the garage. Travis leaned over and handed me the small rectangle of refolded paper, grabbed a notebook from the car floor, and disappeared into the house. I settled back into the driver's seat and unfolded the sheet.

The dim light in the closed garage blurred the page. Only the headline was legible.

DIOSESAN BASKETBALL PROGRAM - 1994-95

I refolded the paper, put it in my jacket pocket, and followed Travis into the house.

Maddie was setting the kitchen table. "I hear you're coaching Travis's basketball team," she said, sporting a knowing grin.

"Come on. He's way ahead of himself."

"We'll see." Her grin broadened.

"Okay. It might be fun."

"Rickie and Casey will be on the team and you like them."

"True."

"The other kids should be fine, too. I talked to Rita Horvath the other day, and she told me there're no problem children in this year's class. No discipline issues."

Rita volunteered at St. Jerome's and Maddie knew her well. She was our inside source, a constant stream of information about the school and its activities that we couldn't seem to find anywhere else.

"What happened to Charlie? He was an obnoxious kid."

"Charlie didn't enroll this year," Maddie said.

"Just as well. I can handle a Charlie, though I'd prefer otherwise. But my concern about coaching is logistics. The practical stuff. I can't just walk out of the office when basketball calls."

"I'm not saying, 'do it,' Doug. But I know you and I know Travis. He can talk you into just about anything."

"That's silly."

"All right. Maybe not procrastinating on his homework; maybe not sleeping late in the morning; and maybe not wearing that God-awful sweater he seems to like so much. About everything else seems negotiable. Though, thinking about it, maybe not even the sweater."

"You're as bad as I am."

"That's lame." Maddie giggled, a reaction foreign to her. Laugh, yes. Hardily on occasion. But giggle, no. Frivolity wasn't in her character. But Travis brought out a lightness in his mother that no one else could elicit. She adored the boy as one might expect, but there was something else, something special between them. I could never describe their bond, but I could see it every time she looked at him.

Maddie had changed little in the years I'd known her, though she was now almost 40. She was a handsome woman, not stunning in the sense of a beauty pageant contestant or a Hollywood starlet, but attractive in an understated way. My wife was the All-American girl. She wore a dash of makeup to tint peach-velvet soft skin. She kept her dark hair short, and though she occasionally changed styles, she never colored it; she didn't need to. A single quirk crept into her otherwise conventional wardrobe. Maddie always wore skirts. I doubt that she owned more than a pair or two of slacks. Certainly not a pair of jeans. I teased her that she wore skirts to show off a pair of long, shapely legs. She looked irritated whenever I mentioned her legs, but I think she liked that I noticed.

I sat down in the living room and drew the paper from my jacket pocket. When I switched on the table lamp beside me, the words fell from the page. Below the headline was a "Dear Parents" letter. The first few paragraphs were boilerplate about the basketball program. I skimmed them. All schools in the diocese involved; every student encouraged to participate; practice after school; games Sunday afternoons; and, so forth. Tucked near the bottom on the back side appeared a final section: "Volunteers Wanted". My eyes followed.

Volunteers Wanted

Volunteers organize and operate the League. Teachers and school administrators don't take part in any official capacity. That means the League — your children — need parents willing to give their time as coaches, assistant coaches, scorers, timekeepers, equipment managers, and assorted helpers.

> The League operates from late October through mid-March with time-off for the Christmas holidays.
>
> The League's most urgent need is for coaches. Several teams do not yet have one. We require no experience, though it helps if coaches have some familiarity with the game and its fundamentals.

Someone must be desperate to let guys coach who don't know anything about the game. Poor kid who gets one of those, I thought as I continued to read:

> Coaches and assistant coaches must be able to attend all practices (twice a week) and Sunday games.
>
> Most other positions require volunteers to be present only Sunday afternoons when the game site is St. Jerome's school gym (about twice a month). Volunteers managing equipment and uniforms can perform their jobs when convenient.
>
> The League pays no one except referees, who are sanctioned and assigned to games by it.
>
> Please consider volunteering. For further information, call Bart Anderson, Director, St. Jerome's Elementary School Athletics, between 6:00 pm and 10:00 pm, Monday - Saturday at (817)523-6586.

I was lucky; I had a great boss. Ty Finchly was a 'meet your objectives and I can be flexible' type of guy. He had three sons and a daughter older than Travis, and I knew he'd helped his kids in their school's sports program. I hadn't noticed whether those activities required his absence from the office, but my job, like his, didn't demand me to spend every moment at my desk. If I needed an afternoon for personal business, I could make up the time later. Still, a few hours here and there weren't equivalent to scheduled days of afternoon absence for an entire winter. I couldn't coach Travis's team without flextime or a similar arrangement where

I could substitute time working outside office hours for time working during them. However, my boss had an office policy against such arrangements. Ty considered flextime 'the latest non-productive management fad that would wither away to be followed by another equally goofy'.

Before I called Anderson, I warned myself: *volunteer for one of the Sunday-only jobs; don't take advantage of a good thing at work; don't get carried away; be sensible; forget coaching.*

"Anderson here."

"Mr. Anderson. My name's Doug Elliot. My son, Travis, is in fourth grade at St. Jerome's. He came home with an announcement about the school's basketball program looking for volunteers. Count me in."

"Great. Thank you." His enthusiasm made me feel as if I were the first volunteer he'd ever enlisted. "We couldn't operate the League without people like you. There's just no budget to pay anyone. Excuse me while I get my volunteer book here." I could hear pages turning on the other end of the phone. "You say your son's playing."

"Yes. He and his buddies are amped up about it."

"Love to hear when kids get excited about playing. What do you want to do?"

"I'd like to keep the scorebook. It's been a while, but I kept score three seasons for a high school JV team when I was younger. The learning curve should be low."

"I doubt there'll be any. About the only difference nowadays is a fancier book with more room for statistics you won't keep anyway. Sorry, I missed your name?"

"Doug Elliot."

"What grade's your son in?"

"Fourth."

"Oh." His drawn-out tone signaled disappointment. "I'm sorry. The fourth-grade scorer's job's taken."

"But we just got the notice?"

"I got off the phone a few minutes ago with another fourth grader's dad who volunteered for the job. Sorry. I'd forgotten the grade. There must be something else you want to do? We always need coaches." The energy returned to Anderson's voice. "No need to be Red Auerbach. Assistant coaches require no experience. Heck, they don't even need to know anything about the game. They just follow the coach's lead and more or less baby-sit when the coach can't be there." St. Jerome's athletic director took a breath and then halted. "Just a minute. What was your name again?"

"Doug Elliot."

"You've a son in the fourth-grade, right? I can't remember his name, but a bigger kid, kind of blondish hair, a lively youngster, said his dad would make a great coach."

"Did he say, 'great coach' or 'good coach'?"

"Made a mental note to follow up and forgot. I remember now."

Anderson seemed to forget a lot. I'd given him my name three times already. Within a minute or two, he'd forgotten Travis was in the fourth-grade. And, he didn't remember the scorekeeper's job was filled until he checked his book. Inattentive? Confused? Best scenario, hard of a hearing. Regardless, nothing to this point in our conversation gave me confidence that Anderson managed this basketball program well.

"Sounds like Travis volunteering me again," I said.

"A couple of other kids seemed to like the idea, too. Give me a chance to tell you about coaching. You may want to change your mind."

The recruiting began, the second round within less than two hours. Anderson launched into his pitch, likely polished during countless spiels to coaching prospects. Over the next five minutes, he made a persuasive case that coaching is an opportunity to spend time with your son working toward a common purpose. "When was the last time you did anything like that? Bet it's been a while. Take my case. I spent so much time working when the kids were young, I was cheating them. I don't like to think about it that way, but I was. Then, one winter, I did something about it. I eventually coached my oldest son for three years and my daughter for two. Best decision I ever made. The kids loved it, and we're a closer family as a result. I had fun, too. Lots of it."

"That's an attractive endorsement," I replied.

"My time with the kids was terrific. I know several other guys who've had similar experiences. With your boy's enthusiasm, I'll bet you'd have a great time."

"I probably would. No, I'm sure I would. Initially, I was interested in coaching."

"Then, what are we waiting for? Let me put you down."

I visualized Travis and me sharing a grand experience. However, reality quickly blotted the image. "I appreciate the interest Mr. Anderson, but I don't think it's a match. I work downtown and don't get off until 5:30. When does the fourth-grade practice?"

"That could present a problem." I heard pages in Anderson's volunteer book turning again. "Fourth-graders. Four o'clock on Tuesdays and Thursdays. The younger kids practice earlier. No one wants to leave them much time between dismissal and the start of practice."

"I can't see any way I can make it to school by 4:00. None. Travis will be disappointed, but maybe there'll be something else I can do. The timekeeper's job? For now, put me down for the time keeper's job. If circumstances change, I'll circle back."

The conversation ended, though neither of us liked the result. He wanted coaches; I wanted to be one. I was a timekeeper for now, but I had nothing to lose by asking Ty for flextime to coach. I'd make my case, even when I knew the answer before I asked the question.

COMMUNITY SERVICE

The brass from Dallas, company headquarters for Steiger Bros., was in the office when I walked into work the next morning. Their unannounced arrival wasn't something Ty was likely to relish. While the office was doing well and more than meeting its numbers, the visitors' sudden appearance meant the pace and direction of normal office activity would change for the day, and perhaps longer.

I planned to stop by Ty's office to ask him about time-off to coach. A drop-by normally wasn't a problem. His office was typically open. Ty's secretary confirmed the boss would be closeted with the Dallas crowd through lunch. However, she thought they might leave in the early afternoon.

"I'll let you know when he's free," she said.

Late that day my desk phone rang. "Ty has a few minutes if you want to come down."

When I arrived, I thanked her with a head bob and a smile and entered Ty's office. "Got a minute?"

"Sure. I've kissed enough 'you know what' for an entire month. Sit down." He bent his graying head toward an easy chair to the side of his desk. "You've dropped a few pounds," he said, scouring my frame from top to bottom.

"Matter of fact, I have. Back to around two hundred. College weight."

"On what? A six-one, six-two frame. Your doctor must love you." Ty looked down at his own spreading midriff and a pained expression crossed his face. "What's up?"

"I've got a personal situation. I'd like to coach my son's fourth-grade basketball team this winter."

Ty glanced at his watch as if to confirm an outside-the-office topic wasn't premature. He looked satisfied and brightened. "Good for you, Doug. I coached

Ralph and Sandra you know." He leaned back in his chair and unbuttoned the collar of his starched white shirt. "Ralph was …"

"Before we get too far. There're complications." I rose and closed the door, an act rare in the office except for personnel matters. But my topic was just that sort.

"What complications?" Ty asked. His pleased expression converted to bewildered.

"I can't do it; I can't coach without some arrangement for time-off."

"Time-off? You mean like an occasional hour or two in the afternoon to coach a game?"

"No. We practice at St. Jerome's every Tuesday and Thursday afternoon at 4:00. It takes an hour to get there."

I watched Ty's initial enthusiasm drain. "You know how I feel about flex-time, Doug. If I give it to you, I'd have to give it to everyone who asks. If I didn't, I'd have a rebellion on my hands. Last spring, an unnamed employee asked if she could work four ten-hour days and take Fridays off. With all the new development out where she lives, the traffic's getting bad."

"Yes, Mae complains about it to everyone."

Ty didn't seem surprised I could identify the 'unnamed employee'. The office was small enough so that someone complaining about traffic in the hinterland could only be one person.

"Can't blame her, Doug. Thank heavens I don't have to fight it. I sympathized but had to turn her down." Ty squirmed in his chair and pulled on his tie. "It wasn't that she'd be loafing those extra two hours when no one else was in the office. I don't think that for a minute. She may be the most conscientious employee on staff. Dallas thinks a lot of her, too." He sheepishly retreated. "No offense, Doug. You know where you stand here."

I smiled. Ty was right. Mae was good at what she did and worked hard at it. And I had no room to complain. My annual evaluations from Ty were always flattering.

"Others in the office though aren't like Mae, or you. They'd abuse a 10-hour, four-day-a-week schedule, even if unintentionally. But if I let Mae do it, what do I say when a less reliable person asks?"

"But you evaluate each of us every year. Couldn't you implement …?"

"That's difficult without measurables. Most of Mae's job is measurable. Not everyone's is." Ty shifted in his chair and leaned over the desk, his weight sliding forward. "There're other things, too, Doug. Ten hours a day? That's a long day. As we grow older, and Mae's no spring chicken, long days become harder. If it were one day, no problem. Two days, no problem. Even four days, maybe still no problem. But week after week after week? I don't think so. I also worry about covering the office with professionals during business hours. This is a mortgage insurance firm and we need people here, ready to help or sell clients when they want to talk, not when we're available."

Ty was becoming animated as he added to his argument. "What if a new employee needs help from Mae on Friday?" He pointed at me as if expecting an answer. "You guys, you, senior people, are mentors, too. You can't mentor on the telephone."

"Aren't you worried about losing Mae?" I asked. "If you won't give her the flexibility she wants, maybe she'll find an employer who will."

"That's possible I suppose." Ty slumped back into his chair, his face clouded by the thought. "But not likely. Mae isn't far from retirement. Her financial interests dictate she stays. She's in no position to do otherwise. I know." As Ty spoke, his voice dwindled and then vanished. His ample jowls sagged, and his face turned dark. He slouched. His pasty skin seemed to shrivel. The transformation came in seconds, as if he'd been peacefully coasting until he drifted off an unmarked ledge.

Ty thought of himself as a people person, and he was. He was caring and pleasant to everyone, from the most senior employee to the most junior, from the highest ranking to the lowest. While there were only a few dozen people in the office, he knew everyone's name and most of their spouses' and children's, their outside interests, and personal goals. He made a point of it. He wanted to help his people succeed, and his employees felt it. But Ty had blind spots and a stubborn streak. I'd just landed in one of them, a newly discovered open sore.

Mae's productivity and health with the longer hours and office coverage were legitimate concerns, as was equitable treatment of other employees, even those likely to abuse Ty's generosity. However, those reasons now appeared excuses, formal justifications for exercising the authority he held over her. His altered manner confessed that he had denied Mae's request, not so much out of principle, but because he could. She had no leverage. She couldn't change jobs without significant adverse financial consequences. He knew it and had taken advantage.

Ty's narrowed eyes were almost closed. They stared straight ahead, vacant. He was motionless and didn't make a sound. Damp spots began to circle beneath his arms and deep wrinkles appeared in the crisp twill inside his bent elbows. He seemed alone. I could only guess what he was thinking, but it had to be unpleasant.

Our conversation had taken an unforeseen direction, one neither of us could have expected. "I understand Mae won't press the issue, but eventually someone will. I won't be that guy, either. My situation's too much like Mae's. But you'd better plan for the day when someone does challenge you, and the distasteful choices that'll follow."

Ty remained immobile, his expression unchanging. "I'm sorry, Doug. I can't let you do it," he almost whispered.

My boss was uncomfortable, more than I'd seen in the 14 years I'd worked for Steiger Bros. It wasn't denial of my request that bothered him, or so I believed. That decision conformed with announced office policy. Nor was it the denial of Mae's request *per se*. What bothered him was the leverage he'd used to deny her. He mumbled almost inaudibly, "I made the right decision, but if I made the right decision for the wrong reason, was it really right?" What little voice audible, tailed off.

"Excuse me?" I leaned toward him, not certain I'd heard correctly.

"Oh. Nothing. Nothing," Ty said.

The late afternoon sun lit the darkening office. Neither of us reached for a light switch. "I didn't mean to make Mae the topic. But since we're here, maybe we can make the best of it."

Ty rolled his hand to wave my thinking forward, though his face showed little interest.

"If I do this coaching thing, I must leave early on Tuesdays and Thursdays."

"Excuse me." Ty straightened and shifted his gaze directly to me. "I thought I said 'no'." He extended his gaze beyond the sentence to underscore his point, and then slipped back into his slouched position.

"Hear me out. For argument's sake, let's say I'm out of the office five hours a week until the season ends. Let's also say, for the moment, we could make some arrangements and you don't object. How do you sell that to the other employees in the office?"

"But I do object."

"Please. Stay with me." I knew I was pressing him. Hard. I had no idea how much farther I could go.

Ty sat. Silent. His eyes focused on me, and he was listening, but his scowl told me he suspected the entire endeavor.

"Let's call this thing community service. I take five hours a week during the winter to help kids, one of whom is mine. I remain accountable for all work-related activities. When the season's over, we re-evaluate. Or maybe I should say evaluate. What's my productivity? What are others saying? Complaints from clients? Favorable publicity? Feedback from Dallas? You get the idea." Ty's expression didn't change. "The beauty is that it's temporary. No one is committed. It's an experiment."

"Experiment?" Ty repeated lifelessly. That single word seemed to spark a modicum of interest. "Suppose I go along with your little experiment. Mae …? How do I explain this to Mae?"

I thought for a moment, more for affect than indecision. Ty couldn't think my response flippant or rehearsed, or I feared I might lose him.

"How about this? Announce to the office I'll be doing community service on an experimental basis this winter. Emphasize I'll continue to carry my normal load during the period. If the experiment is successful, which you can define anyway you like, you'll be open to community service requests from other employees. Then, take Mae aside and tell her that if my situation works, you'll favorably entertain hers."

"You're telling me to surrender." He said, again sitting erect. "Your proposal reverses my flextime policy. I can't do that, and I won't."

"Think about it, Ty. How many people in the office will want flextime for community service with the conditions you attach? A few young idealists? Maybe. But they can do good at other times of the day or week and not confront your conditions. Situations like Mae's are more difficult, I grant. But you could use seniority, for example. After you've been here 10 years, you can do this; 15 years, that; and so on. It's a perk, an employee benefit."

"What about young people with no seniority wanting to go back to school part-time?"

"That's easy. You hire them as part-time employees."

"Steiger Bros. doesn't hire part-time employees."

"My point."

Ty lightened for the first time in the last 15 minutes.

"Okay. Okay," Ty said, though I could tell he still was unhappy. "Write it up. I want this whole thing on paper, including measurables for your performance. And I want you to explain how the company benefits."

"Fair enough."

Ty swallowed, and looked off into the distance. I heard him breathing. The room was almost dark now. He turned the switch on a large brass table lamp sitting near the edge of his desk. It didn't light the room but did illuminate the immediate area.

Ty returned the conversation to our initial topic, one he obviously felt more comfortable discussing. He stretched his arms high above his head, the dampness under them now pronounced, then clasp his hands and positioned them behind his neck and leaned back. "When I coached my son, Ralph, I had this father. He called a couple of times a week about … 'the team'. Dad wanted to assess the previous week's game and talk strategy about next week's opponent. Hell, most of the time I didn't even know who we were playing next week, and he was scouting them. Anyway, after we finished those preliminaries, the conversation always turned to his kid. How could we get his kid more shots? Or how could his kid occupy a more central position on the team? Mostly, it was about getting his kid more shots."

Ty relaxed telling the story. He took off his tie, folded it, and lay it on the side of his desk.

"Was the kid any good?" I asked.

"Short, fat kid. Built like his dad. Modest skills. I'd have rated him about third or fourth best on my team. If I were to get any kid more shots, he wouldn't have been my choice." Ty leaned back again in his chair and repositioned his hands behind his neck. "I think the old man considered the kid a Division-I prospect. Probably already had school admission forms on his desk so the kid could walk-on, just in case Coach Knight missed him in the recruitment process. If not Indiana, then Duke, Kentucky, North Carolina, or some other college powerhouse."

"Was the kid as clueless as Dad? Or did he just go along to gig the old man?"

"Interesting question." Ty reflected and then rendered judgment. "It was mostly Dad, I think. Kids watch TV and identify with elite teams. But turn off the TV and the fantasy fades. They're on to something else. At least most kids. Some are more delusional. Yet when a guy flashes around you for an uncontested bucket, you quickly get the idea. You recognize there's a pecking order and you're not even on the tree."

"And Dad?"

"Dad's different. He isn't on to something else. His playing days are over. But he goes on dreaming through his kid. The more television portrays exceptional athletes growing up in unexceptional neighborhoods, the more they see their sons as possibly one of them. Everybody wants something special for their kids. But I mean … get real. All kids can't be Michael Jordan."

"The odds of playing in a major college basketball program have to be tiny," I said. "Somewhere I saw that three percent of all seniors playing high school basketball play in college. Any college. And how many grade school players get to play in high school? It has to be a tiny fraction."

"Tried every way possible to avoid the guy." Ty sighed. "Never had so many business dinners as I had that winter. Dad couldn't take the hint. If he didn't catch me at home, he'd show up at practice. I began to wonder if the guy ever worked."

"Nothing you could do?"

Ty answered with sad eyes wandering to the dimmest corner of the office. "Be rude, I suppose. It's probably the only way, though that seems excessive. This stuff is supposed to be fun. It's supposed to be about kids, not parents." Ty swiveled his head and returned his gaze to me. "I wish you luck. With the parents."

I rose to leave. "Hold on? How could Dad scout next week's opponent when he was watching his son's game? Didn't the league play all its games at the same time?"

Ty chuckled, the color returning to his face. "He didn't; his older son did. And that was strange, too. Would you believe ... the only time Dad let the poor kid use a family car was Sunday afternoons to scout the opposition. That meant the only way he could to see his girlfriend was to take her along. A completed scout sheet was the price they paid for a date."

Later that evening I reported first to Travis and then to Anderson that I'd coach St. Jerome's fourth-grade basketball team in the coming season.

ONE GRADE: TWO TEAMS

"Remember, Dad. Be sure to get Rickie and Casey. We want to play together." Travis had his priorities for the team, and a unified *Troika* was priority number one. If I returned from this evening's meeting without the three as members of the same team, any good will I'd earned from my son by agreeing to coach would be lost. The three of them got into this together, just as they got into practically everything else together, and they assumed nothing would prevent the same from recurring. I didn't expect a problem either. Until one surfaced.

Fifteen of the 18 boys in the fourth-grade class signed up to play basketball. The number was too many for a single team. Ten would have been ideal, resulting in two groups of five, equal numbers to scrimmage against one another in practice, and few enough to provide ample minutes for every player in games.

The St. Jerome's fifth-grade team was also oversubscribed. It had 13 boys who wanted to play, two of whom hadn't played on the fourth-grade team the year before.

Anderson resolved the numbers problem for both classes with surprising dexterity. He ordered one fifth-grade team and two fourth-grade teams. The two fifth graders who hadn't played the year before would drop to the fourth-grade players' pool, forming two fourth-grade teams of eight and nine members. He recruited another fourth grader's father to coach the second team, and the numbers headache vanished.

That night, the three of us - Anderson, the other coach, and I - would meet at the St. Jerome's gym to sign out keys, review potential safety issues, and decide who would play on which team. There'd been no try-outs. Neither coach knew the skill level of any player compared to any other. I'd never seen my son play basketball, though I had an idea of his athletic ability and competitiveness. The same was true for Rickie and Casey. But other than that, I had no basis to select team members.

"I don't know how we'll choose teams, Travis. Mr. Anderson didn't tell me, but I'll do everything possible to ensure *The Troika* stays together."

Travis didn't seem to consider landing the three friends a problem. He was on to another concern, filling the rest of the roster with other close friends and the best players possible. "You should get Zack, Dad. He's really good, the best player in our grade. By far."

"Is he a friend of yours? I haven't heard you mention him before."

"Yup. But he lives across town. We don't do a lot of stuff together outside school."

"Then, how do you know he's so good?"

"Everybody says so."

"Has everybody seen him play?"

"We shoot baskets on the playground sometimes when we don't play dodge ball. Zack's better than most of the bigger kids. By far." Travis's voice became more excited and his words spilled more rapidly. "You should see him dribble, Dad. He can go behind his back. He's been on a team before, too, on a city league team." A city recreation league team apparently burnished Zack's basketball credentials.

"What kind of kid is Zack? Sometimes guys who're really good hog the ball. No one gets to touch it but them. That's no fun."

"Not Zack, Dad. Everybody likes him. Besides, he and Casey are the smartest ones in class, girls or boys."

"So, I should choose Zach if possible?" I asked, awaiting final instructions.

"Yup. And then you want to get George Kovac," Travis said, adding another name to his list.

"Who's George Kovac?"

"He's tall. The tallest kid in class. He's new this year, so I don't know him like the other kids. His Dad picks him up right after school lets out. I always try to get him on my dodge ball team. He's really good picking off guys. He throws the ball hard, too. No one wants to get hit by George." Tall helps in basketball, but I didn't see the immediate relevance of the boy's dodge ball skills. Still, Travis had more insight on the available talent than I did.

"Okay. *The Troika*, Zack, and George in that order. Is there anyone I should avoid? A jerk? Someone who can't get along or is going to be a problem? Maybe a kid whose parents are always visiting school? The last thing I need is an overly protective parent."

Travis shrugged. "Not really," he said. His assessment mirrored the intelligence Maddie received earlier from Rita Horvath, her school informant. That meant I could choose kids for my team without worrying about behavior problems.

"There're some guys who are bad," Travis said.

"You just told me there were no behavior problems in your class?"

"No. I mean play bad."

"You mean play poorly, not bad."

"Okay. Poorly. Carleton and Freddie, they're nerds. I like them. There're good guys. But they trip a lot."

"Like trip and fall?"

"They don't fall. Carleton did the other day at recess. But not most of the time. They just trip."

"You mean they're not coordinated?"

"I guess so. They trip a lot."

"Did they sign up to play?"

"Yup."

"I don't want kids who trip a lot. Anyone else I should try avoid, or get?"

"Maybe, Andy."

"Okay. Maybe, Andy. Do I try to get him or avoid him?

"Get him."

"Do you know anything about the two fifth-graders, Wilfredo Hernandez and Randal Wise? They'll be on one of the fourth-grade teams. Are they good guys?"

"Geez. I don't know." Travis's mood changed; his face soured; and his eyes blazed as he looked straight into mine. "The fifth-grade has a lot of jerks in it, Dad. Always talking big and pushing around the little kids. I don't like them. No one in my class does."

"Are Hernandez and Wise jerks?

"I don't know," he said, his curt tone unchanging. "If they're fifth graders, choose somebody else. The fifth-grade is the worst of the worst."

I met Anderson and Carleton's dad, Jordan Whitley, the other fourth-grade coach, at the entrance to the school gym promptly at 6:30. The single security bulb hanging over the metal double doors dimly lit the area, providing enough glow to disclose Whitley as an early middle-aged man, short, and slightly built, particularly compared to the hulking Anderson. Close to nothing else about Whitley was nondescript. He sported heavy-lensed horned-rim glasses and a handle-bar mustache that nearly blocked the parts of his face uncovered by frames and lenses. More striking, his swirling bush was bright crimson. Masses of flaming red curly hair fell over the top of his receding hairline to complement the thicket below. He dressed in Ivy League issue: blue blazer, diagonally stripped blue and light green tie, and gray slacks. The embroidered crest on his blazer pocket was too faint to decipher, limiting what I could further surmise about my new colleague. Though he hadn't uttered a word, I already considered him the most interesting person I'd met in a long time.

I held out my hand. "You must be Whitley. My son told me you're coaching the other fourth-grade team." I glanced sideways at Anderson, who had had more than one opportunity to tell me he had formed a second fourth-grade team and either had forgotten or chosen not to do so. "Glad to meet you. I understand you have a son in the class, too."

"Yes." His hand reached for mine. After a couple of abrupt pumps for a handshake, his right arm rolled mid-way into the air as an actor might when highlighting a character's line. "I do. Carleton. He's excited to play basketball. I was surprised at his interest. Look at me." His eyes scanned his body from chest to toe. "If you looked at Carleton, you'd see me minus the mustache. We aren't exactly the athletic type." Whitley laughed in a self-depreciating manner. "I'm excited about it, though. Exercise, a good father-son bonding opportunity." He moved his head up and down as if to confirm his favorable appraisal.

I turned to Anderson and held out my hand. "We've talked on the phone. Nice to meet you in person." Other than his immense size, height and weight, nothing in his appearance was memorable.

"Same here." The loquacious, ebullient personality he'd shown to recruit me had disappeared sometime between then and now.

Anderson unlocked the door and turned on an overhead bank of lights, partially illuminating St. Jerome's home court. The gym was laid out as a practical, multi-purpose facility. Eight rows of wooden bleachers flanked us on both left and right as we entered. Across the court was a darkened stage, elevated three feet above the floor, purple curtains wide open at their sides. A small set of chorus' risers rested in its center, fronting a medieval castle wall designed for a class play. Black metal piping suspended from the ceiling anchored two basketball hoops framed by large rectangular glass backboards, one set at each end. An electronic scoreboard hung from the wall high, behind the basket to the right. A yellow color covered the exposed cinder block walls except for a large, contrasting purple script, "Saint Jerome's, Home of the Scholars," highlighting the two unbroken sides.

It didn't take Anderson long to show Whitley and me the equipment closet, the first aid kit locations, and the school's three pay telephones. Four leather basketballs, hand numbered 'one' through 'four' with a black felt pen, constituted the program's equipment inventory. They never left the gym. The result was a basketball shortage when St. Jerome's played as a visiting team. There were no school basketballs for those games. Players brought their own. Most were of the cheaper rubber variety. But if no player brought a ball, the coach was the last resort.

"I don't understand," said Whitley as he filtered escaping saliva through the crimson hairs growing on his upper lip. "Are we dependent on some kid bringing a basketball to an away game? Or do we just borrow balls from the opposition? What am I missing here?" He was almost yelling, the spit congealing on his mustache faster than he could vacuum it back.

"That never seems to be a problem," Anderson replied. "The kids usually have balls. They may not be the best. But they work. The home team produces the game balls and they're always leather. League rules."

"I understand economizing," Whitley said to him. "But economizing with the most essential part of the game, the basketball? What do three or four basketballs cost compared to a full set of uniforms?"

All of St. Jerome's teams had cool uniforms, at least according to Rickie. I was curious. "Do we have pull-over warm-ups, too?" I asked Anderson, who by now had drifted away from his two rebellious volunteers. He didn't respond, though I couldn't tell whether the reason was out of pique or he was too far away to hear. "Misplaced priorities drive me nuts. A pet peeve," I said in a deadened tone meant only for Whitley's ears. "I see it too often at work. And here we go again. The relative consequences are different here, but the principle's the same. Why's it so hard to separate the critical from the trivial?"

"Basketballs or uniforms?" Whitley said, peering down at one upturned palm and then the other. He dropped the left and raised the right; he dropped the right and raised the left. "Basketballs or uniforms?" His eyes jumped from palm to palm as if he were debating each option. "Basketballs or uniforms?" Then he looked up with a broad grin. "I'd say basketballs are the higher priority."

I looked at my fellow coach, the man who had initiated the Anderson prod, and returned his grin.

The three of us soon finished the minutiae. The evening's most important agenda item, selection of teams, followed.

"So, how are we going to do this, guys?" Anderson said. "The usual way? Alternating choices? One guy picks a kid, then the other picks, and so on? Remember, we have 15 fourth graders and the two fifth. I told you earlier about the fifth graders."

"Let's talk about this before we start," Whitley said. "I'm here to be with my son. He has friends he wants to play with. This is new for Carleton, out of his comfort zone. I hope he can have some of his closest friends on his team. Maybe that'll happen if we choose up sides in the usual way. But maybe it won't. What do you think, Doug?"

"Travis has close friends he wants to play with, too."

"Whatever you guys want to do," Anderson said.

"We both want our sons. That's a given," I reasoned aloud. "My son Travis has two particularly close buddies, Casey Costello and Rickie Hansen. We call the three *The Troika*. They hang out all the time. Went to camp together last summer. You get the idea."

"That's fine," Whitley said. "They should be on your team." He pulled a piece of paper from his pocket, glasses teetering on his nose as he examined it. "Carleton wants to play with Freddie, for sure. I remember Sam coming over to the house. Jason, likewise. I'd like them on my team. Okay? That would give me four." He looked at me and then back at the paper he held.

Travis would be happy. I'd already satisfied his minimum requirement. The rest would be extra credit. "Is that a list of everybody who signed up?" I asked Whitley.

"Yes."

"Mind if I look? I forgot mine."

He handed me the paper, and I glanced at it. What I said was true. I'd forgotten my copy of the roster. But I didn't need a piece of paper to know who was available. I had the list memorized. My request was a small ruse to keep the conversation casual. A strict alternating choice format might alert Whitley to the fact I intended to claim the best athletes in the class. After a brief perusal, I returned the list. My task now was to secure Zack and George and avoid anyone who was terrible. But after the two, I had no idea of any player's skill level.

"Travis mentioned Zack several times. Can I have him?" Whitley looked back at the list. He said nothing. Silence. He seemed somewhere else. My pulse quickened; I grew afraid he may be onto my ploy. I took a deep breath and waited for an answer.

Whitley appeared to regain consciousness. "Oh, sure. Sorry. When I heard the name 'Zack' it triggered a thought about a business matter and ... " His explanation tailed off as if he'd already said too much.

Four targets selected. One to go. "Travis tells me there's a new kid in class, George. A bit shy. No siblings in school. We'd like to bring him into the group. *The Troika's* pretty good at that. Not that the kids on your team aren't."

"That's a nice thought," Whitley said.

Anderson had dragged out a small notebook and was engaged with it. He seemed satisfied to let his two charges complete their work. Absent a cacophonous row between us, the program director didn't appear likely to meddle.

"You have five and I have four," Whitley said. "That leaves six from our class and the two fifth graders. I wish Carleton were here to help. There're a few familiar names on the list I recognize. In fact, I think I served on a committee with this boy's father." He pointed at 'Wozniak, M' below 'Wozniak, F' on the paper. "Yes. I forgot there's a set of twins in the class, and I'm sure their dad and I shared some committee." His cheeks bulged from his broad grin, pushing the frame of his glasses up on his nose while dribbles of spittle appeared at the lower edge of his mustache. "They'd fit with my team. Good to have twins play together. It also saves me a phone call whenever I have to reach the team."

Anderson interrupted, "You'll want a telephone tree. It saves time. The mothers usually take charge of it." Except for doling out keys, this trifling piece of advice was Anderson's major contribution for the evening.

Player selection went smoothly. Everyone seemed happy. One bothersome issue remained.

"Do you know anything about the fifth graders?" I asked Anderson.

"Just what I said. The fifth-grade team was over-subscribed, and these were the two kids who didn't play last season. Beyond that, I don't know if they're big or small, good or bad. I guess I should say skilled or unskilled, behavior problems or not. But I don't think it's hard to figure out that if the kids could play, their classmates wouldn't let them go."

"Travis likes everybody in the fourth-grade," I said. "When I asked him about the fifth, he was decidedly negative. 'Mouthy' and 'pick on smaller kids' were the two phrases I remember. I asked him about the two names on the list. He didn't know either one."

I gave Whitley my best 'what-do-you-want-to-do' look. His up-turned palms rolled outward, and his arms and shoulders rose. His mustache twitched. His expression broadcasted, 'Don't ask me. I don't have a clue'.

Guilt began to seep into my conscience. I was taking advantage of Whitley. Travis had given me some idea of who could play and who couldn't, and I'd drafted all of those who could. Whitley seemed to have the best of intentions. He wanted to work with his son and his son's friends. I felt the same, but I also wanted to win. Perhaps he did, too, though my guess was he hadn't even thought about it.

"Tell you what, Whitley. Travis says there aren't any jerks in the fourth-grade, just some kids he likes better than others. Does Carleton have trouble with anyone in the class?"

"Not that I know of. He's not spoken ill of anyone I can recall."

"Okay. I'll take the two fifth graders, sight unseen, and hope for the best." I needed to salve my conscience. "Throw in Andy. I've heard Travis mention him. You take the remainder of the fourth graders."

Whitley's face crunched. I could see him in deep thought as his tongue darted across the bottom of his mustache. He studied the player list, running a forefinger up and down the paper. Then, with a grand swoop he held out his hand and with the corners of his mouth rising said, "I think we've got an arrangement that makes everyone happy. You have eight and I have nine. You have the two fifth-graders." He then read each name on his list, assigning it to the team he understood they would play for.

Whitley seemed pleased; I was ecstatic; Anderson was ready to go home.

"Do you need a list of the two teams now?" Whitley asked Andersen.

"Not really. Mail me one. However, I hope you'll have time to call each kid when you get home tonight and tell them they're on your team. They understand we're meeting and will want to know the outcome as soon as possible. That's my experience, anyway."

As Anderson started to turn off the lights, Whitley and I headed out the metal double doors. I'd scarcely planted both feet on the sidewalk behind the building when Whitley grabbed my elbow. "Do you mind if I call you from time to time for help? I bought a couple of basketball coaching books. One of them looks pretty good, but it focuses more on older kids." Glancing over his shoulder, he said, "Anderson seems more interested in filling slots than helping those of us who occupy them."

I nodded. "You're right about that." I reached into my pants pocket and pulled a business card from my wallet. "Here's my card. I'm writing my home number on the back."

Travis met me at the door like a puppy waiting for a bone. "How'd we do? How'd we do?"

"*The Troika* will play together."

"Yea! Way to go, Dad. Me and Casey and Rickie are on the same team." Travis was almost dancing, his feet not sure if they should be going up and down or side to side. But whatever direction they headed, they did so energetically.

Maddie joined us amid the commotion.

"Mom, Mom. You won't believe it. Me and Casey and Rickie are playing on the same basketball team."

"So, I heard. The neighborhood probably did, too. By the way young man, it's Casey, Rickie and I, not me and Casey and Rickie."

"That's what I said."

Maddie beamed as she shook her head.

Travis's feet slowed as he poised for his next question. "Who else is on the team?

"Zack."

"Zack?"

"Didn't you tell me to choose him?" I said, laughing at his excitement.

"Our team's going to be good, Dad. Really good." Travis was dancing again. "Mom, Zack's on our team and he's the best player in school. By far."

"I've heard that."

"Who else? Who else is on the team?" Travis asked.

"We have George and Andy."

Travis swept into a little twirl as he threw his arms into the air. "Yea. Yea."

"Do my choices meet your approval?" I asked, knowing the answer.

"Way to go, Dad." His grin said more than his words. "Who else?"

My glow lifted and I adopted a more business-like tone. "The two fifth graders, but I don't know anything more about them now than I did before. We'll just have to see what kind of guys they are."

Travis immediately exchanged his grin for a somber look. His feet stopped, planted. Then with a deep sigh, he said, "Maybe they'll be okay." Recovering his sparkle, he ran for the phone. "I have to call everybody. They'll want to know they're on my team."

"Time out, young man. I need the phone to call everyone's parents. You can talk to your buddies in the morning. Now, finish your homework."

"Dad."

"Homework. Now."

I needed to notify the parents of each team member that evening that their son would play for me this season. The task had to be completed swiftly because it was nearing the hour when phone calls were inappropriate. I decided to first call the parents I didn't know personally, starting with my two fifth graders. Friends and acquaintances would likely be more tolerant of late calls.

Wilfredo Hernandez's parents were first on my list. I dialed. A female voice answered.

"Mrs. Hernandez? My name is Doug Elliot. I'm a basketball coach at St. Jerome's school and Wilfredo will play on my team this season." I didn't know if I should use the verb "selected," "drafted," "chosen," "assigned," or whatever to describe what had taken place earlier that evening. I settled on 'will play'.

"Oh, that's nice." Her heavy Hispanic accent bubbled. "He'll be so happy."

"I'm glad to have him, Mrs. Hernandez. You understand that Wilfredo's a fifth grader, but he'll be playing on a fourth-grade team. That's because he hasn't played organized basketball before."

She either didn't understand or didn't care. She hurried on. "Wilfredo isn't here now. He's with his papa at the bodega."

"I don't need to talk to him." I felt myself speaking slowly, enunciating every sound to be clear. "Please tell Wilfredo that he's on my basketball team, on Doug Elliot's team, and I'll contact him soon about our first practice."

"Oh. *Si. Si.*"

"I'll also mail you and Mr. Hernandez a letter with a schedule of practices and games, the behavior I expect from the players, and so on."

"Yes. Yes."

"Do you have any questions for me?"

"No. No." Her excitement was audible. But when she had nothing further, it seemed the perfect point to end our brief conversation.

"Good evening, Mrs. Hernandez, and thank you very much."

"*Gracias.* Thank you, *Senor. Buenas noches.*"

It had been a great night. I selected Travis's friends and the kids he said were skilled. Then one of the unknown fifth graders has a mother who seems as cheerful and pleasant as one could ask. If Mrs. Hernandez' son remotely resembled his mom, he'd fit wonderfully with the team and its coach. I hope she'd attend our games. I wanted to meet her.

My next call was to the parents of the other fifth grader, Randal Wise. The phone rang only once before someone picked up the receiver.

"Hello?"

"Hello, my name is Doug Elliot." I repeated the information I gave Mrs. Hernandez before the listener could say a word.

"It's a little late to call," responded a stiff, grainy male voice.

"I apologize, but we just finished selecting teams, and we wanted to let the kids know which team they're playing on as soon as possible. We didn't want a situation where some knew, and others didn't."

"Select? I thought Randal was playing on St. Jerome's fifth-grade team."

"The fifth-grade team was oversubscribed. Too many boys wanted to participate. Since Randal hasn't played before, he was assigned to a fourth-grade team, my team.

"Who made that decision?" The voice was abrupt.

It was Anderson, but that seemed irrelevant at this point. "Sorry, I'm not sure," I replied.

"Why should my son play with boys a grade below? He doesn't know anyone in the fourth-grade. It'll just give his classmates another reason to pick on him. Randal already gets enough of that. He doesn't need any more because of a basketball team."

"Another boy from the fifth-grade, Wilfredo Hernandez, will also be on my team."

"Don't know him and I still don't like it. Who can I talk to?"

"The man in charge of the program is Bart Anderson. His number's 817/523-6586. I doubt you can reach him now. He was just at our player selection meeting and had a few errands to run before going home."

I heard Wise spew a muffled grunt.

"Please tell Randal he's on my team, so he isn't the only boy in school who signed-up and doesn't know who he's playing for. I'll contact him soon about the first practice and will mail you a letter with the schedule and so forth. Good evening."

I hung up, hoping the kid didn't take after the old man. But I feared Randal Wise was my penance for hoarding the best players. Then I remembered Ty's advice, 'be rude' with parents when you must, and your coaching life will be much more pleasant.

Conversations with the fourth graders' parents were uniformly enjoyable, each seeming eager for his or her son to play. They thanked me for volunteering and pledged their cooperation and support. Most added that they planned to attend as many games as possible, a prospect I verbally endorsed. A father or two even muttered something about helping should the need arise. A few chats had to be cut short due to the late hour and the need to complete every call. Still, my task ended by 9:30, the self-imposed deadline.

The evening was a propitious beginning to my community service project. Little could have gone better except the conversation with Mr. Wise. It was a sour note that bore attention to ensure it neither deteriorated nor spread. But I felt excited as I lay down to sleep. This was going to be fun.

THE COACHES' MEETING

Only a few vehicles clustered near the front doors of St. Bernadette's, one of the two Catholic high schools in the diocese. As the older and more centrally located, it hosted the annual coaches' meetings for the diocese's grade school basketball league. Tonight, the fourth- and fifth-grade coaches took their turn.

The official reason to separate coaches for grade level meetings was different rules for different grades. However, Anderson cautioned 'the rules' was a pretense to encourage competing coaches to meet and socialize. The theory was that if coaches knew one another as people rather than as competitors, any rancor arising during games would be minimized. Or at least, it would dampen competitive instincts and dull the sharpest edges. Anderson told me he thought the theory was pure garbage. I was inclined to agree.

A white cardboard poster in the dimly lit lobby read *Basketball Coaches' Meeting*, 8:00 pm, Room 8D. A big red arrow near the bottom pointed to the right, down the hall. Two young men walked in the front door behind me and another three mingled just outside what appeared to be the meeting room.

I could smell strong coffee and suppressed a chuckle. Anderson was right. Someone wanted to encourage the coaches to socialize, though an evening beer was more likely to do the trick than an evening coffee.

The meeting was open to anyone. Twelve schools were in the league, each with at least one fourth- and one fifth-grade team, a minimum of 24 coaches. Assistant coaches, referees, team moms, and other interested parties swelled potential attendance. So, when I entered Room 8D, I was astonished. My count was15 people, including the three who entered before me and the two who trailed. A tall, thin, balding man in short sleeves, faded jeans, and sneakers was writing on the board. He presumably was the League Commissioner, Paul Spenser.

The night was pleasant, and the traffic light on my drive over. Still, 8:00 on a work-night is never an attractive meeting time and probably eliminated more than a few potential attendees. Veteran coaches had likely skipped. They'd experienced the rules and probably needed no refresher. Besides, the Commissioner mailed a summary of the meeting and an updated set of rules to every coach. The demography of the room supported that explanation. It was young. Most attendees appeared in their 30s, making me one of two graybeards in the room. The coaches seemed in reasonably good physical condition, as former athletes might, though a few paunches were starting to fall over belts. The contingent was entirely male. Most wore nothing out of the ordinary, a jacket against the evening chill and jeans or khakis. A couple with pulled down ties appeared to be refugees straight from work. But more than one sported a high school, maybe even a college, letter jacket, the kind with a colored wool vest offset with light tan leather sleeves, and a school's initial, its letter, displayed on the upper left chest panel. One large fellow exhibited a dark blue "F" on his chest with *Warriors* scrawled in white across the back of his shoulders; another showed a Kelly green "A", and a third flashed a burgundy letter "P".

For all the good intentions, socializing was not the evening's group activity. No one drank coffee; no one ate doughnuts. A few scanned the ceiling while others checked their cuticle or gazed at bulletin board displays. Anything to avoid talking to one another. Spenser's chalk squeaked across the board, the loudest sound in the room. I didn't know a soul. Whitley was a no-show and if anyone needed to learn something, anything, about basketball and the league, it was him. I later learned St. Jerome's experienced fifth-grade coach was also missing.

I took a final glance around the room before grabbing a seat and noticed a vaguely familiar face off to the far side. I walked over and sat down next to him, an ordinary-looking fellow, the only other guy of my age in the room.

"Hi. My name's Doug Elliot. We've met somewhere. I apologize. I just can't remember where."

"Fred Bauer," the fellow said. His face hardened and his eyes narrowed. He ran a hand down his cheek. Shortly, his lips brightened into a broad smile. "Jonas. You're a friend of George Jonas."

"That's it. We worked together on that fundraiser George chaired two or three years ago."

"Sure did. Raised a few bucks for a good cause, too. Seen George lately?"

"As a matter of fact, I saw him and several of the guys from the fund-raiser a few weeks ago. We had our end-of-season banquet for the golf league over at

Stanky's, in the back room. Remember? We had some organizational meetings there."

"You bet I do."

"Let's get the meeting started," yelled Spenser from the front of the room.

"Talk to you afterwards," I whispered to Bauer.

"Welcome everyone. Thanks for coming. We've got fresh coffee over there for anyone who wants it. Doughnuts, too. Don't be afraid to help yourself. They're free."

The coffee did smell good, but no one budged.

"Let's start with introductions. I'll go first and then we'll move around the room. When it's your turn, tell us who you are, what grade and school you represent, and maybe something about yourself. Okay? I'm Paul Spenser, the League Commissioner. I've been doing this for seven years. The Commissioner's job is to organize the league and handle disputes. I coached for several seasons over at St. Mathew's when my kids were young."

He pointed to the closest fellow on his right, directing him to be the next to introduce himself.

"John Jarasek, fifth-grade coach, Holy Name. Oh yeah, this is my first-year coaching." Jarasek stopped and turned his head toward the next in line. The pattern held for the remainder of the room, including me. Name, grade, school, and coaching experience, nothing more. Every coach was new to the league except Fred Bauer and one other.

Spenser retook the floor. "Look guys. This is a pre-junior high league, a mixed fourth- and fifth-grade activity. It's probably a little different than anything you've experienced. Each school in the diocese has a team for both grades. A few of the bigger schools have more. St. Bartholomew's, for example, has two teams for each grade. St. Luke's has one. St. Jerome's has one for the fifth and two for the fourth. It's pretty much a matter of school size and how many kids come out for the team. When things don't balance, you may notice a few fifth graders on fourth-grade teams and vice versa.

Spenser stopped and looked around. "If you guys have any as questions as we go, give a shout. Don't be bashful about the coffee, either. Now, we have a fourth- and a fifth-grade division. Fourth graders play fourth-grade teams and fifth graders play fifth-grade teams. At the end of season, the winning fourth-grade team plays the winning fifth-grade team for the league championship. Quite frankly, I don't know why we bother. The fifth-grade kids always wallop the fourth graders. They should. They're a year older, bigger and more mature, and they've played more games than their fourth-grade counterparts." Spenser paused and frowned as if he were deliberating the game's future. "We really need to revisit the reasons to play that game. Yeah, we do. But the rules are set for the year. So, there'll be a championship playoff game between the winners of the fourth-grade division and the winners of the fifth-grade division." The Commissioner returned to the agenda. "There're 16 games plus the championship. You'll play some teams once and others twice." He looked around the room as if expecting questions. "Don't ask. The schedule's locked. Half of your games are at home, and half are away. All games are Sunday afternoon at 2:00. Now, let me hand out the schedules. Take one and pass on the rest."

Bauer nudged me, and whispered, "Fourth or fifth?"

"Fourth."

"Me, too. What school?"

"St. Jerome's."

"St. Leo's."

"Got a kid on the team?"

"Don't you?"

I smiled and nodded.

The league scheduled St. Jerome's to play St. Leo's twice, one game early in the season at St. Jerome's and one later at St. Leo's. I expected those games would be fun. Bauer may have been an ordinary-looking fellow, but as I recalled from our brief shared experience, he was intelligent and organized. His team was likely to reflect those characteristics.

Spenser continued. "We play six-minute quarters. That doesn't sound like much, but you'd be surprised how gassed little kids get in that short time frame. Six minutes also gives you plenty of opportunity to play your subs."

A hand shot up from one of the letter jackets.

Spenser recognized him. "Yeah?"

"What are the rules on playing time? I mean, is there a rule that requires every kid on the team to play a minimum number of minutes? And if so, how many? And who keeps track of the time? Or is playing time up to the coach?" And as if his point weren't obvious, he added, "As it should."

"This comes up every year," Spenser said. "I know a lot of you coach Little League baseball and they require every player to bat at least once and play two innings in the field. We don't do that because we have different numbers of kids on the teams. We also can't have people sitting at the scorer's desk with stop watches counting the seconds each kid plays. That being said, these are young boys in a pre-junior high league. We expect coaches, all coaches, to give every kid a chance to play. I also expect you to play them more than some artificial minimum."

Another hand was in the air. A guy with a pulled down tie apparently wasn't satisfied with Spenser's response. "In a league I'm familiar with, they handle the playing time issue easily. Every kid must play one uninterrupted, full quarter. The administrative issue is non-existent. Every kid is assured a minimum amount of playing time, kind of like Little League. Why can't we do something like that here?"

"As I said, not everyone has the same number of players," Spenser responded. "Some teams have 8 and some have 12. A minimum time requirement gives teams with fewer players a competitive advantage. I'll bet the league you're talking about has a fixed number of players on every team. Little League does, at least around here. We can't do that so long as we accept every kid who wants to play and base our league on schools. I don't see either changing anytime soon."

A different letter jacket joined the conversation. The rising pitch and dry wobble in his voice argued the guy wasn't accustomed to speaking in public. "Yeah, minimum times tilt the playing field." He cleared his throat. "They give some teams an advantage over others. That shouldn't happen." He cleared his throat again and sat down.

"What about kids just playing and getting some exercise? When did we get so competitive? They'll learn that soon enough."

The new speaker sat directly behind me. Before I could turn around to see who it was, a pulled down tie on the other side of the room chimed in. "Yeah. These are fourth and fifth graders. Some of these kids can't even bounce a ball and we're worried about tilting playing fields. I like the idea of a one uninterrupted, full quarter minimum."

The first letter jacket took the floor again. "How do you discipline kids if you can't withhold playing time? If a kid skips a practice, I dock him minutes in a game. Period. Every kid understands my rule, and it's a good one. But my rule could violate a minimum time policy, and it shouldn't."

I wondered how closely these coaches would follow their argued philosophies once the whistle blew. Would the faces of kids anxious to get into games persuade the more competitive to play their less skilled more minutes than planned? Would the desire to win persuade the less competitive to increase playing time for the more skilled than they wanted? How would I react faced with a choice between playing time and winning? I wasn't sure. But it presented an interesting choice for more than practical reasons.

I leaned over to Bauer. "Has playing time ever been an issue for you?"

"Yeah. It can be. Every kid wants to play, and every kid wants to win. The two aren't necessarily compatible. Predictably, playing time comes up every year and predictably Spenser disposes of it in a couple of minutes. The rules, he says, have been set for the year."

"I just heard that."

"And you'll hear it again."

Another letter jacket, built more like a wrestler than a basketball player, stood. "The purpose of a game is to win. Some kids are better than others. Everyone on the team wants to win, even kids at the end of the bench." He shifted his stance to assure his voice reached every part of the room. "Minimum time rules don't give coaches any flexibility when they need it in tight games. Sure, you try to get your kids in every game, but you don't want to jeopardize the team in the process. Afterall, one of the concepts we're trying to teach is the team over the individual."

"This shouldn't be about winning. It's about playing, learning teamwork, getting some exercise," a pulled down tie yelled from the back of the room.

"Just a second," Spenser shouted. His booming voice drowned out all other sound. "We're getting a little far afield here. The rules are set for the year. I'm here to explain them and answer any questions. Rules changes should be saved for after the season."

When people have forgotten, I mused.

I looked at Bauer. He gave me the 'I told you so' smile.

"I don't agree," came another voice. "This is my third year in the league. We've never had a coaches' meeting after the season to discuss rule changes. So why not now? I like a mandatory consecutive one quarter playing time rule." He looked around the room for support.

Spenser ignored him and continued, "We have another rule for the fourth- and fifth-grade teams that may seem strange to those who haven't previously coached at this level. Notice on your agenda item six is a 'no press rule.' That means what it says. The team in-bounding the ball has ten seconds to get it beyond the mid-court line. The opposition can't impede, press, or harass a player behind it. When the ball changes hands, all defenders must retreat to the other end of the floor. Is that clear? Once the ball crosses mid-court, the defense can do anything it wants. Not before." Spenser surveyed the room. His face was defiant, almost as if he expected a bitter debate on the issue and wanted to fend off opposition before it arose. An argument came anyway.

"That's a silly rule. It eliminates pressing as a defensive strategy," said the second letter jacket.

"It does," Spenser replied. "Because we want to eliminate that strategy. Some teams couldn't get the ball across mid-court without the rule. What fun would it be for kids to never get the ball close enough to the basket to shoot? Again, this rule isn't open for discussion. I'm just explaining it. It's also one rule I'll also defend for this age group." His extended chin and set jaw terminated consideration of the matter.

The remaining agenda items weren't controversial and quickly dispatched. "Thanks for coming everyone," Spenser said. "My phone number's on the material I'll mail you next week. Good luck and may you all have a successful season."

As others rose from their seats and started to leave, I turned to Bauer. "Any tips for the rookie?"

"Not really. My guess is you'll like the kids and feel more comfortable working with them than the parents." Ty had made the same point. "I signed on to work with kids. Parents came in the deal. For the most part the kids will give you their best effort and not complain. Parents are a mixed bag. I've had strange ones and extremes." Bauer tilted his head backward as if trying to recapture a lost memory. His expression soon softened, and the hint of a smile crossed his lips. His eyes returned to my level and he continued. "This one parent, big guy, maybe mid-50's, a monk's cap for a hairline, had a voice that carried like a bullhorn. Never heard anything like it. He'd perch in the front row with a thin sheet of cardboard rolled into a megaphone and started on the kids from the other team. Never used profanity or called any kid a name. But the noise was constant, loud, grating. He never shut up. 'Dribble, dribble, dribble. Oops,' 'Someone's sneaking up on you. Watch out,' 'Be careful. Be careful. Be careful'. Those slogans were among his favorites. I asked him to stop, and the refs shut him down a few times. The guy argued he was backing our team and not hurting anyone. He had a point. Still, there must be a line between acceptably and unacceptably obnoxious. As far as I was concerned, he was over the line. Just about all of the time."

"Your bullhorn must have been a real sweetheart."

"He actually wasn't a bad guy. He helped a lot at the school. The nuns loved him, though they never saw his Sunday performances."

"Is he still around?"

"Trying to get intelligence for our match-ups, huh." Bauer started to laugh. "No. Mercifully, he and his golden voice deserted us when his kid moved up classes, graduated, and came here, to St. Bernadette's. I hear he's now the noise of area high school athletics."

"If that's the worst parent you've experienced, things can't too terrible."

"I said that's the strangest, not the worst. The worst was God awful." Bauer looked disgusted. His lips puckered as if he were about to spit, and he curled in his seat as if preparing to absorb a blow. "I was coaching a seventh-grade team at St.

Leo's several years ago. I had this kid. He was a marginal starter. Ups and downs for this age are common as you know, but this kid's spirals were abnormal. When he was good, he was terrific. But when he was bad, he was terrible. I played him accordingly, a lot on good days and not much on bad ones."

"That sounds reasonable. What was the problem?"

"Dad only saw the good days; he was blind to the bad ones. So, when the kid was on the bench and something went wrong on the court, a missed shot, a turnover, whatever, Dad started chanting - 'Put Richard in'. 'Put Richard in'. 'Put Richard in'. Kind of like the bullhorn but without the powerful voice and the variety of messages."

"You're kidding."

"You can imagine how embarrassing the chant was for the kid. I could see the guy's wife sitting next to him, wincing. A few games into the season, they sat by themselves. The other parents abandoned them and sat elsewhere. Dad and I exchanged strong words the first time he chanted his advice, and on several subsequent occasions. He persisted regardless. All year."

"Nothing you could do?"

Bauer shook his head and sighed. "Nice kid. I'll never know how Richard got through the season. Truth is, the other kids on the team felt sorry for him, though there was little they could do." A glimmer of satisfaction crept onto Bauer's face. "Still, I saw the kids on the bench squeeze toward him when his dad started, like they wanted to shelter him." He snorted as if in defiance. "I'd forgotten that part. The only decent thing to come out of the whole damned episode."

"Did you play the boy any differently than you otherwise would?"

"I don't think so. I hope not. It would have been wrong to surrender to that jerk." Bauer replied. "As I said, you'll probably like the kids a lot."

The overhead lights flickered as Spenser barked, "Time. Everyone else left ten minutes ago."

"Thanks," I said to Bauer. "I know most of my parents already. I think I'll be okay."

"Remember. It only takes one."

The coffee smell had long since vanished. The Commissioner followed Bauer and me out of the door. He carried a full bag of doughnuts under his arm.

FINGERS, NOT HANDS

The hollow sound of bouncing basketballs echoed throughout the gym, which mixed with the shrill voices of adolescent boys and the incessant squeaking of rubber soles on the wood floor blended to create a cacophony whose only beauty was its symbolism. Basketball season was here.

The release of leather balls from the equipment closet altered the sound's timbre and added volume, but it didn't affect the piercing voices that vaguely resembled a disorganized boys' choir. While most of the team practiced shooting, a sneaker-clad pair of pounding feet lapped the gym, around and around. The boy was coming around yet again for another lap when I held my hand up to stop him, and with a puff and flapping arms he came to a halt.

"Who are you?" I asked.

"Andy. Andy Novak."

"What are you doing, Andy? Why are you running around the gym like that? Why aren't you shooting baskets with the other guys?"

"I like to run."

"Do you run like that all the time?"

"When I can."

"Why don't you shoot some baskets. You seem to be good at running."

"Okay," Andy said. He trotted over to the group shooting free throws and seemed to blend in.

I waited another five minutes to officially begin practice. "Over here, guys." I waved my hand in the air. The noise stopped as the youngsters gathered, the quiet periodically broken by a ball bouncing or one kid nudging another and giggling, followed by in-kind retaliation.

"My name's Mr. Elliot. I'll be your coach this year." I spotted Travis grinning at Casey as if to say, 'That's my dad, you know'. "After practice, take one of these handouts and give it to your parents. The handout has our schedule of practices and games as well as a list of your responsibilities to the team as representatives of St. Jerome's. There's also some parents' stuff. Hang it up on the refrigerator so you don't lose it."

The boys looked up, listening.

"This basketball season should be fun. Everybody'll play in every game. But we keep score for a reason. And what's that reason? The reason is that the final tally tells us ... "

"What's a tally?" Rickie asked. His innocent question ambushed the moment and shred my carefully prepared and updated 'win one for *The Gipper'* speech. What was to have been my motivational *tour de force* to start the season now seemed pointless. It probably always had been. But I was disappointed not being able to deliver it.

"The score, Rickie. Tally's another word for score. As I was saying, the final score tells us who wins and who loses. It's a lot more fun to win than to lose. Right?"

A murmur of assents responded.

"Okay. Let's start with a bounce pass drill. Make two lines, one starting here, one over there. Casey, grab a ball."

For the next hour, the team worked drill after drill. The boys moved constantly. No one experienced down time. I observed and taught, often interrupting their activity to give instruction. Teaching was the important part of coaching to me. Game management and strategy held more appeal for others. I enjoyed that part of the game, too. But I preferred teaching. The kids needed to learn proper techniques and practice them until they became habit. That was the way to improve, and I was intent on seeing they did.

"Guys. Guys." I blew the whistle, and everyone stopped. "You play this game with your fingers, not your hands." I wiggled my fingers to stress the point. "Andy just lost the ball out-of-bounds because he tried to catch it with his palms." I took Andy by the arm and pulled him toward me. "Here, Andy. Put your hands out in front of you with your fingers looking like claws."

"Like this?" he said. His fingers bent forward.

"More bend. That's it." I picked up a ball and tossed it to him. He caught it effortlessly. "Now, put your hands in front of you with your palms and fingers stretched out straight."

"Like this?"

I tossed a second ball to Andy. It banged off his palms while his fingers reflexively closed, struggling to regain the leather sphere. The rest of the team laughed at Andy's struggle, but no one seemed to miss the point.

"Do the same when you shoot the ball. Do the same when you dribble it. Let me repeat: you play this game with your fingers, not your hands."

The next thing I knew everyone on the team was wiggling his fingers, and before long Andy hunched over, raised his hands to eye level and aimed his wiggling digits at Travis. "I'm casting a spell on you," he said in a gasping tone.

"No, I'm casting a spell on you," Travis replied, trying to out-wheeze Andy and wiggle his fingers even more energetically.

"Enough," I said. "No one's casting a spell on anybody."

After an hour of drills, the team grew antsy. They were ready to play, to scrimmage, four on four, shirts on skins. I divided the team equally by skill level and told them everyone should get their hands on the ball and take a shot or two. I wanted to evaluate each player in a competitive situation.

Travis was right about Zack. He was good, much better than anyone else, the best player on the team. By far. He moved fluidly, passed the ball effortlessly, and dribbled with either hand. He may have been naturally right-handed, but one could only tell by watching him shoot. His sole limitation as a player was his size. He was no taller than the average fourth grader. That made it hard for his shot to reach the basket beyond a limited range. Even his free throws had a hint of heave in them.

The two fifth graders on the team struggled. Neither had played before, and it showed. Wilfredo, I called him Willie, panicked when Andy shouted for the ball. He threw it to a player on the wrong team and his hands flew to his head in horror. He screwed a pained look to his face and mumbled something to himself in Spanish.

Rickie razzed him immediately. "Can't you tell the difference between shirts and skins? We're shirts," he said, grabbing the bottom of his T-shirt with both hands and repeatedly flapping it up and down. "The guys without one of these are on the other team. That's why we call them skins."

A quick smile from the fifth grader showed no lasting damage. Rickie relentlessly razzed friends. The jab at Willie was typical Rickie. But I wouldn't know the impact on Willie with certainty until the fifth grader razzed another teammate. Once he did, and I suspected it would be soon, I knew he'd be a full-fledged member of the gang.

Randal was a different story. He was sensitive and a bit slow, though swift to pick up on any perceived slight. He was sullen and said little. He took a basketball when practice opened and never relinquished or shared it with anyone. When I offered suggestions, he scowled and ignored me. When he needed a partner for drills, he refused to team with anyone except Willie, his classmate. Randal resented playing on a fourth-grade team and displayed it in every possible manner.

"Just a minute," I shouted over bouncing balls and squeaking shoes as George lifted a shot through the hoop. "George and Casey just did something really good. Anyone know what it was?"

"Yeah. George made a basket," said Andy, grinning.

"It's not just that George made a basket. It's how he made the basket, and how Casey helped. George go back to where you were."

The largest kid on the floor looked at me, puzzled. Grabbing him by the arm, I pulled the boy back across the free throw lane to a position half-way between it and the side out-of-bounds line. "You started about here, right?" George still looked perplexed and seemed apprehensive. It was almost as if he were afraid of me. I dropped his arm.

"Listen everybody. George was here. Casey had the ball on the other side of the court. George circled around the guys in the middle, the traffic we call it, and ran toward Casey. What happened? Travis was guarding George. When George moved toward Casey, Travis got trapped in the traffic and lost his man." I retraced George's steps to stress the point. "Remember. You'll hear me say this a thousand times. If you want the ball, move to the guy who has it. George moved to get the ball from the guy who had it. Casey made a nice pass. George laid the ball in the hoop. Good job, George. Keep it up." I slapped him on the back, and then pointed to Casey. "You too, Casey. Nice work."

George looked away, almost embarrassed that I'd singled him out for praise. He was a promising player, and I loved him on my team. The challenge would be burrowing through the reticence and mistrust he displayed. I didn't understand the reasons for either but promised myself to help the kids find a way. I'd seen Travis and company in action and knew they could shred George's crust if not in the next few days, within the next few weeks.

The boys milled around, anxious to play again. Soon, Rickie was under assault from Travis, who was guarding him, and in no position to throw the ball to anyone. He'd used his dribble and needed help. Meanwhile, his three teammates ran around jumping up and down with their hands in the air as if to say, "throw it to me, throw it to me."

With a sharp tweet from my whistle, I stopped play.

"Guys. What did I just say? If you want the ball, move to the ball. Rickie needed help. He needed a teammate to run toward him and take a pass. Instead he saw three jumping-jacks waving their hands."

I could hear snickers when I used the term 'jumping-jacks'. Andy hopped up and down to mimic one, provoking further muffled commentary. I was surprised that Travis hadn't mentioned Andy until a few days ago. His playful personality seemed more akin to my son's than did those of *The Troika's* other members.

"Okay. Everybody shoot ten free throws and we're done," I shouted. The boys split and moved to opposite ends of the court to finish the day's last drill. Parents began to gather along the side of the court, waiting for practice to end.

I was elated with the day. The kids were eager and showed basketball skills. They played hard and together, and they seemed to like one another. Their attention spans were short, their collective voices shrill and grating, and their constant picking at one another, tit for tat, irritating. But they were fourth graders, and I couldn't expect anything else. The exception was Randal. He was going to be a problem.

Dusk was chilly when Travis jumped into the car. I turned on the ignition and he turned off the radio.

"What did you think of the first practice, Travis?" I was anxious to get his perspective on what for me had been a great day.

"It was good. I had fun." He buckled his seat belt. "Dad, Casey got a dog yesterday, a little brown and white one. When they got him home, he peed all over the kitchen floor."

So much for basketball practice.

"A new dog in new surroundings. Accidents'll happen. What's the dog's name?" I asked, though I wasn't interested.

"Casey calls him Randolph. A better name would be 'Puddles'." Travis grinned. He was pleased with his joke.

"Zack's a good player," I said. I wanted to goad Travis into some reaction to practice. Anything. Impressions of teammates, drills, the scrimmage, feedback of any kind. He refused to bite.

"Dad, we ought to get a dog."

"I don't think so. As in no. Absolutely not." I meant the firming sound to underscore my resolve.

"But it'd be fun. I'd feed and take care of him. You always talk about learning responsibility. I think a dog's a good idea, Dad."

"Remember last summer, Travis, when the Smiths went on vacation for two weeks? You were supposed to feed Wally in the morning and at supper time, and take him out twice a day for walks. They were going to pay you, too. What hap-

pened? Wally couldn't depend on you. He'd have starved without your mother. If you had a dog, why should I think you'd act differently than you did with Wally?"

"It'd be closer. I wouldn't have to walk so far to feed him."

"Three houses away? The Smiths live only three houses away and that's too far?" My voice was rising along with my exasperation.

We reached our garage. Travis crawled out of the car and ran into the house. I tarried to grab a fruit drink from the auxiliary refrigerator just outside the kitchen door and walked in to be greeted by a sour Maddie.

"I understand we're getting a dog."

"Not on your life. He'll forget about it by tomorrow."

"I don't think so. Travis is going over to Casey's after school tomorrow."

"Did he say anything about practice?" I asked.

"Not a word."

GIORGIO'S

The season opened at 2:00, St Jerome's versus St. Benedict's. A home game. As I sipped my morning coffee, I worried about the afternoon's contest. It was the first game for every one of my guys, except Zach. How would they react? How good were we? How good was St. Benedict's? I didn't have a clue, and I couldn't change anything, anyway. I soon gave up thinking about it and returned to my coffee and morning paper.

"Rickie's mom just called," Maddie said as she walked into the kitchen. "She proposed that after Mass we convene at Hank's Pancake Hamlet and have a late breakfast before heading to the game. Travis thought it was a great idea. But then, your son's never met a pancake when he didn't want a second."

"Hate to dampen the breakfast idea, but the last thing Travis needs is a stack of pancakes digesting in his stomach when the game starts. He isn't the quickest kid to begin with."

Maddie looked at me, annoyed. "Forget the training table routine. There's no chance Travis'll eat a poached egg and a piece of sirloin for breakfast. Now, what am I to tell her?"

"Tell her Rickie shouldn't be eating pancakes before a game, either."

"Come on, Doug. Breakfast at Hank's would be a wonderful runup to the game. The kids could get together and make it a day. Hank's might even turn into a pre-game tradition."

I was trapped. "Let me suggest something else. After the game, let's go over to the pizza place near the school. The kids'll be hungry by then. I'll announce a get together after the game, and they can tell their parents. You and I'll pay for the pizza. Who knows who'll show, but pizza could become the tradition instead of pancakes."

"I'll call her back and see what she thinks."

Maddie closed the deal three minutes later. Pizza after the game; no pancakes before.

St. Jerome's gym was cold when the Elliot contingent arrived. The weather was chilly for the date and the school hadn't yet turned on the heat. The gym's weekend's normal setting, 65 degrees, wouldn't begin for another two weeks. Body warmth from the crowd was expected to maintain the temperature at a tolerable level today, though parents and family from both teams wore every piece of clothing they brought into the gym. One portly fellow in a golf shirt announced, "Getting my coat," as he exited the gym's double-doors.

The previous Tuesday I'd started receiving uniform requests. After Rickie asked for number seven, a rush of number demands followed. Two kids were unhappy because *their* number had been sought by someone else. Randal wanted 99, a number that I told him wasn't likely to be available. I finally told the kids to write their preferences in my notebook. Shoving followed jostling. One kid pushed another to get to the head of the line. A second followed. I bellowed at their boorishness and they calmed down.

Anderson delivered the team's uniforms to the gym Thursday. Travis opened the box with the uniforms immediately after practice and was thrilled to find his number four on top. But his delight quickly disappeared when the jersey didn't fit; it was too small. Other players then started pulling out jerseys and soon discovered that besides number four, the numbers ran from 14 to 23. Anderson had given the popular numbers to Whitley's team. George pulled out number 23, a large size that fit him, and was satisfied. Andy, our smallest player, got Travis's number four. Everyone else had to settle for the medium sizes, numbers 14 through 21, and after a few skirmishes over numbers 15 and 20, uniform distribution concluded.

Today's game was the boys' first opportunity to show off their new outfits, and they posed for their teammates and bleacher audiences as they took off their jackets and strutted onto the court for warm-ups. They seemed pleased with the yellow and white-trimmed purple satin trunks, and the purple rayon jerseys, embroidered with a script yellow *St. Jerome's* scrawled on a white background across the front. However, the fashion show ended abruptly as the chill in the gym forced the kids to put their jackets back on.

I hadn't met the St. Benedict's coach at the league meeting. So, we introduced ourselves during an unoccupied moment as our players warmed-up. He seemed pleasant enough, older than me, and settled in his position. He appeared relaxed as we talked, though he soon barked at one of his players who refused to share a ball. That brief interruption proved a convenient end to our conversation.

We both walked back to our benches, held a joint recitation of a season opening *Hail Mary*, and circled the teams for last-minute instructions.

"Okay, guys. We'll start Zach, George, Rickie, Travis, and Casey. The rest of you'll get in but keep your jackets on for now."

All eight players then extended a hand into the circle, while Travis counted "one, two, three." On three their hands flew into the air as they shouted, "St. Jerry's." Our starting players jogged onto the court.

It was clear from the outset St. Jerome's fourth graders were better basketball players than St. Benedict's. It wasn't just the score. Players from both sides had difficulty getting the ball to the basket's rim. Shots from beyond the free throw line were often heave-and-hope. Still, St. Jerome's players moved the ball fluidly and rarely found themselves tied-up, a common outcome for the St. Benedict's players. The score at the end of the first quarter was 9 - 2, St. Jerome's.

My kids huddled at the quarter's end. "Andy, Willie, Randal, you're in. *Troika* take a blow." Given the weak opposition, I felt comfortable substituting the team's bench early and leaving them in the game for extended play. Zach added assurance. His basketball skills were extraordinary for a kid his age, and he controlled the game. He understood when and where to pass, when and where to dribble, and when and where to shoot. I was confident that if he were in the game, nothing would get out of hand.

Andy and Randal jumped at their first opportunity to play. Andy ran directly onto the floor as if he were chasing a completed homework assignment blown by a brisk wind. He was ready for action; he snapped the elastic in his waistband; bent over and put his hands on his knees; and, waited. Then he looked around and noticed everyone else still in the huddle, pointing and laughing at him. He managed a huge, impish grin on his self-conscious trip back to the huddle, a grin he wouldn't lose the rest of the year.

Willie, in contrast, was reticent. He searched for reassurance in the bleachers where his family, mom and dad, and two brothers, and sister sat. They were dressed as if they had just returned from Mass. Their pants were pressed, blouses ironed, and hair combed. In our telephone conversation, Mrs. Hernandez had sounded eager for Willie to play. Now that Willie was going into the game, she appeared apprehensive.

Our team played more raggedly than it had in the first quarter. Awkward moments became more frequent with our bench in the game. More errant passes, more walking instead of dribbling, more colliding with others. Still, Randal, Andy, and Willie each touched the ball several times. They were in the game, playing, not spectators in uniforms watching the other kids. Twice, Randal even threw the ball in the general direction of the basket in what loosely might be termed a shot. The more the three substitutes played, the more they relaxed and the more fun they seemed to have. Zack, with George's help, kept basketball matters under control and St. Jerome's half-time lead stretched to 15 - 5.

The game ended with a 32 - 11 score, a St. Jerome's victory. The day's win came with maximum player participation, a luxury our team would experience from time to time. Each boy played almost half of the game. No kid or parent could complain. However, the five starters played together only in the first quarter, not long enough to project how they'd perform as a unit over a season. Those five would need to work seamlessly when the competition strengthened, or the team might find itself on the opposite side of today's score. With only eight on the roster, the five starters couldn't scrimmage together at practice. Games were their only chance, and I would have to give them more chances soon.

The team was happy, though perhaps the win came too easily. Zack was almost matter-of-fact, and while *The Troika* was jostling good-naturedly, they seemed distant. Willie still looked lost, though he brightened when he spotted his family standing in the bleachers applauding. The others, save Andy who was running laps while dodging spectators who'd stepped onto the floor, just milled around as I shouted for the team to huddle.

"Way to go, guys." They looked up at me, eager for praise. "Everyone played a good game today. You should be proud of yourselves." Even Zack smiled. "This win is the first. I expect more, but other teams will be a lot tougher."

"Yeah, a lot tougher," said George, flexing his almost adult voice. The other players stared at him, surprised, but they didn't react. George's words were the first I'd heard him speak that afternoon. However, those few announced that the new kid, the big kid, the quiet kid, was now a *bona fide* member of the team.

The game was over. The kids were chafing to find their friends and parents and move on to other things. "See you at practice Tuesday," I reminded them and then muttered to myself, *and we have a lot of things to work on.*

Then, I remembered.

"Hey! Everyone!" I waved my hands above my head. The noise level in the gym fell. Lowering my voice, I said, "Some of us are going to the pizza place around the corner to celebrate. Sorry this is last minute. But please come. Everyone's welcome. I'll pay for the kids' pizzas and sodas. Parents, you're on your own."

"Giorgio's," yelled one of the players, defining *pizza place around the corner* for anyone unclear.

Casey's father sidled up and said, "Doug, let me take care of the soda." We'd discussed him being the assistant coach, understanding that business travel would periodically force him to miss a practice or a game. I told him I appreciated his situation but would welcome any help he could offer. He signed on. Or at least I thought so. Just before our first practice, he called and withdrew without explanation. We hadn't talked since. Offering now to buy the sodas when I needed an assistant coach seemed lame. "Don't worry. I can handle it," I replied.

It was just after 3:30, not an hour most moms and dads want their kids eating pizza. Three parents stopped me and said they and/or their sons couldn't make Giorgio's. Another who I couldn't identify asked for a rain check. I assured him it would be forthcoming. He was the eighth parent I counted and the eighth meant every kid on the team had had at least one parent present to see him play. After the horror stories I'd heard, I was thrilled my players had moms and dads interested enough to come to the game. That was a good sign of the support the kids could expect, a very good sign.

Rickie's mom had alerted Giorgio's that a party of 15 to 20 people would be coming after the game, and requested two round tables be set up, one table for kids and another for adults. When our group arrived, Giorgio had prepared the room as directed. We could hold our little gathering together while the other tables and booths ringing the room could handle the rest of his customers.

The St. Jerome's group crowded through Giorgio's door and into the dining room, the boys crawling over chairs, shoving and pushing one another, and pressing against the table, ready to eat. I suspected most had had nothing since breakfast. All looked hungry. Their chatter was shrill, rapid and noisy. Its focus was the day's game and the plays that, at least the speaker thought, were astonishing or amusing. "Did you see …" was a common start to a sentence coming from their table, soon followed by, "When's the pizza coming?" A giggling young waitress dressed in a red and green uniform with portrait of Giorgio in his white chef's toque emblazoned on her back set out plastic plates and silverware and planted paper cups filled with soda in front of the kids. "I hope one's pepperoni," a voice said over the din. "No. I want plain cheese," shouted another.

I counted six team members at the kids' table, including Willie, who was bantering right along with the others. He may not have known another fourth-grade teammate when the season started, but that didn't seem to be an issue now. George and Randal were the missing.

Three sets of parents circled the adult's table, Rickie's, Casey's and us. Zack's parents left right after the game but arranged for the Casey's to drop him off after our gathering. Andy's parents had made similar provisions with Rickie's.

The boys started breaking apart the two large pizzas, one pepperoni and one cheese, while the adults waited for their food. Maddie ordered a third pizza, half pepperoni, half cheese, as the boy's table was soon almost bare. The kids shoveled their food, talking while chewing, half masticated shreds of pizza often visible. No one graced the table, but Willie was its most civilized occupant, eating slowly and with his mouth closed.

Then I realized, how was Willie getting home? I surveyed the room and spotted Willie's parents and three siblings crammed into a corner booth. I hadn't noticed them before. They sat stoically, waiting for Willie to finish. Their table held nothing but two glasses of water.

I threw in an order for a fourth pizza and walked over to the Hernandez family. "Mr. and Mrs. Hernandez? I'm Coach Elliot. Nice to meet you in person," I said, extending my hand.

Mr. Hernandez said nothing. His face remained expressionless, though he nodded in recognition and took my hand when I offered it. His wife smiled and lowered her eyes. Her behavior baffled me given the pleasant conversation we'd had the night I selected Willie for the team.

"Please come and join us," I said, pointing to the adult table almost lost behind the animated actively at the kids'. They looked horrified. Mr. Hernandez shook his head vigorously. Mrs. Hernandez stared at her husband. They weren't about to budge.

"How about the children? They should get some pizza at the kid's table. It's for all the kids, girls, too." The three Hernandez children eyed the pizza on the kids' table. "They might as well have some pizza while you're waiting for … Wilfredo." I caught myself. Everyone on the team now called him Willie. But I didn't know how his parents would react to the name change, and I didn't want to test it.

Mrs. Hernandez replied in heavily accented English, "*Gracious, Señor* Elliot. The pizza is for the team."

"No. It's for the kids. For any little one who comes to Giorgio's after the game. The pizza's free. The parish has a special fund to pay for the kids' pizza after games." A fib wouldn't hurt anyone.

Mr. Hernandez didn't appear to understand a word I was saying, and Mrs. Hernandez seemed to understand little more. But Willie's siblings did. A short discussion in Spanish ensued. Before it could end, I motioned for Willie to join us.

"Wilfredo, why don't you take your brothers and sister over to the table and get them some pizza and sodas? Introduce them to the guys." I wasn't sure how successful the introductions would be. The Hernandez children, except Willie, were all younger than the team members and I didn't know their level of English fluency.

Willie shepherded them to the table, and spaces magically opened to slide in more chairs. His brothers hopped up on the vacant seats while someone shoved a half-finished pizza in their direction. The little girl, youngest and smallest of the three, stood on her toes and reached for a slice, put it on a handy plastic plate, and retreated to her mother's side. Willie brought her a soda.

The next time I checked the kids' table, Travis had an arm wrapped around the shoulders of one of Willie's brothers. The little fellow seemed content to munch on his pizza slice and to be included. Casey occupied the other. So much for introductions.

The Hernandez family didn't miss a game or a post-game trip to Giorgio's all season, but Mom and Dad never joined the adults' table.

TOBY FERGUSON AND WIFE

St. Jerome's record stood at three wins and no losses. The first and third games had been blow-outs, but the middle contest had been a tussle. The 28 - 18 final score betrayed the game's competitiveness. Every team member played at least one quarter early in the game, allowing me to keep my five best on the floor during its final minutes. Zach, with a huge assist from George, then took over the contest, and the lead stretched from four points to ten.

My starting group was developing a distinct personality. Zack was in charge, directed traffic, and functioned as our leading scorer. George led the team in rebounding and had the second most points. He was learning to use his size to best advantage, and for as shy as he was mixing with other people, including his teammates, his controlled aggression during play often terrified smaller opponents and provided a sterling example for those more tentative. Better, he had built a rapport with Zack and Casey, moving in and out, and back and forth, allowing the smaller boys to pass him the ball close to the basket. Each of *The Troika* had strengths that complemented Zack's and George's. Travis was the "garbage man", diving for loose balls, creating havoc on defense, and was second in the rebounding department. Though not graceful, he was purposeful, the emotional leader on the court and the team's leader off. Rickie was our third leading scorer, making most of his points with shots from the sides. But he was also developing an annoying free-lancing habit, drifting off by himself for no purpose, stopping his dribble, and letting the opponent tie him up before a teammate could arrive. I warned him about his free-lancing, both in practice and in games, but my admonitions had little practical effect. Rickie's selfish habit became more pronounced as the season progressed. His self-centered recklessness had cost us nothing to date, but it posed a serious potential issue. Casey played almost politely, making him the least valuable of the five. I could imagine him one day, pivoting out of the way of a charging opponent, extending an arm and with the palm of his hand open ushering the kid past saying, 'Excuse me. I didn't mean to get in your way.' Still his rapport with other team members and his unselfish play made him useful.

When St. Joseph's arrived Sunday afternoon for our game, their coach, Toby Ferguson, seemed familiar. I was certain I'd seen him before, maybe at the coach's meeting. He carried himself like one of the letter jackets who'd been there, but I'd been too busy conversing with Fred Bauer at the meeting to remember many attendees.

When we introduced ourselves as the teams warmed-up, my sense of familiarity grew even as it turned to disdain. If nothing else, the perfunctory pleasantries were absent. He extended a few fingers for a handshake and flipped them away on contract as if my hand were diseased. He then turned and walked away without comment.

Ferguson looked ready to enter a pickup game on a moment's notice. He wore a red warm-up suit with St. Joseph's in block white letters across the front, a towel draped around his neck tethered under his zipped jacket, puffing him up like an excited prairie chicken. Fading white sneakers and white wool sweat socks protruding from beneath his sweatpants completed the costume. His distinguishing quality was a thick head of coarse, dark hair, so dense it could have been the envy of any male over forty. When I first noticed the mane, I ran my fingers through my thinning hair and fared poorly in comparison.

The game had just started. Zach dribbled up the court and passed the ball to Casey. Instantly, the St. Joseph's player guarding Casey slammed his arm across his wrists, knocking the ball from his hands out-of-bounds. The referee closest to the play blew his whistle, called a foul on the guilty St. Joseph's player, and awarded the ball to St. Jerome's.

Ferguson was on his feet and halfway to the referee before anyone realized what was happening. "What! Isn't it a little early to blow calls? That kid dropped the ball, Ref," the animated coach shouted, pointing at Casey. "It belongs to St. Joseph's."

My team looked at one another, amused by Ferguson's performance. A player wearing red and white had nearly torn Casey's arm off. No rational person could dispute that. Yet, Ferguson was stomping his feet and arguing the call.

The spectators in the bleachers exchanged bewildered glances and rustled uneasily.

The St. Joseph's players and the few of their parents in attendance seemed the only ones in the gym not startled by Ferguson's eruption. It didn't spare them embarrassment, however. The kids on the floor wearing red and white milled around, staring off into space. Those on the bench dropped their heads. None followed their coach's lead or disputed the referee's call. They looked like they just wanted the game to resume.

The target of Ferguson's ire stood frozen. Eventually, the young referee picked up the ball and walked over to the scorer's desk. "The foul's on number eight of the visiting team," he said. "St. Jerome's ball out." He strode back down the court and handed the leather sphere to Casey to put back in play.

Casey in-bounded the ball to Zack who passed it to Ricky and after dribbling for a bit threw it toward the basket. The ball bounced off the glass backboard and fell through. St. Jerome's lead 2 - 0.

Ferguson was back on his feet. This time his target was a stocky St. Joseph's player with a round face and pug nose. "What were you doing, Tommy? You should have been all over that guy!" The coach caught his breath and clapped his hands. "Think! Think! That goes for the rest of you, too."

Neither team scored in the next few minutes, but Zack swiped the ball from the round-faced kid, Tommy, at least twice and constantly frustrated him. Each instance brought another flareup from the St. Joseph's bench. "What the hell's going out there? Can't any of you idiots play this game!" The second 'What the hell' led the older referee to stop play and admonish Ferguson for his language.

"One more use of foul language and you're out of the game," he said, extending the coach a prolonged stare to emphasize his point.

St. Joseph's called time-out. As the team neared its huddle, Ferguson leaned down and pressed his nose against the round-faced kid's. "What's wrong with you? That guy's making you look ridiculous." Nothing constructive came from his mouth, just a steady stream of demeaning criticism. And when the young player tried to turn away, Ferguson grabbed his shoulder and was back in his face. Then I noticed Ferguson and the boy, Tommy, had identical hair, an identical round face, and an identical pug nose. The coach was an older and angrier version of the player. The target of Ferguson's invective had to be his own son.

The other St. Joseph's players remained in the huddle, uncomfortably shifting their weight from foot to foot. They seemed to be waiting their turn, and Ferguson wouldn't disappoint. He turned on them after his last barb for Tommy. But they were lucky. He'd spilled just a few harsh words on them when the whistle blew. The time-out was over, though their coach wasn't through. As the players in red and white fled the huddle and ran back out onto the court, he shouted, "Let's surprise somebody and play good for a change." He turned and grabbed a player about to sit down. "Chris. Get in there for Jason. He's been worthless all day. See if you can be less worthless."

The time-out had been a welcome break, which I hoped to put to good use. My team was playing poorly, and these few moments gave me a chance to explain what we needed to do. The kids had always been attentive in huddles, but this afternoon I kept losing them to the chaos next door. Their eyes darted from me to Ferguson and back. They appeared disgusted by his performance yet captivated by it at the same time. It was if they needed to peek at something that they knew they shouldn't be watching.

Our huddle was a bust. I eventually changed my physical presence, making my kids turn their backs to the St. Joseph's huddle. But I could never recapture the attention that the neighboring circus had stolen.

As my kids returned to the court, the conversations among the St. Jerome's players were intense, yet subdued. They weren't talking about ball movement or squeezing St. Joseph's players. That would have been accompanied by motioning, pointing, and signaling. No gestures fed these exchanges. Just talk and intermittent stares at the St. Joseph's bench.

The unpleasant noise kept pouring from the red and white side as the game continued and became louder as St. Jerome's increased its lead. Ferguson rotated players, again and again, searching for the spark and skill set no one on his team seemed to possess. He exhorted his kids as he threw them onto the court and chastised them when they came off. Those being replaced immediately headed toward the far end of the bench, trying to escape the inevitable confrontation. The tactic never worked.

When it seemed as if the game's character could sink no lower, it did.

A thirtyish woman with no make-up and brown, marginally kempt hair, sat in the first row of the bleachers across from the St. Joseph's bench. She was hunched over, covering the block St. Joseph's across her red warm-up jacket, intent on the game. She first came to my attention, and presumably everyone else's in the gym, when a player in red and white slid across the floor toward her, trying to capture a loose ball. She was on her feet instantly screaming at the referees. "That's a foul, ref! That's a foul! It's been like this all day. Does St. Jerome's have you guys on the payroll?"

The St. Joseph's player had made a valiant attempt, only to show a severely skinned knee for his effort. He rose from the floor, gingerly stepping on a wobbly leg. The injury didn't appear serious, but the sore oozed and surely burned. He'd have a sizeable scab tomorrow. For now, he just needed someone to clean the wound, rub on an antibiotic, and bandage it. He should be able to rest a few minutes and return to the game.

As the boy headed to the bench for treatment, the woman shrieked, "Baby got an owie! Suck it up, wimp!"

Even Ferguson seemed surprised and motioned the referee to escort the boy to the bench. The coach met his player several steps out on the court. "Sit down here, Monty," he said, pointing to a seat. "We'll get that taken care of. You'll be fine." He appeared sincere and human for the first time that day.

Ferguson was mercurial, atrocious behavior alternating with interludes of respite, but the woman across the court was relentless. Once she started, she didn't stop. She paced the sidelines like a coach, blocking the view for other spectators. The first 'Shut up and sit down. I can't see the game,' was not long in coming. She glared into the bleachers, searching for the yell's source. Then came another, 'Sit down!' A third voice, sharper and harsher, sounded. She conceded but kept a knee on the floor and an elbow on the bleacher, ready to pounce should another incident incite her.

The woman was strident and grew more so. The referees initially drew the brunt of her venom. Then she refocused it on the St. Joseph's players, particularly number 12, Tommy. The boy could do no right, and she let him know it. As her disapproving commentary grew louder and more pointed, tears started to slide down Tommy's cheeks.

I called time-out, hoping that a pause in the game would bring Ferguson to his senses. His son was the only St. Joseph's player yet to sit. The time-out would be a good moment to take Tommy out of the game, let him rest, and collect himself. Maybe Ferguson hadn't seen the tears. He couldn't avoid them in the huddle though, and he didn't. "Crying? You've got to be kidding. Get your butt out there and stop embarrassing yourself." And, he pushed Tommy back out onto the floor.

The buzzer finally signaled the end of the first half. Its abrasive noise sliced into me and unleashed a torrent of disgust. I jumped from my seat and ran over to Ferguson, pushing through the referees and assorted players to reach him.

"Get that whack job sitting in the front row out of here or I'll lock the gym! In the front row over there," I yelled, pointing at the caustic woman. Ferguson's eyes followed my hand.

"My wife?"

I should have guessed.

"I don't care if she's the Queen of Sheba. Get her out of here. There's nothing I can do about your vile mouth, but I sure can do something about hers."

He shoved up against me. "I don't know who the hell you think you are, but you can go screw yourself!"

"She goes, or I close it down!"

The crowd could see the confrontation was not coaches posturing over some minor detail. The entire gym - players, officials, and spectators - focused on the two of us. The timekeeper tried to wedge himself between, but he was old and small. The referees proved more effective. They squeezed themselves in the middle. But Ferguson and I continued to threaten one another as the finger pointing grew more vociferous. I was losing my cool and so was he. The crowd filtered out of the bleachers and surrounded us.

"You close it down, you forfeit!" thundered Ferguson.

"You're out of your mind! I'm clearing everyone who's not part of the game. Once they go, I'll kick your behind."

"You can't do that."

"Watch me."

I turned and faced the circling crowd of spectators. "I apologize," I roared in an unmistakable tone. "Adults can't seem to act like adults. Game officials and teams stay put. Everyone else, collect your coats and leave the gym. Immediately."

"What about the kids?" a voice in the crowd asked.

"I'll ensure every one of my St. Jerome's players gets home if you don't want to wait." I stared at Ferguson. "Mr. Ferguson will have to worry about his players."

No one argued. The object of my bile was among the first out the door.

The second half started with no one present except the players, coaches, and officials. Maddie had left with the others. I assumed she and some friends sat in the cold car waiting, but I thought little more of it. I had more pressing matters.

The two teams played the next twelve minutes in virtual silence. At times, I heard the ball bouncing, nothing more. Ferguson said little although my guys were kicking his kid's behind. His team quit long ago. Not one, including Tommy, wanted to compete anymore.

The final score was 42 - 10. There was no endgame coaches' handshake. The St. Joseph's kids picked up their things and escaped through the gym's metal double doors as quickly as they could, Ferguson in the lead.

I asked my kids to remain. I was embarrassed and didn't know what to tell them. However, I believed they couldn't leave the gym without context. I had to say something, no matter how innocuous. We huddled, the puzzled kids standing about me in a loose circle.

"Guys, this afternoon, you saw adults behave badly. My conduct wasn't good. I'm sorry. I started the argument, but I should have done something sooner. I just didn't know what." Feet started to shuffle. Not one kid looked up. I had no idea what they were thinking, though I could see they were as uncomfortable as I was. "The conduct of other adults was worse. Instead of helping kids, they humiliated them. That's wrong. You were here to play and have fun. So were the kids on St. Joseph's team. It didn't happen. I hope you never see anything like this again." I didn't know what else to say.

I picked up my coat and walked toward the exit. "Let's go. If you don't have a ride, I'll take you home."

Maddie had the car running when I slid into the driver's seat. The boys all had a ride so we could go straight home.

"What just happened?" Maddie asked. "The Hansens and the Costellos and I spent the last hour looking at one another, trying to figure it out. Nothing makes sense."

"This was a first for me, too" I said.

"Couldn't you have done something sooner, Doug?"

"What would it have been? I can't tell a guy how to coach his team."

"Somebody has to draw a line somewhere. Coaches just can't act crazy."

"But where?"

"You found a line at half-time."

"Not really. The whack job in the front row gave me the excuse I needed. She was way over the line and had no part in the game. I could come down on her. I couldn't on Ferguson as abhorrent as his behavior was. He was their coach."

"Doesn't the league have rules on things like that?" Maddie asked.

I shook my head. "I saw nothing in the league rules about it and I read them twice. Then again, I wasn't looking for anything like what we saw today. You just assume civilized behavior."

I craned my neck toward Travis, sitting in the back seat. "Travis, what do you think?"

"That was weird, Dad. Really weird. The lady in the bleachers. She was crazy. And nasty. I didn't like her. Nobody did. We just wanted her to leave. And that coach." The intensity in Travis's voice sharpened. "What was he trying to do? Why was he yelling at that kid, Tommy, all the time? Tommy didn't do anything worse than anybody else."

"I guess Tommy's sin was that he couldn't keep up with Zack."

"Nobody can keep up with Zack, Dad. You have to put two guys on him. I'm a kid and I know that. All their coach did was yell and say bad stuff. All the time."

"I yell sometimes."

"Yeah, but you're not mean. That guy was mean. I wouldn't play if he were my coach."

Maddie leaned over. "That sums up my feelings, too."

"Aren't we going to Giorgio's, today, Mom?" Travis asked.

"No. Rickie's mom canceled while you were finishing the game."

"Can we stop at McDonald's, then?" Travis had had nothing to eat since breakfast.

After the family arrived home, my first task was to call the League Commissioner, Paul Spenser. He needed to know what happened that afternoon. I'd behaved badly. But Ferguson had to go. He couldn't be allowed to continue coaching. I didn't care whether another coach was available or whether St. Joseph's had to eliminate its fourth-grade team. Ferguson's behavior was despicable, even abusive. Particularly to his own son. And his wife? She has serious problems and shouldn't be allowed near kids or a basketball game.

I found Spenser's number. It was almost 6:00, mealtime for most families, but I didn't want to lose the outrage I felt. Spenser picked up the phone.

"Mr. Spenser, there was serious unpleasantness today in the fourth-grade game between St. Jerome's and St. Joseph's. Something has to be done about it."

"I heard. I just got off the phone with one of your referees. It sounds like there was plenty of excitement."

"Excitement? That's not exactly the word I'd use."

"Tell me your version."

I recounted the day's events, neglecting nothing, not the yelling, not the crying, not the crazy wife. I detailed my role in the half-time shoving and pushing match and told him I'd cleared the gym to finish the game. "You've got to get rid of Ferguson," I concluded. "He shouldn't be around kids, period. Same for his wife."

"Your story parallels the refs'," Spenser replied. "I'll talk to Ferguson. There's not a lot more I can do, though. This is a parish matter. Parishes select their coaches."

"You're telling me you can't do anything? You're the Commissioner. You're the guy in charge of the league."

"Yeah, but I only have authority when there's a dispute between teams from differing parishes."

"That can't be. One of the refs threatened to throw Ferguson out of the game today for cursing."

"I do have authority over the referees. They can throw out a guy for cursing and I encourage them to do so. But bad behavior? Well. We don't get into that. It's too subjective."

"Bad behavior can be subjective, I grant. But it's no longer subjective when some guy reams his kids at every turn and acts like a total jackass. Ferguson did both all afternoon."

"It couldn't have been that bad."

"It was worse."

"I'll tell you what," Spenser said. "If I'm not satisfied after my talk with Ferguson, I'll call Monsignor Schreiber over at St. Joseph's and report the incident to him. That's about all I can do."

Spenser's indifferent response infuriated me. My anger temporarily numbed my vocal cords and I could only exhale loudly in disgust. "Thanks for your time. Sorry to bother you," I eventually said. I hoped I sounded as exasperated as I felt.

Maddie saw me slam the phone into the cradle.

"How'd it go?" she asked.

"Not well. Do you know a Monsignor Schreiber over at St. Joseph's?"

JORDAN WHITLEY'S PROBLEM

"Jordan Whitley called," Maddie said.

"When?"

"About an hour ago. Seems like a nice guy, but in a hurry. Who is he?"

"He's the other fourth-grade coach."

I dialed the number Maddie left on the pad.

"Whitley. Doug Elliot returning your call. What's going on?"

The conversation was brief. The coaching books Whitley had read didn't help as he'd hoped. He was struggling and so were his kids. They hadn't won a game, and his team had scored fewer than eight points in three of the four contests they'd played. He needed help.

Whitley's office was downtown, near mine. We scheduled lunch at a small, out-of-the-way cafe mid-way between our offices. The place would be quiet, and we could talk. I didn't know what I could do. But I could listen if for no other reason than I didn't want him to quit. Should he resign, Anderson might combine Whitley's players with mine to form a single team. That would be a disaster, and spoil what-to-now had been a delightful experience.

Maddie and I were alone in the kitchen as she prepared dinner. "What's the latest on the dog?" I asked in a hushed voice.

"Haven't heard a word about it lately." My wife eyed the room to confirm our son wasn't in ear shot. "The last time Travis was over at Casey's house, Casey's mom made him help clean up the dog's mess. I haven't heard a word from Travis about one since."

"Bless her," I said.

"By the way, what was the final score of yesterday's game? With all the commotion I never asked."

"We kicked Ferguson's behind, 42 - 10." I smirked. "That jerk."

"You also kicked the behinds of his kids. Were they jerks, too?"

I feared Ferguson wouldn't suffer any consequences for his Sunday's performance. That would force his kids to choose between playing for a crude ass who exhibited disgraceful behavior or not playing at all. Travis knew what he'd do under the circumstances. How many other fourth graders would do the same? But the tragedy was that any kid should have to make a choice.

I was skeptical Spenser would speak to anyone at St. Joseph's, let alone Monsignor Schreiber. Behavioral issues are messy and usually entail degree rather than kind. Without concrete evidence of excess, few want to get involved, and sometimes not even then. The league Commissioner might approach the fellow at St. Joseph's who held the position comparable to Bart Anderson's at St. Jerome's. But even if Spenser did, the guy's primary responsibility was to fill coaching slots, not discipline recruits. He wasn't likely to welcome an opposition coach's challenge to rein in one of his people, let alone kick him out.

Monsignor Schreiber's priorities had to be different. I'd lodge my complaint directly with him. The question was how to approach the man without being shunted into an ecclesiastical bureaucracy. Since I knew no possible intermediary, a cold call seemed my best option.

Five minutes later I was on the telephone to the St. Joseph's rectory, requesting an appointment to speak with Monsignor Schreiber. I told the lady who answered I wanted to schedule a conversation at the Monsignor's earliest convenience but added that 'I wanted it before week's end'. She listened and said, "Please hold."

"This is Monsignor Schreiber. May I help you?" The voice was gentle and kind.

I was prepared to demand an appointment given my prior experiences with bureaucracy in large parishes, particularly where one isn't a member. That left me unprepared to present my case, and at first, I could only stammer, "Oh hello." But I soon gathered my thoughts.

"Monsignor. My name is Douglas Elliot. I'm a parishioner over at St. Jerome's. We haven't met."

"Oh, yes. Father John Doering's parish, a good friend and one of the diocese's most conscientious priests. Good fellow. St. Jerome's is lucky to have him."

"The parish thinks a lot of him, too. He's very popular," I replied. That comment seemed to please the Monsignor as he released a slight hum of satisfaction. "Monsignor, I have a serious matter I want to bring to your attention.

It concerns St. Joseph's fourth-grade basketball team and its coach, a Mr. Toby Ferguson."

I heard mumbling on the other end of the line. "Excuse me, Mr. Elliot," the Monsignor said in a hurried voice and I heard more mumbling. "I'm very sorry. An emergency. I must go. We'll have to continue this conversation at another time." The line went dead.

I stared at the inert receiver in my hand and slammed it into its cradle. "What a brush-off."

"What happened?" Maddie asked.

"Everything progressed smoothly until I mentioned fourth-grade basketball. When he heard that, he was gone. How convenient."

"Just a minute. You don't know he didn't have to leave. You made a cold call. He came to the phone. Then, he had to go." Maddie was playing her role as the family's calming influence.

"It's not like he'll return my call when he gets back from the so-called emergency. He didn't even take my number."

"You gave him your name and our number's in the book. You're the only Douglas Elliot listed."

"I'm sure he'll remember my name."

"Lighten up, Doug. Give the man a chance."

"Ferguson can't be allowed to coach another game. I'll have to find an alternative method to reach Schreiber. You know Father Doering, don't you, Maddie?"

"Yes, and he knows who I am."

"That's a start. We can't wait for this thing to fester."

Tuesday came quickly, and I made my way to lunch with Jordan Whitley. He'd arrived at the cafe before me and greeted me as if we were long-lost friends. His mustache bounced as he started the conversation by asking about Travis, and I reciprocated by asking about Carleton. A dark-haired hostess seated us and before we could speak further our waitress unfolded two menus and asked to take our drink order. Her bus boy soon swooped down with two glasses of water. At that point, Whitley and I agreed we'd order immediately, eat leisurely, and linger over coffee to discuss his basketball problems.

Despite the plan, Whitley wasted no time launching into his woes. The waitress had just taken our order when he began to release more than a month's worth of frustration. He said that coaching his son on a sports team filled with his son's friends was supposed to be fun, and mutually gratifying. Instead, the experience was turning into a miserable affair for both father and son. He regretted ever volunteering.

The problem Whitley told me wasn't losing a game or two. It was losing every game by lopsided scores. His players lacked basketball skills and competitive temperaments, at least compared to the fourth graders they played. His kids were disheartened and embarrassed. Worse, he felt helpless to do anything about it. One boy had already handed in his uniform.

"I don't know what to do," he said. He dropped his eyes and cut the volume in his voice. His tone grew reflective. "Going into this, I didn't understand the difference in kids' basketball skills at this age. Since none of the kids had played before I just assumed we'd all be starting from more or less the same point. How naive."

"Don't get discouraged," I replied. "You haven't done this long. Part of the fun of coaching is watching your kids improve, and they will. Things change over a season."

The waitress set our plates on the table and, after asking if she could bring us anything else, left. Whitley sighed and nibbled on a French fry. He picked up his cheeseburger and put it down again.

"What do I do now?" His outstretched hands begged for help. "I need something, anything. I talked to Anderson about the situation, and he was useless. Without saying so, he said, 'you volunteered. You're on your own'." Whitley shrugged his shoulders and picked up his cheeseburger once more before saying, "Got any ideas?"

"Have you asked anyone to be your assistant coach? Have you asked another dad to help? Maybe a kid's uncle or older brother. Sometimes you can find a mom or older sister who's played."

"Yeah. After Anderson, that was my first route. Seems basketball is as alien to the other families on my team as it is to mine. Nobody knows anything about the game. I didn't bother following up with any of them. Two blind men stumbling over one another is likely worse than one stumbling alone."

"I sympathize. I tried to recruit an assistant coach and was no more successful than you've been." I sipped my iced tea. "Anderson offered nothing?"

He shook his head. "Zip. Nada. Nothing."

"That's not surprising."

Whitely took a healthy bite of his cheeseburger. Catsup seeped from between the bun halves and dripped over his lower lip onto his chin. He wiped his mouth and the recess beneath his lower lip with his napkin and appeared ready to converse again.

"Let me throw out a couple of ideas, Doug. Both require your help."

"I don't know what I can do, Jordan." I empathized with the man and found myself calling him "Jordan" for the first time.

"I was hoping you might come to one of my practices and take a look. Afterward, we could catch a beer and you can tell me what you think. Maybe offer some suggestions."

"I don't know if that'll help you much, but I'm willing to try." Despite my affirmative response, I feared attending a practice would be nothing more than a hollow show of support for a beleaguered colleague. His idea was a 'Hail Mary'. It put too much faith in my ability to identify problems and suggest solutions, and his ability to translate anything I said into something that he could teach his players. The train was too long, and the track contained too many softwood ties and curves.

My agreement seemed to buoy him however, and I saw the smile that had made such an impression on me a few weeks earlier.

"When do you practice?" I asked.

"We practice on Mondays and Wednesdays, tomorrow afternoon, at 4:00."

I clung to my happy face, but my thoughts were far different. I'd have to leave work early, once more pressing my luck with Ty.

"Jordan, I can't promise tomorrow. But I'll check my calendar when I get back to the office. Monday's more likely." '*And that too is problematic,*' I thought.

"You have my number. Call me."

"You said you had a couple of ideas. What's the other?"

"This one's a little crazy and requires more organization. But do you think we could hold two or three joint practices?"

I breathed deeply and eased back into my chair, shifting my gaze from Jordan's horned rims to the droplets skirting my iced tea glass. There were a hundred reasons his request was a bad idea and not one to recommend it. Joint practices would be a waste of time for my kids. They would learn nothing. Those kinds of practices would only help if we worked against our basketball peers, even our betters if the difference wasn't too great. The same principle applied to Jordan's group. And his team wouldn't be working against its basketball peers, or any team resembling it.

Jordan had given me no reason to think him devious. But his joint practices idea contained a second, more ominous drawback. Joint practices would underscore the yawning skills gap between our two groups. They would make the gap appear so colossal that Jordan, or a parent, or even Father Doering might ask for an immediate redistribution of players. They might demand I trade Zack and

George for two of Jordan's least skilled kids, or something equally unacceptable. I grew angry picturing it. Still, I had be careful dousing Jordan's joint practices idea so as not to stimulate designs that didn't already exist

"The logistics of a joint practice would be difficult," I said. "A lot of parents would have to rearrange their schedules which won't make them happy."

"I have a big van. I could pile all the kids in it after a joint practice and drop them off at home. The trip would take longer than usual, and some dinners might get cold in the process. Still, I think I could get my parents to agree."

"I don't know, Jordan. I have a delicate balancing act at work. If I start messing around with my practice schedule, things could change there, and not for the better."

"I could have my team temporarily shift to your practice schedule, Tuesdays and Thursdays. What do you think?"

I didn't like the conversation's direction. If I helped Jordan with his practices, I'd feel obligated to attend more of them. That meant more time off work and more time off was a non-starter. I'd never consider his joint practices request, though I saw no reason to be blunt about it. Neither proposal appealed to me, and I had serious doubts either would be useful to him. I thought about picking up the check and telling Jordan there was nothing I could do. But I couldn't watch a hapless novice sink alone on a melting iceberg a hundred miles from nearest land.

"Let's postpone the joint practices idea, Jordan. I'll attend one of your regular sessions and we'll see. Maybe I can help and maybe I can't. But we'll give it a shot. I'll check my calendar when I get back to the office and call you."

We finished our drinks and chatted pleasantries, split the tab, and went our separate ways.

When I returned to the office, I reviewed the following day's schedule as promised. I had a long-time client who was a longer-time friend in the book for a 1:00 lunch. Those lunches were legend in the office. While we usually concluded them in a gentlemanly two hours, they'd been known to last into the dinner hour, and beyond. I'd cleared my calendar accordingly. I now planned tomorrow's lunch to be of the two-hour variety, after which I'd head to the gym for Jordan's practice. I called to let him know.

THE MONSIGNOR'S COMMITMENT

I arrived at the gym just as Jordan was beginning practice and took a seat in the bleachers. I removed my jacket, grabbed a small notebook and ballpoint, and started to observe. It took no time to confirm what Jordan had told me. No one could catch; no one could dribble; no one could shoot the ball with any hope of scoring. His kids possessed zero basketball skills. Worse, they possessed zero athletic ability on which to build them. It was as if Jordan had driven the length of the state to find the nine boys with the least talent.

Ironically, the team's greatest asset was its coach. Though Jordan was clueless about the game or the skills needed to play it, his innate cheerfulness and enthusiasm spread to the kids. He laughed at himself, allowing his players to feel comfortable laughing at themselves, too. Despite all their problems, they looked to be having fun.

Practice was still painful to watch. The drills were conducted without purpose and players committed serious errors without correction. Scrimmage involved nine boys running around chasing the ball as if it were a greased pig at the county fair. Nothing was accomplished.

Jordan's kids exited the gym just as the eighth-grade girls were coming in to start their practice. He had arranged for Carleton to go home with a friend so he and I could discuss the last hour and a half without young ears present.

"Why don't we go over to Giorgio's and talk. I don't know if it'll be any quieter over there, but at least we can have a beer," Jordan said. He and I walked over and found an unoccupied booth under a flashing neon sign. It emitted enough light for me to read my notes and for Jordan to take some if he wanted. No table service appeared, so I walked over and ordered two drafts.

"What do you think?" Jordan asked when I returned. He took a small notepad and pencil stub from his jacket pocket and set both on the table. He looked as eager as a college freshman attending his first class.

I pulled out my notes. They were extensive. After a quick glance at them, I leaned back into the booth and ran both hands down over my eyes and cheeks.

"That bad, huh." Jordan's excitement drained.

"No. That's not it." I returned to the notes and flipped a couple of pages. "Most of this scratching is about specific items. We can talk about them later. Let's start somewhere else. Jordan, your kids seemed to have fun today, at least most of the time. Is that usual at your practices?"

His face exhibited a puzzled innocence. He obviously wasn't expecting my question and mulled it over for several seconds. "I think so. For the most part, I'd have to say 'yes'. They seem to have fun."

"Any feedback from Carleton? The other kids? Parents?"

"About practices, you mean?"

I nodded.

"No. Not really."

"Do the kids come to practice?"

"Yeah. Occasionally, someone misses school, so he misses practice, too. That's about it. Don't forget about the kid who handed in his uniform, though."

"So, the kids have fun at practice, don't bitch, and show up."

"I guess." Jordan brightened as the logic penetrated the cloud he sat under. As he began to smile, his mustache started pushing up his glasses. "It's not a total disaster, is it? At least not yet."

"No. It's a darn good start. You deserve a lot of credit." Jordan beamed. If my purpose had been to boost his morale, I'd succeeded beyond any reasonable expectation. And my compliment wasn't flattery. It was the truth.

"We know why the kids don't like the games. That means we have to figure out what they like at practice and transfer that to Sunday afternoons."

I took a swig of my beer and fell silent.

"And?" he said, waiting for my solution.

"I don't know. You'll have to help me with that one."

As matters stood, to have fun in one venue, Jordan's players had to swallow persistent humiliation in another. They'd accepted the trade-off to date. The question was, would they continue to do so? His task, our task, was to improve their play enough or otherwise relieve their humiliation in games enough to make the implicit exchange tenable, and to do so before most tired of the current arrangement.

I emptied my beer and dropped my eyes to review my notes. Jordan grabbed it and headed to the bar for a refill. He seemed to believe that the secret to keeping me engaged was a full glass.

"Let's start with a couple of things you need to emphasize at practice. They're the same things I tell my kids. You play basketball with your fingers, not your hands."

Jordan grabbed his pencil stub and started to write. This was a new idea. My first pointer apparently hadn't been in his coaching book. As I elaborated, he wrote faster as if the wisdom would be lost to the ages if not put on paper instantly. I illustrated with my palms, and fingers and he drew pictures of them. I was fascinated and flattered. I couldn't recall anyone giving anything I said such authority.

"Second. You play on your toes and the balls of your feet, not the flat part." I slipped out of the booth for a quick demonstration while Jordan watched. He nodded and returned to his pad and pencil, while I pawed though my list of observations.

"Your kids react differently to the basketball than mine. My kids hang back and wait for the ball to be thrown to them. I badger them constantly to move to the ball if they want it. Your kids, mob the ball. They all run to it at the same time. Neither works."

"You're losing me," Jordan said.

"I have an idea. Your kids are lost now. They just run around without purpose. That needs to change. I'll show you a system that gives your kids a place to start and a place to go. It isn't magic and it won't make your kids all-stars. But at least it'll give them direction and should make playing games more fun."

Jordan flipped the page in his notebook and pushed his glasses back up to the bridge of his nose. He sipped his beer, the head leaving a white banner across the belly of his crimson mustache and then hunched back over his notebook, ready to write again.

"Start by spreading your kids over the floor. One kid runs toward the guy with the ball. That guy passes it to him and breaks in a different direction. When the first guy makes his pass, the others move to their new, pre-assigned spots. Let me show you."

I seized my notepad and diagramed the process. The player layout and their movement were easy to draw and easy to understand. But its simplicity also represented a flaw for if it were easy for Jordan's kids to understand and learn, it would be easy for his opponents to recognize and frustrate. The process needed variation to be successful, and that's where Jordan's troubles would begin. His players needed to adjust their movements in response to their opponents, but nothing was instinctive or natural about his kids. Unscripted adjustments would be impossible for them. That ultimately doomed the process, but the process allowed them to have fun in the interim.

"The plan is for your kids to move, and move with a purpose, a direction. If nothing else, they'll feel like they're playing, not just running around waiting for something to happen."

"I like it." Jordan gushed. He slammed his notebook shut and shoved it back in his shirt pocket. "It's on the agenda for my next practice."

"Your kids can't learn it overnight." I chuckled at Jordan's enthusiasm.

"At least, we have a blueprint. Can you come to my next practice Monday and help me introduce this? I think I understand, but it's new to me, too,"

"I'm sorry, Jordan. I can't. I was lucky to get away today." I understood his quandary but saw no possibility of again leaving work early.

"How do I practice this? Do I draw it out on paper for the kids?"

"Forget paper. Get some inch and a half athletic tape and make five big X's on the floor, spread like we talked about. Start each kid on an X and rotate him from X to X. It's kind of like musical chairs except everyone has a landing spot."

"That's it. That's the name for our system, 'Musical X's'." Jordan snickered; his eyes glistened; his mustache bobbed. He was pleased.

"Show the kids where to pass and where to run. Once they learn, they can use the system on Sundays."

"You know … we could really turn things on their head," Jordan said. He deliberately twisted the tips of his mustache.

I returned a puzzled look.

"Suppose, just suppose, that my team wore game uniforms to practice and practice uniforms to games." He tilted his head, locked his jaw, grimaced, and, after a brief, uncomfortable moment, dropped any pretense and shot a smile that radiated impudence. "Why not? You wear dressier clothes to have fun and work clothes to slog. Right?"

"It would change the mood." I chuckled and then broke into laughter. "Why not? You'll raise some eyebrows. So long as the kids are fine with it, go ahead."

Jordan took his biggest swig of the evening, slammed his glass on the table, and pumped his fist in the air. "To hell with Anderson and his uniforms. Let him think what he wants."

I couldn't tell whether Jordan's new dress policy was a reaction to Anderson's snub or an appreciation of paradox. It made no difference, though. Jordan was attempting a fresh start, and his uniform change amounted to a dazzling announcement.

"Hate to dampen things, but you just can't wear T-shirts during games. Every player must have a number on his back," I said.

"That's what magic markers are for. We'll draw a number on the back of our T-shirts before the game."

"What will the kids' moms think?"

"A measly T-shirt lost to a magic marker's ink pales compared to the long-term genius of the move." Jordan leaned back, stretched out and relaxed. Delighted with himself.

"I'm getting a refill. Want one? Maddie'll probably be unhappy. But now that you have a complete plan, a little self-congratulation is in order." I squeezed out of the booth. Before my foot hit the floor, I looked back at my colleague lounging across from me. "You aren't conventional, you know. You're also a bad influence. I'm starting to think like you."

"I hope that doesn't offend you, Doug." A goofy grin plastered his face from ear to ear.

Leaving Giorgio's, we agreed that the best time to implement the uniform plan was Monday. Jordan's team would still wear their classy purple and yellow uniforms to Sunday's game and get drubbed again. Change would begin the following day.

When I arrived home, I saw a note waiting for me on the telephone pad. Monsignor Schreiber had called and had left his number. I lifted my eyes from the pad to the ceiling and mouthed, *'Hallelujah! The Monsignor returned my call.'* He left the message at 7:40 and my watch showed 9:30. The meeting with Jordan had lasted considerably longer than expected, and there were more beers drained than prudent. I was in no condition to discuss a sensitive matter with a priest, and decided to organize my thoughts and return the Monsignor's call in the morning.

I telephoned the Monsignor just after 9:00.

"Good morning. This is Monsignor Schreiber. Can I help you?" The voice was gentle and kind, his tone unchanged from the last call.

"This is Douglas Elliot, Monsignor, returning your call. I have a serious matter I would like to discuss with you. Is now a good time to talk?"

"Please," he said.

I don't know why, but I believed I had only one opportunity to persuade the Monsignor to act. So, I opened my case directly and carefully.

"Last Sunday St. Joseph's fourth-grade basketball team played its counterpart at St. Jerome's. I coach the St. Jerome's team. A fellow by the name of Toby Ferguson coaches your St. Joseph's team. Mr. Ferguson's conduct during that contest, to put it generously, was reprehensible. And the conduct of his wife, sitting in the bleachers was worse. I immediately reported the matter to league officials. They claimed a lack of authority over anything that's not a basketball dispute *per se*. This isn't a basketball dispute. It's far more serious. It's a matter of adults mistreating kids."

My words flowed, and I laid out the entire episode as accurately and in as much detail as I could remember. I didn't minimize my part in the confrontation. It was a significant component of the day's events, and I didn't want any follow-up to show me shirking responsibility. Yet my focus remained the Fergusons. Monsignor Schreiber didn't interrupt, and while it was impossible to determine how intently he was listening, he remained on the phone.

"Monsignor, when this conversation ends, I'm through with the Fergusons. My team won't play his again. Hopefully, I'll never see the man or his wife again, either. But every time the Fergusons perform like they did last Sunday it reflects badly on your school and on your parish. Worse, Ferguson puts those boys in the position of accepting his ridicule or not playing. It's wrong. I implore you to change this situation immediately. That's what I have to say. Thank you for listening."

With those last words, I felt instant relief. I'd discharged my responsibility; I'd done everything I could. The matter was now in the hands of others, people who could act on the information I'd provided. The tension in my shoulders began to unwind, and the stress in my neck eased. My pulse rate even fell. It was if I'd slipped into a warm shower after a long walk in freezing rain.

An extended silence followed. I had no idea what the Monsignor was thinking or if he even heard what I'd said. I couldn't hear him breath. I wanted to blurt out, 'are you still there?' But I'd made my case. Responsibility for further conversation lay at the other end of the line. At last, the gentle voice replied. "Thank you, Mr. Elliot. I'm deeply sorry this situation occurred. I don't go to the games often anymore. I remember them as good fun for everyone. It'd be disappointing if that were no longer true." He coughed softly. I heard the extended squeak of an office chair's back reclining. "Mr. Elliot, may I ask you a few questions?"

"Surely." I was eager to fill in any missing details.

"Mr. Elliot, have you coached children's basketball before?"

The question surprised me, but I responded respectfully. The Monsignor continued the same line of questioning, seemingly more interested in me and my team than in the event we should have been discussing. At one point, he even asked the score of last week's game.

"Boy, you really whipped us," he said.

His questions continued for almost 15 minutes. My first appointment of the day was sitting in the lobby, and I was eager to conclude these seemingly pointless questions. Finally, the Monsignor said, "Thank you again, Mr. Elliot. This has been a useful, if painful, conversation. I'll get back to you. God bless."

Monday night couldn't come soon enough. I wanted to hear how Jordan had made out with his team at practice that afternoon. Travis reported Jordan's kids had been beaten by almost 40 points the day before, a thrashing of monumental proportions. But this afternoon was the start of a new era for his team. Inverted dress and Musical X's.

I planned to call Jordan at 7:30 for a report on the day's practice. But as I sat reading my newspaper, I grew increasingly impatient and found myself checking my watch every five minutes. I was like a kid on trip, 'are we there yet, Dad?' At precisely 7:30, my forefinger hit the first button.

"Jordan? Doug. How'd it go today?"

"Good. Good." His voice sounded more enthusiastic than analytic. "The kids responded better than I expected given yesterday's trouncing."

"I heard. Travis told me the score."

"That was Sunday. Today, we did it, Doug. We wore our game uniforms to practice. A couple were a little rancid and rumpled from yesterday, probably piled in a corner overnight. Only one kid forgot about the attire switch." Jordan warmed to the subject. "The change seemed to energize them."

"Your idea was great, Jordan. I've always thought when something's going badly, change is more important than what the change is. And you did it in about the craziest way possible. But let me ask: how did practice go? Did the kids get Musical X's? Did they have fun with it?"

"You'd have laughed, Doug. I got to the gym a little early with my yardstick and roll of tape. I taped the X's to the floor in the spots just as you drew them up. The kids noticed the X's as soon as they walked in."

"Five large white X's taped to the gym floor are hard to miss."

"They asked about them right away. But I made the kids wait until after warm-ups. You could see their little minds trying to figure out what all that tape was doing on the floor. Eventually, I had each one of them stand on an X and we walked through the system." Jordan began to chuckle, his intonation somewhere between a cackle and a titter. "You could call the next several minutes confusion amidst chaos. The first problem was that once a kid passed the ball, the others forgot to run, well, walk, to their new spot. Carleton's friend, Freddie, was a primary culprit. When he remembered, he'd go to his new spot and just as he was about to reach it, he'd jump as high as he could and land with a big flat-footed plop, right in the middle of the X. Freddie's exclamation point." Jordan interrupted himself. "I never thought, Doug. Should I have let him do that? Because the others immediately followed."

"Why not? Sounds like the kids were learning and having fun at the same time. Besides, when they're moving full speed, they won't have time to plop on their X."

"We weren't moving full-speed. Today's performance tells me we won't be moving full speed for a while. Definitely not next Sunday."

"I didn't think you would. If you can weather one more Sunday, maybe you'll be ready the following week. The schedule says you're playing that game at St Jerome's. Home court should make your kids more comfortable in their new system."

"Good. If the game's at home, I can tape down the X's."

"Afraid not, Jordan. The rules don't allow foreign objects or markings on the floor. But after a while you may not need them. I remember a time when a coach taped down the X's for practice. The area grew dirty. So, when someone pulled the tape up for a game, the dirt on the floor stenciled an outline of the X's. That wasn't technically legal, but no one could do anything about it. The tape might as well have stayed in place."

"It'll be several games before enough dirt builds to make our stenciled X's visible," Jordan replied.

"Were you able to convert anything you did today into a game or a competition?"

"We did. I'm emphasizing free throws. It's about the only way we can score in a game. Over half of our points come from them. Today, we had a team free throw competition. Every kid shot half of them underhand and the other half the usual way. Somebody left a chalkboard on the sideline, so I kept score."

"Sounds like a productive activity."

"It was and I plan to close every practice from here on in that way. I hope someone leaves the chalkboard again. Something about the score visually in front of you rather than in your head seems to heighten interest. There was something else, Doug. Every kid shot his free throws better underhand. The team made twice as many that way. The kids could toss the ball to the basket rim easily; they didn't have to heave it. Underhand may be old-fashioned and my kids may not like it. But if it works, I may make them shoot that way in games."

"Twice as many?" I repeated Jordan's statistic.

"Yeah. Every kid shot better underhand. Of course, I had kids make only one free throw during the entire competition. But it was underhand."

"That's interesting. Will you keep tracking those numbers?"

"Yeah."

"Keep me informed. I'm not above stealing your idea. A free throw experiment for my kids is now on tap for practice tomorrow. For what it's worth, I think you're onto something."

THE ANNUAL REPORT

The holidays were approaching and the school's annual fund-raiser, the Christmas Bazaar, was in full swing. My team was displaced from its scheduled practices for an entire week because of it. The timing was poor. We were to play Fred Bauer's team Sunday, and I knew he'd have his kids prepared. Without practice, I couldn't do the same.

The Bazaar recess gave me much-needed time at the office, however. While our flextime experiment seemed to be progressing smoothly, extra facetime on Tuesday and Thursday afternoon would reassure Ty I wasn't taking advantage of his good-will. Christmas was a slow period in our office. Holiday festivities occupied clients and staff, leaving sizable chunks of time for office interaction. Under the circumstances, my hours this coming Tuesday and Thursday would be more visible than ordinarily.

I was walking down the hall about 4:30 Tuesday afternoon, half scanning a file and half trying not to wander into a wall when Ty emerged from his office. He headed my way. "What are you doing here? Aren't you supposed to be at basketball practice?"

"Canceled. No gym availability. You know us parochial school types. We have to raise money for the school, and this is the week."

"No bingo?"

I grinned.

"Where're you headed?" Ty inquired, glancing at the open file. "Important?"

"No."

Ty took my shoulder, made a U-turn, and escorted me down the hall and into his office. "How's it going?" he said as he slid into the black leather chair behind his desk. "Run into any crazy dads yet?"

"Well. So far, so good. We're 6 - 0. The best part is I have great kids and the parents have been very supportive. I guess it's easy to be a genius when you win, and every kid plays a lot."

"That's terrific. Kids *and* parents. Lucky."

"I've got this one kid, Zack. If he grows, he may be Division-I material."

"Oh, come on, Doug. You may be undefeated, but let's not get carried away. Everyone knows a kid who can play in a big-time college program. But somehow, they always seem to fall short. Nice to have a special player though." Ty wasn't buying my assessment of a fourth grader's potential to play Division-I college basketball. He knew those types are unicorns. "I had a lot of fun coaching," he said. Ty looked contented as he lounged in the chair behind his large mahogany desk. "Good memories."

"Yeah. It's been fun," I said. "I'd do it again. A single glitch and there was nothing I could do about it."

"What happened?" The boss slid forward and planted his elbows on his desk.

"It's a long story. Sure you're interested?"

Ty nodded. So, I related the Ferguson episode from its beginning to my last call with Monsignor Schreiber. The story took several minutes, but Ty remained attentive as he followed it. His head bobbed and shifted with each new detail. His facial expression mutated at every additional absurdity. He twisted in his chair as the tension rose and steadied as it fell. The guy was engaged without saying a word.

"This had to be the oddest behavior I've ever seen," I concluded. "Not what I expected when I signed up to coach. I had no choice, though. I had to do something. Except for my disgust, the entire matter's over. Everything now lies in the Monsignor's lap."

"Hard to believe, isn't it?" Ty said, again relaxing.

"I've heard of stuff like this before. I thought it was all exaggeration. Just a good story, somebody's tall tale. I don't anymore. Hard to imagine much worse."

"I've experienced worse." Ty reflected as he slid forward in his chair again and hunched over the desk. "Okay, the wife's performance may have been over-the-top. But, let me tell you about a game I witnessed."

"Worse? Come on. You've experienced something worse?"

"It was at a tournament." Ty got a faraway look in his eye, the one he got when he shared an experience or told a story. He leaned back, way back, in his chair and put his feet on the corner of his desk. "My team and I were sitting in the bleachers waiting our turn to play," he said. "Only a few minutes remained in the game before ours when I noticed a player on the bench using his elbow to push away an adult sitting behind him. The adult didn't touch the kid in response to his shove. But he bent over and got into the kid's ear. I don't know what the adult said, but whatever it was his lips moved in an uninterrupted stream. The kid pushed back, visibly upset. The rest happened so quickly I missed half of it. But from that point forward things vacillated between a brawl and Keystone Kops." Ty grew animated as he told the story and dropped his feet to the floor. He slid his chair under the desk and scrunched his hands into loose fists as if he were ready to enter a fray. Then he bent his head down and started to laugh and to laugh harder. He struggled to speak. "After the kid on the bench pushed back, his coach took up his cause. Within a few seconds, Coach threw a roundhouse punch so wildly he tripped and landed face-down in the crowd." Ty's right shoulder jerked forward as if he were launching a pulled blow. "The kids on the bench ran. A guy a few rows back in the bleachers tried to jump on the coach but managed only to slide over the pile of spectators onto the gym floor face first. Soon, another scuffle broke out next to the original brouhaha."

"That's ridiculous. A brawl at a grade school basketball game?"

"The refs came running." Ty struggled through his laughter to spit out the details. "They plunged into the fracas doing their best to separate the combatants. No one knew who was swinging at whom or why. A 95-year-old, okay, a not so pleasingly plump elderly lady dressed in a ridiculous gray and yellow security guard's uniform, brass buttons, epaulettes ... the whole nine yards ... waddled out of the hall toward the melee. What she could do wasn't clear to anyone, including her. All she did was hop up and down and scold the belligerents who were still throwing haymakers. 'Stop it! Stop it!' she shrieked."

Ty folded over his desk in laughter. When he righted himself, I could see tears running down his cheek. He coughed several times and struggled to recover his composure.

"Come on, Ty. You're exaggerating."

"Honest to God's truth. I'm not making this up." He raised his right hand as if taking an oath. "The guys with fat lips and bloody noses headed for the door. The refs called the game, which was lopsided anyway. The coach who threw the initial punch, which hit no one I could see, left the gym cheered as royalty, split-lip, black eye, broken-nose, and all." Ty collected himself. He took a deep breath and rolled his chair back until it hit the credenza behind. He flipped his forefingers under his eyes to wipe away the remaining tears. "It was outrageous behavior and I should be incensed and I am. But geez it was funny."

"And pathetic." I wasn't as amused as Ty.

"The important thing, Doug, is that you didn't get a black eye from your confrontation. You have to look pretty."

"What are you talking about?"

"Come on." Ty was smirking, and with an extended hand guided me to the door. "We're on our way to see Barney."

Barney Ambrose was the most over-paid and under-worked person on the staff. At least, that was the office consensus. His official title was Director of Public Relations and he glad-handed everyone. Still, no one seemed to know what Barney did. Few interacted with him professionally and I wasn't aware of a single individual who did personally. He was just there.

Ty and I walked into Barney's office, and he greeted me. "How's our new media star."

"Doug, remember when you said we ought to consider your time away from the office coaching kids' as community service?" Ty said. *Payback time.* I could feel it. "You also thought it might be a good public relations ploy. 'Ploy' isn't the word I'm searching for. Let's just say, 'recognition', or perhaps an 'edge'." *Definitely, pay-back.* "I bounced the idea off Dallas, and they loved it. They want to feature you and your team in the company's next annual report."

"You're kidding," I said, incredulous. "Why would a stockholder care about a company's employee volunteering as a grade school basketball coach?"

"They tell me we're in the new touchy-feely era," Ty replied. "Stockholders want to earn their money, but they also want to think the company is doing good. Don't ask me what 'good' means. No one knows; no one cares. The brass just wants to present a respectable front that leaves everyone feeling warm and fuzzy."

"It's the latest thing. Part of 'corporate social responsibility'," Barney added.

"You mean fad. You've always fought that stuff, Ty." I first looked toward the boss and then at Barney. Someone needed to be rational.

"I don't think so, Doug," Ty said. "This one's here to stay."

Barney nodded to confirm Ty's opinion. "I agree. We're in a new era."

I wasn't happy, but recognized when the fix was in. "Guess I have no choice. If that's what Dallas wants. What happens now?"

"They want me to interview you about your experiences with the kids. Then, I'll go to one of your games and report on it. As context for the larger story, not for the game itself."

"You're coming Sunday?" Poor timing. With no practice this week, I feared my kids would be stale and I didn't want Barney to see a poor performance.

"That's the plan. Dallas requested it," said Barney.

"I have a responsibility to my kids and their parents. So, here're the conditions for your coverage. The big one is that you can't talk to the kids. You can't interview them before or after the game like some pro athlete on TV."

"You're tying my hands, Doug. The kids' reactions are the payoff. Their feelings are indispensable. No one cares if they win or lose. Readers will be interested in a company employee using company provided flextime to help kids in the community. Helping kids is the story here and I need to talk to some of them. Get their perspectives."

"I don't care, Barney. My kids are too young and vulnerable to be interviewed by someone from the media. That includes you."

"Be fair, Doug. I don't want to embarrass your kids or anyone else. I'm 'puff' media, not 'gotcha' media."

I felt a need to protect my kids. From what? I wasn't certain. The media was new to me. But read enough, long enough, and it's obvious that reporting can be twisted to the advantage or disadvantage of people interviewed. I couldn't let that happen to my kids.

We both looked at Ty to resolve the matter. "Now that Dallas is enamored with the idea, they'll want us to run with it. We might as well get credit. I can't let you forget, Doug, you're complicit in this little agreement. You don't have a lot of room to complain."

I was cornered.

"How's this going to work as a practical matter?" I asked. "Someone has to check the kid's comments, the whole thing in fact, before any piece goes to print. Is that the parents?"

"Parents would be awkward and take too long," Barney said. "What if all the parents but one liked the piece? Then what?"

"We change it and change it until they're all happy." My tone was curt. I meant it to be. "Which kids do you interview?"

"Your son. A couple of others. We'll see."

"Think about that for a moment, Barney. Every kid on the team will know if you interview even one. How'll those you left out feel?"

Barney scowled. "How many kids do you have on the team?"

"Eight, if all the parents' consent."

"I could do that if I kept the interviews short."

Ty looked surprised. Eight interviews required effort, and here was Barney volunteering to expend it. I guessed our PR guy was making a reasoned calculation. A feature in the company's annual report would earn him recognition, and possibly a bonus.

"Two things to consider, Barney. We don't practice this week and I have to get permission from the parents. Any time after that works."

"We're not under severe time constraints, Doug. How about I watch Sunday's game and talk to the kids at practice right after Christmas. Can you get permission from the parents by then?"

"I'll see."

A JANUS DAY

"Fred, I haven't seen you since the coaches' meeting. How's everything?"

"Not bad, Doug. Not bad. I've been happy. The kids have been terrific. Maybe not so much as ballplayers. But it's been a satisfying season so far, the experience everyone says should happen when you coach your kid, but rarely does."

"Which one's your boy?" I asked, spinning to face his team.

"The one over on the far right with the long, floppy blonde hair. Number eight. He and his mother have a pact about the locks. I think he needs a haircut." After a moment watching the kids warm-up, Fred looked back at me and said, "I understand my guys are walking into a buzz-saw."

"What?" I hoped the faux shock in my face was noticeable.

"I saw you guys are undefeated and from the scores, it looks like the games aren't even close."

"How do you know that?"

"Spenser's Monday update. The League Commissioner's report he sends out every week."

"Guess I'm not on the list."

"You should be. All coaches are supposed to get it. Call Spenser. It's fun to follow the league standings. The bulk of teams are win some, lose some. Except for you guys. Everybody else has at least one loss and there're just two one-loss teams.

"I'll bet St. Leo's is one of the two." I shot Fred a knowing look, and he returned it.

"I understand you've a kid who's special. I talked to the St. Benedict's coach the week after you trounced him, and he was telling me about the guy."

"Don't jinx him. Zack'll probably play terribly today now that you mention him. But, yeah, he's special. All my guys have contributed. Zack's just head and shoulders above." I pointed him out to Fred. "I shouldn't be giving away my secrets, but you'll see him soon enough."

We watched the two teams warm-up and continued to talk. "I have a peculiar situation," I said. "A journalist, he's just a PR guy, wants to interview my kids about their experiences on the team."

"You're kidding. Getting press. You guys must really be good."

"Come on. He's just some guy who works in our office."

"Still."

"Have you had any experience with anything like that?"

Fred shook his head.

"I guess I should be flattered and happy for the kids. But I have a bad feeling."

The cheerfulness faded from Fred's face and he became pensive. "Do you control the process?"

"Not really."

"Maybe that's what's bothering you. I hate responsibility without authority."

"I hadn't thought of it that way."

"Do you trust the guy with authority?"

"It's complicated. I trust the guy who has ultimate authority, but I don't know how engaged he'll be. I have qualms about the guy handling the project day-to-day."

Just then I saw Barney flop onto a seat in the second row of the bleachers across from our bench. He was overweight several pounds ago and while he struggled to peel off his coat, he reached into a pocket and hauled out a reporter's notepad and ballpoint. He squirmed to find a comfortable position and settled.

"That's the guy I'm talking about, Fred," I said, shifting my eyes to the new arrival.

"At least he's trying to get a first-hand look."

The players were leaving the court to join their respective huddles. Fred and I turned to one another for a sincere handshake.

"Good luck, Fred."

"You, too, Doug." He put his left hand over our grip.

I liked Fred. I was sorry I didn't know him better.

My players crowded around me, and I stooped to ensure they could hear. "We'll start the same five as last week. Okay, guys. St. Leo's is the best team we've played so far. I know their coach and he'll have them ready to play hard. We'll need our best effort to win today. I want to see guys on the floor scrambling for loose balls; guys pounding the boards to get rebounds; guys all over their man."

My voice ratcheted louder. "Play smart and play hard." Every player then raised a hand, joining the others high above their heads and shouted a loud, if shrill, "St. Jerry's."

It was clear from the opening seconds that St. Leo's was ready to play. They scrambled for loose balls; they pounded the boards to get rebounds; they defended their man all over the court. They played hard, and they played smart. My team seemed stunned by St. Leo's aggressiveness. Even Zack was on his heels. In no time we were down 5 - 0 and St. Leo's controlled the game.

I called time out. My kids jogged off the court and settled into the huddle in disbelief. They were quiet. We were accustomed to dominating, not being dominated.

"Didn't I tell you they'd play hard? St. Leo's wants to win more than you do."

"The guy guarding me is pushing all the time," Rickie complained. "Those are fouls."

"If the ref doesn't call them, they're not fouls. No excuses. We're standing around too much on offense and are lackadaisical on defense."

"Lackadaisical?" Rickie asked.

"Lazy. Stay all over your man. You go where he goes. On offense, move when you don't have the ball. You just can't wait for a pass. How many times have I told you that, Rickie? You and Casey swing back and forth, like we practiced. Let's see if we can get the ball to George in the middle. Travis, you pick the guy guarding him. Stand there like a big tree. Let him run right into you."

Andy stood stiffly upright, chin tucked, arms rigidly clenched his sides, doing his best to impersonate a big, old oak. The kids giggled.

"Set your feet, Travis. If you move at all, even sway, the refs will call the foul on you." I looked around the huddle for reactions. No one budged. "Okay, play defense as hard as they are, and everything'll be fine."

Zack had been playing lethargically. He was too good and too energetic to perform as he had the first few minutes. I blamed his lapse to the lack of practice the prior week, though perhaps I was searching for an explanation where one didn't exist. No team we played had been as aggressive as St. Leo's. Maybe Zack was reacting to that. But if he didn't play up to his standards soon, St. Jerome's would be in trouble.

Our team took the ball. Zack brought it down the floor, dribbling left-handed, and after three quick passes, he had an easy shot. He propelled the ball softly toward the beckoning hoop, but the ball rolled off the rim and into the outstretched hands of a player wearing St. Leo's green and white. I looked out and saw the heads of the guys wearing purple and yellow droop. Drooping heads is a terrible sign. Fred's team had momentum.

Momentum is strange. It exists, though no one can explain it. It's here one minute and gone the next. When teams ride momentum, they can do nothing wrong. They see the path ahead glassy smooth and downhill, not a pebble or rise in sight. And should something deviate, it autocorrects and ends well. But when momentum rides them, they can do nothing right. They see the path ahead strewn with boulders blocking any way forward. And should a favorable course appear, it proves ill-advised. Why momentum comes, why it goes, is anyone's guess. Usually a magical event, flips it and teams find themselves on its other side. The event's never predictable, and rarely planned, but creates transformative change once it appears.

I needed a momentum change before the game snowballed out of control. A magical event. But how to create one? My options were limited. I'd already called a time-out to interrupt St. Leo's surge, and I had no substitute who could bring new energy. I could only stand on the sideline and shout encouragement, like a cheerleader without the colorful costume.

Then St. Jerome's found magic. The attention of a St. Leo's player cradling the ball momentarily lapsed and Travis noticed. He slapped the ball from the kid's hands. It fell against the leg of another St. Leo's player and rolled out of bounds. Our ball.

Zack dribbled up the court, right hand this time, and passed it to George. Travis set the pick, feet spread firmly, expecting a blow. As George rolled around Travis, the St. Leo's player defending him ran into the big tree and collapsed. George took the ball to the basket unimpeded and laid it in. St. Jerome's scored.

St. Leo's came back. A small boy in green and white threw up a shot, and it fell short. Casey retrieved the ball. As my players headed to the other end, I stood up from the bench, raised three fingers, and yelled, "Everybody got it?" My players looked at one another, knowing that three fingers meant we would send the ball to Rickie in the corner and let him take his favorite shot. The maneuver worked, and Rickie hoisted the ball toward the basket. It didn't fall, but when I bent forward in disappointment, I glimpsed the ball shoot back up toward the hoop, ricochet off the backboard and drop into the net. Travis, the garbage man, had picked up the missed shot from the floor before anybody could react and threw it through the basket.

As our team retreated to the opposite end to play defense, Travis had become the de facto on-court team leader. Zack had been the leader out of sheer competence. He was better than everybody, so the others followed. In the last minute everything changed. Leadership passed from authority of competence to authority of emotion. Travis was now all over his teammates, prodding them to play harder, run faster, compete more energetically.

I just stood and watched, and cheered. As a coach, I was thrilled to see an ordinary player take charge at a critical juncture. As a father, I was beyond thrilled. I was proud. Travis was the unquestioned leader of *The Troika*, but this was different. He assumed leadership of the entire team when the group needed it. He didn't wait for anyone to assign it or vote to confer it. He took it because someone had to fill the vacuum to avert calamity. Travis wasn't about to let calamity occur, and the leader within him surfaced.

The half-time score stood 17 - 17. We'd broken St. Leo's momentum and stabilized play, and my confidence in a favorable outcome grew. There was one caveat. Fred had played all his substitutes for at least a few minutes. I hadn't. I'd played my starting five the entire first half. With them, we'd struggled for a tie. What was I to do with the three substitutes sitting on the bench? I didn't like my options.

The team huddled prior to the start of the second half. "Andy, Willie, you're in. Rickie, Casey, take a seat." The frowns on the faces in the huddle, including the faces of those who were about to see their first action, told me my decision wasn't popular. But I had no choice. It would be best to start the two substitutes to begin the second half and see where we went from there. Randal still sat on the bench, and I had no idea how I'd deal with that situation.

"Here's what we'll do. Andy, run up and down the court as fast as you can. Be ahead of everyone, all the time. Make them find you."

Andy smiled. "I can do that."

"Zack, look for Andy if you get a chance. One of their guys might fall asleep."

Travis slapped Andy on the back, a vote of confidence.

The second half opened and instantly St. Leo's had two more points. This time it was Fred's son who scored. He had taken advantage of our weakest defender, Willie, who had forgotten who he was supposed to guard.

Minutes elapsed. Travis seemed to secure every loose ball, and George captured more than his share of rebounds. But Zack didn't score. Though he had missed most of his shots in the first half, I urged him to continue throwing up the ball. He was too good to keep missing. The law of averages, if nothing else, had to turn in his favor. Eventually it did. Zack dribbled around a defender, stopped, and threw his shot through the hoop. Soon after, he made another for our first lead of the game.

Then things got interesting. A St. Leo's substitute grabbed the ball and rifled it at the basket. The ball slammed against the front of the rim and flew beyond the horde of players waiting to rebound it. Zack grabbed the ball and peered down court. There was Andy, all by himself, under the basket. Andy caught Zack's pass and tossed it in, and without celebration, put his head down and ran as fast as he could back to the other end of the floor.

Andy may not have celebrated, but our bench did. It exploded. The boys jumped up and down and threw fists into the undefended air. They were reacting to an added two points in a tight game. They were also reacting to Andy, a placeholder, making the basket. St. Leo's would now have to account for the kid who ran up and down the court full speed and would never tire. If they didn't, he might score in the same way again.

The third quarter was nearing its end, and the contest grew wilder and stranger. Willie collected himself after his mistake to begin the second half. His man hadn't scored since, and while he wasn't helping us, he wasn't hurting us. His face was grim as he moved up and down the court, jaw set, eyes fixed on the man he was guarding, looking terrified to make another mistake. He seemed to be working hard and not having much fun.

Willie had scarcely touched the ball. When he did, he treated it as hazardous waste, and immediately returned the object to the player who delivered it. Following one of those back-and-forth exchanges, Zack took the ball and threw it to George. The entire St. Leo's team collapsed on our tallest player, and while he looked for a place to distribute it, he spotted Willie standing alone in the corner. George passed him the ball. Willie instinctively looked to pass it back. But two green and white jerseys descended on him. Travis, standing under the basket, howled, "Shoot!" Sheer panic launched Willie's shot. The ball floated through the air for what seemed like minutes before it rattled around the rim and dropped into the net.

Willie froze, a contorted look on his face. He stood immobile, looking at the bench. He'd made a basket, in a game, in a close game. Willie seemed paralyzed, but no one else was. The team ran to Willie and started pummeling him, slapping him on the back, and tousling his hair before realizing St. Leo's was still playing. Even as Willie retreated on defense, individual players stepped out of place to run over to him with a congratulatory hug or hand slap. They seemed thrilled for Willie, and he repaid them with a grin as bright as the freshly polished hardwood floor he stood on.

In the bleachers everyone was standing, clapping, and cheering. Willie's family, too, was on its feet, even Mr. Hernandez. He stood erect, unsmiling, but applauding. Mrs. Hernandez was crying, a handkerchief daubing her eyes. Parents in the bleachers reached over to extend congratulatory handshakes. Willie's basket was a big event for the entire team.

The eventful third quarter ended. St. Jerome's led by three points, including the unexpected contributions of two substitutes. Zack had begun to score. Travis played like a man possessed. I faced a difficult decision, however. Randal hadn't played, and if he were to play a full quarter, he'd be in the game for the duration. That didn't portend well for the game's outcome. Andy and Willie would accept instruction and do their best to fulfill their assigned roles. Randal would say, 'Yes. Yes.' and then run around as if I'd said nothing. At times, he'd even obstruct guys doing what they'd been directed to do.

"Randal, you're in." My tongue pressed on my lower lip as Randal eagerly moved to courtside. I needed to watch him carefully. "Willie, you and Andy are out." I looked down at both, standing side-by-side. "I want you to know what a good job you guys did. You should be proud of yourselves." Willie looked relieved; Andy looked disappointed. Their faces brightened, however, when the rest of the huddle murmured, 'nice job,' 'way to go,' 'good work,' expressing well-deserved praise, for their performances. "George take a seat. Rickie, you and Casey are in."

I'd considered my line up before the season began. In a close game, I planned to rotate playing time among everyone except Zack, our best player, and George, the tallest and our second-best. Today, I needed to revise the plan. Travis had been the team's energy and almost single-handedly had cracked St. Leo's momentum. He had to remain in the game even if he were the coach's kid.

Our huddle broke to start the fourth quarter. Within the first minute, Zack dribbled the ball down the court and passed it to Casey, who threw it to Randal. Whether inspired by his fellow fifth-grader, envious of Willie's unexpected basket, or prodded by some mysterious demon, Randal hurled the ball one-handed in the general direction of the hoop. His attempt more closely resembled a javelin thrower unleashing a spear than a basketball player shooting a ball.

I bolted to my feet. "Randal, take good shots. Don't just throw the ball up." He acknowledged me by waving a hand, which from experience meant 'I hear you, but I'll do what I want to do, anyway'.

Randal was no more helpful playing defense. He liked to chase the ball, abandoning his man to roam unescorted wherever he wanted. His teammates covered for him as best they could and were usually successful. This time they weren't. While Randal was off chasing the ball, St. Leo's made two sharp passes, finding his uncovered man under the basket. St. Leo's led by two.

I called time-out. When Randal reached the huddle, I exhausted every scintilla of willpower to keep myself from screaming. I remained composed, but was visibly irritated and in his face. "Randal, who's your man? Who are you supposed to guard?"

"That player over there." He pointed to a small, brown-haired boy, barely visible in the St. Leo's huddle.

"What's his number?"

"I don't know."

"Why not? We've talked about this since the beginning of the season." I was increasingly irritated. "You have a man. He's wearing a jersey with the number five on it. You stick with that number. Wherever he goes, you go. If he gets a drink of water, you get a drink of water. If he goes to the bathroom, you go to the bathroom. Got it?" As I turned away from Randal, I hastily reversed course. "And don't throw up any more shots from downtown!"

After a few instructions to the rest of the team, I released the boys back out onto the floor. Zack was at mid-court when I motioned him to return. He leaned in and I said, "Don't let the ball get anywhere close to Randal. We don't want him throwing up another wounded duck."

"Got it, coach."

Zack listened to instructions, acknowledged them, and followed through. Given that he handled the ball most of the time we possessed it, I was confident we wouldn't see another hurling exhibition from Randal. I was too optimistic.

Zack tied the game with a shot over an extended hand. Travis forced a turnover at the other end of the court, giving our best player the ball, again. He sent it to Casey. While Casey waited for Rickie to come open, Randal ran from ten feet way, wrestled the ball from Casey, dribbled twice, and without even looking, heaved a shot that landed in the black metal piping behind the backboard anchoring the basket. When the ball fell to the floor, Randal pounded a fist into his open hand in a gesture that said, 'I should have made that one' and turned to run to the other end of the court. The team retreated in disgust. But Casey stood frozen, staring at his hands and trying to figure out what had just happened.

I'd had enough. One quarter minimum playing time be damned. Randal was screwing everything up. He wasn't just playing poorly, which I expected; he refused to follow any instruction and appeared to be ruining the play of others; he was his usual selfish self, and the rest of the team and their coach, me, resented it. Less than half a quarter was enough for Randal today.

"George get back in the game for Randal."

The remainder of the contest was anti-climactic. Zack began to score with help from Rickie. George collected rebounds, and Travis, the garbage man, did a bit of everything, even sinking two free throws, a first for him. Casey went through the motions and little more, seemingly still stunned by Randal stealing the ball from him. St. Jerome's lead at the end was eight points, a margin that masked the game's intensity and parity.

After praising my kids for their effort, congratulating them for the win, and highlighting Willie's first points, I turned to meet Fred who'd given his kids a similar talk. "Nice game, Fred." I was relieved and must have shown it. "You know we're scheduled to play another one of these after Christmas."

"A good match, Doug. I thought we had you a couple of times."

"Only twice? I thought you had us more often than that."

"You have those two kids who changed the game. The one's an amazing player."

"Believe it or not, this was his poorest showing of the season."

"That's hard to believe."

"I kid you not. He didn't start playing like himself until into the fourth quarter. Then, he went back to being Zack."

"It must be fun coaching a kid like that." Fred's sigh contained more than a hint of envy.

"It is. My worry's that I'll ruin him before somebody who knows what he's doing gets his hands on him."

"What's your explanation for the other one, the one who plays like a wild man."

"His mother may not be glad to hear that."

"Your kid?"

"Yeah.

"Is there a competitiveness gene?"

"I don't know."

"Well, if there is that kid inherited it in spades."

"Thanks, Fred. But don't forget your boy threw in a couple of critical baskets."

"Walt? He's a lot like your son, willing to do anything, help any way he can, follows directions, but Walt lacks an edge. Your boy has an edge, and I don't mean that in a pejorative sense. He just doesn't quit."

"An edge cuts in more than one way, you know."

"I've heard that. But you should like the way your son's cuts."

"Today was fun. Like it should be."

"A different outcome would have improved things. But, yeah, a good day," Fred said.

We shook hands, again.

"Looks like your group's heading out." I watched the people who had filled the bleachers wander out the metal double-doors in the back of the gym.

Fred saw his group leaving. He turned his head back toward me and put his hands together as if in prayer. "Just be gentle with us next time. Gentle." His voice fell to a whisper.

"Go home."

Fred bounced out of the gym with his son in tow, surrounded by other team members and their parents. Watching him leave, I wanted to believe we would've had the same conversation had the outcome been different.

Our side of the bleachers was leaving, too. Many in the group headed to Giorgio's for our now post-game ritual. I picked up my jacket and started to follow when a small, gray-haired man wearing wire-rimmed glasses and nestled in a tan canvas car coat intercepted me.

"Coach, do you have a minute?"

"Surely." I didn't recognize the fellow, but we stepped aside as the remnants of the crowd streamed toward the metal double-doors.

"Coach, you behaved badly, today. You were terribly unfair, and I didn't like it." His tone was firm but controlled.

"Excuse me. Who are you?"

"Montgomery Wise, Randal Wise's father."

I should have known.

"You wrote in your letter to the parents you'd play every child at least one quarter in every game, and if I remember correctly, you said you'd try to make it more."

"That's right," I replied.

"At the time, I didn't think that was fair. Playing time should be evenly apportioned among all of the children. I didn't object then because I wasn't familiar with this sports thing. I was wrong. I should have objected. But today you not only didn't do the decent thing, you violated the shameful principles you, yourself, set out. Randal didn't play a quarter. I watched the clock. He played half a quarter, if that." Wise paused, presumably to let me absorb a fact I may have overlooked. "Your son played the entire game. So did that boy, Zack. It's not right. Why should they play four quarters and Randal play half of a quarter? This is grade school, not the professionals."

"Mr. Wise, my policy is to give every kid at least one quarter of playing time per game. I've more than honored that commitment. The boys have had virtually equivalent playing time in most games leading up to this one. Today was an exception. I defy you to find another coach in the league who has done as well."

"I don't care about other coaches. I don't care about other teams. I care about St. Jerome's. I care about my child. You weren't fair to him today."

"One day isn't the season. I've been more than fair to Randal when you assess the season in its entirety. Agreed. I changed priorities today, and I don't regret it."

Our conversation had grown testy and soon attracted attention from the few people remaining in the gym.

"You put winning first, didn't you?" Wise said.

"I did, and I'd do it again given the circumstances." I wanted to say that if your kid followed instructions and played with a sense of team rather than as an undisciplined, selfish brat, he would have played more. Better judgment prevailed. Wise was no doubt unhappy about my playing time decisions, but I sensed that Randal presented his father other, deeper troubles, and I didn't want to rub a wound to find them.

"I see no use in continuing this conversation. You show no remorse and you obviously don't intend to apologize," Wise said.

The latter remark angered me. Apologize? To whom? For what?

"You're correct about one thing, Mr. Wise. Further conversation on this matter is pointless."

Our increasingly sharp exchange lasted only a few minutes, but it unsettled me. I suppose I expected universal approbation for my coaching. When I received admonition instead, I was irked. Wise's initial charge generated a flash of guilt, though I dismissed it instantly. I was the one who'd been affronted. Wise was just an old nut case with a loser kid.

John Hansen, Rickie's dad, joined me as Wise stalked off. "What was that all about?"

"A vociferous objection to my coaching."

"What? We won the game, didn't we?"

"True. However, that gentleman thought I did so in an unethical manner. He didn't like the way I distributed team playing time."

"That must have been the Wise kid's old man." I nodded. "What did he expect? His little, you know what, stole the ball from Casey. Stole it. A teammate. The kid then threw one up from so far away he needed binoculars to see the basket. A coach can't let that happen any time, let alone in a close game. It's not fair to the other kids."

Hansen's use of the word 'fair' jarred me. I hadn't thought about my decision to bench Randal in those terms, but he was right. Randal's recklessness wasn't fair to the rest of the team. His irresponsible play jeopardized their effort. Old man Wise had used the same word to criticize the same decision. He didn't think his son's playing time 'fair'. *Two opposed perspectives justified by the same word,* I mused. *So, what's fair? Whatever's in one's personal interest?*

Hansen and I walked toward Giorgio's. We were the last to arrive. The first pies were being served to the kids. His wife had been late ordering them as she, too, had been absorbed in the game, a conversion from her tepid interest earlier in the season.

The entire team except Randal surrounded the enlarged kid's table. The two younger Hernandez brothers, now part of the regular crowd, were packed in with the others. I even saw George, who'd participated only once before, sitting at the table's end next to a visiting cousin. He was reserved, but the other boys more than compensated. They were noisy, energetic, and voracious.

Mr. and Mrs. Hernandez sat in a booth with their young daughter, two cups of coffee on the table, an upgrade from the water of their earlier appearances. Perhaps their splurge was to celebrate Willie's first score. And there, in an unnoticed dark corner, sat Barney Ambrose, notebook out, scribbling between slurps from his beer glass and attacks on his chicken wings.

A MONOPOLY CHRISTMAS

The adjacent Christmas and New Year's holidays don't line up well for families with children, particularly in the belt just south of the Great Lakes. The winters in the region are normally miserable: damp, windy, and cold, though not consistently cold enough to maintain a snow cover. Their months-long inclemency forces kids inside to either overdose on Christmas toys or passively stare at paraphernalia intended for outside pursuits. The Elliot family was exhibit number one.

Travis had itemized a series of Transformers he wanted for Christmas. Robots, action figures and vehicles. The days of sending a letter to Santa had passed. While his list seemed narrow, Maddie and I both liked that our son showed interest in mechanical objects, gadgets that would stretch his imagination and afford him a greater understanding of forces, leverage, and similar physical phenomena. We joked that Travis was a budding engineer, but we both would be pleased if he ventured in that direction.

Maddie and I, under Santa's name, supplemented Travis's wish list with a packet of dress socks and two large bags of chocolate-covered peanuts for his Christmas stocking, and a sweater for school, a new catcher's mitt, and two board games, *Sorry!* and *Monopoly*, for under the tree. The loot this year was thinner than usual because of the recent emergency replacement of the furnace. Yet, Maddie and I thought it more than adequate to satisfy our son. We were mistaken when, after opening and examining his last package, we heard Travis say, "I wonder what I'll get next year?"

Christmas fell on Sunday. The team would practice the following Tuesday per the schedule I'd distributed before the season began. Not all parents, including my wife, were thrilled with the mid-holiday practice. But given the Christmas Bazaar interruption and our subsequent mediocre play against St. Leo's, I wanted to work with my team over the holidays. The school janitor, Mr. Louganis, agreed to keep the gym thermostat at a tolerable level while verbally wondering if my wife had yet filed for divorce, and if the parents of any player would bother to send their kid.

Tuesday's practice arrived. Everyone showed except Randal. Since Montgomery Wise hadn't left notice at the house or with another parent that his son wouldn't attend, I didn't know whether Randal's absence was pique or an unannounced pre-planned family activity. Still, I was torn. How could Randal learn to discipline himself on the court and play unselfishly with his teammates if he didn't practice? Yet, was it even realistic to think Randal could improve given his performance to date? And what about his father who seemed to think of basketball practice as wasted time?

The season had gone well, beyond expectation. The kids were happy, and the parents seemed satisfied. Our win-loss record was spotless. The single blemish, the Wises, couldn't mar an otherwise wonderful experience.

Practice that day had a special addition. Jordan Whitley walked in the door with Carleton and his friend, Freddie, as we were starting.

"Jordan. Merry Christmas. What did Santa bring you?"

The two of us were increasingly comfortable around each other. Perhaps it was because I was no longer concerned that he'd attempt to poach my players. Perhaps it was because he was a good guy, and the more you knew him, the better you liked him. Perhaps we were just compatible. I couldn't speak to anything in particular, but his increased warmth toward me seemed genuine.

"Just fine, Doug. Thanks. I heard you guys were practicing, so I thought I'd stop by and … supervise." He tittered and grinned as he elongated the word 'supervise'.

"You'll be pleased …" I stopped and turned to my team. "Two lines. Layups. Come on, Andy. Pay attention. Let's not get sloppy." The team moved into its first warm-up drill, and I returned my attention to the visitors standing next to me.

"Carleton, I see you and Freddie have your gym shoes on. Why don't you join in?"

Jordan's son looked up at his Dad with a questioning face and then back at me. "No, thank you, Mr. Elliot."

"Freddie?"

"No, thank you, sir."

"We have to leave, anyway," Jordan said. Carleton and Freddie looked relieved. "I just wanted to stop by. I neglected to include the holidays on my practice schedule. When I hinted at calling one, I realized I'd be the only guy present."

"Not even Carleton?"

"He was the first to say 'no'. Right, Carleton?" Jordan looked down at his son. Carleton gazed into the distance with an 'I've never seen this guy before' expression. I was familiar with the look. Travis had given it to me on more than one occasion.

"Jordan, before you go, I want to tell you we'll end practice today trying your experiment with underhand free throws. Maybe it'll work; maybe it won't. But, it's worth a try. Thanks for the tip."

"I plan to continue having my team work on it, Doug. I'll be keeping statistics, too."

"Hey, Travis, sharp passes. Don't get lazy," I yelled. The playfulness that Travis exhibited often intruded on moments calling for a more serious demeanor. I was watching an example. "Sorry, Jordan. I've got to get on these guys before they start throwing balls back over their heads."

"What?"

"I'm exaggerating."

Jordan smiled and left, and I returned to my players as they wound up opening drills.

"Willie, that was a cool basket you made Sunday." I paid my compliment loudly. I wanted the others to hear.

He beamed, and the boys took turns slapping him on the back and congratulating him.

"What did your mom say when you got home?"

Willie blushed and looked uncomfortable. "She was happy. My dad was, too."

"What did your little brothers say?"

"Bet you can't do it again."

"They're wrong. You can and you will," I said. "Andy, you got a hustle basket."

"What's a hustle basket?" Rickie asked.

"It's a basket you get when you hustle more than the other team. Andy ran past all the St. Leo's players and got to the basket before anyone else." His teammates turned their attention from Willie to Andy and started smacking him on the back. Willie was the first.

Practice resumed. Balls echoed. Shoes squeaked. Rims rattled. And all the while stinky perspiration dampened the T-shirts of my kids. Fifteen minutes before practice was to end, I announced that we would shoot free throws. The players automatically split and headed toward opposite ends of the court.

"Hold it guys," I said. "We'll do our free throws differently today. I want everybody to shoot five the way you usually do. Count how many you make. Your next turn, I want you to shoot five underhand."

Groans flew in my direction. 'Only little kids do it that way!' 'Not me!' 'That's for girls!' 'What for?' 'No way!'

Several took steps toward me in disbelief and protest. I persisted as the grumbling continued. "We shoot free throws poorly. On a good day, we make half. That could cost us a game. Each guy gets four turns today, ten throws overhand, ten throws underhand, and I want you to give the underhand tosses an honest try. I'll be keeping track of the numbers."

The team split again and returned to their places at opposite ends of the court. The guys were still grumbling, though not as loudly. Willie and George were exceptions. They said nothing, neither endorsing nor dissenting. Willie's response could be expected as he likely didn't understand the social connotations involved. George was another matter. Yet, he took my direction as he did any other.

The first round with the overhand throws had the expected results. Zack made three of five, but four of the guys, including Rickie, the loudest grumbler, made only one. Andy made none. The trial with underhand throws then began. Rickie threw his first ball wildly into the air in an act of defiance. I saw his performance and yelled. "Rickie! Do that again and you're welcome to leave. For good. I won't put up with that garbage from you or anyone else." The gym went silent as Rickie retrieved the ball and made a second … this time genuine attempt.

At the other end of the floor, George, who'd made one of his five overhand attempts, was taking the trial seriously. His first underhand shot rose toward the basket, rolled around the rim and fell off. He tried again. This time the ball rewarded him as it slipped through the hoop. By the time George finished his turn, he'd made three of five.

Before the second round began, I gave a few minutes of instruction shooting the ball both over- and underhand. The temper of the room had thickened. The kids wanted to prove that overhand was the better way. I know they believed shooting free throws underhand made them look dorky, and no fourth grader wants to look like a dork. But I hoped that at least some minds would be open to the possibility that a different way might produce better results.

The day's free throw experiment ended, and the outcome shocked the kids. Only Zack shot better overhand. Willie and Casey were equally good, or bad, with either method. The rest proved more proficient underhand.

George was ready to switch. I'd have predicted him to be the last. The rationale for the experiment was that fourth graders aren't strong enough to shoot the ball from the free throw line overhand with much chance of success. George was the largest and strongest, and the one most able to reach the basket without excess effort. I expected him to consider underhand free throws a test of his manhood. He was also the new, shy kid in a class filled with natural leaders. Accepting the free throw change meant bucking teammate opinion. And when he did, it wasn't only an act of rationality, it was an act of social courage.

"The change works for me, Coach," George said. "I make more free throws that way."

"You look like a dork," Rickie said. He chided George, dipping his knees excessively to mimic an underhand free throw.

George swung around to face Rickie. "You calling me a dork?"

Rickie reeled backward. "Well, no. Shooting underhand is just kind of funny. That's all."

I let the confrontation play out. This was good for both boys. George was reticent to stand up for himself. Announcing that he preferred the underhand free throw method was as assertive as he'd been all season. Rickie, in contrast, deserved a good comeuppance. He was mouthy with his teammates, and I still worried about his recurrent free-lancing.

Rickie eventually drifted away, but George refused to budge until it was clear Rickie had no further commentary.

Parents began trickling in to pick up their sons. "Thursday, we'll work on our free throw experiment again. Okay?" Then I remembered. "Everybody. I have a letter for your parents. They have to sign it and you have to return it next practice. Any questions?"

"What's it about? Are we going to a tournament or something?" Andy asked.

"No," I said. "We've a lot of games to play in the league. A tournament isn't in the cards. When you're older. Maybe."

I gave each boy a folded letter, stapled closed, with the parents' name scrawled on the outer flap.

"Can we read it?" asked Casey.

"Take the letter home. If your parents let you read it, that's fine. Just be sure to return it Thursday with a signature."

The day was wretched: cold, damp, sporadically spitting rain, spread by a wind that rose and fell, but never stopped. The weather begged everyone to find shelter.

I was relaxing in the front room, reading the morning newspaper in my favorite chair, and trying to avoid going anywhere. Maddie lounged in her recliner reading a book. The doorbell rang. She rose to greet Rickie and Casey, who had run through 50 feet of nastiness that passed for weather to our front door. I could hear the boys piling in, peeling off layers of wet clothing as they did, and making their way to the family room, across the hall from where I sat.

The *Monopoly* board lay on a card table, the money issued and tucked under each side by denomination, 500's to 1's. *The Troika* slide into their seats around the board awaiting Zack, who would claim the fourth chair. I could see that Travis had already positioned himself as the banker, Santa's hand calculator by his side. "I'm the shoe," said Rickie, picking his token from the game's cardboard carton, and placing it on 'Go'." I watched him sit back satisfied as he shoved a hand into the overflowing popcorn bowl on an adjacent table.

"Give me the car," Casey said, staking a claim to the token. Travis had sited his favorite, the cannon, on 'Go' an hour before.

"Did you see *The Lion King*?" Casey asked his friends. The movie had been released not long before.

"I liked the old king," Travis growled in his deepest voice, a terrible attempt to impersonate James Earl Jones, the cinematic voice of the old lion king. A rasp in Travis's young voice was supposed to substitute for Jones's *basso profundo*. He tried to cover the discrepancy by pulling sounds from as far down in his throat as he could. I thought his impersonation ridiculous, but Casey and Rickie considered it hilarious and booed him. The boos only encouraged Travis. "I'm the king. You're my servants," Travis said, pointing an extended finger toward them. Rickie and Casey burst into laughter, so much so that when Rickie flipped his arm to applaud, he sent the popcorn bowl and its contents flying.

"Whoops!" Rickie's offending hand rushed to his mouth, and he traded an expression of total merriment for one of abject guilt. "I'm sorry," he said from his hands and knees while grasping the bowl with one hand and cupping the other to sweep popcorn back in.

"You should be sorry." Travis's impersonation was growing raspier, though not deeper. He shook his finger at his prostrate friend while roaring like the old lion king. "Roar!" "RoAR!!" "ROAR!!!" Casey, already on the floor helping Rickie, started to roll and hold his sides.

Maddie came rushing from the kitchen with a concerned look. "What's going on?"

Travis refused to leave character. "My vultures are cleaning the forest." He pointed to the boys on the floor. "Quick, before the hyenas get here." The two friends flew into stitches, again.

Maddie looked around the room, her face puzzled. She didn't understand Travis was impersonating James Earl Jones and that she was now an unwitting character in *The Lion King*.

"Doug. What's going on here?" she asked from across the hall.

"The movies, dear. The movies." I was laughing, too, long since distracted from reading my morning newspaper by the shenanigans coming from the family room.

The doorbell rang once more, and Maddie escaped *The Troika* to answer.

I heard the door open. "Zack get in here!" Maddie said. Rain noisily pelted the doorstep while a waft of cold air spread down the hall. The door slammed shut.

"Let me take your jacket, Zack. I see it's still nasty outside."

"Sure is, Mrs. Elliot." I could hear the crackling of a canvas coat and the squeak of galoshes escaping leather-soled shoes. "Thank you, Mrs. Elliot."

"What's that?" Maddie asked.

"A paperback. I carry one when I go anywhere in case I have extra time."

"You've a *Monopoly* game this afternoon. There won't be much time for reading."

"I hope not. That'd mean I'd gone bankrupt early." Zack knew the game.

Maddie marched Zack by the shoulders toward the family room where *The Troika* had yet to recover from Travis's earlier hijinks.

"Hi, guys. What's going on?" Zack asked.

"ROAR!!!" said Travis. Rickie and Casey burst out laughing again, though less energetically than before. Travis's schtick was tiring. Zack looked on, baffled. Casey collected himself and explained. "I asked if anyone had seen *The Lion King*. I thought it was cool, a cartoon, but better. Then Travis tried to sound like the old lion king in the movie, and … you know."

I couldn't see Zack's reaction from where I sat, but I heard him say, "I haven't seen the movie, but I've seen Travis in action."

"You understand," said Casey.

Calm now and seated, Rickie picked up the dice. "Shake to see who goes first." The *Monopoly* game was officially in progress.

I sat down with my newspaper twenty minutes ago and I still hadn't finished the front page. It was time to find a quieter spot. I was about to get up and leave when Zack said, "My dad says somebody's writing an article about the team and we're all going to be in it." My curiosity was roused. I wanted to hear this conversation, so I sat back down … to eavesdrop.

"You mean we'll be in the paper?" Rickie asked. He wiggled enthusiastically.

"It was in the letter Coach Elliot sent home yesterday. Travis, you should know all about it," Zack said.

"I forgot to ask." The coach's son was expected to be the team's unofficial inside source of information. Travis had failed in his responsibility. "There're too many letters coming home from school these days. I can't keep track of them all."

"It's your dad's," Casey shot back. His voice was incredulous.

Travis had no reply. The room was silent until Rickie's voice interrupted. "Hey! I shook double fours. Move me to Vermont Avenue. I get another shake."

Zack returned to the letter over the clatter of Rickie rattling dice. "The guy who's writing the article wants to talk to everybody on the team."

The noise of dice stopped.

"About what?" Rickie asked.

"The team," Zack said.

"Just like the pros," Rickie said. His tone was reverential.

"What are we supposed to say?" Casey asked Zack.

"I don't know. We should sound smart, I guess."

"How do we do that?" Rickie asked. He looked at Zack, then Casey.

Casey shrugged.

"Did the letter say anything else?" Rickie continued.

"It said the parents have to agree," replied Zack.

"That would be cool to see my name in the paper," Rickie said. "I'll talk to my parents. They have to sign something, right?"

"I wonder if we'll get our picture in the paper?" Casey asked no one.

"Maybe an action shot." Zack speculated. "You've seen those."

"Do we pose? Or do they take pictures during a game?" Rickie inquired.

The *Monopoly* game had all but ceased while the boys considered the possibilities. They didn't understand that a feature in Steiger Bros.' annual report differs from a newspaper article. I knew they thought every family member and friend would read about their basketball exploits in the local gazette or magazine. I couldn't tell them the piece would be buried in a high-gloss, small-circulation, fat booklet that only a few investors and financial analysts would see. At least not yet. They were too excited.

"What if we lose a game?" Casey asked. "Do we still get in the paper?"

That thought stopped them. Lose? The table went silent. "We won't get in the paper if we lose?" Zack asked looking around the table.

"I don't know. I just thought I'd bring it up," Casey replied.

"They don't write stories about losers." Travis rejoined the conversation, following a brief exile for failure to provide the expected inside intelligence.

"We're not going to lose. It's not going to happen," Rickie assured.

"We've played seven games," Zack said. "There could be one or two really good teams we haven't played yet."

"Seven and zero. Dad told me we're the only undefeated team in the league."

"Guys. We're not going to lose. It's not going to happen," Rickie insisted.

"I didn't say I thought we would," Zack responded. "It's possible. That's all."

"It's not going to happen," Rickie repeated. He sounded exasperated.

Audible relief spilled from the room following Rickie's last declaration. I could hear their breathing relax. Someone rummaged in the popcorn bowl. Someone else counted money.

"Rickie, it's your turn," Casey said.

Rickie picked up the dice and rolled. "Eleven. Put me on Community Chest and give me the top card!" He read the yellow card aloud: '*Go directly to jail. Do not pass Go. Do not collect $200.*'

UNPREPARED

Thursday's practice began with unspoken anticipation of the final fifteen minutes, the time when the free throw experiment would resume. The prevailing opinion among the team was that only overhand free throws were manly and respectable. Underhand tosses were for sissies and dorks.

Travis was a social animal, and in the fourth-grade social hierarchy, dorkiness is about the lowest rung. Since conclusion of our initial experiment, he hadn't said a word about free throws. It wasn't like him to remain silent on matters of dorky decorum. Yet, whenever someone mentioned underhand free throws, he broadcasted his opinion with a shriveled nose and puckered mouth, the same grimace he wore last month when he mistakenly drank from a glass of unsweetened grapefruit juice.

Practice proceeded without incident. Randal was still vacationing from the workouts, but the rest of the team was present. The kids ran their regular drills and then scrimmaged. The level of chatter was depressed. Other than that, everything seemed normal.

As practice neared its end, I shouted, "Free throws."

The players divided and went to opposite ends of the floor. Balls soon headed for their respective hoops propelled by overhand throws. The success rate was poor, but as usual it varied by individual. Zack made four while Willie didn't make any. I roamed the court from end to end, clipboard in hand, to record results.

The first underhand round followed. Then, a second overhand round and a second underhand. After all four rounds ended, I didn't need to recap the experiment's result. Every kid knew his scores.

"What do you think?" I asked, hoping the players would recognize the outcome of the free throw experiment, and accept it. Even grudgingly. Shooting free throws underhand made sense regardless of the social stigma attached. But the kids had to reach that conclusion on their own, or they would never fully commit to its success.

No one said a thing. Several heads dropped to avoid eye contact. Feet shuffled; eyes focused on sneaker laces. I needed someone to step forward. Casey eventually did. "If we shoot better one way than another, who cares if we look like dorks." He didn't lift his head when he spoke, and his voice was passionless. His words came from his head, not from his heart. I appreciated Casey's effort, but that endorsement wouldn't sway anyone.

Travis had made twice as many free throws underhand as overhand that day and was the team's leader. I shot him my most insistent look. He averted my eyes. I could see he wanted no part of underhand free throw shooting and the dorkdom it conveyed.

The shuffling continued; eyes still focused on sneaker laces; hands rested on hips; no one said a word. We just stood.

Zack broke the silence. "I'll shoot underhand if everybody else does." The others stared at him. They all realized he was the only one to perform better overhand. Yet, if the team on average made free throws underhand at a higher rate, Zack would sacrifice his personal interest and shoot underhand, looking like a dork in the process, just like the others.

"That's stupid," Travis finally blurted, revulsion covering his face. "Guys should shoot the way they shoot best. Zack shoots best overhand. I shoot best underhand." Travis spit his words. He sounded as if he were fighting every one that spilled. Yet, a compulsion stronger than dorkdom kept pushing them from his mouth. Turning to Rickie, he daintily dipped as if throwing up an underhand free throw and said, "And, you're going to join me looking like a dork." The sour look on Rickie's face curdled.

"Travis is right," I said. "Every guy should shoot free throws in games the way he's most successful. We're looking for results, not style. No one's locked in. We'll continue to practice free throws. If you get better overhand, you can switch back." The kids needed to know they had a path out of dorkdom.

Maddie and Travis headed to the family room to watch television after the evening meal. I grabbed my newspaper and headed to the front room. The phone interrupted.

"Mr. Elliot," Monsignor Schreiber greeted me. "How are you this lovely evening?"

"I'm very well, Monsignor. Thank you. Merry Christmas. I didn't expect to hear from you during the holidays."

"Yes. It's our busy season as my merchant friends would say." He showed a bit of humor for the first time. "A good spell to profit, no pun intended." He chuckled at his own terrible pun. The Monsignor's unexpected levity was short-lived however, and his tone changed when he reached the call's purpose. "The matter you brought to my attention was too important to defer. Mistreatment of children is a serious charge. I wanted to attend to it as soon as possible," he said.

Weeks had passed since my initial call. During that interval, I'd often questioned Maddie about following up in some fashion. Each time she counseled patience and each time I'd heeded her advice, more than once reluctantly.

"Mr. Elliot. We've found a temporary new coach for our fourth-grade basketball team. Sister Martha assumed control last week. She'll be our head coach until we can find a permanent replacement. Mr. Ferguson will change roles. He'll be an assistant coach, more in title than in responsibility. I've also spoken with Mr. and Mrs. Ferguson about acceptable behavior at basketball games. The school's sports director will look in on practices and games, and in case of inappropriate behavior report back to me." He cleared his throat. "Mr. Elliot, I'm sure you have several questions that I regrettably can't answer. Many things have happened because of your call, but I hope you can appreciate the confidential nature of my discussions with the Fergusons."

I noted the word 'discussions'. Plural.

"I do have questions, Monsignor. Mr. Ferguson remains an assistant coach. Why is he even around the team? What authority does Sister Martha exercise on paper and in reality?" I had an extensive mental list of questions, but the Monsignor cut me off.

"I'm sorry, Mr. Elliot. I'm not at liberty to answer those inquiries. The reasons behind the changes we've made and discussions with the people involved remain private. But let me say, I appreciate your report enormously and your patience in its resolution. Without your concern and diligence, the changes that have taken place, and I think they're very positive changes, would never have occurred. You should be proud of that."

"Thank you, Monsignor. That's kind of you."

"May God bless you, and Merry Christmas, Mr. Elliot. Good evening."

I stood in the hallway holding the dead phone. "Maddie. Maddie." I headed toward the family room to find my wife. The Monsignor had just delivered the final act of the Ferguson affair, and I was confused. I didn't know what to think. I needed to talk to my wife and make sense of what had just happened. We met between the front and family rooms.

"What's wrong, Doug? Are you all right?" My raised voice had upset her.

"I'm fine. I just want to talk. Sorry, I didn't mean to scare you."

Visibly relieved, Maddie walked into the front room and sat down. I trailed her.

"Monsignor Schreiber just called." Maddie's attention sharpened as I recounted our conversation. She tracked every detail and didn't interrupt. I knew her well enough to know she feared any intrusion might muddle my train-of-thought and, in my eagerness to recount the conversation, skip some critical comment or observation. "It's clear the Monsignor believes the matter settled."

"At least he shared that with you." She had a point.

The Monsignor had told me what he thought I had a right to know, which was little. He said, 'changes have taken place', and I had no reason to doubt his word. But I'd never know what those changes were: substantive or cosmetic? Wide-ranging or narrow? Expelling the Fergusons or embracing them? No one other than those directly involved ever would. Then, there was the possibility nothing had happened or would, and I'd never know that either. I'd only know what I'd been told and no more.

The ambiguity of the outcome left me unsatisfied. I was invested in a positive result. I'd hoped that my time and concern would be rewarded, and I needed to believe they would. I'd even have accepted an argument against my case. Maybe a 'mind your own business.' But nothing. Nothing. I'd never know the outcome.

"I feel ..." My voice trailed off.

"Frustrated? Disappointed? Empty?" Maddie said.

"All the above."

"That's understandable."

I fidgeted in my chair, exasperated.

"Doug, if you didn't care, knowing the outcome of your actions wouldn't matter. You care; so, they matter."

"You understand why I'm so angry. 'Angry' isn't even the right word."

"I know you well enough to appreciate why you're upset. The Monsignor left you in a void. Still, look at it from another perspective. Suppose someone at St. Joseph's saw the Fergusons' performance and decided that they needed serious counseling. Maybe the Monsignor then exerted his authority to see that counseling happened. One element was to relieve Ferguson of the coaching job. However, the counselor didn't want to humiliate or isolate him, so the counselor kept him on as an assistant under the supervision of a new head coach. If that happened, should the Monsignor have told you? You may have felt better, but what about the Fergusons? Should they have had their private affairs broadcast to ease your sensitivities?"

"That's a stretch, Maddie." I felt her hypothetical made light of my irritation.

"My scenario's possible, isn't it? Perhaps unlikely, but possible? How many similar possibilities exist? Too many to count." Her voice level and tone hadn't changed the entire conversation. "I'm not saying you don't have real, deep-seated frustrations. I'm saying there may be good reasons you have to endure them."

"I suppose, but that doesn't make me feel good about it." My voice was louder than I expected or wanted, while my hands flew from the chair's arms as if they had a mind of their own. I waved my elevated arms. "I'm just venting." My voice melted as my hands fell back to the chair's arms. "It infuriates me."

"I know." Maddie smiled supportively, leaned forward, and took one of my hands into hers, squeezed and softly rubbed it. "Come on," she said as she rose. "Let's watch some TV. *Seinfeld* should be on tonight. You always like that show."

I didn't remember whether *Seinfeld* was on Thursday or not. It didn't matter. Maddie had worked her magic as she always did, and I felt better. Not satisfied, but better.

St. Jerome's fourth-grade basketball team continued to win. Since I'd started receiving Spenser's weekly account of Sunday games, I could track how we were faring compared to other teams in the league. We led at 9 - 0. Every other team in the league had at least two losses, and we'd defeated both two loss teams. Seven games remained in the season and our lead appeared healthy.

My team was not only winning, it was getting better. A major reason for its improvement was Jordan. I stole his free throw idea, and though my kids' initial resistance created tense moments, they stopped worrying about looking dorky once the balls started to fall. All the kids on the team now shot free throws underhand except Zack.

Wins made it easier to find playing time for the three substitutes. Andy and Willie played as many minutes as *The Troika*, and just a few less than George. Randal, having returned from his Christmas sabbatical, got more and less time depending on how he blended with the unit on a given day. Despite my constant prodding, Randal never grasped the relationship between the way he played and the minutes he played. He continued to throw up shots from anywhere on the court, to dribble the ball when he needed to pass it, and to forget the man he was supposed to cover. His teammates, including Andy and Willie, grew increasingly annoyed. Randal, who was never popular, continued to lose any good will he ever had. He either didn't notice or didn't care.

At the opposite end of the league standings sat St. Jerome's other fourth-grade team. Jordan's team. They hadn't won a game. St. Bernard's, a position above them in the standings, had won a single contest and Jordan's team still had them on the schedule. That match offered his team a reasonable chance to win a game. I could only hope.

The changes Jordan had instituted since our meeting a few weeks ago hadn't resulted in more success on the court, but they did cause a stir. His policy of uniforms at practice and T-shirts for games confused everyone, particularly Anderson, who took pride in St. Jerome's uniforms and treated each as if they were clerical vestments. Jordan reveled in his reversal, and if the change tweaked Anderson, so much the better. The Musical X's system was a different matter. Jordan told me it helped his team improve play early in games and the kids loved to make flat-footed plops on their imaginary X's. But as I'd anticipated, opponents soon caught on and his players were unable to adjust, usually erasing the system's benefits by the end of the first half. Jordan claimed Musical X's made games more fun for the kids, though it didn't substitute for a win.

Two generic types of defensive strategies dominate basketball. Man-to-man and zone. The first assigns each player an opponent and expects the player to prevent his assigned opponent from scoring. The second makes each player responsible for an area on the gym floor, a zone, and expects the player to prevent any opponent in the zone from making a basket. One type of defense guards a player while the second guards an area.

St. Jerome's played man-to-man, as did every other team we had encountered. But when we faced Holy Redeemer, we found a team that employed zone.

Holy Redeemer was 6 - 3 in the standings. When we entered their gym at about 1:30 for our 2:00 game, they were warming-up in their marine blue uniforms with *Holy Redeemer* scripted in red across their jerseys. They appeared the same as any other any team we'd faced. They were the same size, shot the ball with the same exaggerated effort, and picked at one another in warm-ups with the same patchy energy. Even their sweat-stained white sneakers looked the same.

The Holy Redeemer coach was different, however. He didn't resemble the other coaches I'd met. His gray flattop and wrinkled face depicted a man significantly older than his counterparts, including me. He wore glasses with plastic frames, colored on top and clear on the bottom, a style that took an abrupt exit in the early 1960's. A huge key ring bulged from beneath a brown plaid sweater vest that covered his ample paunch. And, after I watched him sort through that ring to find a key to the storage closet, I realized the fellow was not only Holy Redeemer's fourth-grade basketball coach, but also the school's janitor.

By now the news of St. Jerome's success had spread, and with our success, the number of followers increased. The families of all the players, often including more distant family members, such as cousins or aunts and uncles, now attended every game. The Hernandez contingent had risen from five to seven, for example. Other contingents had grown more. So, I wasn't surprised to look across the court toward the bleachers facing our bench and see the stands filled. Most of the people I knew or at least had seen before. And then I spotted a face I knew only too well. Barney Ambrose squatted in the front row with his note pad.

I initially had had no strong feelings about Barney, but his handling of the annual report's feature on our team reduced any stature I may have given him. I'd followed through as he requested and obtained permission for him to interview my kids. The conversation with Montgomery Wise was less than pleasant. I didn't care whether Randal spoke to Barney or not, but it was only fair to inform Wise that everyone else had agreed and that Randal would be the odd man out should he deny his son permission. The word 'odd' triggered a loud reaction from Wise, and I held the telephone receiver at arm's length while he ranted. When the decibel level dropped, I asked 'in or out?' He answered 'in' and continued to rant. I hung up.

The kids were excited about Barney's visit. None of them had been interviewed before and the thought of talking to a reporter, just like their athletic heroes, electrified them and elevated their status among their peers. The kids constantly asked when the man who would write the article would show up and ask them questions. They wondered if he'd bring a camera. I didn't know and when I marched into Barney's office looking for answers, he battered me with deadlines, timelines and printing schedules, none of which I knew a thing about or cared to learn.

"Tell me, Barney, when are you interviewing my kids?"

There he sat viewing the game, and I still didn't have an answer.

This week's opponent, Holy Redeemer, scored immediately. Zack dribbled the ball back down the floor and encountered something new to us, a zone defense we weren't prepared to face. I'd made a serious error of omission and could only hope my players were good enough to bail me out.

I called time-out and my team jogged to our huddle, confused. Time-outs were reserved for correcting mistakes arising during the game's progress. This game had just begun.

"Guys. Holy Redeemer's doing something different on defense. They're playing a zone. Remember a zone defense? We practiced against it several weeks ago."

Zack understood, but it took the full time-out to jar most memories about the different defenses and how to play against each. I stretched the time-out to the maximum, trying my best during the seconds available to explain how and why we needed to adjust our normal play. When the referees demanded we return to the court, I wasn't confident my players understood. My embarrassment was compounded when I glanced over at Holy Redeemer's bench to see if their team had made any substitutions and noticed that the guy with the large key ring bore a knowing smirk. He'd fooled me and my team with his gambit, and he knew it.

"Andy, sit next to me," I said when we returned to the bench.

Holy Redeemer's players fell back on defense into a compact group, impenetrable to any of our players, including George, the tallest kid on the floor. The thicket they created near the basket meant that our team couldn't get the ball close enough to get good shots, and the good shots we did get refused to fall. We struggled to score, but we made Holy Redeemer struggle, too. When the first quarter ended, the tally was 7 - 4. Our team, the team that led the league and was undefeated, the team that had thrashed most of our opponents, had scored a mere four points in the first quarter. And had battled to do that.

Since the initial minutes of the game, I kept my arm around Andy's shoulder pointing out positions, movements, passing lanes and other keys to playing against a zone defense. I hoped that with the added instruction he might go into the game and contribute in ways that our current players weren't. I doubted Andy would realize my hopes, but he was a willing learner with boundless energy and our team needed a change. Perhaps he was the tonic.

Casey was our weakest link, so I substituted Andy for Casey and was rewarded with a surge in the team's play. Yet, for all the élan that followed Andy's entrance, the ball still wouldn't drop. Poor shooting from over the thicket mixed with a lack of short, easy shots from within were proving a deadly combination.

Though the team scored more points in the second quarter than the first, Holy Redeemer led at half-time by four. It grew. But by early in the fourth quarter the lead of the team in marine blue and red shrank to two points. We never got closer.

My team had played hard. It was also a bit unlucky. But Holy Redeemer played with uncommon discipline. Sporadically, one of their kids would dash from the crush under the basket to challenge Zack, but other than those limited forays everyone fell back into a pack under the hoop, sliding from side to side depending on the ball's location. No one ever seemed out of place.

Our team had more basketball talent than did theirs. Only one, maybe two, of their players were good enough to start for us. But that didn't matter today. We were a superior team that lost to an inferior one.

The truth was Holy Redeemer imposed our first defeat because our team, my team, was unprepared to play against a zone defense. That wasn't the players' failure. That was the coach's failure, and I was the coach. I'd let my kids down and I felt terrible about it. What had I been thinking? It was inevitable there would be a team that played zone. It just happened to be Holy Redeemer, and it just happened to be today. I had no excuse.

When the final buzzer sounded, my kids headed for our bench. They were distraught and hurried to put on their clothes over their damp uniforms, collect lingering parents, and escape. I couldn't let that happen. They had to learn they couldn't run. They had to face the fact we lost. I also had to tell them their coach let them down.

"Huddle up, guys." The kids grumbled. Damp and disheveled, and in various states of dress, they slowly rose to join the huddle. Randal was the exception. He was ready to have fun and picked at Willie, though Willie was in no mood and as upset as the others. I disliked Randal more and more, and sensed the kids did as well.

"We lost today," I said. Looking across my players, I saw nothing but hair above their lowered heads. Not one eye, not one nose, not one mouth was visible. Except Randal's, who wandered around the gym looking for who-knew-what. "Who had fun, today?" I asked. Not one head moved. "I didn't either."

The crowd was dispersing. Barney had left.

"Remember how this feels," I said. "We never want to feel like this again. The referees didn't rob us. The crowd didn't interfere. No one was hurt. We have no excuses. I believe we're a better team than Holy Redeemer, and if we played them again, the score would be different. But we don't." No one moved a muscle.

"The weakest link today and the major fault for the loss was your coach. Me. I didn't prepare you. You can't do what you haven't practiced. That's my fault, not yours. I'm sorry." Heads began to rise, and I saw a few questioning eyes. Then other heads popped up, and more eyes fixed on me. "That won't happen again. You'll always be prepared. I'll see to it. I promise. Now, let's pledge to one another, we won't lose another game. Ever."

The team's attitude changed instantly. Cerebral, soft-spoken Casey shouted, "Yes! We're not losing again!" Grumbling transformed into, 'Yeah!' 'Right!' 'Come on, guys!' 'Losing stinks!' 'No more!' They spat their resolve at one another, all seven who remained. Randal had left the gym and was on his way home.

We'd ended our huddle. I thought all the boys had gone. "Mr. Elliot." It was Rickie tugging at my sleeve. "Does today's loss mean that no one will write an article about us now? That the man won't interview us?"

"No, Rickie. The man will still write the feature." The boy's face illuminated, and he ran out of the gym. Sometime soon I would have to explain the difference between a feature in a corporate annual report and a newspaper article.

The coach with the big key ring was packing equipment into the storage bins and locking up. His kids were gone. I was preparing to leave, but I lingered. The guy intrigued me. He hadn't attended the coach's meeting, and I hadn't seen or heard of him. He gave no hint of being personable, but his team played well, beyond the capacity of its individual players, and made a marvelous example of the whole being greater than the sum of its parts. That couldn't happen if some guy just threw out a ball and said, 'go play'.

He hadn't approached me for a post-game handshake, but I felt compelled to say something. "Coach," I called walking in his direction, "your kids played with discipline and poise, today. How do you get that out of them?"

He didn't stop packing equipment. "They're good boys."

I could tell he didn't intend to elaborate, so I tried something more personal.

"Do you have a son on the team?"

"Not this year."

"You've obviously done this for a while. I'm new to the league." I thought flattery might open him up. "What do you do at practice? That zone was stifling."

"The kids work hard." He declined to elaborate.

I could have prodded further, but a fourth simple sentence from him was unlikely to add either insight or enjoyment. Whether his hollow responses were reserved for me or whether they were standard fare wasn't a matter I cared to consider. I extended my hand and as he took it an 'I enjoyed kicking your behind' expression sprouted across his face. It was the most emotion he'd shown all day.

THE PROFESSIONAL PHOTOGRAPHER

When I stepped into the office Monday morning, Barney was waiting at the receptionist's desk. "Sorry about your loss, Elliot. Still, one loss makes a better story. The boys seem more human that way, not a bunch of basketball-playing robots trained by a professional coach. The feature needs normal kids and you need to look like a normal volunteer."

I ground my teeth. Barney didn't have to tell me he relished watching Holy Redeemer beat us. His manner televised it.

"While we're talking about the feature, Barney, when are you coming to interview my kids. They're waiting."

"I've about finished my background research. I should be ready to interview your kids soon."

Background research? I would have thought he could collect all the information he needed with two or three phone calls.

"When is soon?" I asked.

"A week or so."

"That's what you said two weeks ago."

"Some things came up."

"Are you bringing a camera?"

"No."

"Should my kids wear their game uniforms?"

"No."

"Anything they need to know beforehand?"

"No. Not really."

"Keep me advised," I said as I turned to walk to my office.

The first practice following our loss was different. The normal horseplay was absent, and the good-natured banter silenced. When Andy tried to resurrect them, Travis shut him down. The sound of bouncing balls was still loud and ubiquitous, but its echo was pure, uninterrupted by the usual cacophony of clashing voices and noises. Following initial drills, the boys huddled. Quiet.

"We got our behinds kicked Sunday. What did you learn from that?" I asked. They stared at the floor. No one moved or said a word. I could only hear breathing. "All right, how do you feel about it?"

I noticed Travis, standing to the side, squeezing a basketball between his hands. The harder he squeezed, the more his neck and arms contracted, and they began to quiver. When his clenched mouth and shaking muscles signaled he could squeeze no harder, Travis blew. "I hate to lose! It stinks! Damn!" He slammed the ball into the floor, and it shot back into his open hands. He cupped the recaptured ball on a hip and turned his face away in disgust.

Heads snapped with Travis's first word, but his fury elicited little overt reaction. I heard a muted 'yeah' here and there. Then crickets. The hush surprised and puzzled me.

"Is that all anyone has to say? Is Travis the only one upset?"

Rickie answered. "It's no fun to lose."

"Yeah. But why isn't it?"

"Because losing's embarrassing," Zack said.

"Why's it embarrassing? People lose all the time."

"Because I missed a lot of shots, ones I should have made." Zack's bent head and hunched shoulders aired his disappointment.

"Nobody shot well, Zack. You didn't. Nobody else did, either." My reassurance didn't satisfy him. He held himself to a higher standard than did the others, an unspoken burden that the more talented often assume. "Zack, what did I say about blame? We win as a team and we lose as a team." I knew all the basketball clichés and swore to avoid them, and here I was delivering one of the tritest when I wanted to make a serious point. My players needed to understand the reasons for our loss.

"George, were you bothered by Sunday's performance?"

He looked me in the eye. "Yes sir. I was."

"Why?"

Zack interrupted before George could reply. "Because we're a better team than Holy Redeemer and they beat us."

"No, Zack," Casey said. "They didn't win. We lost."

The conversation about the loss to Holy Redeemer made everyone uncomfortable, except Randal, who had checked out long ago and hung around only because his ride wouldn't show up for another hour. I didn't want to press the matter too hard or too philosophically for fear my kids would miss the principal idea. Yet, here were the two smartest kids on the team, Zack and Casey, attributing the cause for our loss to subtly distinct factors. Their difference was too sophisticated for most high school kids, let alone for most fourth graders. I knew I'd lose the group if I pressed it.

"Whatever," George said. It was our fault we lost. We can't blame anybody else,"

Heads nodded. I was proud of my guys. They looked at themselves, not others. No excuses.

"If it's our fault, what do we do about it?" I asked.

I expected someone to pop up with 'work harder', 'play harder', or a fix of that nature. It was the logical conclusion for boys taught that work brings reward. George had a different idea.

"We were too big for our britches," he said.

His teammates looked at him as if as if he had just propped open the gym door in the middle of January.

"We thought they weren't as good as us, and we played like it."

"Is George right?" I asked.

"I thought we'd win," Travis said.

"Me, too," agreed Rickie.

"But, is that what George means?"

Eyes turned to me, most perplexed. "Isn't it good to think you're going to win? Did George and Travis say the same thing?"

The blank stares from all but Casey and Zack told me that none of this made sense. A wise coach would have dropped the whole thing, but I was stubborn. My team needed to learn something from Sunday and not just that they didn't like to lose.

"Guys, George and Travis are saying different things. But both are right." The boys were listening, except Randal, who was now exploring the mechanics of the drinking fountain.

"Travis said we should think we're going to win. We should feel confident before and during a game. That is, if we've done our homework and are prepared. Anyone disagree?"

Heads bobbed, and even glimmers of smiles appeared. That idea met universal approval and understanding.

"We should feel good about ourselves going into games. Then, what did George say?"

"He said we were overconfident," Zack replied. "We didn't respect Holy Redeemer until it was too late."

"George, is that what you meant?"

"Yeah. Zack says it better than me. But I meant what he said."

"Anybody disagree with that?" I looked around the huddle for a glimmer of appreciation for George's observation. "Casey, what do you think?"

He nodded. "I think so. George's right."

"Rickie? What about you?"

"We're better than they are. We should have smashed them." He was combative and restless.

"You miss the point, Rickie. Why didn't we? George said we got too big for britches. Do you agree?"

"I suppose."

I looked at the team's expressions, more and less understanding, more and less attentive, more and less patient. It was time to move on. "We've spent a lot of time talking," I said. A whispered 'yes' from behind drew restrained smiles. Their interest was waning. Most visibly wanted to put their long-idling engines into gear. "Okay. So, what's the point? Why all the talk? We wanted to understand why we lost and what we could do about it. Right?" I studied the boys. "And? … And?" I hoped for a response but didn't expect one.

Willie came through. "We got too big for our britches." Willie likely had never heard the expression before it came from George's mouth and he probably didn't even know what britches were, but he'd seized the idea and internalized it.

"Then what do we do about it, Willie? If we know the problem, how do we ensure sure we don't lose again?"

"Take everybody seriously. Pretend every team is the best we'll ever play."

"Is Willie, right? Is he?" I asked. "You bet he is. Everybody understand what Willie said?" Heads nodded, some vigorously, others less so, corresponding to those who I suspected understood Willie's point, more and less.

Willie just smiled. He took the ball he'd been holding and started dribbling toward the other end of the court. Soon the sound of bouncing basketballs echoed throughout the gym again.

Watching the kids, I reflected on the past several minutes and recognized that I failed to highlight the salient caveat. I wasn't sure I failed because the matter never seemed to fit or because I was too embarrassed to present it. Yes, a team should feel confident going into a game. If they're prepared. My kids weren't prepared, though they didn't know. They had no reason to know. Their coach didn't know they weren't prepared, either. But he had reason to.

The next game couldn't come soon enough. Everyone wanted redemption. Last week's loss had embarrassed us, and this would be the team's first opportunity to prove the prior game was an aberration.

Barney was in the bleachers again, this time accompanied by a guy carrying a camera with a huge zoom lens, the type used by photographers at major sporting events. A closed tripod and an assortment of unzipped leather cases lay beside him.

Barney hadn't notified me of his plan to bring a photographer. However, I knew of no league rule that prohibited taking pictures at games. Parents often snapped shots with their Instamatics and Polaroids from the front bleacher. An outsider with a serious camera felt different though, something league rule-makers couldn't have anticipated. Still, the end product is a photograph regardless of the camera's or its operator's sophistication.

During warm-ups, I strode across the court and collared Barney. "What's going on?"

"I brought along a guy to take a few action shots for the feature."

The photographer adjusted the settings on his camera while Barney and I spoke.

"You might have said something." His lack of communication irritated me.

"I didn't want to tell you because you'd tell your kids, and everybody would be upset if things didn't pan out."

"Sure," I said. "Where's he taking his pictures from?"

"Don't ask me. He's the pro, works a lot of the big games around here. I only got him because nothing's happening in the area today."

"Where's he going to take the pictures from, Barney?" I repeated.

"Ask him. Hey, Bert." He motioned to his guy, who was now standing on a bleacher, checking his light meter. "Come on over."

Bert Pratt climbed down two steps with cameras and related equipment swinging from straps hanging around his neck and joined us.

"Bert, this is Doug Elliot, the guy I work with," Barney said. "He wants to know where you'll take your pictures from."

The photographer looked at me blankly for the briefest moment, dumbfounded by the question, and throwing an arm toward the court, said, "Everywhere. The more perspectives, the more interesting the pictures."

"You'll be standing or crouching in front of people watching the game?"

"Yeah." Bert replied, stretching the word. "You do that. You take game photos from the front, not the rear. Sorry, I'm not transparent, but I do move around a lot."

"Okay, Barney. Here's the deal. Do what you have to do, but Bert must take a least one action shot of every one of my players. All of them need to have at least one souvenir. Deal?"

Barney didn't consult Bert. "Not a problem."

Bert didn't react well to Barney's acquiescence. "How'm I going to that?" the photographer asked. "I'll be making a lot of pictures and probably will have an ample supply of every kid. But I can't guarantee it. How do I keep track? I don't know these kids."

"Doug, make out a sheet with every kid's number listed. Give it to Bert." Then, turning to the unhappy cameraman, Barney said, "Bert, just check off the kid's number the first time you get his picture."

"Anyone got an extra pencil," Bert groused.

The game was to start shortly, and I still hadn't told St. Katherine's coach or the referees about Bert. The three congregated at the scorer's table and I joined them to explain his presence and purpose. The young coach consented instantly. However, he wanted a *quid pro quo*. "Print a few pictures of my kids and I'm happy to agree," he said. Our final arrangement was that I'd send him copies of pictures in which his kids appeared prominently.

The referees weren't as cooperative. The older one asked about rules regarding pictures at games, and after a brief discussion concluded none existed. Then they expressed concern about a photographer blocking their line of sight. They couldn't referee a game dodging a guy shooting pictures.

"Bert's a professional who works college games around the region and knows what he's doing. He understands his role and appreciates the jobs that officials have to do." I embellished both Bert's credentials and the referees' importance to the game. I wanted to kill their reticence and, after noting that both coaches didn't mind a roving photographer, they agreed to let Bert take his pictures.

Heading back to the bench, I wondered where Barney found the money to pay Bert's fees. They had to be substantial, and I doubted that Bert would reduce them for the honor of documenting a fourth-grade basketball game. Barney told me he'd just about finished his background research, over two months of it and counting, and today he was attending his third game, this time towing a professional photographer. For a small feature in an annual report? It made no sense. There had to be more.

My team huddled in front of our bench. "Guys, there's a photographer here. He'll be taking pictures."

"Action shots?" Rickie asked.

"Yes, action shots, Rickie." His response was the one I dreaded and from Rickie most of all. "Forget about him. Play hard and you won't notice him. He warned me. If you try to pose, you're not interesting and he won't take your picture. You're only interesting when you're in action."

I drew the team closer to lower my voice. "I don't know much about St. Katherine's. But they have a good record. So, Willie, what do we do?"

Willie recited his formula on cue. "Take everybody seriously. Think St. Katherine's is the best team we'll ever play."

"Right?"

"Right," echoed the loud response.

"Hands in."

"St. Jerry's," the team yelled as their arms flew toward the ceiling.

Soon, we'd see whether my team had learned anything over the past seven days.

From the start, it was clear a new energy permeated the kids. Passes were crisper and guys other than Travis regularly hit the floor fighting for loose balls. Mistakes were mistakes of aggression, not indecision or reticence. Most of all, the team focused. They weren't just happy to be playing, they were intent on playing to the best of their abilities. Even Rickie, who'd gone on an early preening spree for a camera that ignored him, caught the fever. The team committed more fouls than usual, but those were a fair trade for the added edge they displayed.

St. Katherine's proved a creditable opponent. Their players fought as if they were in a championship contest. But my kids were relentless and showed skills I hadn't seen since the second half of St. Joseph's game, the Toby Ferguson fiasco.

The final score read St. Jerome's 46 - St. Katherine's 34, an outcome that in no way captured the intensity and quality of the match. At game's end, I believed that if we hadn't lost last week, we would have lost today. St. Katherine's was a superior team to Holy Redeemer, but last Sunday's toasting made us better. Much better.

Everyone adjourned to Giorgio's. Attendance at these post-game gatherings kept growing as more parents and families of players recognized the occasion as part of a day-long outing. Mass, game, and Giorgio's for an early dinner. Barney understood the routine better than most. When Maddie, Travis, and I rounded the corner next to Giorgio's, there stood Barney with Bert and his camera focused on the entrance. I'd no idea what they were up to. We pushed past Barney and his paraphernalia-toting sidekick into the pizza place.

As usual, the kids assembled at their table with pizzas and sodas. The adults sat at tables located against one wall and drifted from table to table, drinks in hand. The Hernandez family hovered in their booth. I tried to temper their self-imposed seclusion by periodically stopping to speak with them and compliment their son. I loved Willie. He was a terrific kid. His teammates thought so, too. And, as Willie grew closer to his fourth-grade companions, the other fifth-grader, Randal, grew more isolated. Giorgio's gatherings exemplified their differing trajectories. Willie was a regular; Randal never appeared.

No one noticed Barney and Bert had slipped into the place and occupied a booth near the Hernandez family. Bert had holstered most of his cameras and stored the rest of his gear in the back of the booth. But he carried almost as an appendage a smaller version able to take pictures in minimal light.

Before long Maddie noticed Barney. While Maddie had never met the man, she recognized him from my descriptions.

"What's he doing?" she asked, nodding in the PR guy's direction.

"I don't have a clue. He was supposed to write a two- or three-page human interest feature for the company's annual report under the heading 'Employee Volunteers'. Now the feature seems a major production." I turned my head as inconspicuously as I could toward Barney's booth. "See that guy with Barney?"

"Yes," she said, straining to look.

"That's the same guy who took all the pictures at the game, today."

"It is. I recognize him now."

"Barney's up to something; I can feel it in my bones; I just can't figure out what?"

Zack's parents dropped by our table and joined us for several minutes. Maddie struggled the entire time to avert her eyes from Barney's booth. But once our guests left, she devoted her full attention to his corner and interspersed among my conversations with others provided regular updates of its activity. Her latest update, the third, was identical to the prior two: Bert was taking pictures of kids, parents, and whoever walked in the door, and Barney was wolfing down whatever it was on the plate before him.

"Even with Giorgio's approval, this is out-of-hand," I said. "The pictures, particularly their number, make no sense."

"How well do you know Barney?" Maddie asked.

"I know him, but we don't associate much."

"What's his reputation around the office?"

"His reputation? He doesn't have much of one. He's pleasant enough to people, but then few see him. I've never heard of him in the office after hours. He never volunteers to help with anything, like the office Founders party or the annual blood drive. Can't remember if he even showed up for either event last year. Professionally, no one seems to know what he does. He's the office PR director. Yet all the office PR I see goes through the Dallas headquarters. If you forced me to summarize his reputation in a single word, I suppose it would be 'indolent'. Maybe that's a bit harsh. 'Lethargic' might be better."

"Then why do I see this flurry of activity? That doesn't stem from a lethargic person."

"Beats me. But I'm going to find out." The trouble was, I didn't know where to begin.

BARNEY'S FEATURE

The annual report of a publicly traded company may be the dullest publication known to mankind. It features remarks from the company's Chairman of the Board and its Chief Executive Officer about the firm's performance and its plans followed by page after page of numbers in fine print that only a financial analyst or serious investor could appreciate. Its primary purpose is to show the financial face of the business, but companies over the years have spiced things up by adding color and pictures, design features to communicate their story in words and illustrations to complement the numbers. Barney's job was to prepare a feature for the Steiger Bros. annual report, and unless it differed from traditional reports, his *magnum opus* would run about two small magazine size pages, just four eight-inch columns.

I'd promised Maddie I'd investigate Barney's motives prompting yesterday's photo extravaganza. While I could imagine several scenarios his actions might support, I couldn't verify any of them.

On Monday, after I said 'good morning' to the receptionist, I detoured to Barney's office. He had his back to me when I walked in and with a raised voice, I greeted him, "What the hell's going on, Barney?"

He swung around. He wasn't pleased.

"What do you mean?" The tone in his voice matched mine.

"Bert. A professional sports photographer for a fourth-grade basketball game?"

His glowering expression blossomed into a huge smile.

"Like that, huh?"

"Not particularly."

"Aw, come on, Doug. Stop being such a fuddy-duddy. Everybody liked it, including your kids."

He had a point I refused to concede. "What I really didn't care for was all those pictures at Giorgio's. What was that all about? These are just kids and their parents having fun after a game. Maybe a shot or two of people celebrating, but a raft of them? What will you do with all those pizza pictures? Sell them to Giorgio?"

"My buddy, Giorgio." Barney almost cooed. "He said the pictures were fine with him. Bert showed my pizza man his credentials, and I told him we were taking shots for a national publication and his name would appear in every picture we used of his place. He liked the idea."

"I don't care about Giorgio. I care about the kids. By the way, what national publication?"

"The annual report."

Barney sat in a low-slung leather chair behind his desk, relaxed and entertaining my protestations as minor irritants. He had his plan, but he hadn't bothered to share it. Whatever it was, it impacted kids for whom I was responsible. That was a big problem, and Barney's flip attitude didn't soothe my apprehension.

"Everything's shaping up," he said. "I plan to talk to your players week after next. Bert said he'd have the pictures ready by then. So, I'll have a personal action shot to hand every one of your little darlings."

My kids would like Barney's bribe. A lot. Not just a posed picture like our team photo, but a real action shot like in the newspapers. Score one for Barney. The photos would be a hit.

"Barney, you've been spending all this time collecting background on the team. You attended three games. You brought in a professional sports photographer to shoot God-only-knows how many pictures at a game, followed by another gazillion shots at Giorgio's. You aren't doing that for a piddling two-page feature in an annual report. You've got something else in mind, and I want to know what it is." My voice was rising.

"There's nothing going on, Doug," Barney said. He remained unruffled. "I just want to be sure the feature's first rate. This is a big chance for me, you know. Recognition from Dallas for a job well-done wouldn't hurt my career." Barney paused. Then he changed tone. "Why can't you appreciate my perspective for a change?"

"I've no trouble with you receiving credit when you finish, Barney. Good for you. As long as that's what it's all about." I rose to leave, convinced he wouldn't tell me more. "Remember, we need pictures for the St. Katherine's coach, too."

"Have that on my list." Barney was again cheerful. "I'll bring a handful when I come to talk to the kids." I turned to leave. "You know I have to interview you, too, Doug," he said as I passed through the door.

I scheduled lunch with Jordan for later in the week. I wanted to hash over the Barney problem with a peer. Maddie had told me what she thought, but like me, she may have been too close to appreciate the situation's subtleties. I'd conversed with Jordan only a few times, but he seemed like a reasonable guy and one worth consulting.

"Fill me in, Doug," Jordan said. He looked as dapper as ever, today sporting an expensive-looking reddish-brown striped suit to complement his red hair and crimson mustache. He accessorized the suit with a starched pale-yellow shirt and a white collar and cuffs, amber stones in his gold cuff links, and a patterned dark yellow tie. His get-up verged on garish, but Jordan Whitley pulled it off in style.

I started my story at the beginning and brought Jordan up to date on developments with Barney and his feature. When finished, I asked, "What do you think?"

"You're suspicious of something or we wouldn't be talking. But suspicious of what?"

"I don't know, Jordan. I have a built-in conflict-of-interest here. The purpose of Barney's feature is to promote my company. Fine. I like Steiger, Bros. It's a good company. But I also have a responsibility to look after my kids."

"From what you tell me Doug, I'd be suspicious. There's just too much activity for such a small project. In my opinion, the question isn't whether there's something going on. Of course, there is. The question is, what is it? Then, you need to know whether this extra-circular activity, whatever it may be, is harmless or not. That's the ultimate question you need to answer."

"I can't if I have no idea what Barney's up to."

An aging, but attentive waitress laid our lunch before us and quickly left.

"Let's think of some explanations," Jordan said.

"I prefer to consider harmless ones first, beginning with the idea that Barney doesn't have enough to do and uses the feature to fill time. I haven't seen him do anything else. If that's what's going on, I'm probably getting out of sorts for nothing."

"That's the best scenario," Jordan replied. His strained expression plowed deep furrows in his brow. The mustache twisted. "If I were a betting man, it would be the scenario with the best odds. Still, if you're worried about this guy's behavior, you have reason. A lot of things you describe are strange."

"It's hard to imagine anyone with so little to do. I see nothing out of his shop, at least nothing I can remember."

"Then, consider other, less pleasant possibilities. Think for a minute," Jordan said, closing his eyes. "Why all the pictures, not just during the game, but after? Doesn't that seem odd?"

"I pressed Barney on that yesterday and got no answers."

"What would he use pictures for?" Jordan held his head in his hands, elbows on the table skirting his plate. I could see him thinking behind his shuttered eyelids. He eventually opened them and said, "Maybe, he's not interested in pictures of the team at all, but pictures of one kid and is using the others as decoys. Any parents have a lot of money?"

"What?" I jerked backwards. "What are you talking about?"

Jordan leaned in. His eyes scanned the diner as if looking for an eavesdropper. "Kidnapping."

"Come on, Jordan. Be serious." I expected him to burst out laughing any moment, a good joke on me and my inflated concerns. But neither his demeanor nor his expression changed. He was serious.

"Do you have another explanation for all those pictures?"

"That's what we are trying to do here, think of possibilities. But don't you think kidnapping is a bit extreme?"

"It's unlikely, sure, but it's a possibility. Now, any parents with money?"

"Not that I know of."

"What about that fifth-grade Hispanic kid?"

"Willie?"

"Maybe his family escaped the home country for political reasons, and someone wants revenge or something?"

"You're hallucinating, Jordan. Are you sure those aren't funny mushrooms?" I pointed to an exposed mushroom slice sitting atop his half-eaten cheeseburger.

We both took another bite of our meal and chewed as we thought until I threw out another possibility. "What if Barney wants to sell those pictures to a magazine or as stock photos? Something like that?"

"He could. But he'd need a signed release from the kid in the picture."

"What if he were working on a book of pictures about kids or kids playing?

"How can he do a book of pictures when someone else is taking all the pictures?"

We continued picking at our meals. The waitress stood not far away, on alert should we beckon.

Looking up from his now almost finished cheeseburger, Jordan said, "Maybe we're focusing too much on the pictures. You said the guy's been doing a lot of research."

"Supposedly."

"Maybe he's writing a book about your team. That explains both the research and the pictures. He's seen some games."

Jordan attacked his fries while I pondered his latest thought. After a moment, he became impatient. "What do you think?"

"That idea's worth considering. The research and pictures make sense if that's his purpose." I leaned back in my straight-backed chair, its two front legs three inches off the ground. "Still, after watching Barney over the last few years, two things reduce the likelihood of a book. Writing one takes effort, and effort isn't Barney's strong suit. He, should I say, lacks energy. He also doesn't write very well. What I've read of his isn't good."

"That doesn't matter. A book doesn't have to be well-written. A lot of guys who write books can't write. I worked for a bunch of professors in college who wrote stuff all the time and they were functionally illiterate." He stopped to reconsider. "That may be an exaggeration, but not much."

I smiled when I recalled the same issue from my college days and the number of student editors used to rewrite professors' work.

"Do we have anything else?" I asked.

Lunch was ending, and it'd been unproductive. The only reasonable idea that emerged was a Barney-authored book, and it wasn't satisfying. Too many pieces, all about Barney himself, didn't fit.

Still, Jordan wasn't finished. "Let me try this on you. Suppose, just suppose. Think about this." The volume in his voice fell. "Barney's a front man for a sports agent. That kid, Zack, they tell me is an unbelievably skilled basketball player for his age. I read these sports agents are trying to recruit younger clients all the time. Barney could be helping some guy evaluate a prospect."

I raised my hand. "Waitress. Check."

Barney and I had agreed that he'd interview the kids one at a time during a practice. While the interviews would interrupt the team's preparation for the following Sunday's game, nothing else seemed workable given the need to coordinate every kid's schedule with Barney's. I initially wanted a parent present at each interview to protect the interests of their child, but after discussing the matter with several parents, I realized that the idea was too clumsy. Then, I thought I'd sit in on them all. Barney objected. He argued that my presence might influence the kid's comments, considering he planned to pose questions about their coach. I had to agree. A different parent might do. Then I thought of Jordan. No kid on my team knew him. Better, he understood my concerns and would listen carefully. He agreed the moment I asked.

Interview Thursday arrived. All eight of my players were present. And excited. It had been weeks since I'd announced Barney's plan and their role in it. The longer they waited, the more excited they grew. The boys followed their big-time athletic heroes, and they read their interviews in newspapers and sports magazines. They would now follow. They'd experienced the thrill of a real-life sports photographer taking action shots of their play. Their words would soon accompany their pictures. This was heady stuff for a group of fourth graders.

Barney was half-way up the bleachers, perched among so much equipment he might have been on an overnight camping trip. Tape recorders and microphones were strewn across the wood benches, interspersed among boxes stuffed with tape cassettes. Manila envelopes crammed with photographs were piled to the side. A folder filled with notes and assorted materials rested near his right hand, and each of his outer jacket pockets housed a note pad. The inner pockets held rows of ball points, a supply adequate to write *War and Peace*. Twice.

Jordan arrived, and I marched him up the bleachers to see Barney. "Barney Ambrose, I want you to meet Jordan Whitley. Jordan will represent the parents during the interviews. He coaches the other fourth-grade team and has a son in the class."

"The son isn't on your team, right?" Barney asked.

"Right," replied Jordan. "He's on my team." Jordan sat down among Barney's clutter and waited to start.

"Doug, to rest your heart, I'm recording the interviews on two different tape machines," Barney said as he pointed to the two decks resting on the bench. "We'll have two tapes of each kid. I'll keep one and give the other to the kids to take home to their parents."

Jordan's head jerked upward, surprise painted on his face. Mine shared his expression. Once I'd absorbed Barney's offer, I wanted to ask Jordan why a kidnapper would give the parents a copy of his target's interview. But with Barney sitting there, I thought I'd save my question.

"What a good idea, Barney," I said. "Copies will make everybody feel better, me included."

"The process is a little awkward," he said, pointing to the two microphones hanging around his neck, one feeding the sound to one recorder and the other feeding it to the second. "The kids will have to talk into two microphones at once, but that should be manageable. Let's get started," he said. "You've got a kid by the name of Andy, right? Send him up."

Jordan looked at Barney and said, "I plan to just sit here. Won't say a thing unless I think you're pushing a kid too hard or asking something inappropriate. I intend to be inconspicuous."

I left them and found Andy. He ran up the bleachers and sat down in front of Barney. I watched my colleague fish in a Manila envelope and pull out a letter-sized glossy photo. He took a quick look at the picture, then at Andy, and then again at the picture. I assumed he wanted to be sure the right photo landed in the right kid's hand.

After a few minutes, I knew we wouldn't accomplish much at practice that day. The kids had one eye on the basketball and the other on the bleachers. I half-heartedly tried to impose discipline, but I had one eye on the bleachers, too.

Barney's first interview didn't appear to go well. The action shot Barney handed Andy gripped the boy's attention despite Barney's best efforts to ask him questions. Even worse, as Andy's gaze drifted from Barney to the photo and back, his moving head kept pulling his mouth away from the microphones. From my vantage on the court, Barney couldn't be sure he was capturing any intelligible sound.

Jordan sat motionless.

Barney released Andy after about ten minutes and the boy bounded down the bleachers, photo in hand. The rest of team accosted him as soon as he reached the floor. 'Let's see. Let's see,' they shouted, followed by a chorus of 'Cool'. By the end of practice someone, likely Rickie, would judge whose picture was best. Andy held the clubhouse lead.

After everyone had had at least a glimpse, Andy stuck his photo on a bleacher under his winter coat and returned to practice.

Casey was next on Barney's list, and I sent him to the bleachers. I saw that Barney had learned at least one lesson from Andy's interview: do the work before handing out the candy. The interview with Casey, from where I was standing, seemed to progress much better. Casey's body movement suggested engagement. I caught his eye peeking toward the Manila envelope bearing the pictures, but it was only a peek and only once.

If interview length equated to interview success, Casey's was smashing. It extended for twenty minutes, a pace that, if continued, meant the interviews would last well past our practice time. Barney had six more to finish in less than an hour.

As I brought Zack up the bleachers, I reminded Barney of his potential time problem.

"Got it, Doug. I'll make the rest shorter."

"How did your interview with Casey go?"

"Smart, articulate kid," he replied, and stuck his head back in his notebook.

As Barney started to interview Zack, I could see Jordan's expression become more intense. He sat straighter and stiffer. I knew he took his sports agent hypothesis seriously, and he'd parse every word of the interview for evidence to support it.

Meanwhile, our practice was chaotic. We carried on, though the primary reason now was to occupy time until everyone could be interviewed, and their action shot exhibited. The team wouldn't accomplish anything basketball-wise today.

We had a match on Sunday, and we led the league by one game. A sloppy performance could pitch the team into a tie for first place with a single contest remaining. Because of today's distraction, I felt compelled to remind the team of our precarious position in the standings. Randal was now being interviewed, so the present seemed an opportune time. I motioned the kids to huddle.

"Guys, who played in the Super Bowl last month?"

Andy popped up. "The 49ers and the Chargers."

"That's right. And do you remember the one thing both teams talked about before the game?" No one remembered. I hadn't expected them to. "They talked about all the distractions, all the non-football things they had to do that took their minds off the game. They had dinners and hoopla and press interviews. What happened to us today?"

"We had press interviews and hoopla," George said.

"That's right. And we can't let the press interviews and hoopla distract us from our purpose: winning Sunday's game."

A murmur spread across the team.

"Willie, what do we have to do?"

"Take everybody seriously. Believe every team is the best we'll ever play."

"Right. There're two games left on the schedule. We play the first one Sunday and the last one the following Sunday. We have to play each of them as if those two teams are the best two teams we'll ever play."

My kids returned to their drills and soon their parents began to wander in to claim them. The boys threw on their heavy coats and cradled their personal action shots as they walked out the door, proudly showing them to anyone in sight. Practice was over, though effectively it had never begun. Barney finished with Randal, and Travis hopped up the bleachers. I again warned Barney about time. I knew both he and Travis liked to talk, and feared that once they began, we might not get out of the gym until midnight.

While waiting for Travis to finish, I opened the Manila envelope stuffed with photos featuring the St. Katherine's kids. My deal with the St. Katherine's coach was to provide pictures with as many of his players as possible. I smiled as I rummaged through the envelope's contents. Bert may not have caught every St. Katherine's player in action, but he caught most of them. I soon had assembled about twenty pictures of St. Katherine's kids to send to their coach. Then I turned to the St. Jerome's envelopes.

Despite giving a single picture to each of my kids, the photo envelopes bulged, and I scolded myself for not demanding multiple shots. Yet Barney had held up his part of the bargain and every team member had a treasure, perhaps even more valuable because there was only one rather than a handful.

I thumbed through the photographs. Bert's work was impressive. He was a true professional. Each photo caught the subject in motion, feet off the floor, an arm thrown carelessly, a body leaning at an unsustainable angle. A number centered on Travis, and I was disappointed Barney hadn't selected for him the one where he was sliding on his chest toward the camera with eyes bulging and a big black circle for an open mouth. That was an action shot.

Several of the Bert's best featured George. Bert caught him far more often than any of the others, an album's worth, and he'd done so beautifully. I hadn't noticed before, but George was expressive when playing. If the boy had been less self-conscious, I'd have teased him about it. Instead, I was satisfied to admire Bert's professional portfolio.

As Travis came bounding out of the bleachers from his interview, I closed and replaced Barney's envelopes. I hoped he wouldn't lose those pictures.

A CHANGED PERSONA

The last two games on the schedule, both played at St. Jerome's, were runaways. My kids overwhelmed the opposition from beginning to end in each, and the margins of victory were substantial. I found it rewarding that they played so well and continued to improve throughout the season, individually and, more importantly, as a unit. The difference in our play between our first practice in October and our last game in March was appreciable. I still corrected mistakes and bent ears, but as a group their mistakes were increasingly subtle. Many of the early season's obvious errors now appeared infrequently. The team was fun to watch, particularly when they performed a skill or ran a play that I'd taught them. Travis continued to lead aggressively, and Zack continued to perform astonishingly well for a fourth grader; Rickie went off on tangents less often and I stopped worrying about them; George improved more than anyone else and became a force near the basket; Casey, Willie, and Andy put forward their best efforts; and, Randal? Randal continued to throw up shots any time from any place and ignore any instruction. Every team member played approximately the same number of minutes in each of the last two games, satisfying Montgomery Wise and any partisans he may have had. The only celebration to mark our winning season was the usual Giorgio's pizza gathering after the finale, and those festivities were little different from the ones following any other home victory.

Maddie, Travis, and I were home finishing a bowl of ice cream. I was telling them about all of Bert's photos in the Manila envelopes, including the large number of George.

"I wonder why so many of him?" said Maddie.

"Bert shoots what's interesting. Probably a random thing. George got just one action shot like everybody else."

"How do you like yours' Travis?" Maddie asked. "I see it's hanging in your room."

"It's really cool, Mom."

The telephone rang. I looked at my watch and frowned. "Dinner-time is no longer sacred."

"You had your dinner at Giorgio's, and it looks like your dessert's gone, too," Maddie replied.

I answered.

"Doug Elliot? This is Paul Spenser, Commissioner of the basketball league. I believe we've spoken before." He had to be referring to the Ferguson matter, the call where he begged off taking any action because he supposedly lacked authority. Other than requesting to get on the mailing list for league scores, I'd neither spoken to nor thought of him since.

"First, congratulations," he said. "Your team won the fourth-grade competition. One loss is really good. It's been a while since any team has had a 15 - 1 season. Three losses are usually enough to win, or at least tie."

"Thanks. The kids played well all season. Which reminds me, do they get a medal or trophy or something?"

"Sorry. It'd be nice, but we don't have money for hardware. Only enough to pay the refs." The plea of poverty was becoming an old and irritating saw. Maybe the parents should take up a collection to get the kids something. They deserved a keepsake. They were champions in every sense of the word. I knew a bauble recognizing their accomplishment would only collect dust as they got older, but at least for a while it would be a memento they could highlight somewhere in their rooms.

"Let me get to the purpose of my call, Elliot." Spenser adopted a more business-like tone. "Remember the coaches meeting when I talked about this being a fourth-grade/fifth-grade league? I said the fourth-grade winner would play the fifth-grade winner to determine the league champion. A playoff game if you will."

"I also recall you thought it was a waste of time because the fifth-grade never loses. So, you're telling me my kids are this year's sacrificial lambs?"

"I wouldn't put it that way." He was audibly annoyed. "As I said at the meeting, we should reconsider this game. Perhaps a champion for each grade. But that's not the way it works now."

"You want to be sure my kids will show? Is that what you want me to say?"

"That's a little cold, don't you think?" He'd lost all pretense of solicitousness.

"Okay. My team'll be there. When, where, and who?

"The playoff is set for next Sunday, 2:00, at your place, St. Jerome's gym."

"I like that. Home court advantage." Our fifth-grade opponent would be bigger, more mature, and experienced than we, so any edge my team could gain, including home court, would be helpful. "Who do we play?" I asked. I didn't think the name of the opposition would make much difference. Scouting their team or otherwise preparing for them wouldn't be possible at this late date. Still, I was curious, and wanted to put a name on the school we'd play.

"St. Jerome's," Spenser said.

"No. That's us. We're the fourth-grade team."

He laughed. "Surprise. It's St. Jerome's fourth against St. Jerome's fifth, an intra-school battle for the championship.

"You're kidding. Are you sure?"

"You heard me correctly. St. Jerome's fourth against St. Jerome's fifth."

"When was the last time that happened?"

"Never, to my knowledge." Still laughing, Spenser continued, "If you think you're surprised, you should have heard Bob Kartz when I told him who he would play."

"Bob Kartz?"

"He's St. Jerome's fifth-grade coach. You ought to get to know him."

The kids often talked at practice about what's happening in school, particularly in their homeroom. While I don't eavesdrop, one can't help but learn who's angry with whom, which teachers are mean and which are nice, who's in trouble and for what, and other current gossip. I knew the fourth graders disliked the fifth graders as a class. They didn't mingle in school or out, making it unlikely any fourth grader knew, or cared about the success that the St. Jerome's fifth-grade team was experiencing. Randal and Willie must have known. Yet I'd not heard a word about it from either.

I knew the announcement that the fifth-grade would be our opponents in the championship game would jolt the fourth graders. But how would they respond? Would they roll-over and play dead for the upper class? Or would they pursue the fifth graders with the defiance and contempt I'd so often heard them express? The answer came swiftly.

Empty ice cream bowls sat on the table when Spenser's call ended. Four eyes stared at me in anticipation.

"Well?" said Travis and Maddie in unison. It was almost as if they'd rehearsed.

"That was Paul Spenser, Commissioner of the league. He confirmed that St. Jerome's won the fourth-grade division, which we already knew. And then he told me that our opposition in the fourth-grade/fifth-grade playoff game next Sunday would be none other than …" I paused to make a slight bow and a sweeping gesture with my right arm as if introducing a celebrity. "St. Jerome's. Our fifth graders."

Within an instant Travis's expression flipped from curiosity to dismay to disdain. His eyes narrowed, his lips crumpled, and a scowl crossed his face. It told me everything I needed to know. Travis was wired for the game the moment I announced the opponent.

"Dad, I've got to call people," Travis declared. He burst from his chair, noisily dropping his spoon into the empty bowl.

Maddie and I normally wouldn't have allowed our son to make calls after dinner. Now, she said nothing. Nor did I.

Travis commandeered the phone for the remainder of the evening and wouldn't rest the line until eventually ordered to do so. He talked to the other members of *The Troika*. Zach was also on his call list. He likely phoned the other two fourth graders on the team as well, though I was certain his list failed to include either Willie or Randal. I knew he wouldn't want to compromise Willie, and he didn't trust Randal. Those two would learn soon enough.

I caught Travis between calls. "What are you telling these guys?"

Travis set his jaw before replying. "I want to beat those jerks so bad. I want to show them up in front of every kid in school. They're losers. They talk big all the time and always pick on the little kids. They do all kinds of mean stuff. I'm telling people how they'll rub it in if they win. I'm saying we have to beat these guys no matter what. I want to be sure everybody on my team feels the same."

"Remember Travis, the fifth-graders enjoy huge advantages over you guys. Don't get carried away. I don't want you to be too disappointed if things don't work out."

"I don't care, Dad. I don't like the fifth-grade."

"Doug, you won't believe this," Maddie said.

I was just walking through the garage door, home from work. The first day of the week is the busiest at the office and I was tired.

"Take off your coat and sit down." I didn't have my first arm out of its sleeve before Maddie began. "Rita Horvath called shortly after lunch. Seems like the school's atwitter about the game between the fourth- and fifth-grades. Sister Cecelia learned about it this morning after Mass and wasn't a happy camper."

"When was the last time she was a happy camper?" I said pulling off my coat.

"According to Rita, Sister thinks this game will be a divisive grudge match between two classes that don't like one another. She sees nothing good coming from it."

"How does Rita know that?"

"She helps at school. Remember? Rita said Sister was busy all morning doing everything she could to dampen any potential adverse effects from the game. She told the faculty of her concern and made it known that the match wasn't a matter for open class discussion. No posters or other forms of partisanship will be tolerated in the building or on school grounds. She told the staff to remain neutral. She also ordered cafeteria and playground monitors to be alert for any signs of fourth- and fifth-grade class rivalry, or anyone fomenting it. She then said the same thing to the students over the public address system during afternoon announcements."

"Don't you think Sister's overreacting? It's a basketball game."

"I'm just reporting what Rita told me. Sister runs a tight ship over there, you know."

"So I've learned."

"Everyone in school knew about the game long before the afternoon announcements," Maddie said. "Sister's trying, but there's not much she can do about it."

"She can halt any excess, and that's a good thing."

Travis's broadcast the night before ensured the kids knew of the game before anyone else, including the school's administration. While Maddie and I assumed the purpose of his calls the prior evening was to inform teammates of the championship game's opponent, their tenor and language made it clear his objective was to incite rather than to inform. Beating the fifth-grade was to be a crusade.

"Rita said that the fourth-grade is just about everyone's favorite, but nobody believes they can make the game close, let alone win. I guess the fifth graders are big and have a nasty streak."

"At least we're the sentimental favorite."

"Rita also says, no fourth-grade team has ever beaten a fifth-grade team in the playoff."

"How does Rita know that? She's right, though. Spenser doesn't think we even need to play the game." I rose from the chair to hang up my coat. It'd been lying across my lap for the last several minutes.

"She also said the upper classes are having a field day teasing the fifth graders about playing the 'little kids' for the championship. They're saying things like:

'You'll blow it.' 'Watch out for the little kids.' 'You guys are overrated.' Anything to annoy them."

"How've the fifth graders reacted to the harassment?"

"She didn't say."

What had once been an afterthought became central. Word of the league championship game had begun to spread. Jordan called to offer me his team's practice time slots in case I wanted extra practice this week. He'd forgotten that his slots ended with his season, but I thanked him. Later that evening, a reporter from the neighborhood weekly newspaper called. He wanted to cover the game as a human-interest story and asked for a few comments. I referred the guy to Sister Cecelia, who I had every confidence would find an appropriate response.

I needed to ask Ty for two more days and expected pushback. Instead, a championship playoff game whetted Ty's interest and he quickly granted my request. The downside was that Ty called in Barney, who advised Ty he'd attend the match and would incorporate it into his feature.

Tuesday night's practice was different. It was intense and focused, much like the first practice after our loss. Only more so. I didn't know whether the kids thought we had a chance to win or not, and I wasn't going to ask. Travis would have considered the question irrelevant. He was so consumed by winning, the possibility of not being able to do so likely never crossed his mind. He saw his job as ensuring that every kid on the team felt as strongly about a win over the fifth-grade as he did.

It was all out-of-character. Travis was this laid back, well-liked, talkative personality who had seemed to do an about face. Early in practice he accidentally slammed into George who stumbled backward and frowned. "What are you doing, Travis?"

"Get used to it. That's nothing like you'll get Sunday. They'll start the game pushing and shoving, and never let up." Travis's tone was sharp.

Not long after, Travis rifled a pass to Casey who let the ball slide through his hands and fall to a defender. Travis immediately was on him. "Catch the ball."

"You were only that far from me." Casey pointed to the nearby spot from where Travis had launched the throw.

"That's how we'll have to play to win Sunday. No dipsey-doodle passes. Catch the ball."

Casey stared at him as if he weren't sure this Travis was the same guy he knew.

I'd seen Travis take over the team from Zack several games prior. Emotion had replaced competence as the team's driving force. The leadership change was more evident at practice today than it had been. Travis prodded his teammates at every turn and fiercely cursed himself when the error was his.

Shortly before practice's end, Travis knocked the ball out of bounds. When it ricocheted back to him, he viciously kicked it against the wall, and it bounced high across the floor to the opposite corner of the gym.

"Travis!" I shouted. "Cool it and grow up. Take a seat." He glared at me. I couldn't remember him doing that before.

"Are you all right?" I asked Travis as we drove home. His intensity in the gym had almost been disturbing. Though he typically was the one responsible for translating a non-descript incident into an object of merriment, he saw nothing light or humorous in anything today.

"I'm fine," he said. He turned off the radio. "Why?"

"You didn't quite seem like yourself at practice. I thought something might be on your mind."

"Not really." Travis gazed out the side window. "I have this book report I have to hand in next week and I haven't started reading the book. Don't tell, Mom, though."

"Hey, I won't let you get away with a late book report, either." Neither of us spoke for several seconds.

"What do you think about Sunday's game, Son?" Travis was still gazing out the side window.

"What do you mean, Dad?"

"Are you guys up to it? They're big I hear."

"No choice, Dad. No choice."

His answer struck me as odd. What does a fourth grader mean by 'no choice'. I let the remark slide. But I couldn't imagine what my son was thinking, and that bothered me. Whatever it was, I wasn't happy. We didn't speak the rest of the way home, a rarity for my verbose boy.

I was troubled. Travis's mood seemed dark. Dinner would come first, but I wanted to talk to Maddie as soon as I could. She might have a better perspective. I didn't know what to think, but I believed that a silly grade-school basketball game lay at the center of the muddle my son was in, and that it was foolish and unnecessary. Maybe even harmful.

When the family finished its evening meal, I sent Travis to read the book on which his report was due shortly. Maddie and I then sat down, and I spilled everything that was bothering me about Travis's recent behavior. My problem was, how do you spill what you don't understand? I described today's practice to her and my subsequent conversation with Travis. My words were as garbled, confused, and as contradictory as our son's behavior.

"You're worried?" Maddie said.

"Yeah."

"Why?"

"Travis isn't himself. It's as if he's taken on a new persona. He seems consumed. I don't know whether he's even preparing for a basketball game anymore. It's more like he's preparing for battle and demanding his friends join him. When I asked after practice about anything bothering him, he plead ignorance. That's hard to believe." Maddie's face expressed rising concern. "Travis is like me. We're competitive. We both want to win and win badly. But there're limits, limits of fair play, limits of balance, limits of possibility, limits of obsession. Has he passed a limit? Is he trying to win or to prove a point?"

"You're telling me that Travis wants to win to prove a point."

"I don't know."

"What point? To whom? Why?"

"I don't know."

Maddie and I stared across the corner of the table at one another. I could feel no air circulating. The light seemed dim. The chair grew hard.

"Do you think you can win, Sunday?" Maddie asked.

"I haven't the slightest idea. But if today's practice offers a hint, I'd say, 'Yes. Damned right. We have a chance.' Travis has infected the team."

"Is that good? What happens if we don't win. I worry the boys will be so upset that they'll forget their season's success. It's been a wonderful year, Doug." Her eyes pleaded. Tears formed in the corners. "You can't allow one disappointment, in a game they can't reasonably expect to win, erase everything else. The kids need a sense of proportion. It's your responsibility to see they have it."

"I know I should agree." My thoughts were still scrambled. "This whole thing just seems different and I don't know why."

THE RULES

Thursday's practice was terrible. Every player on the team was chippy, ready to take affront at any nudge or comment. The boys appeared more eager to bicker and scrap than to play, and they recoiled when I collared them for a silly mental mistake or an inexplicable error. The exercise was useless, so I threw them out of the gym fifteen minutes early.

Sunday came none too soon. We arrived one hour before game time so Maddie could get a seat. The intra-school match was drawing considerable attention despite Sister Cecelia's efforts to quash it. A small piece on the game had appeared in the neighborhood weekly, and it was a featured item on a local radio station's community events program.

Maddie held the day's newspaper under her arm, ready to consume the front page while she waited for the game to start. On the floor, Travis peeled off his jacket and trousers while I headed to the equipment closet.

Two teams using one set of equipment was cumbersome. The fifth grade was the designated home team and received all the home court advantages. That made matters all the more unpleasant for my kids. Our regular game jerseys were identical to the ones used by the fifth graders, so we were compelled to wear yellow T-shirts with numbers scrawled in black magic marker on the backs. The fifth graders sat on the home team bench, and we sat on the visitors. The same designations appeared on the scoreboard. The only concession we received was half of the school's four leather basketballs to warm-up.

I hadn't seen the fifth-grade team play, but as they trickled onto the court for pre-game warm-ups no one could miss their size. I immediately christened two of their players *The Twin Towers.* Each measured at least a half of a head taller than our tallest player, George. And they were muscular. They wouldn't flinch when bumped or wince from a sharp elbow.

There were no pre-game formalities. Sister Cecelia had seen to it. But the bleachers were crammed with hopeful fourth-grade fans. Among them were sprinkled a few fifth-grade partisans, anticipating a crushing triumph. An overflow eventually developed, and people lined the walls underneath the two baskets and clustered on the stage behind the team benches. The house was full.

For all the pre-game hype, the actual contest began almost unnoticed. The fifth-grade grabbed the opening tip and soon *The Twin Towers* went to work, playing catch. One threw the ball at the basket and, after missing, the other rebounded the errant shot and threw it back up. They alternately took the first four shots of the game. George and Travis jumped as high as they could but weren't able to reach the outstretched arms of their older and taller counterparts. *The Twin Towers* continued their two-man barrage and then the ball took an ugly carom off the rim. Casey caught it, threw it to Zack, and our team finally had a turn.

Rickie launched the fourth-grade's first shot, a hurried toss that arced high over the arm of his taller defender. It didn't reach the basket and fell harmlessly to the floor. Heads and arms and knees scrambled for the loose ball. Suddenly Travis rose from the pile, ball in hand, and threw it through the hoop before the larger boys could regain their feet. No matter the game's outcome, the fourth graders could always claim that they held the lead for at least a while.

As our team retreated on defense, I knew we couldn't allow *The Twin Towers* to play catch like the last time they possessed the ball. So, I positioned George and Travis where *The Twin Towers* had stood. That forced the two taller boys into unfamiliar spots on the court. I also directed two of our players to guard any fifth grader trying to dribble, which they did often and not well. Zack was the first to steal the ball from an unsuspecting dribbler which he then threw to a wide-open Rickie running under the basket.

My kids couldn't stop *The Twin Towers* completely. They were too big, but by robbing their preferred spots and constantly harassing their teammates with gnat-like peskiness, the smaller fourth graders limited the fifth grader's effectiveness.

At the other end of the floor, Zack couldn't miss. Everything he threw up seemed to fall. The display was stunning, and when their coach, Kartz, assigned two and sometimes three of his players to guard Zack, the smaller boy would pitch the ball to a moving George who would force *The Twin Tower* guarding him to foul. George, undaunted by the jeering fifth graders, made most of his free throws. Underhand. By the middle of the second quarter, our team led 18 - 10 and *The Twin Tower* guarding George went to the bench for the rest of the half with three fouls.

My kids played as I could only have dreamed. Except Rickie's opening airball, the team had made no obvious mental mistakes. Their play was crisp and alert, and they exerted maximum effort. I didn't want to wake up, but reality soon intruded. I had substitutes who needed to play. With one *Twin Tower* in foul trouble on the bench, now was the time. Still, I vowed that so long as the score was close, I'd limit the substitutes' minutes. To hell with Montgomery Wise.

"Andy, you and Willie, report into the game for Casey and Rickie."

Within minutes we lost ground. I couldn't complain about the two substitutes' play. Both did everything I asked and performed to their capacity. It just wasn't enough. When he saw my substitutes on the floor, Kartz had his team swarm Zack, and ignore Andy and Willie. Zack responded by throwing the ball to open teammates. But when either Andy or Willie, the usual open teammate, got the ball, they were so nervous or intimidated they immediately tried to return it. We were paralyzed. Half-time came and our lead had shrunk to four.

I worried. Not only did I have Randal yet to play, but the seated *Twin Tower* would return when the second half began. Zack had scarcely missed a shot while few shots the fifth graders had taken found the basket. Statistically, neither was likely to continue. A few poor minutes or even the slightest decline in our effort would doom us. Yet, my team had a two-basket lead. If anyone would have guaranteed me that half-time margin before the game started, I'd have been overjoyed. Better, my kids seemed juiced by the score. I could tell they were eager for the half that lay ahead.

The other bench remained flippant, dismissive of the 'little kids'. The fact the 'little kids' had whipped them in the first half seemed to have made no impression. I think they felt it was only a matter of time before the earth's axis would regain its proper tilt and all would be well. Their brashness was palpable. Between halves they threw balls at the basket with little attention or focus. They seemed not so much to be practicing shots as loosening their muscles. Kartz passed among his charges without offering direction. No critique; no instruction; no help. His demeanor showed that he thought the fifth graders only needed to appear on the floor for the second half, and the remainder would be a foregone conclusion.

The third quarter started with Randal substituting for Travis, and Rickie and Casey back in the game. The fifth-grade team immediately scored and retreated back down the floor sporting smug looks. The earth's axis was righting. But Zack returned fire with another successful shot, snuffing any ideas of an immediate turnabout.

My players knew to keep the ball away from Randal. Isolate him. His reputation for launching shots from any place at any time was well-earned. The other kids were conscious of team. Not Randal. To him, team was a meaningless concept, and the tightness of the score didn't influence his play one iota.

Randal's classmates compounded the boy's court isolation. They rode him mercilessly, constantly reminding him he'd been sent to play with the 'little kids'. I heard one say, 'You aren't even good enough to play with the fourth graders.' But their favorite taunt was 'Demoted.' 'Demoted,' 'demoted,' 'demoted,' they chanted. Even when they ignored him as a player, which they usually did while the game clock was running, the word, 'demoted,' was never far from their lips. The mockery was almost enough to transform Randal into a sympathetic character.

Seconds elapsed at a crawl. While our team was holding its own, I couldn't continue to effectively play our four against their five. The only thing saving our team was the fifth grader's sloppiness. The balls they threw continued to fly in every direction except the one intended. Each miscue was ignored, even by Kartz.

Then the unthinkable happened.

Casey held the ball and looked like he was about to lose it with a defender draped all over him. He had no choice but to pass it to Randal, who was nearly out-of-bounds and far from the basket. Randal caught the ball and somehow averted a charging fifth-grader. Then, with marked exertion he heaved the ball in the general direction of the basket, only to see it glance off the backboard and slide through the hoop. Randal had scored!

His heave was a lottery shot, a million to one that hit by pure, dumb luck. I couldn't believe what I'd just witnessed. Throughout the gym, mouths opened, eyes swelled, and the room filled with a noisy hum of disbelief. Kartz twisted to his feet, arms hugging his head, wearing an expression of pure agony. I was on my feet, too. Laughing. But there was no time to celebrate. Randal had just won the lottery. I had to yank him before he launched his next lottery shot. I didn't like the odds that he'd be a repeat winner.

"Travis, you're in for Randal."

Randal stood on the floor, as shocked as anyone in the gym. His dismissive classmates turned to retreat to the opposite end of the court, and in the process threw him glares and scowls and mouthed 'lucky', 'sloppy', and worse. Not one of them seemed happy for their classmate, even grudgingly.

Randal reached the bench before a teammate could even give him a congratulatory hand-slap. But as he arrived, Andy and Willie were all over him, pounding his back, slapping and shaking his hand, knuckling his crewcut, and applauding him with every conceivable word of praise. They were happy for him, and for his first basket ever. I tried to offer Randal my congratulations without removing my eyes from play. As I watched Rickie make a free throw, underhand, the bench's celebration of Randal's basket continued.

With two minutes gone in the last quarter and our lead stretched to nine points, it finally dawned on the fifth graders that they could lose. Kartz seemed to recognize that fact after Randal's lottery triumph. The fifth graders began to play with greater intensity and focus, using their size to advantage. *The Twin Towers* tossed George and Travis about as if they were throw-pillows. Their pushing grew so blatant I complained to an official. He told me to 'shut up and sit down', and made it clear he was officiating the game and didn't need my help. *The Twin Towers* reclaimed their preferred positions on the court, shoving George and Travis as necessary, and again played catch as they had to begin the game. One *Tower* threw the ball up, and the second rebounded it, and then the second *Tower* threw it up and the first rebounded it, and then the other *Tower* threw it up again and again until the ball eventually fell through the hoop.

My team was defenseless. They were playing as hard as they could, but the newly focused fifth graders overwhelmed them. The bigger team just kept coming, erasing our lead, gradually, but relentlessly. The contest would be a race to the final buzzer. If our kids could hold on long enough, they would score an astounding upset. But that prospect grew increasingly bleak. The fifth graders were scoring faster than time was running out.

The larger of *The Twin Towers* threw the ball in for another basket, narrowing our lead to one point with 42 seconds left in the game. Kartz called time-out to direct the next onslaught. George and Travis, visibly exhausted, had been rendered impotent by the two large fifth graders. The referees hadn't helped as they allowed *The Twin Towers* to shove and push our smaller players without fear of fouling. One more trip down the court and the fifth graders were likely to erase our lead with little hope of recovery. We had to score, something we hadn't done since the beginning of the quarter. Or find a way to keep them from scoring.

The fourth graders huddled, feet shuffling, weight shifting, no one still. I could hear the kids breathing deeply. Willie and Randal were especially fidgety, knowing they would have to face the wrath of their classmates should their team fall short. I then jerked my head out of the huddle and yelled to the scorer, "How many time-outs do we have?"

"Three." the scorer yelled back. His voice was muffled by the rising crowd noise.

"Okay. Here's what we'll do," I said as my head dove back into the huddle. "Casey, throw the ball into Zack. Everybody else take your usual positions. Zack dribble up the floor but don't go past mid-court. Repeat. Don't go past mid-court.

With 36 seconds left, hold the ball and with 33 seconds left, call time-out. You're facing the clock on the score board, so you shouldn't have any trouble seeing the time. Got it?" He nodded. "Thirty-six seconds you hold the ball, 33 seconds, time-out."

As my team walked back out onto the court, I collared the closest referee. "Ref, be on the alert. My guy will call-time out at 33 seconds."

"Your guy has ten seconds to get the ball past mid-court or you lose it," he replied. I didn't tell him that the whole premise of my strategy hinged on never taking the ball across mid-court. Then he looked at me with a smile and winked.

Zack leisurely dribbled down the floor. The reinvigorated fifth graders waited for him, ready to pounce as soon as the ball crossed mid-court. I was on my feet, and with 36 seconds left, I faced Zach and froze my hands, fingers cupped, the breadth of a basketball apart. He paralleled my actions on the court and held the ball. And with a referee counting down the required seconds to cross the mid-court line, "… three, two, one," Zack calmly held his hands in a 'T'. The whistle blew. Time-out.

We had used the first of our three time-outs, and now we had 33 seconds to play.

My team returned to the huddle. I leaned into its midst. "That was fun. Let's do the same thing, again. One difference. Zack, hold the ball at 27 seconds and call time-out at 24. Got it? Twenty-seven and 24. Casey, throw it into Zack. Everybody else take your usual positions."

Fewer visible nerves appeared in the huddle than just a few moments earlier. My fifth graders excepted. The stomachs of the others still likely churned. But Zack didn't seem fazed, and I suspected he even understood what I was doing.

Our players returned to the floor more briskly than before. Casey threw the ball into Zack, who started slowly up the court. Suddenly Kartz erupted on the fifth-grade bench. "That's chicken!" he cried. I saw him swallow the word he wanted to follow. "That's total chicken!" He was on his feet, stomping and pacing. Kartz now realized what I was doing, and he was helpless to respond.

Kartz's outburst riled the crowd, though few understood its cause. His words may as well have been spoken in an extinct language. Still, he created an unwanted distraction and Zack couldn't miss the countdown despite the commotion coming from the fifth-grade bench.

" … four, three…" I looked out, myself having momentarily lost concentration, and there was Zack, holding the ball. "… two, one …" And he gave the referees a 'T'. Time-out. It was our second time-out. We had one left. Twenty-four seconds remained in the game.

I repeated the tactic a third time. Zack dribbled the ball to mid-court but remained unobstructed behind the line. It was as if he were taunting caged wolves secure in the knowledge that the fence between would protect him. Kartz was howling; his kids were confused. They anxiously looked back to the seconds ticking off the clock while standing impotently on their side of the fence. The fourth-grade team had bought another nine seconds.

We took our final time-out. Fifteen seconds remained, and the crowd was buzzing. The players walked off the court and into their respective huddles. This time our strategy couldn't be as simple. The rules required that a player, hopefully one of ours, touch the basketball across the mid-court line before ten seconds expired. If that didn't happen, we had to surrender the ball to the fifth graders. Even if Zack dribbled across mid-court in the allotted time, he wasn't likely to escape the horde of opposition waiting for him and we would lose the ball with time left on the clock. Kartz would then call his last time-out, station *The Twin Towers* under their basket and one of them almost certainly would score.

Everyone in the gym seemed to understand Zack could and would run off the first nine seconds of the remaining 15 by dribbling behind the mid-court fence. Then what? We had to kill that remaining six seconds, too.

"Here's the plan, guys," I said. Every team member leaned in to listen as the crowd noise grew. I instructed each player where to position himself when Zack dribbled down the floor. "At the 11 second mark, the four of you start running back and forth across the court like we practiced. Don't just put your head down and run. Look for a pass. If you get one, dribble it anywhere toward our basket. Don't shoot. Just kill as much time as you can. Zack, you should be close to mid-court still dribbling with 10 seconds on the clock."

The buzzer sounded, demanding our presence on the floor. My team exited the huddle. I held Zack. "Whatever you do, make sure someone touches the ball over mid-court before your ten seconds expire. It should be one of our guys. If not, make sure one of theirs does. Throw it at their feet if you have to. Remember, we have no time-outs left."

He nodded.

The crowd was the loudest it had been the entire game. Partisans of both sides were on their feet cheering. The fourth-grade fans hoped for a David and Goliath ending, while the fifth-grade cheering section hoped to avoid total humiliation.

The noise level receded momentarily as the crowd anticipated the game's final seconds. With complete composure, Zack dribbled the ball toward mid-court accompanied by a rising clamor from the crowd. He surveyed the floor as the clock advanced and with 11 seconds remaining *The Troika* plus George started running back and forth across court to free themselves for a pass. With the clock ticking down, Zack edged closer to the legal fence, hoping to throw the ball to George just after his shoulder clipped Travis's as they passed one another. But neither George nor anyone else came open. Two fifth graders in their defensive stances loomed. Just as the referee's count reached "one", Zack, with cobra-like speed, hurled the ball at an opponent's leg and watched it carom out-of-bounds. The fourth-grade still possessed the ball.

Five seconds remained in the game. I had no time-outs to position my team and hoped Kartz would help by using his last time-out to position his. He didn't oblige.

The referee retrieved the ball, handed it to Casey standing in front of our bench, and started to count the five seconds Casey had to throw the ball to someone. My guys immediately initiated their out-of-bounds play, trying to free a teammate for a pass. But no one got loose. The fifth graders clung to their men as plastic wrap to a leftover. Casey just held the ball and as the crowd grew louder and the referee counted … two, one … I yelled, "Throw it." Reflex released the ball, toward no one in particular. A mass of hands reached and then grabbed and twisted while the ball slipped across outstretched fingers and fell to the floor. I saw a tuft of light brown hair flash toward the free ball as a football player might trying to recover a fumble. Through the swarming legs and feet, it was impossible to see the face of the figure on the floor, arms hugging the ball now lodged under chest and chin. But when I finally could see, there, on top of it lay the garbage man, Travis. He refused to budge, and by the time a fifth grader thought to snatch the ball from him, the clock had run out.

When Travis realized the game was over, he leapt from the floor and in one motion pitched the basketball toward the gym rafters and joined the melee already in progress. The fourth graders were going berserk. They jumped up and down, punched the air, and threw themselves all over one another. When they finished, they looked around and saw nothing more to do, so they did it again. George extracted himself from the bottom of the pile of players, and then, not seeing another pile, jumped on top of the original. When they finished piling, they hopped and ran without direction, not knowing where to go or what to do, just looking like they had to race or spin or bound, anything to release energy. Andy was the most egregious. He ran and ran and ran, dodging the crowd spilling from the bleachers and the living statues, people too happy or too stunned to move. When the spectator residue flooded the floor, Andy found an empty path near the gym walls to continue.

No one was happier than Randal. In a display of utter reprisal, he danced around his dumbfounded classmates, making faces and gesturing wildly. They'd rejected him and made fun of him, and he'd beaten them. Now it was his turn. It was as if months, even years of repressed frustration from slights and insults, large and small, actual and perceived, found an escape valve to deluge his tormentors. The newly tormented, his classmates, didn't respond graciously, and with raised fists began to chase him. A curt reprimand from an alert parent ended that folly, but Randal couldn't be curbed, and he continued to dance among his fleeing classmates.

Prior to the game I'd sensed a stronger interest in this match than in our others, but as the game wore on, and the fifth graders grew more arrogant and the fourth graders more resolute, the crowd grew more involved, then more intense, and finally more animated. By game's end, it was virtually an appendage of our team. And, as the last seconds gasped, it shared the unadulterated joy of sons and brothers and nephews and neighbors, not just in winning a basketball game, but in winning a struggle they never should have been able to. And they did it on their own, with doggedness, self-confidence, and talent.

Fourth-grade elation couldn't have contrasted more sharply to the silent, stunned guise of the fifth-grade team. Those on the court when the final buzzer sounded stood shocked, unable to move. *The Twin Towers* could only stare at one another in disbelief and then turn to look through the glass backboard and beyond to a scoreboard documenting their single point loss to the 'little kids'. Other fifth graders sprawled on the bench, eyes glazed, looking nowhere. Monday would be a grim day at school.

Though I shared the jubilation of my team, I was as stunned as Kartz. Still, I refused to miss the opportunity. With a smirk, I approached the fifth-grade coach. He waved me off, refusing to acknowledge not only that I'd kicked his behind, but also that I knew the rules and had used them to my advantage. He'd forgotten them and paid for his oversight.

I needed to see my son, to embrace him, to tell him how proud I was of him. I hoped to find a kid with a burden stripped, and a persona returned. I saw him not far away, jumping up and down with the rest of *The Troika*. When I reached him, I grabbed him from behind and lifted him off the ground. I felt unbridled delight, and when Travis realized who had accosted him, he twisted and buried his head in my chest without a word and returned a bigger hug than I gave him. His feet eventually touched the floor, but the embrace didn't end. I knew this was a time and place that could never be replicated or forgotten, right up to the perspiration and stink from his soaked T-shirt. I hadn't known what to expect from my son when the season began, but I'd never have dreamed he would offer an experience like this.

Giorgio's was mayhem. It was difficult to tell which was rowdier, the kids' table or the adults'. Unfettered energy filled the room. Kids yelled back and forth, shifted from chair to chair, and back again. Arms flew everywhere, underscoring a verbal point or demonstrating one of the day's better basketball moves, sending filled and unfilled soda cups flying in the process. Jostling was continuous, and the kids' table consumed two more large pizzas than on any previous outing. Gross-outs multiplied with half-chewed pizza, wet with saliva and sodas, balanced in clumps on extended tongues or strained through sauce-reddened teeth. Casey's mother noticed at some point and put an end to that incivility. But nothing else changed.

Every player's parents found seats somewhere in the room. Even George's dad showed. A first. I'd seen him a few times when he picked up his son after practice in a small pick-up with a construction company logo on the door. He was young and seemed shy, like George. I made a point to meet him, and while conversation was almost impossible in the clamor, I told him we couldn't have won the fourth-grade league, let alone the playoff game, without his son. Dad said he was proud of George and his boy's performance that afternoon. He quickly retreated to a booth near the Hernandez family, where he limited socializing to wait for his son to finish his celebration.

Montgomery Wise was the only missing parent, and Randal the only missing player. I thought Wise would have been delighted to allow Randal to join the other revelers, considering his son had scored, and in a championship game against his classmates. Randal's taunting after the game left no doubt he was ecstatic with the contest's outcome, and perhaps no one had greater reason to be. Still, Randal played only a few minutes in today's game, always a critical factor to Wise. I assumed the boy's absence could be attributed to the peevishness of his old man.

These post-game affairs normally lasted little more than an hour. Once the adults had ordered, eaten, and maybe had a second glass, the kids tired and it was time to go home. Today's party had now passed the hour-and-one-half mark. The racket hadn't ebbed, and no one had budged.

Maddie and I were having a grand time. It helped that my ego was constantly stroked by references to the strategy I'd employed in the game's last minute. 'How'd you think of that? Nobody knew what you were doing until it was too late.' 'You sure know how to use the rules.' 'The other team got out-coached today.' 'Great strategy.'

I basked in their compliments. It was true that if I hadn't used the rules to our advantage, we would have lost. But I recognized my strategy as only the cherry sitting on the whipped cream piled on top of the cake. I emphasized to anyone who would listen that I'd just remembered the rules. It was the kids who showed the extraordinary poise and skill, and who put forward the incredible effort.

Jordan had dragged Carleton to the game, whether for a father/son outing or to motivate him looking forward to the next season. Neither probably understood which. Nor did it matter. Jordan knew of the post-game festivities and decided to attend uninvited, though no one was ever really invited. I saw him throw Giorgio's door open, scout the room, and push a reticent Carleton to the kids' table. He then headed in our direction. He didn't know our table companions, and he hadn't met Maddie, though he knew her by name and reputation through our lunches. It made no difference. The conversation at our table soared, Jordan in the middle, and never subsided.

I'd been making the rounds, glad-handing anyone looking familiar. The Hernandez family was particularly cordial. Mrs. Hernandez told me how much Willie enjoyed playing on my team while Mr. Hernandez nodded in assent. The remains of a half-eaten small pizza lay on their table, Willie's little sister nestled next to her mother, nibbling on a slice. They, too, were celebrating.

People began trickling out more than two hours after the game concluded, one family group after another. Returning to my chair after yet another round of table-hopping, I parked next to Jordan who elbowed me and, using his nose and chin as a pointer, repeatedly jerked it upward as if he wanted to alert me to something. His eyes darted, scouring the immediate area as if to assure himself no one else saw his warning. I knew Jordan could be quirky, though he appeared to go overboard in this case. Until I caught his intent. He was directing my attention toward a dark booth in the back where Barney sat alone, munching catsup-laced fries and surveilling the room. He occasionally jotted a note on a small pad. How I'd missed him until now was a mystery.

PART II

THE SECOND HALF

BARNEY'S GRAND PLAN

Spring came and went, and the summer ushered in a schedule change for Travis. A later breakfast, trips to the swimming pool, and adventures in the local park with the neighborhood gang replaced the daily trek to St. Jerome's. Chores during the afternoon substituted for homework at night. Baseball supplanted basketball as the season's premier sport, though bats and gloves comprised a small fraction of the endless physical activity in his life. The nuns at St. Jerome's were trying to institute a summer reading program, but it was falling flat with my son, and neither Maddie nor I chose to impose it. Bright days pulled him into the fresh air while rainy days inspired endless games of Hearts. When the day took a particularly depressing turn, and it became obvious no part would permit outdoor activity, the *Monopoly* board emerged from the closet. The late sunset meant a late dinner, and after recounting the day's events, cleaning up the kitchen, and taking an evening shower, there was little time left for Travis to read or watch television.

Maddie had cut her volunteer hours at the hospital once school was out. The reduction gave her more time at home to be with Travis though she often questioned her decision when his perpetual motion carried him out of the house from breakfast until dusk, occasionally interrupted by a drop-in for lunch or a snack. Her biggest contribution, she felt, was as a chauffeur, driving Travis to and from the swimming pool, to and from baseball games, and to and from visits to other members of *The Troika*. However, I knew she liked being around should Travis or one of his friends need her.

I envied my family's summer months. While I shared as much with them as I could, my routine at the office didn't change. The job required my presence in winter or summer, on sunny days or dreary ones. That made me start looking forward to our family's three-week stint at the lake almost as soon as the weather warmed.

Steiger Bros.' fiscal year ran July 1 - June 30, and its annual report release was to coincide with the stockholder's meeting scheduled to follow its conclusion. It was mid-June when Ty called me to his office for a meeting with him and Barney Ambrose. I couldn't recall having seen Barney in the office, or anywhere else, since the dark booth at Giorgio's the day my team beat the fifth graders. I guessed the meeting was about the annual report, and I was right.

Ty sat on the edge of his desk sporting a jovial mood and a relaxed demeanor. He pinched the first pages of the company's annual report between his thumb and forefinger. Barney was already present, sitting in a straight-backed chair in front of Ty's desk, wearing a tasteless green- and black-checkered sport coat with a matching bow tie. The coat's checks resembled a Daliesque abstraction of a checkerboard while its pea green hue fell just short of neon.

With his free hand, Ty waived me to a vacant chair complementary to Barney's. "Doug, Barney brought me an early copy of the annual report with the feature about your basketball team." He switched his gaze toward the guy in green and black. "I like it. What do you think, Barney?"

"I was happy with the way it turned out, Ty. A little disappointed they didn't include more material. I gave them a couple extra columns, but Dallas forced me to cut them."

Barney reached into a brief case I'd never seen him carry and fished out another copy of the report. "Here, Doug. Here's a copy for you. Page 15. It's pre-release, so you can't give it to anyone yet, not even your kids."

"Dallas loved the piece, Barney," Ty said. "Kudos. I expect somebody down there will send you a congratulatory bonus. I don't know how much it'll be. Out-of-phase bonuses are usually more for recognition than dollars. It should pad your wallet a bit, though. Let you buy a couple more of those fancy jackets like the one you're wearing."

Barney eyes brightened while I mentally groaned. More than once the office's unofficial fashion maven referred to Barney's jackets as 'horse blankets'. The thought of his stable growing, even by one, was depressing.

"What about that longer piece you were talking about, Barney?" Ty asked. "If you can get that placed in the *Reader's Digest* or some other high-circulation magazine, I think Dallas would be ecstatic."

"I've told Dallas about my plan, and they are." Barney looked simultaneously pleased and wary.

"What?" I bellowed. The noise startled Ty and caused Barney to cower. "You don't have permission to do that. The agreement was for a feature in the annual report. Nothing was said about placing a longer piece somewhere else. What's going on?"

"You don't know about this, Doug?" Ty asked. He looked perplexed.

"No. This is the first time I've heard anything about an extended piece. I suspected something was up long ago. Barney was doing too much research and taking too many pictures for a four-column feature in an annual report. You do know, Barney, *Reader's Digest* doesn't have pictures. Right?"

Ty shot Barney a hardened look.

"Barney, you told me from the beginning that you planned a second, longer piece." Ty was now glaring at him, too. "I thought the idea was to promote the company to a larger audience than just stockholders and financial analysts." Ty's tone indicated he wasn't pleased, but he continued calmly. "What happened? Why didn't you tell Doug about your plans?"

Barney shrank into his chair. "Doug's hard to work with, Ty. He's fought me all the way. He set up a bureaucracy to get parents' permission, a guy to eavesdrop on my interviews, and only in the end did he agree to talk to me on the record about his experiences. I was afraid that if I went one step beyond the annual report, he'd block me with the families. I thought if I could get a good piece placed in a reputable magazine or newspaper, I could go around him. I'd get permission from the families directly." He looked straight at Ty, eyes pleading.

"I'm one of those parents, Barney. You couldn't go around me. What were you thinking?" Jordan would be happy to know kidnapping wasn't part of Barney's ill-conceived scheme.

Ty exhaled, walked around his desk, and fell back into his chair, the good humor gone. "Well, where does that leave us?"

Silence met Ty's question. I couldn't understand Barney's reticence to defend his idea. Perhaps he was backpedaling too quickly to form a coherent argument. I know I was too stunned and appalled to develop a counter. Ty interrupted after a long pause "Well? Where do we go from here? Doug?"

"I know what I've agreed to, though it apparently isn't what others think I've agreed to." I glared at Barney. "The parents of every one of my kids will back me up."

Ty was a compromiser by nature. He always looked for a middle ground when controversy arose, a trait I'd seen him use often and effectively in the office. "Barney, why don't you fill Doug in," Ty said. He was conciliatory. "What are your goals and plans? Let's make sure Doug knows everything there is to know about any piece you're preparing on his kids and his team."

It soon became clear Barney had had a plan almost from the beginning and I was the only one in the room who knew nothing of it. It apparently had expanded and shifted as my team became more successful and then morphed further upon our humiliation of the fifth-grade. And though his plans sounded still fluid and his strategy for implementation amorphous, they remained the center of Barney's attention and the core of his work product. Months after the season's end.

"The first piece I plan beyond the annual report is a serial for the employee newsletter. It starts in late fall and follows the team through the season. I'll have a couple of introductory pieces about how Doug became the coach and so forth, and then I'll report on a different game in every issue until the season's end."

"Hold it. Hold it," I interrupted. "I haven't even thought about coaching these kids again next season. Nor have Ty and I talked about it. Maybe there won't be an opening for me. Maybe someone else will get the job. Maybe I'll get hit by a bus. You're getting a little ahead of yourself I'd say."

"That's not what I mean."

"Then, what do you mean?"

"I plan to serialize your fourth-grade team. We already know it's a good story, so I won't have to worry about how things work out from week to week."

"You mean you plan to write the stories as if they were current when they're a year old?

"Why not? They're exciting and fun. No one will know."

"I'll know. My kids'll know."

"The piece is timeless, Doug. Kind of like a good book. You read and re-read it. Sure, you know the ending. But getting there is the fun. And in this case, most readers won't even know what happened until they read the final issue."

I cringed and squirmed in my chair. Barney wasn't exactly planning to lie to his readers, our colleagues, but I thought his deception unsavory.

"The series will focus on you, Doug, so I'll need more personal insights than you've given me so far." He looked at Ty seeking the boss's support for his request.

"Me? Why me? It was the kids who put in the work. It was the kids who played their hearts out all season. It was the kids who created the sensation. The season wasn't about me. It was about them." It was now my turn to look at Ty in search of the boss's support.

"It's an employee newsletter, Doug," Barney said. "You're the employee. Readers will relate to you more than to the kids. Besides, it's a lot easier for readers to focus on one coach than eight players."

"Barney's right on this one, Doug. The employee newsletter is no big deal, but it'll give our office nice visibility in the company. Your team's a good story. Give Barney a hand with it." Ty had donned his corporate hat to resolve the dispute. I watched his head nod as he listened to Barney's scheme for our segment of the employee newsletter. The only time it stopped was when Barney tried to justify the deception.

Barney explained he had written five versions of the same basic story, each with a different twist and each featuring different incidents and different personalities of team members. The versions were crafted to appeal to different outlets. The one focused on me highlighted private volunteer activity and the role of the business supporting it. That effort targeted a general news magazine or financial newspaper. Another for a sports publication took the upset angle. Barney even drafted one for a popular psychology magazine featuring the two fifth graders playing on a fourth-grade team that defeated their classmates. He planned to submit the piece after he'd interviewed Willie and Randal a second time. The idea made me chuckle. Good luck getting permission from Montgomery Wise to do a psychological piece on his kid.

Barney said that the story he was pursing most aggressively was a human-interest piece he'd earmarked for *Readers Digest*. While no longer the national common denominator it once had been, the publication still held broad appeal and an article appearing in its pages would yield enormous value directly to the company and indirectly to Barney Ambrose. He had determined his first task was to get an article published somewhere, anywhere, and subsequently have the *Digest* adopt it.

Barney's project seemed far-fetched, even delusional. I voiced my skepticism. "Have you tried *Life* or *Look*?" The two popular, mid-century magazines had ceased publication decades before.

"That's not helpful, Doug," Ty said. He then turned to Barney. "Just where are we on this project? You haven't briefed me in a while." Then Ty started to rattle questions he should have been asking months ago. "Just how realistic is this *Reader's Digest* idea? Have you spoken to anyone there about it? Can you publish anything else from the project? What are your timelines? When can I see something?"

Ty's sharp questions befuddled Barney. Today was to be his big day, the pre-release of the annual report showcasing his long-awaited feature. But along the way to his triumph something had changed. I could see in his face Barney recognized there'd been one. All he could do was stammer, "Let me find my briefing notes, Ty. I still have a copy somewhere in my office."

Ty returned to his conciliatory mode. "While we're working on those questions Barney, we shouldn't forget why we're here. This little gathering is to preview your work on company-sponsored volunteerism for the annual report. I've read the feature. It's outstanding. You did a nice job blending the kids, the human-interest aspect, and Doug's volunteerism with the company's side of the story."

Ty swung about and looked at me directly. "Don't you think so, Doug?" It was less a question than a demand for a positive response.

"I haven't read it yet." My fingers began fumbling through the first few pages of the annual report until they found page 15. They pressed the pages apart, and I began to read.

It didn't take long to finish. The feature focused on me as a volunteer and the company's role in making my efforts possible. My kids, the *raison d'etre* for my coaching, received few mentions, and the season's highlight, our win over the fifth-grade, earned only passing reference. The feature was underwhelming, uninteresting, and not particularly well-written. I had no intention of sending a copy to my kids. The let-down would be too great.

When I glimpsed up from the pages, Ty and Barney were both staring at me.

"Well?" Ty said.

"About what I expected. Information's all correct," I replied in a business-like fashion, conspicuously omitting any laudatory comment. Ty's eyes narrowed and the folds around the top of his nose deepened. It was time to make nice, and I wasn't cooperating. "Other than the employee newsletter, is this it? Can I tell the kids to expect nothing from their interviews?"

"Barney still has irons in the fire. I think he made that clear." Ty's frown told me he was irked at my pedantic response to his implicit request. "We'll get together after our meeting and take it from here. You needn't worry further."

Barney nodded.

"Remember, Ty. I still have a responsibility to the kids and their parents. It didn't end with the season's last game."

It was now his turn to reply in a business-like fashion. "I'll keep you informed."

Barney and I rose to leave, but Ty motioned Barney to retake his seat. The two apparently still had matters to discuss. I left the room and headed home, a preview copy of the company's annual report in hand.

The family's summer flashed by. Travis interrupted his routine to spend two weeks with the other members of *The Troika* at Camp Sunk Boat. Soon after,

Maddie, Travis, and I made the trek north to the lake for our annual three-week break at a different location, in a different residence, with a different schedule, and absent familiar outsiders. A place where Barney and my basketball team would be blurred by time and space.

Too soon, our calendar displayed the last week of August. My family would reintroduce itself to its normal routine in a few days. Maddie would be back at the hospital volunteering, and Travis would be back in school with his buddies, now a fifth-grader. Except for the family's sojourn to the lake, I'd never left my desk.

The late afternoon sun silhouetted the roof peaks and gables of the townhouses lining the street where John and Celeste Hansen lived. That evening, they were hosting a back-to-school party for parents, delighted that summer was nearing its end and their children would soon be back in the care of professionals paid to channel their energy and attention.

The Hansen's invited their immediate neighbors and parents of children who were close friends of the Hansen youngsters. Maddie and I fit the latter category. They also invited Travis and Casey to keep Rickie company while they entertained the adults.

The Hansen's house was unique to the neighborhood. It featured a covered wrap-around porch on the right with open green space between it and the neighboring residence. The primary entrance stood at the far end of the porch, facing the street halfway down the length of the house.

Travis, Maddie, and I climbed the steps and headed toward the front door. Travis cradled a shoebox filled with sorted baseball cards, topped by his most recent acquisitions. Maddie carried a small, red cloth sack containing a reasonably priced bottle of chardonnay as a hostess gift. About halfway to the door, I glanced up and noticed construction underway in a small area where the porch ceiling abutted the side of the house. The work wasn't extensive enough to divert guests from their normal path to the main entrance, but the faded blue tarp covering it suggested the job was more than cosmetic. We passed under the construction and rang the bell.

"Welcome to back-to-school night," John Hansen said as he opened the screen door. He seemed delighted with the self-assigned name for his event. The loud laughter and voluminous chatter coming from inside told us his guests were already in good stead.

"Rickie's upstairs in his room, Travis. Casey's there too," Hansen said. Travis hopped up the steps, securing the shoebox with a second arm to guarantee that no part of his treasure spilled. A rolled magazine stuck out of his back pocket, the latest edition of *Beckett.*

"Come on in, folks," our host said. He ushered us through the front hall toward the kitchen. "Maddie, Celeste's on the back porch. There's beer and wine in the cooler. If you'd like something a little stiffer, it's on the counter."

"What's up with the porch, John? I saw the blue tarp tacked to the ceiling."

"Don't know yet, Doug. A lot of water leaked between the wall and the porch ceiling during the last hard rain. Some seeped through last week, too." Hansen was likely referring to the light showers that fell a few days before. "Best outcome, it's just a seal of some type, not rot or a structural problem. The contractor poked around earlier today but left before I could talk to him. I'll know more Monday."

"Good luck. That stuff gets expensive in a hurry." I recalled the costly small job a contractor recently completed on our house. "Did you get bids?"

"Yeah." My host grew a puzzled look. "You know though, an odd thing happened when I was looking for contractors."

"What was that?" The doorbell interrupted, and my host changed direction to answer. I went into the kitchen and opened a beer for me, prepared a tray of sodas and munchies, and headed upstairs to take the first shift serving the boys.

From inside Rickie's room, I heard loud voices trying to consummate a trade for the baseball card of Chicago Cubs second baseman, Ryne Sandberg. Rickie owned a 1994 Upper Deck issue, and Casey and Travis both wanted it. Bidding for Sandberg was getting heated when I disrupted their negotiations. I set my loaded tray on a small uncluttered space of Rickie's dresser.

"Dad, I'll give Rickie a Mike Piazza and a Ken Griffey, Jr for a Ryne Sandberg. Casey only wants to give a Frank Thomas. Tell Rickie I'm giving him the best deal." He looked at me to provide authority for his opinion. "I showed him the price guide already. My deal's best." Their pricing Bible, *Beckett Baseball Monthly*, lay open on the bed, no doubt consulted. A glimpse at the guide's pages showed Rickie was robbing them both.

"Mr. Elliot, are you coaching us again this year?" Casey said, his face peering up from his seat on Rickie's bed. "I sure hope so."

"Me, too," Rickie added. "Travis said you would."

"Travis sometimes gets ahead of himself. Basketball season doesn't start for a few months yet. There's plenty of time to decide who'll coach you guys."

"Don't worry. Dad'll be our coach." Travis picked up his Piazza and Griffey cards and extended them for Rickie to examine. "They're in mint condition. Mine is the best deal, Rickie. Isn't it, Dad?"

Casey just grinned, watching Travis writhe as if he were a hooked trout about to be netted. The fix was in. He knew Rickie was a White Sox fan and his trade offer, Frank Thomas, was a White Sox.

I left hurriedly, closing the door behind me, unwilling to be dragged further into their squabble. They were still wrangling as I descended the stairs.

It was at least an hour before I caught up with my host. "You were saying John that you were looking for a contractor to fix the porch and something odd happened. I'm curious."

"Oh yeah. I called Kovac Construction to see if they wanted to bid on the job. I've seen their pickup driving around. You know, the one with the big red logo on the door. His kid was on last year's team, too. So, I decided I'd give Kovac first shot. I called his number in the book. No answer. I kept calling. No answer. Strange for a business I thought. Then, a couple days later, just when I was about to give up, someone picked up the phone. It was Kovac's cousin. Seems the family moved back to Massachusetts not long after school let out for the summer. I knew I hadn't seen that pickup driving around for a while." Hansen continued to babble.

"What did you just say?" I asked.

"About what?"

"The Kovac family."

"They're no longer around." Hansen seemed oblivious to the consequences of the news he'd just delivered.

I wasn't. George Kovac was gone. This year's basketball season would be different.

Early fall is beautiful in our part of the country. Better, it's the onset of football season and I enjoyed my time refereeing battles between Travis and assorted friends over the relative merits of area teams, the Chicago Bears, Indianapolis Colts, and Detroit Lions. Nothing was ever settled, but that wasn't the point. The point was the argument, the chance to disguise preference for one's team and hostility to rivals as informed opinion.

I assumed throughout the fall that once basketball season arrived, I'd move up a grade with Travis and his buddies to coach this year's fifth-grade team. I understood the new season would bring change to the group playing for me. I'd lose some kids from last year's team and add at least enough to replace them. John Hansen's announcement about the Kovac family at his back-to-school party underscored the altered conditions that lay ahead.

The Kovac family's return to Massachusetts meant replacing George. His loss would be a blow. He'd been the second-best player on our team and his continued improvement over last season heralded an even better player this one. He was also our tallest member, the only truly tall player we had. But George's loss created another less obvious difficulty.

My fourth-grade team had five first-line players before the skill level dropped precipitously. George's loss meant St. Jerome's fifth-grade team would begin with at least one substitute-quality player on the floor. We wouldn't be able to field one full lineup of kids who could play. The team needed at least one skilled recruit to do that, but the prospective replacements were frightening. They all came from Jordan's old team.

Worse, I couldn't even be sure I would be able to keep *The Troika*, Zack, and Andy from last year's group. Jordan had seen my kids play and knew mine were better than his. He would want some of my old group in his lineup this year.

The more I thought about the coming season, the more dubious I was about coaching again. I'd relished my time with the fourth-graders. Everything had exceeded expectation. It was an amazing experience that left warm memories even when the last was a perspiration-soaked, stinking T-shirt rubbing against me. But last season was an anomaly; it wasn't replicable. Anything less would detract, and less was a foregone conclusion. Coaching this year's fifth-graders made no sense. Once had been enough. I'd done my share for my son and his friends. Nor did I need further validation as a coach. Still Maddie was right. Travis could talk me into just about anything.

September slid into October and I stopped to see Ty late one afternoon.

"Ty, I want to coach the group at St. Jerome's again this winter. I hope it'll be the same kids, one year older. I don't have any details or practice times yet, but I assume they'll parallel last year's."

"Nothing can parallel last year, Doug. Beating the fifth-grade team was one hell of an accomplishment. I talked to a guy by the name of Kartz I met at a luncheon a month or two ago. Forgot his first name.

"Bob."

"Yeah. He was the fifth-grade coach wasn't he? The guy was still moaning. He didn't argue that what you did was illegal, but he sure considered it sneaky."

"Why? Saving allotted time-outs and calling them when I needed them? I knew the rules. He didn't. Maybe a fairer way to say it is that he forgot about the options the rules gave me. Until it was too late. My heart bleeds." I gloated.

Ty laughed out loud and then shook his head as if he still couldn't believe what my team had accomplished. "Same deal as last year?"

"Same deal." I stopped and rethought my acquiescence. "Where's Barney in the plan this year?"

Ty hesitated before he answered. "I'm not sure. For all the trouble and wasted resources, Dallas loved his feature in the annual report. They never saw the *sturm und drang* behind it and wouldn't have cared if they had. Barney's feature made the point they wanted made, and it didn't waste much space doing so. That means some of this may be out of my hands. I may not have as much control this year as last. I promise though, I'll keep you informed as best I can."

"Fair enough." I trusted Ty, however exercising less control this year than last was almost laughable. He'd exercised none last year. Barney was a different story. I trusted him as much as I trusted Randal Wise's judgment on a basketball court.

"Anything further on those other pieces Barney was writing about my fourth-grade team?"

"Nope."

"The employee newsletter serial?"

"Dead. Dallas believed it was misleading."

"Who says corporate ethics have gone the way of the dodo."

Two weeks later I walked into the house after work and Travis met me. "Dad, Mr. Anderson came to school today and left this letter for the parents." He waved a piece of paper in my face, his feet gliding all the while. "You're coaching again, right? All the kids want you. They say you're the best. Everybody's excited. You have to do it, Dad. Please. Please. Please."

I raised my hand as if to say 'enough,' and then replied, "I plan to coach, Travis, and I've already arranged for the time with my boss."

"Yes." He jumped up and down, still waving the paper. "I've got to call Rickie and Casey right now."

"No, you don't," Maddie said. "After dinner."

"They're my best friends. They'll want to know now."

"They can wait, and so can you. We don't want to eat dinner cold."

"Mom."

"It's time to eat. Wash your hands."

We sat down to the evening meal after Travis returned from washing his hands for a second time. The running water somehow had missed most of his dirtier hand during the first washing. Maddie suggested a quick, second effort just might fool the running water into falling straight from the tap this time.

"Dad. Don't forget to choose Rickie, Casey, and Zack. We have to play together," Travis said before the first plate had been passed.

"Don't you think you're a little premature? We don't even know who's signed-up, yet."

"Oh, everybody's signed-up."

"Who's everybody?"

"There's me, Rickie, Casey, Zack.

"That's four. Maybe we won't have enough sign-ups for a team."

"There're lots more."

"Like who?" I wanted Travis to understand that four friends didn't represent all the boys in his class.

"Do you have a math test on Friday?" Maddie asked, handing Travis a plate of lasagna. "There's garlic bread on the table and salad in the bowl. I want you to take a little," she said to Travis, pointing to the green mix.

THIRTEEN PLAYERS

I headed to St. Jerome's after dinner. Anderson had left a message with Maddie saying that he had two volunteers to coach the fifth-grade boys this season and that we'd work out the details during a brief meeting at the gym. My appointed time was 8:20, a dreadful hour for a 10-minute meeting.

I arrived 15 minutes early and sat in the bleachers, waving to a few people I knew. Shortly, the metal double-doors at the back of the gym opened with an elongated squeak, and in walked Jordan. Decked out in an exquisite black pin-striped suit with a pink and black bowtie, he joined those of us in our jeans and pull-overs.

I hadn't seen Jordan since the victory party at Giorgio's last winter and regretted it. He was enjoyable company, and though his conspiracy theories were goofy, he otherwise was a thoughtful conversant. Most of our talk related to our basketball teams, and perhaps if we departed from that common denominator, we'd have nothing to talk about. Maybe, we'd even find one another's company disagreeable. But I doubted it. This year was another chance, and I was determined to make him a permanent friend.

"Hey, Jordan. Over here."

He saw me waving and turned in my direction.

"How are you doing, Doug?" he said as he sat down beside me.

"Pretty fancy duds for a gym." I rubbed his lapel between my thumb and forefinger.

"Snazzy, huh? Didn't have time to go home and change."

"Anderson left a message that two guys applied for the fifth-grade jobs. That's you and me, right?"

"I don't know who else it'd be."

"We should be able to work something out." I felt awkward. Last season, I'd selected the best players and Jordan got Carleton and friends. He now knew who could play and who couldn't, and that hard-earned information had to influence his choice of kids. How? I'd learn soon enough.

Jordan's immediate interest lay elsewhere. "Whatever happened to that guy, Barney? He was up to something. Did you ever find out what?"

I told him the story of Barney trying to place articles about the team in the *Reader's Digest* and various other popular publications. I also told him how Barney had been unsuccessful, and how he showed, at least in my judgement, he was in way over his head. "Worse, Dallas, our home office, loved the piddling little item he wrote for the annual report about the team, which was actually more about me. He got a bonus for it. I'll make you a copy. You won't believe it. All the time and effort, and expense, for that?"

"I don't buy the whole thing," Jordan scoffed. He stared into the rafters as if he were seeking answers in the extended universe. "It's in the pictures, Doug. It's in the pictures."

"Elliot. Whitley." Anderson called. He beckoned us to where he was sitting. We got up and walked over.

Fumbling through a file of coffee-stained papers, Anderson started. "Guys, you both coached last year and you both volunteered this year. I've got no reason to choose one of you over the other. You'll need to figure out how you want to do this."

Jordan and I looked at one another. "I don't understand," I said. "Last year the fourth-grade had two teams. Why not for this year's fifth-grade? Same class."

"There aren't enough sign-ups for two teams this year. One of you had eight kids last year and the other nine, as I remember." He checked the yellow pad in his file folder. "Yeah, that's 17 of which two were sent down from the fifth-grade. So, you had 15 fourth graders playing. Only 13 signed-up this year. That's too many for one team, but not enough for two. So, I made an executive decision," Anderson said. "We'll have one fifth-grade team this year consisting of 13 kids."

"That's ridiculous," I replied. "We can't have 13 kids on a team. No one gets to play more than few minutes a game. Kids sit when you scrimmage. The number's obscene."

"Got a better suggestion?" Anderson asked.

"How about sending some sixth graders down or fourth graders up? That's what happened last year. It worked."

"Can't do it this year. Both fourth- and sixth-grade classes have numbers that work for them."

"So, we get stuck?"

"As I said, 'got a better suggestion?'"

"What about seven and six?"

"Don't be silly. That can't work."

"Neither can 13."

"Stop complaining. You had a big year last season."

"I sure didn't have a big year," Jordan said.

As far as Anderson was concerned, the discussion was closed. He'd decided what he would do before he'd opened the gym door. The meeting's sole agenda item was to tell us of his ruling. "One of the two of you'll coach. I suggest the other assist."

Jordan stared at Anderson, his thick lenses bestowing his disappearing eyes with a spacey contempt. "That's easy. Doug's more experienced than I am. More successful, too. He should be the coach. I'll help."

"We'll do it together, Jordan. You and I and our 13 kids." I scowled. Thirteen. I imagined how I might run off a few kids to bring the number down. Force them quit. Rigorous practices and a few directed gruff remarks might do the trick.

"I'm happy to coach with you," Jordan said, as he grabbed my shoulder. His clasp interrupted my mean-spirited thought. I was embarrassed I'd entertained, even momentarily, the idea of running kids off. But 13 was too many.

"I love it when a plan comes together," Anderson chirped. He seemed relieved that his bad news had met only token resistance. He handed us a list of names with telephone numbers. "Here's the roster of the boys who signed-up. You're responsible for notifying them. Your practice schedule is Mondays and Wednesdays at 5:30."

"What was wrong with last year's four o'clock time slot?" Anderson ignored me and called the next group. 'Ty will be thrilled with this season's practice time. My wife will be furious,' I said, grumbling half audibly.

"Let's go around the corner," my new assistant said. "Giorgio's has a pay phone. We can call our wives and tell them we've got important business we're conducting."

We headed to the pizza place, where the two of us sat down over beers to assess the catastrophe that had been dropped on us.

"Thirteen players screws up everything. Nobody gets to play more than a few minutes a game. Think about it, Jordan. Twenty quarters of playing time in a game, five players times four quarters. We have 13 kids. If everyone plays equal time, each kid plays one quarter per game and seven play two. That's nuts."

"We're not going to do that, are we? We'd never win a game. Not even be competitive in most."

"Of course not. But say we play Zack the entire game to maximize our chances. That still leaves just four quarters to spread among the other four starters."

"You're assuming we give every kid at least one full quarter of playing time."

"For now, though we don't have to. Three minutes instead of six as the standard for minimum playing time would make things easier," I said. "Two minutes even more."

"A kid can't break a sweat in two minutes."

The full impact of the 13-man roster was registering. Not only would we have all the extra players to get into every game, they were mostly Jordan's old crew, the ones who had eked out a single victory last year. They were terrible basketball players, on a different plane than the kids from my last year's team. Yet, everyone had to play, and play a reasonable number of minutes.

"I refuse to believe we're locked into 13 but assume for the moment we have no choice. What are we going to do about it?"

"You're the coach, Doug."

"You're the assistant, Jordan. The assistant is supposed to be the smart guy who makes the coach look good."

Jordan's beer was almost gone, and he drained it. "Okay. What are our options?" His question didn't thrill me. The last time we pursued this exercise Zack was clandestinely being tracked by a sports agent and everyone else was in jeopardy of being kidnapped. "Maybe some kid will surprise us," my assistant speculated. His conjecture was characteristically upbeat, which made me smile. But it was also as realistic as discovering gold under the gym floor.

"We'll find out how good we are as coaches. The truth is I didn't have to do much last season. Threw out the ball and let the kids play. I just made sure they didn't beat themselves and everybody got in the game. The only real improvement I made was persuading them to shoot free-throws underhand, and you were the guy responsible for that."

"Yeah. Sure. Don't play that 'aw shucks' game with me. I know better," Jordan said. "But I grant you, this job will be exponentially more difficult than last year's."

Jordan was right. I stared into my beer glass, praying that a positive thought might bob up through the remaining head. None did.

I began to mentally assess the changed roster. Five from my fourth-grade team would return. George was gone. The team would miss him. Badly. I'd also miss Willie, but for personal reasons. Though he contributed little as a basketball player, his unfailingly pleasant disposition and constant effort made him a delight to coach. Randal's disappearance would be a pure blessing.

Seven of Jordan's nine would return. Considering the persistent drubbings his team took last season, the large proportion wanting to play again was a tribute to him. The kids liked the easy-going novice and had fun playing for him. My competitive nature wasn't likely to sit as well. One new player signed-up. He was in school last year but chose not to play. Since Travis had never mentioned the boy, he wasn't likely to be the pleasant surprise Jordan hoped for. That was the sum of the basketball talent we had to work with. Transforming the group into a competitive unit would tax anyone's coaching skills, let alone ours.

By the time I reached home, Travis was asleep in a living room chair, his head on his chest with a crop of dirty-blonde hair falling over his forehead. He didn't hear me enter. "Travis wanted to stay up to find out who was on his team," Maddie whispered. Her face glowed in an affectionate warmth as she gazed down at her son.

I shook Travis's shoulder.

"Dad?"

"All your buddies are on the team." The corners of his lips gradually rose, and Maddie helped him to bed.

"Good for you, getting all of Travis's friends on the team," Maddie said when she met me in the kitchen. "You'll probably need to tell Travis again tomorrow. I doubt he'll remember a word you said."

"He'll be happy to hear about his buddies. When I tell him the rest of the story though, he won't be so pleased."

"Why?"

"We have one team this year instead of two. I'm coaching and Jordan's my assistant. But the big news is that we have 13 players."

"How many?

"Thirteen. Five from my last year's group; seven from Jordan's; and one new kid."

"That can't work. Can it? No one will play much. It's almost like, 'why bother'. Is there anything you can do?" She looked bewildered.

"I don't know. I asked about moving kids across grades, like Willie and Randal last year. Anderson claimed that he couldn't move anyone this year."

"Easy for him to say. He doesn't have to live with the consequences."

"Think. If we play all 13 a reasonable amount of time, we'll get the you-know-what kicked out of us. I don't like it and I'll guarantee the kids from my last year's team won't like it either, particularly when they have to sit on the bench and watch it happen. It may not be as painful for Jordan's kids. They're used to losing, though Jordan says several signed-up because they hope to play on a winner this season."

"Don't get too upset, Doug. Maybe something'll work out. Besides, you've had your glory. Now comes retribution for the pain you inflicted on other teams last year."

I didn't appreciate either her irony or her humor. "You play to win every time you walk on the court. You don't play to win half of your games or settle to win one every now and then."

"I understand. But remember, you're working with a huge handicap. Maybe a 50:50 record won't look so bad at the end of the season."

"What a terrible thought."

Maddie got up from her chair, walked over to a cabinet, and pulled out a bottle of bourbon. She poured a small glass, no ice, and handed it to me. "Drink and go to bed. Your life won't change if you don't have a winning season."

The sound of bouncing basketballs again echoed through St. Jerome's gym. The kids warmed-up while we waited to begin the fifth-grade team's first practice of the season. About half the faces were familiar. However, except Carleton Whitley and his friend Freddie, those from Jordan's old team were new to me. I didn't recall seeing any of them in any context, though I'd attended one of Jordan's practices last season. Presumably, those unfamiliar faces had all been present, but not one registered.

Jordan was missing. We'd spoken on the phone the night before and I knew he planned to attend practice. Then the metal double doors in the back of the gym flew open and in he strode wearing a purple warm-up suit with a yellow 'St. Jerome's' scrawled across the front, a white towel wrapped around his neck, and a pair of new white sneakers on his feet. The aberration was a khaki-camouflage cap, a chapeau that a duck-hunter peeking from a blind might wear. Add curly red hair, a bounteous crimson handlebar mustache, and Coke-bottle hornrims, and Jordan was a sight that caught the attention of the entire team. My old players strained not to burst out laughing; his old players looked amused; and his son, Carleton, looked for a place to hide.

"Sorry to be late, Doug. Had to change." Now I was the one who looked out of place. I hadn't had time to change. A business suit and wing tips, the tie and jacket stripped, was my coaching costume for the day. The only identification I wore to divulge my position was the whistle around my neck, which I soon blew to start practice. Neither Jordan nor I would have made the centerfold of a sportswear magazine.

"Okay, guys, bring it in," I yelled over the din of bouncing balls and kids' voices, and beckoned them into a huddle around Jordan and me.

When it was nearly quiet, I said, "I'm Coach Elliot, and this is Coach Whitley. We're coaching together this year. Whatever either of us says, goes. Got it?" Heads nodded. "We're looking forward to working with you. We'll talk about team rules, and so on, later. Let's get started."

The team made two lines for the layup drill. First in line was a non-descript kid who must have played on Jordan's team last season. I didn't recognize him. He dribbled the ball unsteadily toward the basket and as he neared it, jumped off his right foot and tossed the ball with his right hand at the backboard behind the basket.

"Hold it. You can't do that," I hollered. "If you throw the ball up with your right hand, you jump off your left foot. If you throw it up with your left hand, you jump off your right. Why? Because you stretch out that way. You're closer to the basket when you shoot. Make sense?" The boy nodded. "Try it again. Left foot, right hand." He made an uncoordinated second effort, this time using the correct limbs. "Okay. That's better." I grimaced. This season was going to be as bad as I feared.

Jordan sidled up as the drill continued. "Had trouble with his footwork last season, too."

"I think we can eliminate that kid as your hoped for 'pleasant surprise'," I replied.

Every player took several turns during the drill, and every player performed as expected. No surprises emerged, pleasant or otherwise.

"Split up. Guys in that line, go with Coach Whitley to the other basket. Guys in this line stay here with me." Zack, Casey, and Andy followed Jordan along with three others. Travis and Rickie stayed with me and the remaining five, one of whom was the new boy who hadn't played the year before. The reason he hadn't soon became clear. He could hardly catch the ball, let alone dribble or shoot it, and he recoiled when the ball headed in his direction. He was afraid of it.

The drills at both ends of the floor ran at the speed of spreading molasses. Slow. Very slow.

The team's sluggishness might have been attributed to a first practice. Only Zack played throughout the year, and even he took time off in the summer to pitch baseball. The rest of the team probably hadn't touched a basketball ball since the last game of the last season. But rust wasn't the principal issue. That could be ground away. It was the lack of athletic ability.

Many of Jordan's old crew moved as if they had drafted a plan to execute the drill and then mechanically followed it, step by agonizing step, the whole performed so clumsily as to make the exercise unrecognizable. Their process resembled a foreign tourist asking directions from a local, word for word, right out of a language phrase book, and then garbling the pronunciation so badly as to make even correct vocabulary and expression unintelligible.

Soon, the five who had played for me last year grew impatient. Their thresholds varied with Rickie the first to cross, but all five were visibly eager to stop slow motion and play at full speed. Andy, trapped in a listless drill, even asked Jordan if he could skip a turn and run a few laps around the gym.

I didn't know how much patience I should demand of them. I wanted to avoid dividing the team into two skill groups, effectively into last year's two teams. That would splinter team cohesion. But if we continued this course, team cohesion would splinter anyway, at least among my old group.

The savior for the moment was Jordan. He exhibited unfailing patience and good-humor, and it spilled to others. He walked his old group through drills step-by-step with a constant stream of encouragement and wry comment. My kids liked Jordan's banter too, and it cut their edge. Before long, he had my kids working one-on-one with his. He set up pairs, the more polished working with the less.

Practice neared its end. The team had completed most of the drills Jordan and I had planned the night before. I thought we might finish with a few final repetitions of each, but the kids were tired of drills and wanted to scrimmage. Besides, we could no longer avoid the huge gap in skill sets between some of the team's players and others. Now was as good a time as any to display it.

"Ten minutes left, guys. We'll scrimmage half-court. Carleton, Bobby, Freddie, Sam, and Vince: shirts. Zack, Casey, Travis, Rickie, and Andy: skins. I'll get you other guys in soon." Another instance where 13 players didn't work.

My old team peeled their T-shirts to become skins and let the shirts take the ball unimpeded. Bobby threw it in to Carleton and when Carleton tried to pass the ball to another teammate, Zack casually stepped in to intercept. Zack then passed the ball to Casey who threw it to Rickie who lobbed it to Travis who took a shot from under the basket. The progression had been effortless. The shirts spun in place, trying to follow the ball as the skins moved it quickly from player to player. The following minutes presented more of the same. The shirts never got a shot. I sat Zack, replacing him with Vince on the skins. Little changed. One by one, I made certain that the three who didn't initially play had an opportunity to demonstrate their skills. They had none.

I rearranged teams. This time Zack and Travis were shirts along with three boys from Jordan's old team while Rickie, Casey, and Andy joined the skins with Freddie and Carleton. The two sides were theoretically even. As a practical matter, they weren't, not even close.

The scrimmage became a game of two on three. The five players from Jordan's old team rarely touched the ball and spent most of their time getting out of the way. They weren't playing. They were spectators standing on the gym floor.

That wasn't all. The Zack and Travis tandem dominated because Zack handled the ball at such a high level. Under normal circumstances, Casey could have handled it well enough for the skins. Against Zack, he was no match. I doubted anyone in the league would be. However, the exercise underscored a second chasm in skill level, the one between Zack and everyone else.

How long Zack would tolerate playing with teammates, even opponents, so much less skilled than he, was an open question. To an extent, he had no choice. If he didn't play on our team, he wouldn't play with any school team. But a school team wasn't his only outlet. There were city-sponsored recreation leagues. He already played in one of them. Zack seemed to like the kids on our team, so I expected he'd continue to play with his school friends. Still, he could drop us any time he became frustrated with our level of play, and without Zack, we were dead.

Practice ended. I thanked the kids for their attention and effort. Jordan echoed my sentiments and then sent a message to the players on his last year's team, "We have to play better this year than we did last. I didn't like winning just one game. Coach Elliot's team won a championship. I want to be part of a team that wins, and I expect everyone's best effort to do so."

The players gathered their things and met their parents for their rides home. "Jordan let's have lunch tomorrow. We both have kids to take home now. Besides, my feet are killing me."

He looked down and mouthed, 'wing-tips?' and turned up his nose. "I have a shoe store you need to visit. A more up-to-date appearance would do you wonders."

"Dad, this year's going to be terrible, isn't it?" Travis said as soon as he jumped in the car.

"What makes you say that, Son?"

"I like the kids in my class. Everybody's okay. But most of them are terrible basketball players. We're going to get creamed."

"You're ahead of yourself, Travis?"

"No, I'm not. We're going to get creamed."

"We haven't even started the season. Give everybody a chance."

"Dad, I'm not stupid. George's gone. That's bad enough. Now you have to play all those kids who can't play."

"Don't forget, Zack's the best player in the league."

"Yup, and since when can you play basketball by yourself?"

Travis had evaluated the situation harshly, but accurately, though I couldn't concede it. He was the team's emotional leader, and I couldn't have the emotional leader holding a negative assessment of our prospects. He had to have hope. I had to convince him that his observations were premature. My plan was to beg for time and trust the team would improve, though I knew appreciable progress was unlikely.

"How do you like Mr. Whitley?" I asked, diverting the topic from a discussion I didn't want to have. "He's excited about working with you guys."

"He's nice, and his warm-up suit's funny, but we're still going to get creamed, Dad."

"The kids will improve. That's what Mr. Whitley and I are supposed to do. Help you get better."

"We're going to get creamed, Dad," Travis said without missing a beat.

"What are you going to do for this year's science fair? Any ideas yet?"

"Not yet."

Jordan and I sat down to lunch at our usual spot. We went through the motions of reading the menu and then ordered our standard fare. Neither of us spoke. We were afraid to set a tone or choose a starting point. We just sat and stared into space.

After a full dead minute, Jordan said in a flat tone, "Kind of cold out there today."

I burst out laughing. Jordan froze for an instant and then joined me. We must have sounded like two fools to the diner's few other patrons. Two well-dressed adults exploding into a belly laugh in the middle of day, and all without a glass of alcohol in sight.

From the beginning, Jordan and I had enjoyed a relaxed relationship. Yet there we were, fearing a dialogue that neither of us knew how to initiate. Jordan's opening, an exercise in avoidance, was ridiculous. Yet he'd started the conversation.

"Cold outside," I repeated. Jordan's diversion had been an amusing interlude, but we could no longer escape the inevitable. "We have two very different teams we have to meld into one, and we've got our first game in a few weeks."

"We can try, Doug, but it's not going to happen. The gap's too large. We need a strategy to get around it, both in games and at practice."

"Get around it? How?"

"Yesterday, during the scrimmage, you tried various combinations of kids to see how well they played together. I learned a couple of things watching that exercise. The first is that we won't win many games, maybe not any, if we give every kid substantial playing time every game."

"That's negative," I said, taken aback by the habitual optimist's novel stance.

"I know, but hear me out," Jordan replied. "If we're not competitive, the kids you had last year will lose interest. Wouldn't you, coming off a season where winning was the norm?" He paused long enough to let me agree and then continued. "The kids from my old team aren't going to like it, either. One of the reasons they signed-up after last year's debacle was that they thought they might get to play with some of your kids and win. They don't want to repeat last year. That means we have to win at least a few games, regardless of playing time. We'll lose kids if we don't."

Jordan's comments surprised me. He offered a perspective I hadn't considered. I'd always played every game to win. No exceptions whatever the prospects. That now looked naïve. Jordan's idea was to win at least a few games. If that meant some kids wouldn't put a foot on the floor in those contests, so be it. There would be lots of minutes for everyone in the several we wouldn't win. Playing time for many kids on the team might be lumpy game to game, but we could even it out over the season.

Jordan's idea seemed a reasonable compromise between winning and playing time, yet I hated it. I hated it because I was conceding that we wouldn't play every game to win; I hated it because I couldn't imagine the substitutes enjoying the bench when we won and occupying the court when we got clobbered; I hated it because we would play as two teams, not one; I hated it because every kid wouldn't necessarily play in every game; I hated it because our scheme was cold calculation without a hint of sport in it. The entire concept just struck me as wrong, but I faced an untenable situation and had no better alternative.

"Have you talked to Carleton about your idea?" I asked.

"Not directly. All my players were so excited to win that one game last year. I can't describe it. We didn't like losing. We were just resigned to it. Once the kids found out what it was like to win, their attitudes changed. When Carleton learned there would only be one fifth-grade team this year, the first thing out of his mouth was, 'good, we'll win some games for a change'."

"Your idea could work, I suppose. Last year I adjusted playing time by the size of our lead. The bigger our lead, the more our subs played. Maybe I could reverse the process. The bigger the opponent's lead, the more our subs play." I took another bite of my cheeseburger and wiped my fingers on my napkin. "The problem reversing the process is that it requires an educated guess early in the game. Can we win this thing or not? Hardly a science. Then we have to stick to the plan unless an unexpected outcome becomes obvious. There's not much flexibility. A lot could go wrong."

"That's the best idea I have," Jordan said. "It'd be great if every kid played at least a little every game, but that may not be possible if we want to win. You'll have a real balancing act, Doug."

I was grateful Montgomery Wise wasn't a team parent this season, but how many Montgomery Wises were in the current parental crop, ready to pounce when their sons didn't get in a game? I didn't know, and neither did Jordan. The letter we would send to the parents with the season's schedule and team policies might tip us off to any parental attitude issues. If not, we would likely find out after the first game or two.

A NEW SEASON

"Mr. Elliot! Mr. Elliot! Travis is in big trouble."

"What's going on Andy? Where is he? Is he hurt?" My eyes scoured the gym looking for my son. He wasn't there.

"No, he's not hurt. But if Sister Cecelia finds out, he won't be able to play in Sunday's game."

"What's the big trouble he's in?"

"He got in a fight."

I wanted to talk to someone less excitable than Andy. Casey wasn't far away. "Casey do you know anything about Travis and a fight?"

"Yes, sir. It happened at lunchtime."

"Where? Who was he fighting with? About what?"

A fight wasn't like Travis. I knew that if an upper classman picked on a little kid, Travis would be the first to the rescue. But a fight?

"What can you tell me, Casey? Where's Travis?"

"He's with Mr. Louganis," Andy said.

"Who's Mr. Louganis? Why's Travis with him?"

Jordan walked into the gym in his purple warm-up suit, ready for practice.

"What's the excitement, Doug?"

"Something about Travis. The kids say he's been in a fight." I turned to face Andy again. "Who's Mr. Louganis?"

"He's the janitor," Andy said. Casey nodded in agreement.

"Oh, yeah. I remember. Where can I find him? Jordan, why don't you start practice while I try to find out what's going on. Andy tells me that if Sister Cecelia learns about it, Travis won't be able to play Sunday."

"She's strict," Jordan said.

"Just what we need to start the season, Travis suspended from the team." I still couldn't figure out what was going on. "Andy, where's Mr. Louganis?"

"The boiler room in the basement."

"Show me. Go ahead, Jordan, and start practice. I hope I'll be back soon."

I followed Andy out of the gym, down the cement staircase to the basement. At the bottom of the steps, we passed the boy's bathroom, and I heard Travis say, "Carleton, I'll take this one. You grab the other."

I went in. There were Travis and Carleton. They each held a large spray bottle in one hand and a rag in the other and were cleaning the mirrors on the wall.

"What are you guys doing?"

My voice unnerved them. Travis seemed miffed, and Carleton looked embarrassed. Travis was disheveled, his hair messed, and he had a large smudge on the right side of his forehead. The top button of his shirt was undone, and his underarms showed that he had been perspiring. I didn't pay much attention to Carleton, but he seemed to look little different.

"Anybody care to tell me what's going on?"

"We only have to finish cleaning these mirrors, Dad, and we'll be right up."

"Why are you cleaning mirrors? And, what's this I hear about a fight?"

"Yeah. Carleton and me."

"You and Carleton fighting? About what?" I was incredulous.

"It's a long story, Dad."

"I've got time, and it looks like you do, too."

Carleton, standing on a two-step stool, continued to polish the mirror above the far wash basin. I sent Andy back to practice.

"It's Monday, so Mom fixed me peanut butter and jelly sandwiches for lunch. I got jelly on my hands. So, I came down to wash it off. Carleton and Rickie were already here. I washed my hands and grabbed a paper towel. It got kind of wet. So, I wadded it up in a ball and tried to shoot a basket."

"Shoot a basket?"

"The waste basket over there," he said pointing to a large, cylindrical aluminum receptacle for used paper towels. "I missed and hit Rickie in the arm. It left a wet spot on his shirt. So, he got a paper towel and ran water on it and threw it at me. He hit Carleton instead. Then, Carleton picked up a wet paper towel and tossed it at Rickie. Pretty soon we were just firing wet paper towels. I guess there was a lot of water and paper towels on the floor. Mr. Louganis walked in. He looked around and wasn't happy."

"I can understand that."

"He made us clean up the floor and then said he would tell Sister Cecelia. We said he couldn't do that. If he told her, she wouldn't let us play in the game Sunday."

"And?"

"We made a deal. We'd stay after school all week and empty waste baskets, clean the bathroom mirrors, and sweep the floors if he didn't say anything."

"So, your fight with Carleton was a wet paper towel fight?

"Yup."

"Is that what happened, Carleton?"

Jordan's son stopped polishing the mirror long enough to say, "Yes, Mr. Elliot. We weren't really fighting. We did pull quite a few paper towels from the dispenser, but we didn't hurt anybody or anything."

"We just got wet, Dad."

"Why isn't Rickie down here with you two? I thought you said he was in on it."

"He hid in a stall when Mr. Louganis came in."

"And Mr. Louganis didn't see him?

"He was too mad looking at the mess on the floor."

"Okay." I groaned. The janitor was taking advantage of the kids to get his work done, but it was a good lesson for them. I just hoped Louganis would keep his end of the bargain and the kids would be able to play Sunday. "Wrap it up. Let's get back to practice."

"Can't do that just yet, Dad. Mr. Louganis has to sign off before we can go."

I walked back up the cement staircase to the gym and spotted Jordan supervising a drill.

"You aren't going to believe this, Jordan."

"Oh. I think I will. I've already heard a lot."

"An inauspicious way to start the season, I'd say. Imagine. Both coaches' kids suspended for the first game."

"What are the chances?"

"I don't know. Sister Cecelia supposedly has long ears."

St. Joseph's was the first game on the season's schedule, and we played at home. My fourth-graders had crushed their team last year, partially in response to the behavior of their coach, Toby Ferguson, and his wife. I was eager for the rematch as soon as I saw the schedule because the game would not only be an early test for our untried and problematic team, but for our new 'win-some' strategy. The match also represented a test for Monsignor Schreiber's word. He'd promised appropriate action to stem the Fergusons, despite refusing to divulge its nature. The game might tell me more.

St. Jerome's was already on the floor warming-up when the St. Joseph's fifth graders arrived. There, leading the pack was Toby Ferguson with his wife trailing not far behind. I was stunned. If this was Monsignor Schreiber's version of appropriate action, our ideas varied in the extreme. Then I grew furious. The priest had lied. He'd done nothing. He'd left those kids to the mercies of two crazies. I looked for the Ferguson boy, Tommy. There he was, stripping off his jacket and walking toward the bench.

I spun around looking for someone to scream at and there stood a pleasant, freshly shaved young man of college age. "Doug Elliot?" he asked.

"Yes."

"Hi. I'm Adrian Atkinson, the St. Joseph's coach." I froze. I was confused and my expression must have shown it. Then I heaved a deep sigh of relief. "Are you all right?" he asked.

"I'm sorry. My mind was a thousand miles away. You caught me by surprise." I smiled and extended my hand, delighted to erase my earlier impression. "Nice to meet you. Is this your first game coaching St. Joseph's? As I recall, someone else coached the team last season when these boys were in fourth grade."

"Yes and no," Atkinson said. "I began coaching this group last year around Christmas. Monsignor Schreiber, he's our parish priest, collared me one day after Mass and asked if I'd be willing to coach some kids. He knew I'm a physical education major over at the college and thought a little experience coaching might help my resume."

"Has it?"

"Don't know about my resume, but I love coaching. We didn't win many games last year. But just that partial season convinced me I want to be a coach when I graduate. I'm looking forward to the next few months." Atkinson oozed enthusiasm.

I didn't dare ask how the Fergusons fit into the puzzle. At least not now. "Great," was all I could sputter in response.

"I understand St. Jerome's is the powerhouse of the league."

"Every season's different," I replied. "You'll learn that, and you'll also learn that you often don't know why. Sometimes, the ball bounces in your direction and sometimes the ball bounces backward."

"Backward?"

"The other direction."

"Hmm. One thing nice about this experience: I pick up a lot of practical stuff, stuff I can use when I go out and get a job coaching."

"You'll do much better than that tidbit. Just pay attention. I've found that you never know when or where you'll find something useful."

As my team huddled, Travis and Carleton sat in the bleachers. Sister Cecelia's long ears had heard about the wet paper towel fight and the first thing Tuesday morning she'd marched the boys into her office, reprimanded them for their behavior, and suspended them from Sunday's game. She also told them they were to help Mr. Louganis for the rest of the week and threatened to suspend them from school if they engaged in anymore 'tomfoolery'. The Elliot's and the Whitley's each received a letter detailing the transgressions and formalizing the penalties. I wasn't surprised. Sister had a reputation, though I was amazed how quickly her antennae had picked up the news. From the specificity of the transgressions in Sister's letter, I suspected Mr. Louganis had sold out the kids. But I had no additional evidence, and it made no difference. Neither would play today.

"Guys, here's the deal," I said in our huddle, "We need to get the season off to a good start. That means a win. You can see we're missing Travis and Carleton. They stupidly got suspended. So, the rest of you'll have to carry the extra load. Everybody'll get in the game today, at least for a bit. But it may only be for a few plays. I'll do better as the season progresses and you practice more." My eyes traveled to Jordan. "Coach, anything you want to say?"

Jordan bent into the huddle, his eye level met the kids', and he said in a low, firm voice, "Remember fellas, and I'm talking to those who played for me last year, it's a lot more fun to win than it is to lose."

"Everybody bring it in," I said, and a loud "St. Jerry's" filled the gym as their hands surged into the air. The starting five headed for center court and the remaining six to the bench.

"Doug, is this still a win?" Jordan whispered. "Without Travis, we're thin."

"Doesn't make any difference. Unless St. Joseph's found some *wunderkind* over the summer, this may be our best opportunity for a win all season. We can't miss it. We just can't."

The game got off to a promising start. Zack performed his magic and scored four points the first three times down the floor. Still, problems appeared immediately. Last season George and Travis controlled the game near the basket using George's height and Travis's bulk. Without either boy, we couldn't hold our own in the middle of the floor. We were dependent on perimeter play, which for small kids with minimal strength, was a huge disadvantage. A few minutes elapsed, and Rickie threw in a basket, and then Andy, running at his usual feverish pace, caught a St. Joseph's player napping, slipped behind him and caught a ball from Zack for another basket. We led 8 - 0. When St. Joseph's called a time-out to regroup, the mood in our huddle was a rerun of last season's, bubbling, buoyant, and confident. Jordan and the new players adopted the tone instantly, but I failed to share their optimism, even if Travis had been playing. And he wasn't.

The score stood 12 - 4 to begin the second quarter when I sent in our first two substitutes. I'd instructed Zack that the game wasn't to become a three-man affair with the two new players watching more than playing. Yet after one of them muffed a pass from Casey and pushed it out of bounds and the other bounced a dribble off his foot, our side became a three-man team. The substitutes never handled the ball again. They still played defense and did so credibly. The smaller of the two even made a steal. But three against five doesn't work long-term. I had to pull the two substitutes as soon as I could legitimately claim to have fulfilled my obligation to play them.

The score was soon 14 - 10. The Ferguson kid made the second of two baskets for his team, and when he did, a roar rose from the St. Joseph's side of the bleachers. Mrs. Ferguson led the cheering for her son's two-pointer while Dad sat quietly, a huge grin on his face.

By half I'd played four different substitutes, two minutes each, hardly enough time for them to loosen up. Our lead had shrunk to two points. St. Joseph's tied the game soon after the second half began, and I still had two substitutes who hadn't played. Thirty seconds later we fell behind by a basket.

I called time out and took Jordan aside, "We're going for a win. I want to give the two kids who haven't played their two minutes, but no guarantees. Problem?"

"Okay. I agree. This one has to be a win."

I threw the hand towel I was holding against the bench in exasperation. It hit the back, flew open, and slid underneath. "I'm still irritated with Travis. Wet paper towels? If you get booted, at least do something memorable."

"Like what?"

"I don't know. Paint the monkey bars on the playground purple and yellow or hang the portrait of Sister Cecelia in the hall upside down or nail a 'Closed' sign on the front door of the school. Something worth getting booted for."

"I'm in the presence of an aging juvenile delinquent." Jordan chuckled.

"Travis inherits mischievousness legitimately. From his father. Where does Carleton get his?"

Jordan, still chuckling, and I, still unhappy, returned to the huddle, "Zack, I need you to run St. Joseph's into the ground. Everyone has to help, but Zack is going to take over." It was an onerous assignment to give any kid. Few could absorb it; fewer still could savor it. I believed Zack would do both.

Takeover, Zack did. He ratcheted his game to a higher level and became a one-man show. He controlled the ball; he scored; he passed to open teammates; and when he wasn't doing that, he was stealing it from the other side. What he couldn't do was rebound. He wasn't big enough, and neither was anyone else on our team. Nor did Zack relish scrambling for loose balls, and they constantly fell into the hands of St. Joseph's players. We missed the 'garbage man'. Fortunately, the rest of the team absorbed Zack's urgency. Andy caught St. Joseph's napping again, not once but twice. By the fourth quarter, if the red and white jerseys weren't chasing Zach, they were running after Andy. Casey served as Zack's alter-ego. When Zack couldn't find an outlet for the ball, he sent it to Casey, who would return it when Zack was ready to have it again. Rickie hung out in his preferred corner waiting for either Zack or Casey to get him the ball, and his patience resulted in two baskets. We regained the lead and expanded it to four points mid-way through the last quarter. But St. Joseph's refused to quit, coming back to score again and adding a free throw.

Two minutes remained and I still had two kids who hadn't played. I'd often thought about the choice, winning or meaningful playing time for every kid. What would I do if faced with it? Where would my priority lie? To this point, the choice had only been hypothetical. My team had been good enough to let me avoid the issue. It had arisen only once last year, and Randal's selfishness made that decision easy. This was different. Two kids sat at the end of the bench. Neither were Randal. They were good kids. If I put them in the game, they would follow instructions and perform as teammates, not isolated individuals. They would also doom the team's prospects.

I was angry with Travis for leaving me in this predicament. If he hadn't been suspended, the matter would never have arisen. We'd have had a comfortable lead and playing everyone would never have been an issue. But obsessing over Travis's behavior now didn't help.

Jordan and I had developed a season's strategy before the first game. It required discipline if it were to be successful, and St. Joseph's was a must-win in it. I had no choice. The players on the floor would finish the game while the two kids at the end of the bench would sit.

The final score was St. Jerome's 33, St. Joseph's 31.

The win produced relief, but neither elation nor pleasure for me. The game had been a chore from beginning to end, and now I had a mess to clean up. I had to explain to the kids who didn't get into the game why they didn't play. The win-some strategy was rational, and my decision fit its proscribed formula. To the affected kids however, the rationale for my decision was likely inexplicable, and I wouldn't try.

I brushed past Jordan and ignored the jubilant faces of our kids running off the court. I crouched near the end of the bench, before the two boys who hadn't played. They still sat, looking blankly at me, as if they didn't know whether to be happy with the team's victory or disappointed at not playing.

I felt rotten, worse than I could have imagined. I'd screwed up in so many ways that I'd made a difficult situation nearly indefensible. Like a short-sighted blockhead, I had told the team everyone would play when I knew we were playing a must-win game. I wasn't thinking. Not only that I'd played four substitutes, labeling the remaining two the only players undeserving of floor time.

I squatted in front of them and put a hand on a knee of each. "Don't give up on me. I'm sorry I didn't get you in the game today. That'll change. I can assure you."

A few mumbled words met my apology. Both boys got up and wandered off, still dazed, as if they had been invited to a party only to be told at the door their invitations had been withdrawn, and I'd been the guy who'd withdrawn them.

"Your team's better than last year," I said when Atkinson came to our bench to congratulate me. "I don't know what you're doing with your kids, but you're doing something right."

He smiled and thanked me for the compliment.

"Who's that energetic lady in the front row making all the noise when that one boy made a basket?" I asked. I knew the answer before I asked the question.

Atkinson chuckled. "Oh. You mean Mrs. Ferguson? That was her son, Tommy, who made the basket. They're among my most vocal and enthusiastic parents.

"It's nice to see parents rooting for their kids, not harping on their mistakes."

"That's the Fergusons. They've encouraged me, too, and I've appreciated it."

"Oh? They're helping you? With the coaching, I mean."

"No. Monsignor Schreiber recruited Sister Martha to help me out with the coaching. She's my assistant, though she couldn't be here today. Except for games, I only see the Fergusons when they pick up Tommy after practice. And occasionally at the rectory. That's where I first met them. They were just leaving a meeting with the Monsignor. Do you know them?"

"Now that you mention it, I do believe we've met."

Everyone understood that a home game meant a trip to Giorgio's afterward and Maddie and I headed in that direction. Travis had joined his friends earlier and was likely already seated at the kids' table, in the middle of whatever activity there was. I was still furious with him.

"You realize Travis could have cost us the game today," I said to my wife. "If we hadn't been lucky with Andy catching St. Joseph's napping, we'd have lost. We needed Travis. He wasn't there. Instead he was sitting in the bleachers with you. Watching. Suspended. Does he understand that?"

"Doug, you've been on him all week about it."

"I know, but does he understand the consequences of that little stunt he pulled?"

"There're worse things than a wet paper towel fight."

"That's beside the point. He knows he can't do that. You look crosswise at that school and you're in the Sister Cecelia's office. It's not that he's a stranger there.

"He's not a regular, either. Let it go, Doug. Your team won."

"But without Travis we should have lost to a team we should have beaten."

"Say that again?"

"Travis has a responsibility to his team. He didn't fulfill it, and we almost lost because of it."

"Forget it, Doug. I don't want to hear another word about the matter, especially on the way home when Travis's in the car."

By the time Maddie and I rounded the corner, we could hear the hum of conversation within the team's home away from home. Its rising volume attested to the good cheer over the day's victory and a widely held optimism for the new season. Rickie's dad, John Hansen, greeted us at the door as we walked in. Maddie went ahead to claim a seat at our regular table.

"Nice start, Doug. I was nervous before the game with Travis out. Still, we picked right up where we left off last year."

"I liked the result. Other things could have gone better."

"Relax. We won the game with one arm tied behind our back. So, you didn't get everybody in the game. You've got 13 kids. Well, 11 today. You can make up for it later, and Montgomery Wise isn't here to gripe. Life's good." He clapped me on the shoulder. "See you at the table."

Montgomery Wise may not have been at the game, but another father may have held similar ideas about playing time. Differing from Wise, he would have had cause to be upset.

Jordan intercepted me before I could reach the table where Maddie was waiting. He wanted to introduce me to the parents of two boys on our team who'd played for him last year. Both got in the game today, for limited minutes. However, their brief playing time didn't seem to dampen parental enthusiasm.

"Way to go, Coach," said the taller of the two men. "We're looking forward to a good year. We've already matched last year's win total."

"That was our team," Jordan said. "Doug's fourth-graders won 15, actually 16 games if you include the win over the fifth-graders."

"We heard about that," said a diminutive dark-haired lady standing next to the taller man. "That's why we're so hopeful. Mr. Elliot's team has had success, and success breeds more success."

"A championship?" said the shorter fellow. His comment fell somewhere between a question and an assertion.

"Hold it everybody," I said. "Thank you. But we're getting way ahead of ourselves. Today was just the first game of the season. We've got 15 more to play. It's a little early to be talking about a championship."

"Coach's right," the diminutive lady said. "That puts too much pressure on the kids."

"I suppose. But after last year, and without a critical player today, a player who'll be back next week I would add…" the taller man said looking down at her. He shifted his gaze to me. "You're right, Coach. It's early. But I still can't help but be optimistic. Very optimistic."

"Let's just say, we're off to a 1 - 0 start. That a good way to begin the season." I edged from the group. "Nice to meet you and I hope to see you at the remaining games. Please excuse me. My wife's waiting."

I headed toward the table where Maddie sat with our regular group, Rickie's and Casey's parents.

"What was that all about Doug?" Maddie asked. She almost had to shout for me to hear her.

I leaned in. "Jordan just introduced me to a few parents of kids new to the team. They're bubbling with optimism over the year's prospects. They have no idea." I glanced at the other two couples at our table who were in deep conversation. "Nor do our friends. Enjoy yourself while you can, Maddie. It's going to be a long season."

BARNEY'S FAMILY

I was finishing my newspaper a few days following the St. Joseph's game when the telephone rang. I glanced at my watch. "A little late," I said to Maddie as I rose to answer. She nodded and returned to her book. "Hello. This is Doug Elliot."

"You have to play everybody."

"Excuse me?"

"You have to play everybody."

"Who's this?"

"You coach the St. Jerome's fifth-grade basketball team. You control playing time. Sunday, you didn't let everybody play. You have to let everybody play." The male voice was unwavering, but thin, missing the punch that accompanies most demands. It sounded almost reticent, as if another person stood behind, compelling the voice to deliver its lines.

"Playing time is between me and my players. And their parents. Other than that, it's no one's business. Now, who are you? Are you a parent?" The caller said nothing. "If you won't tell me, I have nothing more to say."

My voice was testy. Maddie must have heard and came out of the front room to stand next to me. She frowned and cocked her head toward the phone, trying to listen.

"I'm not the important person here. You are. Every boy on your team wants to play in the game. That's why they sign-up. It's your responsibly to see they do."

"I appreciate the advice from such an obviously knowledgeable person. However, unless you're a parent and identify yourself, we have nothing to discuss."

"We do."

"I think not."

"If you continue to hold kids out of games, you'll regret it."

"What do you mean 'regret it'?"

"Just what I said. You'll regret it."

The line went silent.

"Who was that?" Maddie asked.

"Some guy who didn't like my playing time decisions Sunday. He never identified himself and I didn't recognize the voice."

"Strange."

"That's what I thought, too. At first. Just strange. Then, he finished, 'you'll regret it'."

"What? He said, what?"

"You'll regret it."

Maddie had already washed off what little make-up she wore. Its absence lightened the color of her skin, as did the pale pink and gray flannel robe she wore. But that simple phrase 'you'll regret it' depleted her color further. She was ashen.

"He didn't elaborate," I said.

"Doug, that sounds like a threat."

"Yeah, it does."

"Let's call the police." She picked up the phone and started to dial.

"I'm not sure we want to do that. The guy didn't sound angry. Or crazy. He sounded more like somebody who wanted to register a complaint."

"He said, 'you'll regret it.' Right? That's a threat any way you look at it."

"Let's go back into the front room and talk about it first."

"I'd just as soon call the police. Right now," Maddie said, raising the receiver.

"Come on." I put my hand around her bicep and nudged her toward the front room. She laid the instrument back in its cradle. We reached our chairs, but neither of us picked up our reading material.

"Let's think about this for a minute," I said. "It's reasonable to assume the caller was the dad of one of the two kids who didn't play Sunday. If not them, then one of the subs who only played a few minutes. That's six kids and five dads."

"Six kids and five dads?"

"We have a set of twins. Remember? Take out the two dads I met after the game who told me how pleased they were with the team, and we're down to three possibilities." My front teeth scraped my curled lower lip as I considered the options. "Maybe I should call each of them on some pretext and see if I recognize the voice."

"Let's say you call and suppose you recognize a voice, then what? That's not a time to play-it-by-ear." Maddie's face wore a troubled expression. She looked washed-out and grim. But her faded appearance contrasted sharply to the crisp sounds coming from her lips.

The phone rang, again. She stiffened.

"Relax. I'll get it." I jumped up and ran to pick up the phone.

"Doug, it's Jordan."

I placed my hand over the receiver and called to Maddie, "No worries, dear. It's Jordan."

"Hi, Jordan. What's up?"

"I just got a threatening phone call."

"From whom? About what?"

"I don't know who the guy was, but it was about playing time in Sunday's game."

"Someone's busy. I think I got the same call about ten minutes ago."

"Really?"

"Yes, and I think I've already narrowed the caller down to one of three dads. All had kids on your team last year. Did you recognize the voice?"

"Geez. No, I didn't. I wasn't listening for that."

"Are you sure?"

"Yeah. What are you going to do, Doug? Threats. That's serious business."

"I'm inclined to let it pass for a while and snoop around in the meantime. Some guy may just be in a pissy mood tonight, though Maddie thinks we should call the police."

"If he were just in a pissy mood, why would he have waited a few days to call? Why wouldn't he have called Sunday night right after the game?"

"Good point. I don't know."

"So, if you've narrowed it to three dads from my old team, but I can't recognize the voice … Something's not right, Doug. I like Maddie's idea. Let's call the police."

"Do you really want to call the cops on one of our kids' parents?"

"If it's a parent, 'no'."

"Who else could it be?"

"What about Montgomery Wise? He's a sanctimonious, holier-than thou, do-gooder who wants to change the world in his own warped image. And he doesn't like you. I wouldn't put it past him."

"You've never met Wise, though I won't argue with your characterization of the guy. But, nah. It's not him. I'd have recognized his voice right away."

"If you're sure."

"It has to be one of the three dads. Who else would even care?"

"Makes sense."

"Let's sleep on it and we'll talk after practice tomorrow."

I hung up the phone and walked back into the front room. Maddie sat, erect in her chair, waiting. "That was Jordan. He got the same call."

"Did the guy threaten Jordan, too?"

"Yeah."

"And? What are you going to do?"

"We'll talk about it after practice tomorrow."

"I don't like it, Doug. Getting threatening calls about a fifth-grade basketball game. That's ridiculous. And scary."

Jordan and I sat in the bleachers after practice while our sons collected their things. "Thought any more about the phone calls?" Jordan asked.

"More than they deserve, but Maddie's terrified."

"I was lucky. Jill was taking a shower when I got mine. She doesn't even know about it, and I plan to keep it that way. At least until we decide what to do."

"Here's my thinking. We won't have to worry about any more threats for the next couple of weeks. Everybody'll get plenty of playing time this Sunday against St. Katherine's. Our prospects against them are dismal. I'm not as sure about the following week's game. But the guys we play then seem to be successful, too."

"That doesn't bring us closer to identifying our caller, though. It just postpones things."

"Not really. The game after next is at St. Jerome's. That means everybody will go to Giorgio's after the game." I handed Jordan a 3 X 5 card. "Here are the names of our three dads. We'll talk to each of them there and pinpoint the voice of our guy. Your job is to be sure they all get to Giorgio's."

"How am I supposed to do that?"

"You're the assistant coach. You're the smart one."

"How can you be so certain it's one of these three? I still think we shouldn't forget about Montgomery Wise."

"It has to be one of them. I repeat: who else would it be?"

"Okay. Let's say we identify the guy. Then what?"

"We read him the riot act, right there."

The second game of the season was the disaster I'd foreseen. We not only lost, we were crushed, and the outcome was decided well before half-time. I wasn't prescient. Last year my team had struggled to beat St. Katherine's playing at St. Jerome's in the infamous professional photographer game. This year we not only played at St. Katherine's, but I was told they added two quality players over the summer and the prior week they'd walloped Fred Bauer's St. Leo's team.

My consolation was that our substitutes played long, though agonizing, stretches. I doubted they were having much fun getting clobbered as they were. Still, they were in the game, and playing, and their floor time allowed me to conserve minutes for our starting group, which I could bank for games we had a chance to win. Neither Jordan nor I would likely receive a phone call this week.

Carleton's pal, Freddie, was on the court with other subs finishing the final brutal minutes. He was one of our poorest players, so it came as no surprise to anyone that while hovering over the ball trying to dribble, he illegally touched it with both hands. The blow-out had left the gym quiet, the silence broken only by the muted hum of casual conversation coming from the few people remaining in the bleachers. Freddie's mistake interrupted the bland monotony on the court and brought an outburst of laughter. Silence quickly returned and individual voices became audible again. "Did you see that kid?" a middle-aged man in a black overcoat said. He elbowed the guy standing next to him. "Both hands? You've got to be kidding me."

"Pretty bad, huh? Looks like he's just slapping at the ball," his companion replied. They both snickered while attempting to cover their mouths with little effort or success.

"If I had a kid like that, I'd be too embarrassed to let him play," said the first.

"Yeah. He should be playing with dolls instead."

The couple seated in the bleachers next to the standing men drew back at the last remark. They didn't seem to appreciate the pair's commentary, or at least its volume. One of them, a prim older lady glared at them, and after a dismissive pause, said, "Couldn't you say it a little louder?"

The commotion caught the attention of three teenage boys seated in the front row not far away. They'd intermittently watched play, but mostly jawed and poked one another accompanied by an occasional smattering of laughter. I saw the middle kid peek up long enough to see Freddie run past him down the court.

"Look at that kid prance. You think he's wearing a diaper under those trucks?" The teen's voice carried above the crowd's murmurs. The entire gym and every player on the floor had to hear him. He nudged his companions who responded to his tasteless humor with a round of guffaws. Then noticing his newly attained prominence, he fell to one knee, swiveled his neck to follow Freddie, and peered upward as if he were trying to look underneath a tablecloth or a skirt. "I don't see anything hanging out," he said.

"That doesn't mean one isn't there," said his buddy on the left. "Look how he's bent over. Butt sticking out. You could easily pack a diaper in there, and no one would notice."

"Do you think it's filled?" the third replied, bending over and laughing at his contribution.

"Could be. Look at him." The obnoxious instigator bounced from the floor and with elevated wrists hanging limp, tip-toed along the sideline, rear extended, knees flaying inward mocking Freddie's unusual and awkward gate. I seethed at their ridicule.

Freddie had to hear the teenagers as he likely had heard the adults prior. Yet his expression remained impassive. He was trying to ignore the sounds, but I saw his lips and cheeks begin to quiver.

"Ref! Ref!" I shouted. I called time-out and jerked my head toward the bench. "Rollie get in there for Freddie."

Freddie ran off the court, head bowed, eyes fixed on a seat at the end of the bench. But before he could reach his destination, I grabbed his attention and beckoned him. He reached me as the final buzzer sounded. I could see moisture gathering in the corners of his eyes. But he seemed determined not to yield to the accumulating water.

"Freddie," I said putting both my hands on his shoulders, "those jerks in the bleachers were just looking for something to do. So, they decided to pick on you. Why? Who knows? Guess they just wanted to show off. To feel important. Well, they showed off all right. They showed they were immature morons. They knew you couldn't fight back because you were playing on a team. You had to think about your teammates first. Not what they were saying. I'm proud of the way you handled the situation, Freddie. You're twice the man they are."

Freddie looked up at me. He tried to smile, but he couldn't dam every tear.

Barney ambled into practice right on schedule. Ty had told me last week that Dallas wanted Barney to produce another feature for the annual report like last year's, only longer and more focused on the boys taking part. His prior feature had been a hit in the corporate suites, and they said a complementary effort would burnish the image Steiger Bros. wanted to project. Both accepted their assignment with relish. It was an easy A. No one had to do much, and the credit rolled in.

When Ty announced Barney's new project, I had three responses. First, the team differed from last season's and wouldn't be as good. There would be no breathtaking finish like last year. Second, I wasn't thrilled with Barney hanging around. It was annoying last season, and I wanted no repeat. Third, I insisted

Barney get the consent of my co-coach for his plans. I fudged Jordan's title to ensure Barney took him seriously while neglecting to mention that my co-coach distrusted him and suspected his motives.

Jordan and I'd arranged for our sons to get rides home with other parents after practice. When the kids were gone, we grabbed our coats and escorted Barney to Giorgio's. The PR guy, first through the door, headed to his favorite booth in the darkest recesses of the place. Jordan and I looked at one another questioning his choice but followed and sat down.

"I believe you two have met before," I said. "You should know Barney that Jordan is my co-coach this season, and he also has a son on the team."

The words had barely escaped my lips when Jordan plowed ahead. "Tell me about the project you're conducting on our kids." I noticed he used the preposition 'on', not 'about' or even 'with'. His word choice tipped that he intended an adversarial discussion.

Barney started to regurgitate the company line. The project was to create a feature for the company's annual report about employee volunteer activity using company-provided flextime. It was the thousandth time I'd heard his spiel, and each time it sounded more inconsequential. But at least he was consistent. Barney didn't change one rehearsed word.

When he finished, Jordan was blunt. "I don't believe you." He glared at Barney, mustache twitching.

Barney looked at me for an explanation, though I was no less taken-aback by Jordan than he was. I'd expected Jordan to question Barney sharply, but starting the conversation by calling him a liar didn't sit well with me. What was Jordan's plan? Did he even have one?

"What's going on here?" Barney was insulted.

"I don't believe you," Jordan repeated, emphasizing his point.

"Doug, what's going on here?"

"Don't ask Doug. He doesn't know."

Jordan was right about that.

"I've been following this entire affair for a while, back to last year when Doug and I were just friends. He smelled something funny about all the months you spent researching his team. We both wondered how you could devote so much time working on so little. I could have written the annual report's feature in an afternoon. That leads to the conclusion you're either the world's biggest goldbricker or the slowest guy not in special education."

"What are you taking about?" Barney protested. "I don't believe in just throwing things together, particularly something as important to the company as its annual report. I'll have you know I got a bonus for that feature. You don't get a bonus for sloppy work."

"That's not the point," Jordan said. "You could have researched and written a novel in the time it took you to write those few column inches."

Our meals had been served quickly, but no one had yet touched them. Their beer glasses remained full. I'd almost drained mine and was searching for another.

"Look," Jordan said, glowering at Barney, "I don't think you're either lazy or a fool. I think something's going on."

"Like what?" I could tell Barney was growing tired of the interrogation.

"You tell me. If it's not lazy or stupid, what else is there?"

"Why do you think something else is there?"

"Because no other explanation makes sense."

"What doesn't make sense?" Barney asked. "This is getting ridiculous." He started gathering his things. "I don't have to take this from anybody."

"Okay. You don't like it. Then let me ask you about the professional photographer and all the pictures you had shot of Doug's team last year. I can't imagine they were cheap, and I'll bet you didn't personally pay for them. Why'd you take them? What did you do with them?"

"Each kid got an action photo of himself on the court. They loved them. Didn't they, Doug?"

I nodded. "They did, Barney. Travis keeps his on the wall next to his bed."

Barney scowled at Jordan.

"You aren't arguing that you hired that expensive professional sports photographer to take pictures as souvenirs for the kids?"

"No. I had plans for them," Barney said.

"Yeah. Doug told me. To put in the pictureless *Readers' Digest*."

"Things didn't go as planned. I had some other thoughts, too."

Barney again reached for his jacket.

"What was that professional sports photographer's name?" Jordan mused, stumbling as if trying to recall one he should know. "Bert … Bert … Bert Pratt. That's it. I should have remembered Bert's handle easily since I just spoke with him last week."

Barney's hand drew away from his jacket.

"I visited Bert's studio because I was interested in him taking some action shots of a fifth-grade basketball team. He said that was a coincidence. He'd taken some photos of a fourth-grade team the year before. Since he'd taken some, I asked if he had any samples he could show me. It didn't take long for him to find the file and for me to examine the photos."

Barney squirmed.

"They were the ones you paid him to shoot."

"So? No secret there."

"The pictures were remarkable, Barney. You sure hired the right guy. But as I was thumbing through the shots, I spotted something strange."

"With the photos?" Barney asked.

"No. In them. I didn't notice at first, but the second time through it seemed George Kovac was in about every other picture. Remember George Kovac? The kid now back in Massachusetts."

I'd observed the same thing when Barney brought the folder of pictures to the gym to give to the kids. He had many more pictures than he needed, and a large share of them seemed to be of George. I remember mentioning it to Maddie. We both had shrugged it off.

"I asked the photographer why he had so many pictures of this one kid." Jabbing a finger straight at Barney's chest, Jordan said, "He told me that you, that's you, Barney, asked him to do it. Why?" Jordan's finger still jabbed. "Why?"

Jordan slid back and took a sip of his beer. Barney and I looked at each other, him seemingly as confused as I felt.

"You know what Bert said when I asked him?" Jordan said, sliding forward again. "He said that he assumed George was your son, or your nephew, or Doug's kid. Someone special. Now I know George isn't Doug's kid and I don't think George is yours. What about a nephew? The son of a friend? Someone special?"

"I don't have to tell you anything," Barney said. His missing chin extended as far as it would reach.

"You're right. You don't have to tell us anything. But the cops might be interested about you wanting pictures of kids. Even if the cops aren't, word will spread. Doug won't have to say a thing. But your boss will hear about it and when he does, how do you explain all the company's money spent on those pictures?"

Barney twisted the beer glass between his fingers and said nothing. The longer he was silent, the more miserable he looked. He threw up his hands in a gesture of futility, then lowered them as if to retract the thought he'd just had.

Jordan said nothing while Barney stewed. I felt sorry for the guy. If he had a plausible explanation, now was the time to disclose it.

"Jordan," Barney said, "get us another round." We didn't need more beers as two of the three glasses were still almost full. Barney obviously wanted to speak with me in private.

"Same for everybody?" Jordan asked as he headed for the bar.

"What can we do to keep this from Ty?" Barney asked. I now knew he hadn't just made an error in judgment or hadn't just miscalculated his abilities to place a promotional piece in a national publication. He had ulterior motives, as Jordan had long suspected, and I'd been too naïve to appreciate.

"It depends, Barney. I have no idea what you're hiding. If it's criminal, or even lurid, I'll have little sympathy. Something else, I'll listen, and you'll have to trust me." He had no other option.

Barney exhaled in a loud breath as Jordan slipped back into place, distributed the beers, and waited.

"My name isn't Barney Ambrose," the interrogated began. "My given name is Rajko, and I'm the son of Vilim and Maja Blažeković, Croatian immigrants. When I decided I wanted to go into the PR business sometime around my junior year in college, no one in that line of work had a name like Rajko. My friends called me Rog, and that worked. But then there was Blažeković, and that didn't. So, I changed my Croatian name to something more familiar, something you might easily find in the business. My parents weren't happy. They felt I was rejecting my heritage. It wasn't that at all. I was just a young guy who wanted to get ahead."

"How did you ever come up with 'Barney Ambrose'?" I asked.

"That's another couple of hours. I'll tell you sometime."

"Can't we just stick to the story?" Jordan said. My interruption irritated him.

"You guys remember a few years ago reading about the war in the Balkans? Bosnia? Serbia? My people come from that part of the world and I still have relatives living there, including a first cousin, Tea Ćurković. She and her husband, Grgur Kovač, and their son, Juro, lived near the Croatian border with Bosnia. Grgur was a contractor. He built and remodeled houses throughout the region with his two brothers. My cousin told me it was a good business which, with her salary as a nurse, provided them a comfortable living."

I was already fascinated by Barney's story.

"The Homeland War, our name for the war of independence from what was then Yugoslavia, ended all that. My cousin lived in a relatively peaceful area with mostly Croat neighbors. Most of the fighting was elsewhere, but between flare-ups of local violence, the displacement of people, and losing non-Croat customers, Grgur's business was severely damaged. Still, he kept it alive."

Jordan groaned. He obviously wasn't as enthralled by the story as I was.

"It was summer. Juro was out of school, and Grgur was planning a quick business trip to see scattered suppliers and customers. Those that remained."

Jordan twirled the tips of his mustache between his thumbs and forefingers. Then he tapped his foot on the floor and rustled through his coat pockets looking for heaven-only knows what. "Barney, could we cut to the chase here," Jordan said. His tone was ill-mannered. "All this family history can't be necessary. Let's move on."

"You want to hear it or not?" Barney snarled. His voice was filled with rage. Soon, he settled back and started again, though the scowl he wore displayed his continuing displeasure with Jordan. "Grgur and Juro were away from home and got caught up in an outbreak of violence. The two went missing. My cousin tried to find them, but she couldn't. Then, hostilities spread to their town, and the violence forced her to flee. Even if Grgur and Juro were okay, they couldn't go back to look for Tea. They were lost to one another."

My second beer sat on the table, untouched.

"Tea contacted everyone she knew, including my parents and me, asking for any information we might have about Grgur and Juro. She hoped that if they couldn't find her at home, they might find her through a relative. Her letter to me asked if I knew anything about her husband and son's whereabouts. I was sympathetic, even though I'd never met her. I wrote her back to say I knew nothing but would reply if something came up. That was two or three years ago."

Barney took a swig from his glass and cleared his throat. "Well, something came up." He stared at me. "When you gave me the list of kids on your fourth-grade team a name flashed off the page, George Kovac."

"So?" Jordan said. He and I exchanged puzzled glances.

"The English translation for Juro is George. Kovač's a common name in Croatia. Croats are mostly Catholic, and George attended Catholic school at home. Interesting coincidences. There's another coincidence you'll recognize," Barney said in a mocking tone. He transferred his stare to Jordan.

"The old man's in the construction business," said my co-coach, who now showed a keen interest in the story.

"Right. The construction business. So, I wrote my cousin, trying not to generate false hopes. I asked her how old Juro was, and then she telephoned. Do you know how hard and expensive that was for her? She spoke no English, and I spoke no Croatian. Total mistake, but somehow, I got the impression that the boy's age was ten. She sent a follow-up letter to confirm Juro's age and a September birthday. Ten years old, the age of a fourth-grader."

"Why didn't you just ask his dad?" I said. "He could have confirmed whether George was Juro."

"How successful were you reaching George's dad, and you were the kid's coach?" Barney asked.

My head tilted, and lips tightened, acknowledging the veracity of his observation.

"Didn't think so. I saw him only once at Giorgio's. Without a wife, I might add. Do you know anyone who engaged him in conversation? Or saw George's mother?"

"Doug, did George have an accent?" Jordan asked. "If he had just come to this country, he must have had an accent."

"He never said very much, and besides, I wasn't listening for one. Now that you mention it, though. Yeah, kind of."

Jordan wrinkled his forehead and scratched his nose. "But was it a Croatian accent or a Massachusetts accent? New Englanders talk funny, you know. Did he say fa instead of far?"

"I don't remember."

Jordan harrumphed, "Weren't you paying attention?"

"I hope you now appreciate the pictures," Barney said. He opened the palms of his hands as if seeking understanding and even a modicum of empathy. "The only way I could help my cousin was to take pictures of the kid. And how could I take pictures of him without raising suspicion? I suppose I could've hired a private detective or something like that. But I don't know that world. Besides, only perverts do that kind of stuff, and I'm certainly not one of them. I wanted pictures for the right reasons, not the wrong ones."

"Okay. I get the pictures of George playing. But all those pictures at Giorgio's? What was that all about?" I asked.

"We were hoping to catch Grgur. I didn't know what he looked like, so I told Bert to take pictures of every adult male in sight. Maybe he'd be in one of them."

"George's dad wasn't even there that day."

"So, I learned."

I hadn't accused Barney of wrongdoing as had Jordan, but my thoughts often were as maleficent. I now felt guilty about that. Barney had always been a non-entity to me until he inserted himself into my business. Then he became an annoyance, and finally a suspect. Of what I didn't know and wasn't inclined to explore as long as he stayed away from my kids and me. His job made that impossible, and now I learned that his greatest intrusion was his last, most desperate effort to reunite a family separated by conflict.

"Did you send the pictures? Have you heard? What happened?" Jordan almost shouted.

"Yes," Barney answered. His voice was flat. "George was not Tea's Juro." He gathered his jacket and squeezed out of the booth. As he was leaving, he turned and looked at me piteously.

"Ty has no reason to know," I said. "For what's it's worth Barney, my assessment of you as a human being has risen considerably over the last hour."

Barney smiled lifelessly, turned, and left.

Jordan and I sat, deflated. We'd expected a story, but not the one we heard. Not one that made Barney a sympathetic character. We'd looked for the worst and found the best, a situation where motive, if not execution, was unassailable.

We looked at one another in disbelief until no longer able to tolerate the silence, Jordan asked, "You don't think he was lying, do you?"

"No, I don't," I said, shaking my head. "Let's get out of here."

I picked up my things and put on my coat.

"Jordan," I asked as we left Giorgio's, "after talking to Bert Pratt, are you going to hire him to take action shots of this year's team?"

"Are you kidding? You should see his rates."

St. Jerome's played its third game of the season against St. James, a new school in the diocese that had won its first two by relatively large margins. But midway through the second quarter, our match remained close. I had yet to substitute. The game was still a potential win though, and I didn't want to jeopardize our chances until I got a better feel for our prospects. As I considered my options, a voice in the bleachers soared above the crowd noise, "Put Freddie in. Put Freddie in." The voice didn't register. Just more untargeted background noise and I ignored it. Soon, a squeakier tone sounded, "Put Freddie in. Put Freddie in." Then, "Free Freddie. Free Freddie." This time the voice caught my attention, and I remembered Fred Bauer telling me about the loathsome dad who kept chanting, "Put Richard in. Put Richard in." The voice was too thin for the story to be repeating itself. But the similarity was eerie.

While Freddie played several minutes the previous week against St. Katherine's, he was one of the two substitutes who didn't get in the opening game. After the third shout to 'put Freddie in', I looked toward the boy sitting near the end of the bench and saw him blushing. A further outburst somewhere in the crowd deepened the color in his face. The two kids sitting on opposite sides of him cupped their hands into mini-megaphones and chattered into Freddie's ears. He swatted at his tormentors.

"Cut it out. We have a ball game here," I yelled at the unruly kids down the bench. "Jordan, find out what's going on."

The score remained close to the buzzer announcing the end of the first half.

"What was all the commotion about?" I asked my assistant.

"I think an older brother and friends are giving a younger brother a hard time," Jordan said.

"Teenagers. Annoying age. Is Freddie okay?"

"Embarrassed. But I think he's fine."

"Any idea where our noisemakers are sitting? I have no problem going into the bleachers and having a little heart-to-heart with those kids."

"I heard them but didn't see them."

I looked over into the half-filled stands and nothing attracted my attention. But then, I didn't know what I was looking for. My interest returned to a more pressing matter.

"Half-time, Jordan. We're down by two. Is this a win?"

"It could go either way." Jordan pawed the floor with the toe of his clean white sneaker.

"Eight kids to play. We used the starting five the entire first half and we're about even. Is this a win?"

Jordan didn't look up. "Let's start the second half with some of our subs in the game and see how it goes. If we slip further behind, we can go back to the first group."

"Sure you want to do that? Slip behind a couple more points and it'll be impossible to recover. We don't have enough talent."

"Yeah. I think so."

"Okay." I had little more belief in our prospects than my assistant did and I recognized we had a strategy to follow. But concession at this point irritated me.

Vince and Carleton entered the game to start the second half. St. James scored immediately and then scored again. Zack returned the ball following the second score and passed it to Rickie, who began to freelance, burying his head and dribbling in circles until his first opportunity to take a shot arrived. When it came, the ball fell nowhere near the hoop, and St. James possessed it again. Perhaps Rickie was frustrated; perhaps he was desperate; perhaps he had panicked. It was possible, even likely, that he had so little confidence in the substitutes, he was trying to compensate for player skills now assigned to the bench. Still, I couldn't blame the substitutes for Rickie's undisciplined performance, and replaced him at the first opportunity. By then St. James's lead had swelled to nine points, and the game was effectively over. Substitutes filled the floor for the rest of the contest, Freddie among them.

We'd never experienced a loss prior to our ritual at Giorgio's, so no one knew how to act when we fell short against St. James. The place was subdued. No one had much to say. The beating wasn't just a 'we got a bad call', an 'if the ball would have just rolled in,' or an 'if we had had one break.' We got blistered for the second consecutive week and no excuses or 'what ifs' could disguise that fact. Despite a competitive first half, the loss was ugly and the faces and voices of the boys eating pizza at the kids' table reflected it.

The sad truth was St. Jerome's fifth-grade basketball team wasn't very good. That was difficult for most players and parents to accept. They'd assumed that the fifth-grade team would pick up where last year's fourth-grade team left off. I was an exception, and so was Travis. I accepted significant differences existed between the team this year and last, none of which worked to our advantage. But even I had underestimated their size, and I'd done so dramatically.

The descent into reality proved more difficult for some than others. I found it harder than Jordan, if for no other reason than because I was accustomed to winning and he wasn't. Most parents found it harder than I because their expectations were so much higher. And the kids? They just looked bewildered.

The day's reward for Jordan and me was that none of the three parents I'd identified as the possible mysterious caller could have been. Jordan had induced the three to show up at Giorgio's where we eliminated each. One because of a heavy, deep voice, and I almost yelled at Jordan for missing that obvious misfit; a second because he'd just returned from an extended business trip that had him out of the country when the calls were made; and a third because of a slight speech impediment, almost inaudible, but distinct enough to remove him from our list. We were happy to absolve them, but that didn't unravel our dilemma. If one of them hadn't been the caller, who was?

JANUARY'S A COLD MONTH

St. Jerome's was scheduled to play St. Stephen's the Sunday after Thanksgiving. We had beaten St. Stephen's soundly last season, and they'd yet to win a game this. The match presented a superb opportunity to balance our win-loss record following an eked-out victory in the opener and two thrashings the ensuing weeks. The season was still young, leaving time for our team to recover and finish decently.

We'd experienced more difficulties than our record showed. Zack and Travis competed as fiercely as ever, but the team had simply played poorly, even during our win. I grew increasingly concerned. Casey, who had always played cerebrally, began to think through every motion before making it. He moved more and more stiffly, one programmed step after the other. The worse our team performed, the more he tried to think his way through his problems. The more he thought, the more mechanically he played, and the poorer the result. I begged him to relax and have fun. But the more I implored him to just play, the more he retreated into his own thoughts and the worse he became. I stopped pleading and tried empathizing, but without effect.

Rickie now free-lanced more often than ever. He would lose track of teammates, playing his own self-indulgent game. Occasionally, his single-minded roving benefited the team. However, those successes only encouraged him to go off on his own more often with a result usually less sparkling. His play grew more aggravating. Other team members noticed, and weren't happy with it, including those who played little. My only recourse was to bench him, but that created its own problems because I had no one capable of replacing him. Rickie seemed to intuitively understand my predicament, and while it was likely he didn't intend to defy me or his teammates, that was the practical effect.

And, Andy? He just ran, enthusiastically, but uncontrollably. No matter how hard Jordan and I tried to integrate his play with the others, he always seemed out of place.

After Monday's practice, Jordan walked up to me and said, "You won't believe this."

"What won't I believe?"

"Rickie just told me he wouldn't be here for the St. Stephen's game, Sunday. He said his family is going to his grandmother's for Thanksgiving and he wouldn't get back in time."

My reaction was anger, but not surprise. Celeste Hanson ran the Hansen household and if she decided Sunday's game wasn't important, neither Rickie nor her husband would challenge her. I'd still call John Hanson when I got home and raise a ruckus. Rickie had signed up to play for the season, not to make cameo appearances when it pleased his mother, and I'd make sure the Hansens understood that.

Later in the evening, I called the Hansen household. Rickie answered and immediately put his dad on the line.

"John. Doug Elliot. What's this I hear about Rickie not being around for Sunday's game?"

"Oh. Yeah. We're going to the mother-in-law's for Thanksgiving and he won't be back in time."

"The game's been on the schedule since the beginning of the year. This isn't something that just sprang up. Players can't show up for some games and not for others."

"This is the first game Rickie's missed."

"So? You're not supposed to miss any games. Ever."

"It's just one of those things."

"One of those things?" I was flabbergasted. "What about commitment? Responsibility? Loyalty? Where do they fit?"

While we were busy exchanging barbed civilities, Maddie walked by and whispered, "They went to Celeste's mother's last year, too, and made it back for the game."

We shared a smile. Ammunition.

"Look, John. I know you went to your mother-in-law's place for your turkey last year. You drove back Saturday, missed all the traffic, and Rickie got plenty of rest for Sunday's game. Why don't you do the same this year?"

"We thought we'd stay a few extra days. Her mom's not getting any younger, you know."

"Come on, John. What's going on?" The line was silent for a long time. "John?"

"It's not the same, Doug."

"What's not the same?"

"Isn't it obvious? We've already lost two games. By big scores. Half of the kids on the team don't know how to bounce a ball. It's not fun like last year."

"For you or for Rickie?" He had no reply. "We're only three games into the season. Don't you think it's a little early to throw in the towel?" I changed approaches. "Look, we play St. Stephen's Sunday. We should beat them, assuming Rickie plays. A win evens our record. Who knows what will happen after that?"

"I don't think so, Doug. My wife's adamant about staying at her mother's the entire weekend."

"And she has the last word?"

Jordan arrived for Wednesday's practice wearing his purple warm-up suit. I hadn't seen him in any other clothing since the start of the season.

"You wear that thing to bed, too?"

"No. I switch to a pair of purple pajamas." I cocked my head in disbelief. "Don't believe me? They're flannel. Nice and warm."

I chuckled and shook my head. "Looks like we'll be short tonight, Jordan. How many kids do you count?

"Seven."

"I guess no one's having Thanksgiving at home this year. They're all on the road with the Hansens leading the procession out of town."

"Ricky won't be here Sunday, then?"

"No. I talked to John Hansen two nights ago. His wife's still in charge and she's lost interest."

"Art's dad called and told me his family would be out of town, too" Jordan said.

"That won't affect the game's outcome. Anybody else going to be missing?"

"Larry's Dad told me a long time ago that he'd miss the Sunday after Thanksgiving."

"Okay. This is a must win, Jordan. Not only is St. Stephen's winless, they've been thrashed in all three outings, including by St. Joseph's, and that's the only team we've beaten. I doubt we'll get a better chance to win. Our best five players, the entire way?"

"I suppose. If this is a must-win, " Jordan said. "I wonder if we'll be entertaining any threatening phone calls next week?"

Only eight members of the team showed to play St. Stephen's. Worse things could have happened. Eight players had advantages as we'd experienced the prior season. The question was, could we put enough skill on the floor at any one time to make a difference?

If all went well, St. Jerome's would claim a win and everyone who bothered to show would have abundant playing time. But all didn't go well. From the beginning St. Stephen's played an unconventional, flat-out crazy, four on two defense with one man floating. They guarded Zack and Travis and ignored everyone else. I couldn't figure out if their play was purposeful or undisciplined. Regardless, it was effective.

Zack, hobbled by the relentless pawing of two, sometimes three, hovering opponents, tried to get the ball to the usually undefended Casey. Yet, Casey always seemed late or out of place. For all his faults, Rickie was never late. His style of play would have fit beautifully against St. Stephen's. He could have scored at will. While that would have made him insufferable in the games to follow, I would've happily overlooked his free-lancing for the time being.

I grew angrier and angrier at the Hansens and their Thanksgiving excursion. What a difference a year makes. Rickie's parents knew little about the game, then or now. But they could read the scoreboard, and so long as the score was favorable, which it almost always was last season, they were the first at Giorgio's laughing and celebrating. A year later they knew little more about the game, but they could still read the scoreboard, though now it posted numbers they rarely liked. So, the Hansen's extended their holiday; enjoyed their relatives; and didn't worry about Rickie's team.

St. Stephen's had its own problems. As I suspected, their team was bad, and the game grew sloppy. One muffed ball followed by one kicked out-of-bounds followed by a player running without dribbling. Fouls regularly interrupted play, though no one seemed able to convert a free throw. The score at the end of the first quarter was 5 - 4. St. Jerome's led.

The quality of play grew no better as the game progressed. The sole interesting part was the score. It remained close. No more than two points ever separated the two teams. Any basket or free throw made was a major event. But St. Stephen's odd defense led to one positive outcome. It made no difference who I played other than Zack and Travis and sometimes Casey. The other kids were interchangeable, and I interchanged them often and without effect.

With a minute left in the game, the smallest kid on the St. Stephen's team threw in a basket, putting his side ahead by three points. Neither team would score again, and the game ended with a 20 - 17 count.

St. Stephen's had won, and though the game was atrociously played, a festive crowd of local parishioners witnessed their team's first victory of the season. And likely its last. I was glad we'd played at St. Stephen's. A trip to Giorgio's would have been unbearable.

Jordan arrived for Monday's practice dressed in his purple warm-up. He was taciturn. His head bowed a little; the bounce in his step absent; his eyes glazed more than glimmered. I'd taken the previous day's loss hard, but Jordan appeared to have taken it harder.

"What's wrong, Jordan?"

"Yesterday should have been a win."

"Sure should have been."

"We're 1 - 3. I was expecting better."

"What did you expect?"

"Hard to say. The only reason I started this coaching thing was to be with Carleton. I achieve that goal every minute I'm with him, every time we talk about a practice or a game, every time I drive him to the gym. It's been great, and I still enjoy it. I really do." Jordan stiffened. "But I want more. I want to win, too. Maybe not every game. But at least those we should win. Yesterday we should've won and didn't. That infuriates me."

I smiled. "Winning's a narcotic, you know."

"I'm not addicted yet, though I may be on my way."

"What about playing just for the fun of playing?"

"Not as long as you keep score."

"And if you don't keep score?"

"You still know the score. You can't escape it."

The change in my friend's attitude was astonishing. We couldn't have had this conversation a year ago. The language we shared today would then have sounded as different dialects. Common words would have held different meaning; common phrases, different nuance. Jordan's single win seemed to provide the common reference point that changed our communication.

"How do you want to handle yesterday's no-shows?" I said.

"Sit them. Put their rears on the bench."

"You know that's just routine for some of yesterday's absentees."

The corners of Jordan's mouth rose for the first time since he entered the building. "For a couple others though, one in particular, it'll come as a real jolt."

"Yeah. Our chances of winning next week with or without Rickie are somewhere between slim and none, so it would be a good time, even a propitious time, to make a point."

We both chortled.

"While we're on the subject," Jordan asked, "how are we going to handle Christmas and New Year's? They're both on Monday this year."

"The kids get off the Tuesday before Christmas and come back the Wednesday after New Year's. Louganis told me the gym will be locked tighter than Scrooge's wallet between."

"Didn't you practice last year during the holidays?

"That was last year. Sister Cecelia changed the rules."

"We practice the Wednesday the kids return, then?"

"Yup."

"King holiday? President's Day? The kids have both those Mondays off."

"I can get into the gym both of those days," I said, donning a sly look. "Have a little juice with the janitorial staff now despite the wet paper towel fight. Louganis and I are buddy-buddy, and it only cost me a case of beer and an hour of listening to his woes. Not a big Sister Cecelia fan."

"You'd better send a notice to the parents about practice on those days. There'll be complaining. With a note, no one can say they didn't know."

"The schedule already claims those Mondays as practice days. I suppose a reminder won't hurt, though."

The kids took home my letter Wednesday reminding the parents of practices on the King holiday and President's Day. Jordan and I also made our point about missing games. We sat Rickie for most of the following contest, and reduced the playing time for other absentees, especially those of the impromptu variety. The reedy blond kid never asked the reason for his seat on the bench. He knew why he sat, even if his mother didn't.

The days between Thanksgiving and Christmas yielded nothing thankful or joyous. The beatings kept coming, and the frustration kept growing. The competitive balance in the league had changed from the prior year. Significantly. Not only were the relative skills of opponents better, ours were poorer. Zack remained the premier player in the league, but even he couldn't compensate for George's loss and the addition of multiple kids with non-existent playing ability.

Jordan and I continued to work with the team despite the lack of success on the court. We took any marginal improvements, of which there were few, as grand achievements. There was nothing else to cheer.

Barney announced he was leaving Steiger Bros. at the start of the new year and would go to work for an outfit in Philadelphia. I wasn't sad to learn of his departure because I'd never thought he contributed much to our operation. Still, I didn't feel I'd treated him fairly. He'd had a job to do, and I'd made it harder than it should have been.

The office arranged a going-away party for him a few days before Christmas. Barney told me that evening that he wasn't being replaced. A PR guy from Dallas would write the feature for the annual report, and he would contact me in the new year. I asked Barney if he'd heard anything new about his cousin in Croatia, and he said he hadn't. With that, my ambivalent relationship with Barney Ambrose ended.

The next practice I told Jordan about Barney leaving. "Odd duck," was all he said.

St. Jerome's won its first game of the new year and the first since the opening game of the season. The opponent had a winning record, usually a reliable indicator of team quality at this point in the season. Our kids had practiced only once in the prior two weeks, and it had merely scrubbed off the rust they'd accumulated over Christmas. Yet, before a sprinkling of followers at home, our team played its best game of the season.

The kids earned the win, and Jordan and I were proud of their effort. Everyone played. But when we adjourned to Giorgio's for our victory gala, the mood was subdued. No one seemed excited, let alone festive. Casey's parents attended. So did Rickie's, though our two families were barely on speaking terms following Rickie's benching for his Thanksgiving absence. Three sets of parents with sons from Jordan's fourth-grade team also showed. I'd met only one set previously. Jordan introduced me to the other two. They shook my hand, saying little about the game or the kid's play, and never took off their coats.

The kids' table was half empty. Even when parents couldn't make the postgame activities, they usually arranged for their sons to join the outing with their teammates. Few did today, even after the win. The table's conversation ranged from homework assignments to Sister Cecelia's latest edict, but it rarely ventured to basketball. It was as if the day's success had never occurred.

The affair broke up almost before it began. Kids shoveled leftover pizza slices into cardboard boxes to carry home. A first. Never had a slice gone uneaten, even if mushrooms had to be picked off the top first.

It was Saturday, and Travis had been invited to Casey's birthday party. Normally, Maddie oversees transportation, but I wanted to spend time alone with my son. Our season was going badly from my perspective. The more important issue was what the kids thought, and I knew Travis would give me a candid assessment.

"Maddie, I'll drive Travis over to Casey's this afternoon."

"Thanks, dear," she called from the front room. "Don't worry. I'll drop him off. I have to run a few errands."

"Let me put it this way, Travis and I need to talk."

She walked into the kitchen where I'd been standing, putting on my coat.

"If it helps, I haven't heard him say anything about basketball or the team for a long time. It's as if he's compartmentalizing. He seems to think about it when he's playing and then discards any thought of it until his next visit to the gym."

"I wish I could do that. Something about this entire season just keeps bugging me. I can't shake it, whatever it is."

"Maybe Travis has a few ideas, but don't you dare spread your misery to your son."

Travis piled into the car for the quick trip to Casey's. He turned off the radio as soon as he could reach it.

"Dad. Casey got a hundred on his math test yesterday. It was his fourth in a row. Pretty good, huh?"

"That's terrific. Anybody else do that?"

"Zack got a hundred, too, but he doesn't have four in a row like Casey."

"And, how did Travis, do?"

"He didn't get a hundred."

"What did he get?"

"Eighty."

"Sounds like that guy needs to work harder."

"He's been working hard."

I chuckled and then changed tone. "Travis, what do you think about the team?"

"It stinks," he replied without hesitation. Travis sat motionless, looking straight-ahead, showing no sign of elaborating.

"What makes you say that?"

"We get creamed almost every week. Our games usually aren't even close. When they are, you send in the subs and we can forget it."

"We've won two games and lost a few by just a couple of points."

My son sat quietly with his eyes now fixed on me. He looked as if he thought I was out of my mind.

"You can't tell me you aren't having fun. You're into every practice. In games, you're the first guy on the floor after a loose ball. You don't do that if you're not having fun."

"Yes, you do. I don't want to be any more embarrassed than I already am. The other team thinks you stink; people in the bleachers think you stink; you know you stink. That's embarrassing."

"It's not that bad."

"Do you know how it feels to get creamed, Dad? Game after game." Travis looked at me intently.

"I'm the coach; I'm part of the team; I'm getting creamed, too."

"It's not the same. You're not playing. You don't have to stand in front of everybody and see a guy throw a pass over your head, or a pass that never gets to you because somebody intercepts it. You don't throw the ball to a guy and watch him drop it or try to dribble it and kick it away." The frustration burst from Travis like a rupturing balloon. "You saw Rollie last game. He can't even bounce the ball. We're as bad as Mr. Whitley's team was last year."

"What do the other kids think?"

"Like me."

"I'll bet Carleton doesn't think like you."

"Maybe not, Carleton. He's used to losing, but even Carleton wants to win this year."

"Are Carleton and the other subs, the guys you say are used to losing, having fun?"

"I don't know. I guess so. Nobody complains."

"But they don't always show up, do they?"

"I guess."

"So, you're telling me the guys accustomed to winning aren't having any fun while the guys accustomed to losing, are?"

"That's pretty much it, Dad."

"I don't believe that. You like to play Hearts and you don't win all the time. You like to play *Sorry!* and you don't win all the time. What's the difference?

"Basketball's skill. *Sorry!*'s luck."

"I'm not sure I agree, but I understand what you're saying."

I was surprised how quickly Travis replied to my questions. He wasn't an introspective kid, making it difficult to believe that he'd consciously mulled the issues I presented him. Still, he must have grappled with them at some point because he knew what he thought and, when asked, didn't hesitate to convey it.

"Why do you keep playing, if you're not having fun? Why don't you just hand in your uniform? You wouldn't have to embarrass yourself any longer."

"You can't do that, Dad." He looked at me as if I'd raised a possibility so outlandish that it wasn't worth considering.

"Why can't you?"

"I can't leave my friends. They'd get beat even worse, and they'd be even more embarrassed."

"Kind of like what Rickie did to the team at Thanksgiving?"

Travis nodded.

"And you and Carleton did the first game of the season?"

"That was different. We didn't have a choice."

Travis's loyalty to his friends was exemplary. He wouldn't abandon them. He'd stay regardless of the humiliation, though I questioned whether he exaggerated his chagrin and depreciated the pleasure he took from playing. Still, he'd earned the right to feel as he did. He was part of a team, and more than most had committed his energy and attention to competing on its behalf. Regardless of what he did personally, however, he couldn't and wouldn't escape his team's fate, and he recognized it.

"Travis, why do you think we're playing so poorly?"

"I don't know, Dad. We just are."

"Am I doing something differently than last year?" I was looking for any avenue to change the team's fortunes and hoped Travis might offer a direction.

"I don't think so."

"Coach Whitley?"

"Everybody likes him. His mustache and purple warm-up suit are funny." Travis giggled and then looked at me. "Dad, what would you look like with a big mustache?"

"What do you think your mother would say if I grew one?" Travis's eyes brightened.

"You should." His grin broadened. "A big red one, just like Mr. Whitley's."

"Red? Not with my coloring. More likely gray."

We arrived at Casey's house. As Travis opened the door, I reminded him, "Don't forget Casey's birthday present."

"Oh, yeah." He lunged back into the car to retrieve it.

The box was enormous and wrapped in an eclectic ensemble of papers. "What's in the package?" I asked.

"I don't know. Forgot to ask Mom." He grabbed Casey's present and headed for the front door.

Later that night, I received a call from Zack's dad. He and his wife had always been cordial, though never warm. I knew he considered me a good coach and a positive influence on his son. Though he'd said nothing, he had to have aspirations for the boy as a basketball player. That wasn't difficult to understand. I would have had them, too, had I been in his position.

"Coach Elliot," he said. "It's been a tough season, and I won't make it any easier for you. Zack can't play in Sunday's game."

"Is he all right?" I asked.

"Oh, yes. He's fine. As you may know, Zack plays on two teams, his school team, your team, and another in a recreation league the city sponsors. His city team has a game at the same time St. Jerome's plays Sunday. Sunday games are rare in the recreation league. This is an exception because it's a make-up. Anyway, Zack's city team is fighting for the league lead. His school team is fighting for respectability."

I couldn't disagree with his assessment of our team.

"Zack's torn. He wants to play for a title, but he also wants to play with his friends. He's too young to make that decision, so I made it for him. He'll play with his recreation team Sunday."

"Isn't this a matter of loyalty and friendships? Zack's allegiance is to his classmates, not to a group of kids that he may never play with again."

"Coach Elliot, I have high regard for your efforts. Zack likes playing for you and with his friends. You've had success. But this is a new year. You have a different team. Circumstances have changed, and everyone must adjust. I understand you're unhappy."

"You're right about that."

"I'd feel the same if I were in your position. You must understand mine, though." He spoke antiseptically and in monotone. He'd made his decision before he called and there would be no reconsideration.

"You have to do what you think best for Zack. Good luck in Sunday's game."

I hung up the phone, dejected, and feeling sorry for myself.

"Who was that?" Maddie called from the kitchen.

"Another poke in the eye," I replied.

A DECISION

The King holiday came with miserable weather, cold, rain, and a chill that penetrated even the warmest parka. The streets were wet and in places slippery from forming ice. There was little to do and few places to go. Every player attended practice, the first time Jordan and I'd seen a full house in weeks.

Nothing changed with the team as the season wore on. We won another game for a total of three, against ten losses, putting St. Jerome's near the bottom of the league. Three games remained on our schedule, leaving no prospect for even a 50:50 season. Still, Jordan and I kept plugging along, doing our best to improve the team's level of play and perhaps win another game or two.

My patience was growing thin however, and my irritability was rising. I'd always tried to be consistent working with my team, never too high, never too low. The occasional gruff word was for effect more than actual anger. I'd always considered myself a teacher, not a game strategist or even a manager. I believed kids needed to learn basketball skills in the gym, just as they needed to learn fractions in the classroom. That meant step-by-step instruction and constant repetition. I knew no other way.

Though the kids seemed to notice nothing out of the ordinary, Jordan sensed my rising irritability and periodically sent me pained glances, cautioning me to relax. Whenever I sensed an imminent outburst, I turned and stared into the rafters. That was as far away as I could reach in the spacious box we call a gym. At times I feared its corners were contracting, a certain signal I needed to direct my thoughts elsewhere, to a refuge further away. That refuge was a dock on a lake where Maddie, Travis, and I spent our summer hours fishing while on vacation. But even the dock was losing its allure.

"Anything I can do, Doug?" Jordan said as we sat on the bleachers after practice. "We only have three games left. The most painful part's over."

"I don't know. I'm so frustrated. It seems like we've made no progress all season. We keep repeating and repeating, drill after drill, but we're not getting better. If anything, we're regressing. We don't seem to learn anything."

"Did you ever think teaching a sport is more complicated than repetition?"

"Maybe. But repetition is basic to learning. Repeat until you learn and then start something new."

"I haven't been around long," Jordan said. "But it seems teaching basketball differs from teaching a classroom discipline. There's no sequence in basketball. You can't just repeat a drill *ad infinitum* until a kid learns the skill and moves on. There's no time. Games, competition, interrupt. They require players to exhibit multiple skills simultaneously. How do you do that? There's the dilemma. So, we return to the same issues and correct them a bit at a time, and hope the kids remember whatever they've learned long enough to use in the next game."

I sat, thinking about what Jordan had said. He crossed a leg and leaned back against a bleacher, stretching his arms along the plank's edge. After a moment, I rolled my shoulders to look at him.

"Maybe that's what's driving me crazy. I can't fix anything permanently. Every time I plug a hole in St. Jerome's sinking ship, another blows open. Correct a mistake from the last game; find a new one in the next; and watch both repeated in the third."

"This is hard, Doug. Last year's success blinds you. I see you try to teach the kids. You explain; you walk them through it; you give them reasons for doing things. I've watched a bunch of so-called coaches in the last two years who neither tell a kid his mistake nor how to correct it. I suspect a lot of them don't even know. So, they yell at the kids and tell them to try harder. You're doing it right."

"Trying to make me feel better?"

"Isn't that what the assistant coach is supposed to do? Make the head coach feel good." Jordan wore a puckish grin.

"No. The assistant coach is supposed to make the head coach look smart. Then the head coach feels good."

I turned back and gazed across the gym. "Let's be honest, Jordan, maybe it's just the losing. Maybe my personality can't handle it."

"I can see why you might feel that way. Losing's a novel experience for you."

"At least in coaching. Losing's always bothered me in any context, though never to this extent."

"It's not as if we're losing games we should win, Doug. Forget the St. Stephen's game for the moment. Our kids' skills can't match most teams we play. And everyone's bigger than we are. You can't teach a kid to grow."

"You're probably right. But even when you understand the reasons for the disparities, losses wear. Why? I suppose competition is more about emotion than reason, or at least it is for me."

"Doug, my team lost more games last year than we'll lose this year. I prefer winning, too, and we've won three. Our losses aren't the end of the world."

I scanned the gym, watching another grade start practice at the far end of the court and then turned back to Jordan. "Expectations play a role, you know. You expected nothing last year. You did this year."

"They do make a difference."

"I've disappointed people, Jordan. Here was this successful coach leading a fabulous fourth-grade team that astounded the little basketball world we travel in. A repeat for the same kids in fifth-grade was inevitable. Yeah. Sure. Not only was there no repeat, the opposite almost happened. Everybody's surprised and unhappy. I suppose expectation and disappointment feed on one another to create greater disillusion than the team's performance justifies. Still, that's where we are."

"You're right. The kids aren't even showing up at practice."

"Remember, Jordan? You weren't winning a thing last season. Your kids still came to practice and had fun. I saw it."

Jordan removed his glasses and wiped the lenses with a tissue he pulled from his pocket.

"You're not tearing up on me, are you?"

"Don't be silly," Jordan said, replacing his glasses. "I have to admit that last season we expected nothing. Maybe that's why we had so much fun at practice." He rose to leave and then stopped. "One of the biggest differences I've noticed between this year and last is the parents."

"They blow hot and cold, don't they? Win and they're all over you. Lose and you can't find them without a telescope. What message does that send their kids? 'Want to be around you when you're successful. Oh, by the way, when you're not, I've got better things to do.' You don't think kids pick up on that stuff?"

"I remember the excitement. The stands were full of fans for your championship game. Then the blowout at Giorgio's. It looked like every parent and half of their extended families were there. That was something."

"Not like this year, huh. Rickie's parents scratch a winnable game at Thanksgiving. Zack's dad chooses an unscheduled make-up game over loyalty to his school's team. Few parents bother to attend games. Only a handful show at

Giorgio's to celebrate a victory. Before Thanksgiving John Hansen told me, 'it's different this year.' He was right, in a lot more ways than he knew."

The kids who'd played on my fourth-grade team were also growing ill-tempered. They were chippy toward one another, and more so toward their other teammates. Increasingly they practiced haphazardly. During games, they seemed almost resigned to losing, even when the contests were initially competitive. They'd play their minutes and then go sit on the end of the bench, looking disinterested, biding their time, waiting for the deluge of the substitute-enabled blowout. The team needed a win. Badly. My old group needed one most of all.

St. Mathew's had won almost as many as they'd lost, but for the first time this season we played a team that was our size. They were small, like us. They also had only eight players on the roster, which gave them an advantage playing against our 13. However, that edge would vanish if we used our win-some strategy and played just five kids. I brightened at the prospect. Here was a chance to add a fourth victory.

Our team fell behind quickly. But being able to look directly into the eyes of your opponent rather than up at them all afternoon has a salutary effect. At half-time St. Jerome's trailed by a single point. Jordan and I consulted while the kids rested. "Is this a win, Jordan?"

"I don't know. It's been a seesaw. Sometimes I think we'll run away with the game. Ten seconds later, I think they will."

"We've been getting better as the game's progressed. We've got momentum."

"You never know if it'll change. Momentum's fickle, Doug. You taught me that."

"We need a win, Jordan. Everybody's had a lot of playing time over the last month. That shouldn't be an issue. Let's go for it."

"What if we do and lose?"

"Possible. We discussed that downside when we came up with this cockamamy win-some strategy last fall and decided to use it anyway."

Jordan and I understood the flaw in our strategy from the outset. It required an accurate judgment early in the game about the team's ability to win the game. If our assessment were correct, we'd earn a much needed triumph. If it weren't, we'd lose twice, once from sitting our substitutes and twice from sitting on the short end of a score.

"True. We did talk about it. But couldn't we put in a sub or two to start the half and see if we can maintain momentum?" Jordan said.

"That's what we did in the St. James' game, third one of the season. Remember. And we never recovered. Please, no *déjà vu* all over again."

"That's not a fair comparison. We would have lost the St. James' game anyway," Jordan said.

"Look. We either have a strategy or we don't. This is the best shot we've had to win a game in a long time. Let's go for it."

Jordan sighed. "If that's what you want to do, Doug."

I could tell Jordan didn't think going all out to beat St. Mathew's was a good idea. His tone was cautionary, even negative. He fidgeted; he clasped and unclasped his hands; and, in what increasingly was becoming a tell, he pawed the floor with the toe of his clean sneaker. Jordan had been the author of our strategy, but when it came to operationalize it, he froze. His stomach apparently wouldn't follow his brain. He didn't want to chance a mistake. I didn't know whether his hesitation was an innate conservatism or a reticence to look a kid in the eye and tell him he wouldn't play today. But if Jordan wasn't prepared to take a risk now, I doubted he ever would.

The five who started the game for St. Jerome's hadn't come off the floor the first half. It was likely they wouldn't come off it the second, either. I'd played our substitutes extensively in most games, so the starting group wasn't accustomed to as many minutes as I would expect them to play today.

Less than a minute into the second half a loud voice in the crowd shouted, "Put in Freddie. Put in Freddie." I heard the noise somewhere in my subconscious but ignored it. Soon the voice rose again. "Put in Freddie. Put in Freddie." This time the sound caught my attention. Damn teenagers. I peeked down the bench to gauge Freddie's reaction. He was gawking to find the voice in the crowd, and then his head swiveled back and forth, as if he were looking for an exit, a place to escape. None was nearby. His face reddened, and he brushed aside the taunts of the kids sitting next to him.

I toyed with asking the referees to shut down the noise from the crowd but thought better of it. A shot caroming off the backboard into Rickie's hands drew my attention back to the game.

The competition moved into the last quarter. I called time-out and brought the entire team into the huddle. "Guys, we're going for a win. We have an exceptional chance to get one here, and we haven't had one in a while. That means most of you won't play today. I'm sorry. I'll do my best to make it up to you in the coming weeks." The huddle dissolved into two camps. Those playing seemed energized. Their faces brightened, and they talked excitedly among themselves. When the huddle ended, they charged back out onto the floor, ready for a win.

The second camp was muted, faces expressionless, and when the huddle ended, they passively retreated to their seats on the bench.

As the game restarted, the same voice in the bleachers yelled, "Put in Freddie. Put in Freddie. Put in anybody." I ignored the noise and hoped Freddie would, too.

My gamble looked good. St. Mathew's substituted during the time-out, even though we had a healthy seven-point lead. We now had our best players on the floor, and they didn't. We held the advantage.

Momentum then shifted. St. Mathew's scored two quick baskets. And a third followed shortly. Our starting five was tiring. They'd played the entire game and it showed. Time was running out, and neither team could gain a commanding lead. With less than a minute remaining, St. Jerome's led by a single point. With less than 15 seconds remaining, St. Mathew's led by one. I called a time-out to give my kids a breather and to organize a final play.

"Travis, stand next to the free throw line with your face to the basket. There." I pointed to the spot on the court I wanted my son to occupy. "Casey, stand to the right of Travis, about a half step forward. I arranged the two in the huddle as I wanted them on the floor. "Zack take the ball on the other side and dribble around them. If there's a shot, take it. If not, Rickie will be open in the corner and he'll take it. Everybody okay?"

I looked around the huddle. My old team appeared confident, ready to attack, and win. They'd been in tough situations before. This wasn't novel for them. They'd been successful, knew it, and expected to be successful again. Last season to be repeated. Jordan was the antithesis. He was anxious, jumpy. Through his glasses, I could see his swelling eyes. He gasped as if an errant chemistry experiment had sucked the oxygen from the gym. The substitutes didn't know what to think seeing the contrasting temperaments and withdrew to find a place to watch the remaining seconds.

My kids positioned themselves as instructed and the play I had designed worked as planned. Except Rickie missed his favorite shot. When the ball rolled off the rim, St. Jerome's had lost by a point.

I looked at Jordan. "I can't say you didn't warn me."

We were finishing dinner that evening when the phone rang. Travis jumped up from the table to answer. "Dad, it's for you."

"Who is it?" I asked, taking the receiver.

He shrugged his shoulders.

"Hello. This is Doug Elliot."

"You have to let everybody play. You have to let everybody play."

"Who's this?"

"You don't know me?" It was the same voice that I'd heard after our first game weeks ago, definitely not one of the trio Jordan and I had screened at Giorgio's.

"I'll tell you again. It's none of your business. The truth is, I let everybody play. Not necessarily in every game. Over the season though, every one of our players has gotten extensive playing time."

"Not today."

"Are you stupid or just willfully ignorant? What difference does it make if a kid averages four minutes a game or plays four minutes in every game? The total's the same."

"It's not. A boy shows up for a game, expecting to play, and he never gets in the game. He just sits and waits, and watches other kids play. Sure, he may play a lot the following game, but he loses the excitement, the thrill of being on a team when he just watches. Why take the trouble to show? You're not really a part of the team. Why put on your uniform? Why not just plop in the bleachers alongside your friends? And then when the game's finished, you can't be certain the same thing won't happen next week."

"The world's filled with uncertainty. It's part of learning," I said.

"I warn you. Let everyone play, in every game."

"And if I don't?"

"You don't want to know." The line went dead.

The receiver never left my hand. I dialed Jordan. He needed to know that he, too, should expect a call. Jordan hadn't told his wife about the first call, and I didn't want her to answer the second. I heard Whitley's phone ring.

"Hello." A female voice, Jill, Jordan's wife.

"Jill, this is Doug Elliot. Is Jordan there, please?"

"He sure is. That was a rough loss today, Doug. I thought we had that one for sure."

"So did I."

"Just a minute. I'll get him."

With the telephone tucked between my shoulder and ear, I rubbed my thumbs across my eyes. I knew why I'd volunteered to coach this team. Now I was asking myself, 'was it worth it?' Nonsense like threatening, mysterious phone-callers made you wonder.

"Hi, Doug."

"Our favorite caller's back in business, Jordan. I just got off the phone with him."

"Was afraid he might return after today's game. I was hoping it was a one-shot deal. Guess not."

"I'm giving you a heads-up in case you want to answer the phone tonight. Didn't want Jill to pick it up."

"I appreciate that. What are you going to do?"

"I'll wait for you to call me back and tell me about your conversation. If you get the same call I did within the next hour or so, I'm phoning the police." I glanced toward the kitchen to be certain no unwanted ears were listening.

"I'll let you know," Jordan said.

The dinner table had just been cleared, and the dishes put in the dishwasher when the phone rang again. "I've got it, Maddie."

It was Jordan. "I got my call."

"A threat?"

"Yeah, not like 'I'm going break your knees', but I heard an 'or else'.

"That seals it. I'll tell Maddie about tonight's calls. I can't hide them from her. The police will want to talk to both of us anyway, so she'll find out regardless. You'll have to tell Jill. They'll want to interview you, too."

"I know. Sorry for the unpleasant news."

"Yeah. Thanks for the update."

I walked into the front room, and Maddie put her book on the end table. I sat down and craned my neck to see whether Travis was watching the blaring television set across the hall. He was.

"Maddie, the guy called again."

"After today, I thought he might." Her voice seemed resigned. The visible strain of the first call was gone. She leaned forward and stretched her hand to touch mine. Her fingers tips fell on its back, reassuring and comforting. "What are you going to do, Doug?"

"I don't think we have a choice this time. I'm calling the police."

President's Day's practice was scheduled for 4:30. Travis and I arrived ten minutes early so I could unlock the gym, turn on the lights, and retrieve the balls from the equipment closet. He grabbed the first free ball and dribbled to the other end of the court to start shooting. A few minutes later Jordan strode in, wearing his purple warm-up, Carleton a step behind. I'd suspected for a while that Jordan's son had been losing interest in basketball but hung on because he enjoyed being around his dad. My suspicions only grew when the boy shunned the chance to grab a ball and instead plopped down on a front bleacher to wait for practice to begin.

Jordan's buoyancy often sanded the sharpest edges of my rising irritation. He always seemed to have a pleasant word to say about everything and everyone, Barney Ambrose the exception. So, I wasn't surprised when he sidled up to me and chirped, "Beautiful day today, Doug. Did you get out?" Before I could respond, he said, "Jill, and I did. We took Carleton over to the park just to stretch our legs and get some fresh air. Had to be in the mid-60s. In February? Okay, late February. Just good to breathe fresh air after the miserable winter we've had."

I didn't need a recount of the day's weather, though Maddie and I, too, had taken advantage of it for a lengthy walk. Still, Jordan's enthusiasm made me smile. "And tomorrow?" I asked.

"Eh. Supposed to be back to normal. Windy, damp, and cold. Into the low 40s."

Casey drifted in and was now shooting baskets with Travis. They bantered constantly while Carleton still sat alone entrenched in the bleachers, waiting for practice to start.

I looked at my watch. It was 4:30. Three boys were in the gym and ready to go. Ten were missing and I didn't have a clue where they were. No one had said a thing about being absent.

Freddie slipped in, huddled in a light jacket, and sat next to Carleton. We now had four.

"Let's wait a few minutes, Doug," Jordan said in a calming tone. He saw my rising anger. "Lots of people on the road today. Our guys are probably running a little late."

"That's pure crap, Jordan, and you know it. If I were a betting man, and I am, how many kids do you think will show up for practice, today? Pick a number, and I'll take the over/under. Loser buys lunch."

Jordan jerked his head back to offer a confused look. "The over/under? What's that?"

"Simple." I was eager to prove a point with a small wager. "Tell me how many kids you think will be here in, say, ten minutes. Once you give me a number, I'll say 'more will show than you predict', that's the over, or 'less will show than you predict', that's the under. If you pick the exact number, it's a push."

"A push?"

"You aren't much of a gambler, are you? Think of a push as a tie, no winner. If you get the exact number, we push, and we split the check."

"Okay. I'll play. Seven. In ten minutes, seven kids will be here, ready for practice."

"Under." I couldn't spit out the word fast enough. "And I hope you recognize even seven is disgraceful."

We tossed a ball to Carleton and his buddy, Freddie, and told them to work on their dribbling. "Take a few with your left hand, too," I said. Practice would begin 15 minutes late.

I was stewing. Jordan and I'd given up part of our day to be at practice. We gained nothing being here. The kids knew we were practicing, and their parents did, too. It'd been on the schedule for over three months and I'd sent everyone a reminder. No one called to say they couldn't make it or offered an excuse for absence. Jordan and I had been stood up, and I was furious.

"A few more minutes, Doug. Just a few more minutes." Jordan couldn't have missed my seething.

"What? And we'll pick up one more kid?"

Zack walked in on cue, raising the total to five. The longer we waited, the more I simmered. Simmer long enough and simmer comes to a boil. The change requires only a little more heat. And the thought of eight missing kids raised my temperature.

"Anybody know where the rest of the team is?" I hollered over the bouncing balls.

Casey held his ball and said, "Rickie stopped by our house around 2:00 with his mom and dad. His mom said they were going for a ride. I reminded Rickie about practice."

The gym was silent. "Anybody else?" I asked.

The gym remained silent.

"A few more minutes," Jordan said, pleading.

"Why? No one else is coming. I know it; you know it. By the way, you owe me lunch. You lost the bet."

I walked over and sat on the first row of the bleachers. Jordan joined me. Neither of us said anything. The basketballs bounced again.

The more I thought about the situation, the angrier I became. I'd always been taught that when something goes wrong, and our season *had* gone wrong, you work harder. Adversity wasn't an excuse for a day off. Yet most of the team had done so with the aid, if not the outright encouragement, of their parents. I understood a single practice wouldn't yield significant improvement, maybe not even any. But at least you tried to fix what was wrong. The kids missing refused to even try, opting to enjoy the pleasant weather instead.

The simmer reached a boil. "That's it, Jordan," I said. "I'm done. I'm out of here. If no one else cares, why should I? I don't need this. The team's yours, if you want it. I wouldn't blame you if you didn't."

"You can't do that, Doug. There're only three games left. You just can't get up and quit."

"Watch me." I said, regretting the sharp tone I used with Jordan. "I didn't quit on them. They quit on me."

"Think, Doug. Don't make a decision you might regret," he implored.

"This has been coming a long time, Jordan. Nothing to regret."

My assistant gathered his thoughts. "A lot of kids have been loyal to you and done everything you've asked. Casey. Our two boys. You can't walk out on them."

"This is a team, Jordan. I'm sorry about the kids you mentioned. I am. You're right about them. But the team is the whole, not its parts. And I might add, you could only mention a few of its parts."

"Please."

"I've made my decision. I'll call Anderson tonight and tell him you're the new coach."

"Are you sure?"

"Yes."

"How much of your decision was the caller?"

"The caller?" I scoffed. "None. If that were a factor, it would have worked the other way. I'd never have stepped down because of some jerk who didn't have the guts to identify himself."

We sat on the bleachers for a moment, saying nothing, the silence broken only by kids' voices and the hollow sound of bouncing balls. After a few minutes, I got up. "I'll take Casey and Zack home. Can you take Freddie?"

I turned out the lights, locked the gym door, and gave the keys to Jordan.

BREAKING THE NEWS

Since marrying Maddie 16 years ago, I'd consulted her on every important decision affecting our lives, and many of lesser consequence. Her judgement was reasoned and temperate. She was dispassionate and coherent. I valued her opinion and believed the decisions I reached were much better for it. Consulting her also meant she was aware of anything relevant in my life and our future, and I liked that.

Maddie was reading *The Bridges of Madison County* in the living room when I arrived home from practice. She looked up, her open book lying on her lap. "You're home early?"

"Not much of a turnout today. Five kids showed."

"What happened?"

"Good question. The answer is that eight kids didn't show."

I plopped down in a chair across from her. Travis was already in the family room with the television turned to a sports channel.

"What are you going to do?" she asked.

"I've already done it."

"Done what?"

"Resigned. As of about one-half hour ago, Jordan Whitley's the new coach of St. Jerome's fifth-grade basketball team."

Maddie looked at me with a resolute expression. Her eyes burned and her lips firmed. After what seemed like an eternity, she placed her embossed leather marker into her book, closed it, and asked, "Do you want to tell me about it?"

I didn't, not then, not ever. But the topic was unavoidable, and I owed her an explanation. "Today brought the straw that broke the proverbial camel's back." The worn saw was the only suitable summary my tongue could find. "Five kids did the right thing and eight didn't. That, by itself, wouldn't have been enough to make me quit. It was just another piece of the horse pucky added to a pile that's been growing since the beginning of the season."

I poured out my tale of self-pity, a recitation of an endless trail of barriers that thwarted my efforts and otherwise made my coaching life miserable. I'd tried and failed and believed nothing further could be gained by continuing. So why bother? An impartial outsider might have judged my complaints petty and conduct petulant. I was angry because I didn't get my way, so I pocketed my whistle and ran home. But I wasn't an impartial outsider. I was the guy affected. And I judged the situation untenable and resignation the only appropriate recourse.

When I finished, Maddie asked, "Who have you told?"

"Just Jordan."

"How did he react?"

"He said I was making a terrible mistake. I was overreacting and that I should finish the season."

"Jordan's right, you know."

"Possibly," I said. My voice held no conviction.

"If Jordan's the only one you've told, I'll bet you could pick up the phone, call him and unresign."

"I don't think I want to do that. I've made a decision, and I'll stick with it."

She showed neither approval nor disapproval, but she didn't pick up her book. She wasn't ready to leave the conversation.

"Does your son know?"

"No. I haven't told him."

"You have to. Sooner rather than later."

"Yeah. I know." I shrugged, climbed out of my chair and trudged into the family room. If it had been unpleasant telling Maddie, telling Travis would be even more so. I knew he was proud that his dad was the team's coach, and he liked spending time together doing something other than homework. My resignation would change his status among his peers and lessen our time together. I could only guess how he'd accept the news.

"Travis, please turn off the television," I said as I entered the family room and sat down. "There's something we need to talk about."

He pressed the 'Mute' button on the remote as if the conversation might not be important enough to turn off the set entirely.

"All the way." He pushed the 'Off' button and his eyes left the television to focus on me.

"Son, I resigned as the coach today. Starting now, Mr. Whitley is your coach."

Travis said nothing. He put the remote on the table next to his chair as he considered his response. "Guess it was because nobody showed up for today's practice. Huh?"

"That was a reason, but not the only one."

"It's been a terrible season, Dad. We stink. You're a good coach, and it's not your fault. Don't quit, though. Quitting doesn't help."

"I have no choice."

"Sure, you do. There're aren't many games left. You can quit after the season's over."

"I was growing too angry, Son. I just might have started telling people off and yelling at the kids. That wouldn't have been good for anyone."

"I don't know." Travis parsed his words in an un-Travis like manner. "You should have been telling people off and yelling all season. A lot of people needed it."

Travis surprised me. He was contending I'd been too lenient, too patient as a coach. He apparently thought I needed to be more strident and abrasive. I needed to push harder. I wondered how many others, players and parents, believed the same? It was a perspective I hadn't considered.

"What makes you say that, Travis?"

"Nothing else seemed to work. The nicer you and Mr. Whitley were, the worse things got. It was like some guys stopped caring."

"But yelling at kids won't make them play better. You can't teach by yelling."

"Sometimes you can, Dad."

"Remember Mr. Ferguson? You wouldn't want me to be like him, would you?"

"No. But he was mean, and he embarrassed kids on purpose. You try to get kids to do it right. You try to help us. Sometimes you have to get loud to do that."

"I understand there's a difference, but I don't think yelling would have motivated this group."

"Dad, some kids think they're trying. They're not. They're only half trying. And, they're only half trying because no one makes them really try. You have to get on kids. Sometimes hard. Maybe they wouldn't like you as much but that doesn't matter. I'll always like you."

"Do you really think that if I'd pushed Freddie or Carleton, they could have helped our team win games?"

"I don't know. But you didn't and we'll never know."

"Even if I had and even if they became better players, which I doubt, would they've had more fun?"

"How do you have fun when you're always getting crushed?" Travis replied.

"Mr. Whitley's team had fun last season, and they lost every game, but one."

"I don't know how that's possible. I sure wouldn't have had any fun. Nor would my friends."

"Why didn't you tell me this before? I've asked."

"Because I didn't think about it before."

"I'm sorry, Son. I enjoyed every minute I coached you. Sorry I can't say the same about others."

I rose to leave. Travis turned the television set back on. Our talk was over, and I left the family room perplexed. I was relieved Travis didn't seem to resent me quitting. But I was bothered that he didn't seem to believe my commitment to the team matched his. I then recalled last year's championship game and Travis's commitment to beating the fifth grade. And the intensity and the focus he'd displayed that led to the improbable triumph. He thought I hadn't reciprocated his dedication; I hadn't measured up. That's what he was trying to say. And that depressed me.

Bad news spreads faster than good. So, it was for my resignation. Everyone associated with the school seemed to know my action by the end of classes the following day. The response among most parents was adverse. Rita Horvath told Maddie that she heard words like 'peevish,' 'immature,' and 'juvenile' flying around school to describe my behavior. Those were among the more flattering adjectives. Rita also said most parents seemed pleased Jordan would replace me.

There were satisfying anomalies. The evening following my resignation, I opened the door at home to find Casey's mom on the porch, tears pouring down her cheeks. She stepped forward awkwardly, hugged me stiffly, and disappeared without saying a word. I also heard from Mrs. Hernandez, Willie's mother. She called and said she'd heard the news and was sorry. She said she didn't understand what had happened, but whatever it was, she was sure I was right. I barely got in a 'thank you' before she hung up.

By the time I reached St. Jerome's athletic director, Bart Anderson, he knew the situation.

"I hear Jordan Whitley will take over for you. Is that right?"

"It is."

"Then I don't have any problems with you quitting." Anderson needed someone to cover so he wouldn't have to recruit another coach. Jordan satisfied that need. He didn't bother to thank me for the time I'd spent in the program. Nor did I expect him to.

Nearly a week later my office phone rang. "Hi. This is Peter Robicheaux with the PR group in Dallas. My boss has assigned me to write a short feature on your volunteer activities with a kids' basketball team for the company's annual report."

"Good morning." I tried to sound as cheery as the caller.

"I'd like to schedule some time in the next couple of days to interview you about your flextime volunteer activities. Last year's feature was quite a hit I understand. We can't repeat the same theme, so I'd like to take a fresh angle for the coming report, possibly comparing the differences in your experiences this year and last. How you've grown as a coach. Something like that."

"Excuse me," I said. "Let me save you some time. I no longer volunteer. I resigned my position with the basketball team."

"But my boss told me you're the coach."

"Your boss probably didn't know about the change. It was recent."

"May I ask why you resigned?"

My first instinct was to tell him it was none of his business, but I'd have to provide Ty an explanation at some point. I might as well practice on this guy in terms he would understand. "Let's just say, there were creative differences among the parties involved."

"This changes everything. I think I should talk to my boss again and see what he wants to do."

"That makes sense." I hoped his boss would tell him to forget the whole thing, though that wasn't likely.

"Let me check my bases down here and get back to you."

I now needed a conversation with Ty. I hadn't told him anything about my resignation. If he'd noticed that I was in the office more hours than normal on Monday and Wednesday afternoons and had asked the reason, I'd have told him. If he'd asked about the basketball season, I'd have told him. I had nothing to hide, but there'd been no reason to flaunt my resignation. That was before Dallas jogged my memory. They would ask Ty about my situation and I didn't want to blindside the boss. I made an appointment to see him as soon as possible and hoped Dallas didn't reach him before I could alert him to the changed circumstances.

The earliest I could see Ty was 3:00 that afternoon, and only for a few minutes. His schedule was solid for the day. However, a phone call from Dallas was likely to pass straight through and the resulting conversation could prove embarrassing to both Ty and me. I needed a favor from Ty's secretary. I asked her to hold any call from PR in Dallas until I'd spoken with the boss. A long-time friend of Maddie's from the hospital, she didn't even ask why.

Three o'clock came and went, and I grew antsy. It was 4:00, and I still hadn't heard from Ty's secretary. I didn't bother her. She'd phone when Ty was available, though my trust in her didn't diminish my anxiety. It was almost 5:00 when she rang. Ty had just a few minutes before he had to leave for a dinner engagement.

I mouthed a quick 'thank you' as I rushed through her office. When I passed her desk, she held up a pink telephone message slip: *Robert Bonson, PR Director, Dallas.* She had intercepted the call, and I could have kissed her.

"Doug, can't this wait until morning?" Ty said. "I have a dinner scheduled and I'm already late."

"Not really. I need to be sure you're not blindsided and made to look foolish." 'Look foolish' caught Ty's attention.

"I'll give you the summary tonight. Tomorrow I'll give you the details, but it must be before you talk to anyone in Dallas. I don't want you to be the only guy who doesn't know."

Ty sat on the edge of his chair, overcoat still on. "Make it quick," he said.

"Last week I resigned my coaching job at St. Jerome's. The reasons are long and varied. That's for tomorrow. This morning I received a call from Dallas PR about a second version of Barney's feature for the annual report. I told the fellow I was no longer a volunteer. He said he'd consult with his boss about what to do. You now have a telephone message from a guy by the name of Bonson who heads PR in Dallas. He probably wants to discuss the feature."

The room was quiet. Ty looked up quizzically. "That's it?" He jumped to his feet and headed for the door. "Geez, Doug. You had me worried. I thought it was something important." As he hurried through the office door, he turned and said, "Come up with a few options tonight that I can give the PR guys in the morning." As the door closed behind the departing figure, Ty shouted over his shoulder, "And, piss on the feature. The corporate suites will forget about it by next week. It was the flavor of the month."

"What?" I ran into the hall behind him. "I thought you liked it."

"Nah. A feature on a volunteer coach in an annual report? Dumb idea. I just needed a reason to justify our flextime experiment, and Barney's drivel was it. A genuine article in a real publication? That may have been a great idea, but I was confident Barney could never pull it off. The most useful thing coming from the affair was keeping him busy." Ty brightened. "I did get some nice exposure in Dallas, though." He hopped into the elevator.

I developed an options paper for the feature that evening as Ty had requested. The first and most prominent option was to dismiss the whole idea. The options paper was the last I heard of Barney's feature, or anything resembling it.

THE SEASON ENDS

The doorbell rang. I set aside my newspaper and went to answer. Two large men stood at the door in the gathering dusk.

"Mister Elliot. I'm Sergeant Ludlow and this is detective Svaboda. We'd like to talk to you about the threatening phone call complaint you lodged."

"Please, come in." I held the door open for the two policemen and lead them into the living room. "Excuse me. Let me get my wife. She'll be interested."

The Sergeant had just removed his overcoat and seated himself in an easy chair when he reached into a pocket and pulled out a small cassette player. "Before we go too far, please listen to this tape and tell me if the voice is familiar."

He pressed the machine's 'On' button and out-flowed the voice of the threatening caller. It took only a few syllables for me to recognize it. "That's him. No doubt about it."

"Your identification confirms what we suspected," the Sergeant said.

"You found him then? That's a relief. What can you tell us?" Maddie asked.

"This whole affair is about a kid's basketball game. It's absurd, but my job is filled with absurdities these days. You have a kid on the basketball team you coach by the name of Freddie Marnoca.

"I do. He's one of my players. Or was. I recently gave up the team."

"Seems Freddie has an older brother, Frankie. A teenager. Eighteen."

Maddie leaned in.

"The brother, Frankie that is, played basketball when he was in grade school a few years ago. He told us he liked basketball a lot. I gather he wasn't very good. He rode the bench most of the time. A lot of games he never saw the floor. He believes it wasn't fair other kids got to play a lot every game, and he didn't get to play at all. That made him angry, but he couldn't do anything about it. His coach was intent on winning, regardless of who played or how much. So, the kid just picked up splinters and grew angrier. He went out for the team the following year. Same coach. Same result. He didn't play."

"I understand the kid's anger," I said. "But what does that have to do with our situation?"

"The kid, Frankie, thought he saw the same thing happening to his little brother, Freddie, the one who plays on your team. He said Freddie didn't get in a game. Frankie didn't think that was right."

"Just a minute, officer. That's not correct. Freddie played as much as most kids on the team."

"Not according to the brother. But that's beside the point. He said that since he was older, he could now speak up. So, he spoke up. Not conventionally, but by veiled phone calls."

"That explains the two calls and when they came. Freddie didn't play in those two games."

"Frankie mentioned that. Vociferously, I might add. He holds strong opinions on the subject."

"Why didn't he just say something to me after a game or make a normal phone call?"

"I asked him that question. He didn't think you'd take him seriously," the Sergeant said.

"He was probably right," I conceded. "An 18-year-old kid. Why didn't he go to their father and have him call me? And I can answer my own question as well as you can. Because his father was out of the country on business. At least the first time."

"What are you taking about, Doug?" Maddie asked.

"Remember when Jordan and I tried a little detective work at Giorgio's. We eliminated three dads as suspects that day. We took Freddie's dad off the list because he'd been out of the country on business. Never considered it might be a different family member."

"Exactly," the Sergeant said. "Once the kid called, he couldn't ask his dad to make another one. It would have identified him."

"How did you discover the caller was Frankie Marnoca?"

"It wasn't hard. We were interviewing parents and asked if they'd seen or heard anything unusual at a game. One mentioned periodic shouts of 'put Freddie in' or something like it. Once we confirmed that information, it didn't take long to find who we were looking for."

I leaned back in my chair and looked at the ceiling. "Did I have that wrong." I drew out the words to emphasize my error.

"What wrong?" Maddie asked.

"I thought those shouts to put Freddie in were just kids ragging on poor Freddie. Why else would he blush when he heard them? The shouts were directed at me instead, and I was too obtuse to recognize it. They actually meant, 'put Freddie in the game'."

"Even if you'd understood their intent, would you have done things differently?" she asked.

"No. Not likely."

The two officers collected their coats, preparing to leave. "Do you have any questions for us?"

"Yeah. What was the threat? What was he going to do?"

"Nothing. The boy just wanted you to take him seriously."

"What happens to him?" Maddie asked.

"He's a legal adult and threatening phone calls are serious matters. After talking with the kid and his parents earlier today though, you won't need to worry about any more mysterious calls. In fact, expect an apology. The old man was so angry the kid may spend for next millennium in his room. What happens legally though is up to the district attorney."

"Doug, do something."

"About what?"

"You don't want to ruin that boy's life with a criminal conviction over a kid's basketball game."

"It's not a game, Maddie. Remember the calls. You were terrified, at least during the first one."

"I was. But let's be reasonable. Match the punishment with the crime."

I sighed and nodded. "I agree with my wife, Sergeant. She's the aggrieved party here. Can't you just scare the kid a little and forget about it?"

"Sounds like a fair resolution to me. You'll need to write a letter to the DA, though. He has final say. Mr. Whitley will also have to agree."

"Neither will be a problem."

I'd filled two roles for my son, coach and dad. I'd resigned the former but not the latter. As a father, I'd attend the rest of St. Jerome's games, sitting in the bleachers cheering for Travis and his team as any other dad. It'd be awkward, since parents of other team members would also attend those games. Avoiding them would be next to impossible, and I knew I'd have to endure strained conversations with those encountered. My first game in the bleachers was at St. Leo's, the team my friend Fred Bauer coached. St. Leo's was a considerable distance from St. Jerome's. That meant I would encounter few parents, which pleased me.

Sunday afternoon I drove Maddie and Travis to the game as I had for the past two seasons. But when we entered St. Leo's gym, I took an unfamiliar path. Travis headed for the St. Jerome's bench alone while Maddie and I climbed the bleachers together. We went as high as we could and then we both lounged among the coats and other winter apparel piled near the top while waiting for the game to start.

Zach's parents arrived and took a place near Maddie and me, though not within speaking distance. They waved when they entered. Otherwise we might as well have been in separate worlds. A few familiar faces dotted the stands, all parents of kids from Jordan's old team. Rickie's and Casey's parents were no-shows, as were Andy's. They'd been regulars last season and vocal fans, but as our fortunes ebbed, their attendance became increasingly hit-or-miss. Someone else had brought their boys to today's game.

Jordan introduced himself to Fred, and I could see Fred scanning the bleachers. Jordan likely had told him of the circumstances behind the regime change. Fred waved when he spotted me.

The kids liked Jordan and I knew they would play hard for him. He'd do his best, though he wasn't likely to prevail. This Sunday the team numbered 11. Kids no longer showed, even for games.

To everyone's surprise, the match with St. Leo's was competitive to begin. Fred's team was like ours. It hadn't progressed much from the prior year, though more than we. The score was tied at half, 18 - 18. Jordan had done an admirable job substituting early, putting him in a decent position to use his best at game's end. An unexpected win seemed possible, and Maddie and I closely watched, hoping for the best.

Fred's team took a four-point lead early in the fourth quarter. It stretched to eight before Zack went on a binge. To that point Zack had played at par, which meant far better than anyone else. But now his play shifted to a different and higher gear as he almost single-handedly whittled the score to two points with less than a minute to play. The game meant nothing in the standings. Neither team had a winning record, but the kids on both sides played as if the season depended on the outcome. Zack struck again to tie the score and the St. Jerome's bench exploded. Fred could only shake his head.

Seconds now remained. Tied, Fred's son dribbled the ball down the court. Fred wanted his team to take the last shot. If they made it, St. Leo's would win. If they didn't, the game would go into overtime. The kids in green and white passed the ball cautiously, trying to get one good final shot, and with less than five seconds remaining one of Fred's players launched an attempt that bounced off the rim. In the ensuing frenzy, a kid wearing purple and yellow knocked the ball out-of-bounds under the basket. St. Leo's still had possession with two seconds remaining.

St. Jerome's played man-to-man defense. I could see that Jordan had assigned Andy to guard St. Leo's number five, but the guy had moved from his regular place, far from the basket, to a spot right under it, and Andy couldn't find him. Unguarded, number five clapped his hands, eagerly awaiting the ball. Jordan saw the developing disaster. "Andy! Andy!" he shouted, leaping to his feet. Andy was too far away. He couldn't recover. "Time-out! Time-out!" Jordan yelled. The referee blew his whistle to stop play.

An animated discussion immediately flared at the scorer's table.

"Oh, no," I said.

"What's wrong?" Maddie asked.

"Jordan just called a time-out he didn't have."

"I don't understand."

"Each team gets three time-outs in a half. Jordan just took a fourth."

"So, what happens?"

"A technical foul. St. Leo's gets to shoot one uncontested free throw. If they make it, game's over for all practical purposes. If they miss, they still get to keep the ball."

"That's not good," she replied.

Fred selected his best player to take the free throw while the kids from both teams remained in their respective huddles. The referee handed the ball to the designated St. Leo's player standing alone at the free throw line. The boy bounced it two or three times, twirled it in his fingers, and then bounced it again. He steadied himself, took a deep breath, and propelled the ball toward the basket. It hit the rim and fell off to the side.

Reactions from the respective benches were predictable, cheers from one, silence from the other. The shooter remained at the foul line until the ball hit the floor and began rolling away. He dropped his head and returned to the St. Leo's huddle.

The coaches sent their teams back out onto the floor for the final two seconds. Overtime was almost certain.

"Andy. Who's your man?" Jordan yelled.

"Number five," Andy shouted in reply.

"Right. Now stick to him."

In the tumult over Jordan's fourth time-out, Fred had substituted. He replaced number five with number seven, a player much different in appearance, taller, thinner, and darker-haired. While Andy searched the floor for number five, number seven hid to the side of the basket where no one noticed him. Before anyone on St. Jerome's recognized the change, the ball had been thrown from out-of-bounds to number seven, who immediately twisted and unguarded tossed the ball into the basket. Everything happened quickly, and the game was over. Andy was still looking for number five.

Maddie and I lagged in our move down the bleachers. I didn't want to see or hear from another parent but did want to congratulate Jordan on a marvelous effort. Despite Fred outfoxing him, Jordan had done well motivating and keeping our kids in the game.

I shook Jordan's hand and patted him on the back. "Next time. For what it's worth, I thought you did a terrific job today. Look at how well the kids played for you."

"I made at least two horrible goofs." Jordan said. He was upset with himself. His head sagged; his shoulders slumped; he ran his fingers through his rumpled hair.

"What did you expect? It was your first appearance in prime time and Fred's been doing this for years."

"Still."

"Forget it."

I was almost out of the door when Fred saw me. We shook hands.

"What's going on, Doug?"

"I wish I knew. Let's just say, this season and last are two different sides of the same nickel. One side's an Indian and the other's a buffalo."

"I know. I've been following the scores in Spenser's weekly report to the coaches." His eyes widened. "You guys have been taking some real beatings."

"It's a great example of when you don't get better, you get worse. We didn't get better. This year's team as fifth graders couldn't beat last year's team as fourth graders."

"You've still got that amazing kid, though. He doesn't belong in this league."

"Remember, I told you I had a potential D-I player. Imagine what he'd be like if he were on a team with kids having equivalent skills?"

"You don't need to convince me. I saw with my own eyes." Fred continued to shake his head in astonishment.

"Now, let's get to the important point, Doug. Why aren't you on the bench? The new guy told me you left a week or so ago."

"I blew after a frustrating season, triggered when most of my team didn't show up for a practice. Granted, the practice was on President's Day, but it'd been scheduled from the beginning of the season."

"That's not hard to believe. How many?"

"Five of 13 showed."

"Oh, boy. When a team starts losing, it's amazing how quickly interest fades." His eyes fell to the floor. "I'm sorry. You produced one hell of a team last year, Doug. I couldn't believe when I read that you guys beat the fifth graders in the playoffs. Incredible."

"That was part of this year's problem. Last year was fantastic. In every way." I felt a smile crossing my face until I remembered the current situation. The glower returned. "The total opposite of this season."

"It happens."

"So I learned. By the way, where did you come up with that hocus-pocus substitution at the end of today's game? Bet you've been practicing that for weeks."

Fred threw back his head and laughed. "Fooled you."

"That ploy is older than you and I put together. How did you ever think you could get away with it?"

"It worked, didn't it?" We were both chuckling.

"You should be ashamed of yourself. You took advantage of a rookie."

"I wouldn't have even bothered trying if you'd been on the bench. If I can get a little edge on a rookie, I'm not going to miss it."

I shook Fred's hand and left. We were still both laughing.

Travis sat in the back seat on the way home. "Dad, you should have been our coach today. You wouldn't have made the mistakes Mr. Whitley did."

"That's not fair, Travis. I thought Mr. Whitley did a terrific job. St. Leo's is a better team than you are. He helped you guys almost pull it off."

"He made a time-out mistake you wouldn't have made."

"I'm not sure that's true. Andy put him in a tough spot. If he hadn't called time-out, the kid under the basket probably would have scored. You never know, but it didn't look good."

"Maybe," Travis said. He didn't sound convinced. "Still, I know he did things you wouldn't have, and Zack knows it, too."

It seemed my legacy as teacher had been overtaken by my legacy as strategist/game manager. I wanted the kids to remember me, if they ever did, as someone who taught them something, as someone who helped them get better, as someone who showed them how to compete. Instead, they seem to have pigeon-holed me as a guy who understood and applied rules and situations better than other coaches. That disappointed me.

Two games remained. Prospects for a win in either were poor. Regardless, Maddie and I attended both as supportive parents. The outcome of neither was surprising. St. Jerome's lost convincingly in both. Almost nothing had changed from the first game of the season. Zack and Travis still played hard every minute and could still be described as the skill and emotion of the team. Elsewhere there wasn't much of either. Casey's play had grown increasingly tentative. The old phrase 'paralysis by analysis' applied. By the end of the season, he was a poorer player than when he started. Rickie? He did his own thing. He could be brilliant or atrocious, but one thing was certain, he did it alone. 'Team' may have been ever present in his vocabulary, yet it fell further and further from his mindset as the season progressed. And, Andy? His highlight was the first game of the year against St. Joseph's. He never equaled it, or even came close.

No other emerged as a player of promise or even adequacy. Nice kids all. Someday they were likely to fill the ranks of our country's doctors and lawyers and scientists. One thing they weren't likely to do is to be associated with any serious athletic endeavor. That didn't minimize them as people, but it did minimize them as contributors to the St. Jerome's fifth-grade basketball team.

When the final game was over, I walked across the gym floor to thank Jordan for a full season of effort, perseverance, and caring. He did what I wasn't able to do, and I appreciated that. I told him I hoped our friendship wouldn't expire at season's end, though I rarely saw him from that point forward. It was my loss.

As we left the gym, Maddie asked if I'd like to go to Giorgio's for one last hurrah. I considered the alternatives and said, "I don't think so. Rickie's parents aren't people I want to see right now."

"But dear, you have no choice. Who'll pay for the pizza?"

She grabbed my arm, and we headed to Giorgio's.

EPILOGUE

Spring Brings New Life

The last remnants of winter still lay in scattered piles. Crocuses had been blooming for a week and tiny green noses began to stick out of the damp soil in the front garden. Spring always made Maddie happy. Travis and I could tell when its first inklings arrived. She would hum to herself, and while the constant drone grew annoying, neither of us wanted to intrude. If that were Maddie's pleasure, we wouldn't bother her. Let her enjoy the seasonal change and the mood it brought.

Basketball hadn't come up since the last game a few months ago. That experience ended badly. The kids liked me when we won, but that was a season ago. This season we didn't win, and no player other than Travis told me he was sorry I left.

Travis signed-up to play Little League baseball in the spring. He'd been playing ever since he was old enough. I'd thrown the ball with him for as long as either of us could remember. Maddie had, too. We'd never missed a T-ball or Little League game or an assignment to bring after-game refreshments. Travis excelled. He was a good baseball player, very good, a much better baseball player than a basketball player.

Maddie and I enjoyed watching him from the bleachers and agonized when vocal parents embarrassed themselves and their kids. We allowed Travis's coaches to teach him the game without interference and were generally pleased with the result. A season of baseball seemed just the cure for last winter's debacle.

Travis's baseball coach this year was Major William Taylor, or Bill, a Marine officer assigned to the college's ROTC program. He'd played baseball at the Naval Academy when he was a student there, and while he became a professional soldier, he never lost his love for the game. He radiated that passion when coaching kids. Typically, he guided teams on a military base, but due to his assignment, Major

Bill coached in our league for a second year. Travis was delighted playing for him, and Maddie and I were as excited as our son.

Travis had just come home from the season's first practice when I walked in the door. He greeted me, "Dad, Major Bill's leaving. You've got to be our baseball coach? You'd be a good one."

"What? Why's Major Bill leaving?" I asked cautiously.

"He told us that the Marines had sent him someplace else and he had to go right away. We need a new coach. You'd be a good one, Dad. Please. Please. Please." Travis was recruiting again.

Maddie stood behind our son, listening to every word and gauging my every reaction. Her arms were crossed. Her face was stoic, and her expression warned, 'no hasty decisions'.

"I don't know, Son. It didn't work very well last time."

"Yes, it did. You were a good coach and the kids liked you. Maybe not Rickie, but most of the kids. You just shouldn't have quit."

I looked at Travis's upturned face, unable to respond. Then for the first time I acknowledged my mistake, "I know, Son. I know."

The End